T0271654

BLACK WOODS, BLUE SKY

By Eowyn Ivey

BLACK WOODS, BLUE SKY

BLUE SKY

EOWYN IVEY

TINDER
PRESS

First published in 2025 by Tinder Press
An imprint of Headline Publishing Group Limited

1

Cataloguing in Publication Data is available from the British Library

Hardback ISBN 978 1 4722 7904 0
Trade Paperback ISBN 978 1 4722 7905 7

Offset in 11/15.75pt Albertina MT Std by Jouve (UK), Milton Keynes

Printed and bound in Great Britain by Clays Ltd, Elcograf S.p.A.

Headline's policy is to use papers that are natural, renewable and recyclable
products and made from wood grown in well-managed forests and other
controlled sources. The logging and manufacturing processes are expected
to conform to the environmental regulations of the country of origin.

Headline Publishing Group Limited
An Hachette UK Company
Carmelite House
50 Victoria Embankment
London EC4Y 0DZ

The authorised representative in the EEA is Hachette Ireland,
8 Castlecourt Centre, Dublin 15, D15 XTP3, Ireland (email: info@hbgi.ie)

www.headline.co.uk
www.hachette.co.uk

Now are the woods all black, but still the sky is blue.
May you always see a blue sky overhead, my young friend;
and then, even when the time comes, which is coming now for me,
when the woods are all black, when night is fast falling, you will be
able to console yourself, as I am doing, by looking up to the sky.

—MARCEL PROUST, *Swann's Way* (translated by C. K. Scott Moncrieff)

PART ONE

FAIRY SLIPPER ORCHID
Calypso bulbosa

Chapter 1

Birdie knew her mistake as soon as she cracked open her eyes. She was wholly sick, like she had the flu or been clubbed all around her head and body and, in the confines of the one-room cabin, she was increasingly aware of her own stink, how her skin was emanating the odor of cigarette smoke, digested alcohol, and vomit. She slid her arm out from under her daughter's head, and Emaleen rolled onto her other side but didn't wake. Little Emaleen, with her messy blond hair and her warm, pink cheeks—Birdie wanted to cuddle with her and go back to sleep. But the pounding in her head was only getting worse. She eased into a sitting position on the side of the bed and slowly stood up. A cold sweat trickled down the small of her back and from her armpits. She put a hand on the wall when it felt like her knees might go out from under her. When she looked down, she saw she was still wearing her same blue jeans and T-shirt.

The Wolverine Lodge had been packed last night. A dozen or so of the regulars had driven from Alpine and Stone Creek, a couple of long-haul truckers had stopped for the night, and Charlie Coldfoot and his buddies had come out from Anchorage on their Harleys for the first ride of the season. Nearly twenty people crowded into the small roadside bar for no other reason than to chase away the darkness. The jukebox played Billy Idol and Emmylou Harris. Outside, the spring puddles had iced up and a light snow had fallen across the mountains, but Birdie remembered feeling on fire. Her hips brushed against the men's legs as she handed out shots of hard liquor and cold bottles of beer. Everything she'd said, everything she'd done, had been effortless and flawless, like she was a perfect flame dancing across the wooden tables, a touch of heat reflected in the men's faces. The music rose up into her feet through the plank floor. She'd let Roy twirl her like a ballerina. Even Della had laughed. Every single one of them—the entire goddamned world—golden and beautiful.

It was tempting to blame it on Roy, but it wasn't a big deal, the cocaine. In fact, she'd hardly gotten a rush from it, so she and Roy had gone back a few more times. Each time they tumbled with laughter out of the bathroom, Della was watching them, unsmiling from behind the bar. Birdie remembered her tongue and nose going numb. Then even her teeth, so that her face felt like it belonged to someone else. It wasn't the coke that tripped her up, though, as much as the drinking. It was as if she had been granted a superpower—the ability to down tequila like it was water.

And that's when she'd made her mistake. She hadn't stopped. When she should have called it a night, counted her tips, and helped Della hustle everyone out of the bar, instead she had doubled down. True, she'd been goaded by Coldfoot or somebody calling her a lightweight, and the coke made it tricky to judge just how drunk she was getting. But the real problem was her bizarre sense of hope. Maybe, somehow, this time, she would be able to suspend herself in that perfect moment when you've had enough to fly, but not so much as to be sick with yourself.

In the cabin bathroom, Birdie put her lips to the faucet and drank several gulps of water and splashed some on her face. She needed a shower and a cup of hot coffee. First, she picked up her lighter and pack of cigarettes from the dresser and stepped outside in her bare feet. The single wooden step was cold and damp with dew. She folded her arms tightly against the chill as she smoked. After months of winter with no direct sunlight, the sun had finally risen high enough in the sky to shine down on the lodge. In all directions, the mountain peaks were sharp white with snow against the blue sky, but the air smelled green, like cottonwood buds and blades of grass and creek water.

Birdie put out the cigarette, went back inside, shoved her feet into her sneakers, and pulled on a sweatshirt. Emaleen was a heavy sleeper. She'd be out for another hour or two. Birdie closed the door quietly as she left.

The small guest cabins didn't have any storage space, so she kept some of their belongings in a back shed. Crammed in a corner, beside Emaleen's bicycle and sled, was the spinning rod that Grandpa Hank had given Birdie years ago. One eye had been duct-taped back onto the rod, the line was brittle with age, and the reel had a hitch in the mechanism. But in the beat-up tackle box, she found a few Mepps spinning lures still in their packages and a tangle of snap swivels. No matter how much her head hurt, Birdie always remembered how to tie a fisherman's knot. *Best cure for a hangover.* That's what Grandpa Hank had always said. Carrying the rod and tackle box, Birdie walked around the back of the other cabins and the lodge, past the picnic table and firepit. Della would still be in bed. Clancy was probably just now brewing coffee and heating up the grill for breakfast in the cafe.

The trail into the woods led to Syd's place, but she wouldn't pester him this early in the morning. Instead she followed it a short way through the trees, and then she left the path and set out for the creek down in the ravine. The summer birds—thrushes and warblers and ruby-crowned kinglets—were returning after the winter, and they fluttered and trilled through the birch and spruce boughs. She had to climb over a storm-fallen spruce tree, but the wild grass was still low to the ground and the devil's clubs hadn't grown to their full, spiny height, so the walking was fairly easy. When the mosquitoes found her, she pulled the hood of her sweatshirt over her head. Even with her ears covered, she began to hear the murmur of the creek before she could see it.

It was only as she was fighting her way through an alder thicket that she realized she'd forgotten her rifle. She'd fallen out of the habit of carrying it on her walks because there was no need in the winter. But the bears would be out of their dens now. She stood quietly in the dense brush, held her breath, and listened. There was only birdsong and the creek, and farther away, the low, steady roar of the Wolverine River.

"Hey bear!" she shouted and clapped her hands. Just in case.

Most often, bears behaved the way you expected, when they came around at all. They avoided people and, when they heard your voice or caught your scent, they gave you a wide berth. Black bears were often spotted on the hillsides, grazing among the soapberry bushes. The more mischievous among them would raid the garbage bins behind the lodge. A shot fired into the air was usually enough to chase them off. The larger, more fearsome grizzly bears were rarely seen, leaving only paw prints or piles of scat in the woods. But now and then, a bear would surprise you. They were too smart to be entirely predictable. Jules lived just down the highway from the lodge, and several years ago a black bear had stalked her as she walked along the power line picking cranberries. Whenever she turned her back to the animal, it loped more quickly at her. When she faced it, it stopped and paced side to side, as if trying to build up the courage to go after its prey. This went on for more than a mile, and Jules said it was like a hellish version of red light, green light, with the bear steadily gaining on her. She was only saved because Stan heard her shouts from his house and came out with his .375 and shot the bear.

Jules had told and retold that story, and others would pipe up with their own. It was a favorite pastime at the lodge, telling bear stories. Part of the fun was frightening the wide-eyed tourists who might overhear, but in truth, you were an idiot to not be somewhat afraid. The most terrifying stories were about grizzly bears, because of their astonishing size and force. Hunters told of grizzlies circling their camps at night, huffing and clacking their teeth in displays of aggression. A surveyor said it was like being hit by a silent freight train when he was attacked by a sow near Alpine. He still bore the scars on the back of his neck and scalp where the bear had clamped down on his head and shook him fiercely, before running off with her two cubs. Just last summer, on the tundra north of the Wolverine Lodge, a grizzly bear had dragged an elderly man from his tent, killed him, and partially eaten him before caching the body under a pile of moss and dirt.

All these stories ran through Birdie's mind as she waited and listened. But how many times had she hiked through these woods and seen nothing more than a spruce grouse or porcupine? Not once had she come across a bear near the creek. In her entire life growing up along the Wolverine River, she had seen only a few, mostly at a distance through binoculars.

Just 'cause you don't see them, doesn't mean they aren't around, Grandma Jo would say. And she'd argue an alder-choked creek is the worst kind of place to be without a firearm. The brush is too dense to see far and sounds are drowned out by rushing water. Nothing is more dangerous than a startled bear in close quarters.

If Birdie turned around and hiked all the way back to get her rifle, though, the morning would be lost. Emaleen would wake up. Birdie would take a shower, then they'd go over to the lodge cafe for breakfast. In no time at all, Birdie would be back at the bar for the evening shift, her head still hurting and her brain in a sick fog.

Birdie pushed on. Once she'd gotten clear of the alders, the trees were sparse and the land gently eased down to the creek. The fiddlehead ferns were just beginning to uncoil. The lady ferns on their thin stems seemed to float like pale green lace just a few inches above the ground. If there was a bear nearby, she would be able to see it.

The creek, which flowed out of Juniper Lake and into the Wolverine River, was narrow enough for Birdie to leap from one side to the other as she followed it downstream. A month ago, there had still been ice at the water's edge and snowdrifts along the banks. That was all gone now, and among the moss and boulders, tiny white-and-purple bog violets bloomed.

Downstream Birdie spotted the old cottonwood that had fallen across the creek long ago. The water pooled deep and dark behind the log and then cascaded over the wide trunk. This had always been the best fishing hole, but the rainbows overwintered in Juniper Lake, and Birdie wasn't sure they were in the creek yet. She hadn't noticed any swimming in the shallows.

Birdie crouched on the bank and opened the tackle box. She found the hunting knife she kept in there, and she used it to cut the old, rusty swivel off the line. After she tied on a new swivel and clipped on a lure, she walked out onto the cottonwood log, careful to not slip on the wet, rotten wood where the bark had fallen away.

Her first casts were duds. One caught on a willow bush until she yanked it free, and the other smacked clumsily into the water directly in front of her. She reeled in again, flipped the bail, and tried an underhand cast, and the lure dropped perfectly into the far eddy. She let it sink for a few counts, gave a tug to get the spinner working, and reeled slowly. She could feel the lure bumping against something, but it was probably only snagging on a sunken tree limb or the bottom of the creek.

She varied where she cast and how fast she reeled. She knew she might be fishing an empty hole, but it didn't matter. It was enough to be out here, to let the sunlight and the green of the forest, the sound of the creek and the summer birdsong, wash over her. What if she could stay out here all day, walking along the bank and casting her line, not thinking about anything but finding the trout? Moss under her feet, birch branches and blue sky over her head, no one demanding anything of her. Why couldn't that be her real life? But it wasn't. Eventually she'd have to go back and face Della, who would still be pissed off about last night. And she would need to call Grandma Jo to see if she could watch Emaleen because it was Saturday and the bar would be busy again. Birdie should have asked sooner, but lately Jo seemed put out whenever Birdie needed something. To make it worse, Jo would have to drive to the lodge and pick up Emaleen. Birdie's car was still broken down, something with the transmission that was going to cost more money than she made in a month. She found herself doing the math for the umpteenth time. Twice-a-month paycheck plus her average tips, minus monthly expenses and the pile of fees she still owed at the bank for the checks she bounced a while back—if she had to pay for childcare, she might as well quit her job and go on food stamps. As it was, even if she scrimped here and saved there, she couldn't see being able to get the car fixed until fall. She was sick of begging rides and money, shuffling Emaleen around like a piece of luggage. It was like trying to win a dull, monotonous game someone else had invented, a game that, in the end, didn't matter one lick. The drinking and partying, she knew it was stupid, but it was just a way to feel some excitement at being alive.

As soon as your thoughts drift away, that's when the fish strikes. Birdie felt a sudden tug on the line, and as she yanked upward on the rod, her right foot slipped, so that she nearly fell. She caught her balance and continued to reel, letting the trout take line when it swam hard away from her. The fish leapt and splashed, and then there was nothing. She was sure it had broken the old line, but as she reeled, she saw the lure dragging across the water. She just hadn't set it well enough. She reeled all the way in, untangled the line from the lure, and checked that the hook hadn't been bent or damaged. She cast again.

In that moment, the ache in her head began to fade and that other sensation—the mess of guilt and resentment that made her want to gasp and thrash and fight—vanished. It was as if her mind narrowed to a point that ran down the clear line and into the cool, dark water. She cast to the far side of the creek again and again, poised to feel any bump or tug.

And then she had it. This one was bigger than the first, and it bent the tip of her rod and took out line, but she worked it lightly, pulling up, reeling down, keeping the line taut. *Don't horse it in,* Grandpa Hank would say. *You got it, you got it.*

Birdie jumped down from the log and carefully reeled the fish up onto the bank. It was a beautiful rainbow trout, easily eighteen inches long and in its vibrant spawning colors—a dark, iridescent greenish brown with black flecks that reminded Birdie of hazel eyes, and a distinct blush stripe down its sides. The hook came easily out of its mouth. She could slip the trout back into the creek and let it swim away, but she would keep it. It'd been a long time since she and Emaleen had fresh trout to eat.

She took the hunting knife and stabbed the trout through the top of the head to kill it, then crouched at the water's edge to clean the fish. As she pulled out the entrails, the mosquitoes and gnats began to swarm. She wiped them away from her face with the back of her hand. Inside the trout's body cavity, she ran her thumb along the backbone to remove the dark-red kidney, and then she rinsed the fish and her hands clean of the blood.

She glanced at her watch. It'd been nearly two hours. She needed to get back. She hadn't brought a backpack or sack to carry the fish—she hadn't truly expected to catch anything—so she hooked an index finger through the gill plate and out its bony mouth, and with the same hand picked up the fishing rod, and with the other the tackle box. She pictured sneaking into the cabin and holding the trout's cold lips to Emaleen's cheek as she slept. Emaleen would wake with a gasp. *Hey, Sleeping Beauty,* Birdie would say, *you're going to turn into a frog now,* and Emaleen would laugh. *No, Mommy. You're all mixed up. A prince! A prince! That's who kisses Sleeping Beauty.*

But what about the frog?

Ummm, you have to, you have to kiss it and then maybe he's a prince?

See! So we should give him a kiss, don't you think? And she'd hold the trout up to Emaleen's face again, and Emaleen would wrinkle her nose and shake her head and giggle.

Okay, okay, we don't have to kiss him. How about we eat him for lunch instead? Maybe Clancy will cook it up for us? And Emaleen would cheer.

Partway into the alder thicket, the tip of the fishing rod caught in the bushes ahead of Birdie. She'd forgotten to carry it backward, the way Grandpa Hank had taught her, with the tip following her through the brush. As she tried to pull it free, the line wrapped around the end of a branch. She set down the trout and the tackle box and began to untangle it, swearing quietly as she worked.

When she was done and she bent to pick up the tackle box, the sound of breaking branches continued. Something large was moving through the alders toward her.

Before she could decide to run or yell, a man appeared out of the bushes. It was Arthur Neilsen. He looked just as startled, and when he tried to step back, he stumbled over a low alder bough and nearly fell.

Birdie laughed. "Scared the hell out of each other, didn't we?"

He gave no reassuring laugh or smile and continued to look as if he wanted to flee in the opposite direction. He was a big man, well over six feet, but he'd leaned out since Birdie had seen him last fall. His choppy, golden hair looked like he'd cut it himself with a dull blade, and his beard was full, except where a deep scar ran down the side of his head and cheek. All that remained of his ear on that side was a small flap. Maybe because of the disfigurement, or his awkward behavior and strange way of speaking, people tended to shy away from Arthur. Birdie had always been more curious than anything.

Arthur looked down at the fish and moved closer. "The trout," he said. "I come here to see if they are in the creek again."

"Yeah, me too. I thought I might be too early, but I ended up catching two. Lost the first one." She picked up the gutted trout and tried to wipe away the leaves and grass that had stuck to its drying skin.

"Got this one, though." She held it up for him to see, and his expression took on an intensity, like a man moving in for a kiss, or a cat winding up to lunge at a mouse. Birdie became aware of how deep they were in the woods, how if anything went wrong out here, no one would hear her shouts.

"Okey dokey," she said with a little laugh. "Well, I'd better get back. Everybody's expecting me."

He tried to step out of her way but there was no room in the tight bushes. As she brushed against him, she was fairly certain she heard him take a sharp breath in through his nose, as if he were sniffing her.

Birdie walked quickly, looking back over her shoulder. Once she saw that he was continuing toward the creek, she called out, "Good luck fishing!" A few strides later, though, she felt stupid for saying it—he hadn't been carrying any fishing gear.

Chapter 2

Emaleen didn't know what to do. Her mom had been gone a very, very long time and she was scared, except she didn't want to think about that, about how scared she was, because the fear might bubble up out of her and grow and grow to a terrible size. Instead, she was trying to keep it wound up in the smallest, tightest little knot, and she could feel it somewhere by her belly button.

Emaleen used to be scared of the dark. That was when she was little. Now if it was night time and she woke up alone in the cabin, she knew her mom was just working late at the bar. She would stay under the covers and squeeze her eyes tight and count to one hundred or whisper stories to Thimblina until they both fell asleep, and when she woke up again, her mom would be in bed beside her.

But it wasn't night time. It was day time and the sun was up over the mountains and even the dandelions were awake and starting to open their flowers. Emaleen had watched out the window as her mom walked into the woods all by herself. Emaleen had watched and waited and watched and waited, shivering in her pajamas. She thought her mom might come right back out. But she didn't. Now it had been a very, very long time, like a whole hour or maybe ten hours, and she didn't know what to do. The longer she waited, the farther her mom went away.

Emaleen wasn't supposed to leave the cabin by herself. She might get smooshed by a car if it drove too fast into the parking lot from the highway, or she might fall into the river and get swept away and drownded because it was a powerful cold river, and she wasn't ever, ever supposed to go into the woods by herself. There were black bears and brown bears and stinging nettles and witches and moose in there. Moose didn't want to eat you, they only liked leaves and flowers to eat, but moose were very tall and very strong and sometimes grumpy. If they got mad because you were too close to their babies or you didn't get out of their way, then they would stomp on you. This one time, that happened to Aunt Della's dog. He got stompled by a moose until he was dead. It was in the winter time and Aunt Della was sad. She said she always liked that dog, even though he was so dumb and chased moose.

Emaleen was allowed to leave the cabin only in an emergency, and then she was supposed to go straight to the lodge and find a grown-up and it would be a big deal and she and her mom might get in trouble. Aunt Della didn't like it that Emaleen sometimes stayed by herself in the cabin, even though she wasn't a baby.

That's how come she didn't cry, and that's how come she didn't go to the lodge. Instead, she got dressed. She and her mom had gone to the laundromat in Alpine yesterday, so her favorite outfit was all clean and smelled nice—the purple T-shirt and the yellow corduroy pants that were the same pretty color as dandelions. Once she was dressed, she opened the drawer to the nightstand and took out the silver thimble where Thimblina lived. A long time ago, she lost Thimblina under her pillow and she couldn't find her for days and days, and when she did find her, the thimble was under the bed with the spiders and dust mites that you couldn't see but Emaleen knew were down there and it was disgusting and scary and she felt bad for Thimblina. So now at night time, she put Thimblina carefully in the drawer so she would be safe and not get lost.

It's okay, Emaleen said to Thimblina, except she didn't say it out loud because Thimblina was imaginary, so you could talk with her inside your head and she'd still be able to hear you. *I'm going to make us hot cocoa. Don't worry, Mommy will come home soon.*

If you weren't very careful, you could burn yourself on the teapot that plugged into the wall, so you had to be super-duper careful. Emaleen scooped hot cocoa powder out of the tin and put it into her cup that was pretty and white with pink roses on it. Emaleen wished she had a tiny little cup for Thimblina, but instead she pretended to pour hot cocoa into an invisible cup, which was okay because Thimblina was invisible too.

Emaleen set the table with their hot cocoa, and a spoon and a paper towel napkin for each of them, and she tried to drink her hot cocoa slowly and she tried not to think about where her mom was going or how fast she might be walking. But she couldn't help it. She looked out the window toward the place in the woods where her mom had gone, and the knot down by her belly button squirmed and grew until she couldn't take it anymore. She stood up and put Thimblina in the pocket of her corduroy pants. She had real toys, like a plastic baby doll and Ernie, who said "Rubber Duckie you're the one" when you pulled the string on his back, but Thimblina was the best because she was a secret. You could carry her in your pocket wherever you went, and you could talk to her inside your head and nobody knew. Big kids didn't make fun of you and grown-ups didn't ask you embarrassing questions like, "What's your doll's name?"

Emaleen looked out the window again, and then she walked across the one-room cabin to the other side of the bed, and then back to the window again, back and forth, back and forth, four, five, six. Grandma Jo said this was pacing, and grown-ups did it when they were upset or worried. It wasn't working, though. She was still worried, and if she only stayed here and paced, her mom might get so far away that she wouldn't ever be able to catch up with her. So she put on her water boots, in case she had to wade across any puddles or creeks. And she put on her ball cap so the mosquitoes wouldn't bite the top of her head. And then she peeked out the window one last time, hoping to see her mom, but when she didn't, she opened the door and ran fast as a rabbit around the back of the cabin so nobody like Aunt Della or Clancy would see that she was breaking the rules.

Emaleen's mom knew how to do lots of things. She could start a campfire without even any gasoline. She could swim and use a pocketknife and shoot guns and drive a truck with a stick, even though Emaleen wasn't sure what that meant. Her mom also knew all about wild animals, and she would never get lost in the woods because she knew which way to the mountains and which way to the highway and which way to the river.

Emaleen wasn't scared about any of that. The reason Emaleen was scared, the reason she needed to catch up with her mom as fast as she could, was a secret she couldn't tell anybody, not even Thimblina, because it made her feel ashamed. Like she'd told a lie or ruined something.

Emaleen found a branch that had fallen out of a cottonwood tree, but when she whacked it on the ground, it broke into three pieces. So she walked farther behind the cabin until she found a better stick that didn't break when she whacked it on the ground.

If she saw a moose, she would be like the polite elephant and get out of the way fast. And if she saw a bear, she wouldn't never ever run, because Grandma Jo said that only makes bears want to chase you. Instead, she would yell real loud and wave her arms, and if the bear tried to bite her, she would hit it with the stick. She didn't let herself think about the witches because she didn't think being polite or yelling or whacking sticks would work against them.

Emaleen was out of breath when she made it to the path into the woods, so she stopped to rest, and she looked back toward the lodge. Nobody was outside and if somebody was looking out a window, they wouldn't be able to see her now because she was hidden in the trees. She liked that feeling, like how Thimblina must feel in her pocket, where nobody can see you and you're a secret. She turned back into the woods and started following the path. It was quiet and darkish because the spruce trees were close together. Uncle Syd had sawed away some of the branches so you wouldn't get scratched by their needles.

When you're in the woods, you're supposed to keep your lips about you, which meant being quiet and looking around and noticing things, so that's what Emaleen did. Sometimes she used the stick like a walking cane, and sometimes she tried to touch the high-up tree branches with it, and when she saw a beetle on the ground she didn't use the stick to squish it but she did poke at it a little bit. Inside her head she talked with Thimblina about where her mom might be going and about how if she didn't find her soon, she would have to go back to the lodge and ask Aunt Della for help, and that wouldn't be any fun at all. *We have to watch for Mommy's tracks,* she told Thimblina, but neither one of them could see anything in the dry dirt and spruce needles and grass.

This one time, Uncle Syd showed her how even when you can't see footprints, sometimes you can see where an animal has walked because they knock down the grass and plants. Emaleen started looking for that. She did it for a long time as she walked, looking down at the plants, and it was boring and she didn't see a single interesting thing and she thought about how long it was taking for her to walk because she was looking so hard.

But then she was surprised because she saw a plant that was broken and squashed to the ground, and she looked up and saw lots of plants and grass that had been stepped on. Somebody or something had walked off the trail and down the hill.

Emaleen was thinking. It was a big choice. If she went the wrong way, she might not ever find her mom. If her mom was at Uncle Syd's, they were probably only drinking coffee and sitting in his garden. But if her mom had made this trail down the hill, then she could be walking farther and farther away.

Emaleen stepped off the path, and she had the feeling that maybe she was being very brave, or else she was being very bad.

For a little ways, it was easy to follow the footsteps because lots of grass and stems were knocked over, but after a while, they got harder to find. She would look and look and finally see a broken stem and she would go there and begin looking for the next one. She was going past a gigantic spruce tree when she saw some witch's hair on the end of a branch. The hair was long, gray green, and scratchy-looking. The witch must have flown too close and her hair had caught. Emaleen had seen this before in the forest. And she'd heard the witches, too, laughing and screeching at night. Her mom said it was probably coyotes or old trees squeaking in the wind that made all that noise, but she only said that so Emaleen wouldn't be too scared.

Emaleen walked way, way around the tree because she didn't want the witch's hair to touch her, and then she watched the ground for more footsteps. When she came to all the bushes, she wanted to turn around and go home. It was dark and scary in there. But she had to find her mom. She looked back at the spruce tree with the witch's hair and tried to memorize it, so she would be able to find her way home again.

The bushes were very hard to walk through because the trunks were thick and crisscrossed. Sometimes she climbed over them and sometimes she climbed under them. Then she got to a place with lots of tall, yellow stalks with long, poisonous barbs on them. Grandma Jo said those were called devil's clubs, and Emaleen had to step sideways around them and suck in her belly so she wouldn't get poked. And that's when she almost stepped in something yucky. It looked like a big mud cake with lots of seeds in it. Emaleen wasn't all the way sure, but she was pretty sure it was a bear's poop, or maybe a wolf's. She touched it with her stick. A grown-up would be able to tell what kind of animal it was and if it was here a few minutes ago, or maybe days and days ago, or maybe even a whole year. Emaleen didn't know how to tell. She hopped over the mud cake, and she scooted around the poky plants, and she climbed over and under and on through the bushes. She didn't drop her stick this whole time, and she kept thinking about how if she saw a wolf or a bear, she would hit it on the head.

As she went deeper and deeper into the bushes, though, she started having a nervous feeling. Inside the thicket, she wasn't hidden away like a fun secret. She was very small and alone and kind of shivery.

Up ahead, it looked like the bushes came to an end. But they didn't—they kept going and going and going. Emaleen's throat was dusty, and her legs were very tired. She wished she'd brought her mom's water canteen, and maybe a snack. That tight little knot of worry by her belly button was squirming. She sat down to rest on a thick, low branch, and it was kind of bouncy so that it would've been fun except she was tired and worrying, worrying. She decided it was time to go home and get Aunt Della, because maybe she needed a grown-up.

When she stood up from the bouncy chair, though, she didn't know which way she was supposed to go. If she turned this direction or that direction, it all looked the same. Like a magic trick, like maybe a witch had built this to catch her. And that's when she got really, really scared. Her cheeks turned hot, and she started to cry, just a tiny bit. She couldn't run because the branches tripped her and grabbed at her, but she climbed and shoved her way straight through without stopping or changing direction. Even when the bushes scratched her face and smacked her shins, she kept on and on until she was free. And there was a creek, and on the other side was a spruce tree with the witch's hair. It was confusing. She didn't remember crossing a creek to get here, but that was definitely the witch's tree, so that meant she needed to be on the other side of the creek and up that hill to get back to Uncle Syd's trail.

When Emaleen stepped into the creek, she found it was too deep for her water boots. But she could see a place where the water spread out wide into lots of little streams that went around ferns and boulders. Emaleen balanced on the boulders and hopped to the ferns. Every few steps, the water seeped in over the top of her boot, and one time she even fell backward in the cold water, but it wasn't very deep. By the time she reached the far bank, her boots were full of water and her bottom was wet. But she was almost home now. She just had to go up the hill to Uncle Syd's path.

She climbed and climbed forever and when she finally got to the top of the hill, the path wasn't there. Emaleen looked all around. She searched farther and farther away from the creek, but there were so many trees she couldn't see the mountains or the highway or the river. She was having a hard time seeing at all because her eyes were full of tears. Maybe she could follow her own trail backward. But then she would have to go across the creek again and into the scary bushes. And also, wasn't she already on the right side of the creek?

Grandma Jo, one time, she told a story about a little boy who had gotten lost in the mountains and all he had was a bag of marshmallows. He'd been very smart and hadn't eaten them all at once, but instead had made a place to sleep under a tree and had eaten just one marshmallow each morning until the rescuers found him. That's what you were supposed to do if you got lost—stay in one place and save your food. But she didn't have any marshmallows, and she didn't want to sleep outside with the spiders and mosquitoes.

"Mommy! Mom-my!" She yelled as loud as she could, because maybe her mom wasn't so far away yet and maybe she'd hear her and come find her. She called and called until her throat hurt and her voice sounded funny. "Mom—" Her yell cut off right in the middle, because all of a sudden she thought about the bear or the wolf, how it might hear her and come find her and eat her. She got very quiet.

It wasn't any fun to sit in one place and wait and wait, and it didn't seem like a very good plan except Grandma Jo had said so. Sometimes Emaleen thought she could hear footsteps, walking, walking, but Thimblina would say, *It's only a squirrel,* and sometimes she heard growling far away, but Thimblina would say, *It's only the river.*

Emaleen took the thimble out of her pocket. It was shiny silver and looked like a tiny, fancy hat. Grandma Jo said it was to put on your fingertip when you're sewing, but Emaleen liked to put it on her thumb because it fit perfectly. She held it up in the air so Thimblina could fly out and not get squished, and then she put the thimble on her thumb. She wasn't sure exactly what Thimblina looked like. Maybe like a dragonfly, except without creepy big eyes and prickly feet, or maybe like a fairy with moth wings and long, lacy feelers coming off her forehead. But also, Thimblina could turn into a small, shiny light, like a star that you could cup carefully in your hands. When she was sleeping inside her thimble, she was very small, but then she could get big when she flew out into the world, because she was magic.

Emaleen wished Thimblina could keep her safe and help her find her way home. But that was silly. Thimblina was just pretend. Only moose and witches and bears were real.

Chapter 3

Emaleen was gone. Birdie had searched through the cabin, even opening the cupboard under the bathroom sink and pulling back the shower curtain, all the places Emaleen used to play hide-and-seek when she was a toddler. She went outside, calling "Emaleen! Emaleen!"

It was the last thing she wanted to do, but finally she went to the lodge. Della was still asleep in her upstairs apartment over the bar, and she looked elderly and confused when she opened the door.

"Gone? What do you mean gone?"

"I don't know. I looked everywhere. She was in bed sleeping when I left..."

"You left? When?"

"This morning. I just went down to the creek for a while."

She waited for Della's fury, but instead Della immediately swept into full-bore rescue mode. "Tell Clancy to go to Syd's. Maybe she's there." Her voice was brusque, efficient. She got dressed as she spoke, buttoning her jeans under her nightgown. "And if not, we need Syd to help us look."

She and Della moved in larger and larger circles near the lodge, going through each guest cabin, the shed, anywhere and everywhere. When Syd showed up, he hadn't seen Emaleen at his place or along the trail. He would head toward the river and work his way back, while Clancy borrowed Della's truck to drive along the highway and Della went to search near the creek. They wanted Birdie to stay at the lodge because most likely Emaleen was nearby and would turn up eventually.

An icy terror was seeping into Birdie. Her mind skipped from one scenario to another. If something had happened to Emaleen . . . if she was gone from her forever . . . but she wouldn't give herself over to that panic. She had to stay calm. She needed to think. Where would Emaleen go? She returned to their cabin, irrationally hoping that Emaleen was asleep under the covers and somehow Birdie hadn't seen her, or that maybe Emaleen had come home without being noticed while they were all out searching. But the cabin was still empty. Birdie stepped back out into the bright sunshine.

On the other side of the gravel parking lot and grassy yard of the lodge, an impossibly tall figure emerged from the trees. Birdie shielded her eyes from the sun with her hand. It was Arthur Neilsen, and, riding on his shoulders, was Emaleen. When he saw Birdie, he lifted Emaleen off his shoulders and set her down. They ran to each other, and Birdie got down on her knees and grabbed Emaleen in her arms. Emaleen's face was scratched and tear-streaked, but otherwise she seemed all right.

"Oh, Emmie. God damn it. Are you all right?"

"I'm sorry, Mommy." Emaleen was sniffling and wiping her nose with her arm. "I'm sorry I got lost."

Birdie held her and rocked her, even as a part of her wanted to throttle her.

She looked up to Arthur. "Where was she?"

"She is on the other side of the creek. I hear her cries and find her. She is safe now."

Birdie held Emaleen and kissed her again and again on the side of the head.

Della's anger came, just as Birdie knew it would, and it didn't take long. As soon as Clancy returned to the kitchen and Syd headed home, Della set Emaleen up at a cafe table with a cinnamon roll and hot cocoa and beckoned Birdie into the side hall.

"I am sitting here, just trying to fu—" Della stopped herself and spoke more quietly. "I am just trying to understand. But I don't get it. What the hell are you thinking? First you get completely shit-faced last night. Then you wander off and leave that baby alone like that?"

"I didn't wander off. I went fishing. For like an hour. I thought she'd be asleep that whole time." *And I'm not a baby anymore,* she could hear Emaleen arguing. Birdie felt a smile flicker at her lips.

"Nothing is serious, is it?" Della said. "It's all one big party to you."

"I just needed to get my head straight. I need that sometimes, you know. Just two fucking seconds to myself, without everyone keeping tabs on me."

"That's not how it works. You're her mother. Like it or not, you're the most important person in her life. You're supposed to be looking after her, keeping her safe. Just that quick" —Della snapped her fingers—"she could get snatched away from us."

Birdie's anger was rising. "You're my boss, Del. I get that. You get to tell me how to do my job. You can tell me when to pay the rent, and when to show up for work. But don't tell me how to raise my kid. What do you even know about being a mom?"

Della looked like she'd been slapped, and Birdie knew she'd gone too far. "I'm sorry, Del. I didn't mean . . ."

"Just get your act together, that's all I'm saying." Della's voice was tight, unwavering, but then she hugged Birdie and said more gently, "I don't want to lose you two."

Birdie understood all the implications of those words. Della housed a considerable amount of patience and compassion, but even she had her limits, and when Della was done with someone, it was absolute. The loss would be more than a paycheck, or even cheap rent for Birdie and Emaleen. Della had said that watching Birdie live her life was like watching a tightrope walker, Birdie teetering, swaying one way and then the next, and Della was afraid that one of these days she was going to fall and no one would catch her in time.

She didn't fire Birdie, though. Instead, she switched her to the day shift. She insisted it wasn't punishment, even if it meant a significant cut in the tip money Birdie would earn. Della said the bar had quieted down most evenings and she could use Birdie waiting tables in the cafe and washing dishes, but Birdie knew the truth—Della wanted to manage her away from the partying, and she'd never liked her leaving Emaleen alone in the cabin at night.

"I don't want to go, Mommy. I'm tired. Let's cuddle and watch cartoons. Please." Emaleen was limp as Birdie tried to stretch a turtleneck shirt down over her head and shove socks onto her feet. It was like dressing a defiant rag doll.

"Come on, Emmie. Can't you help me? The cafe opens for breakfast in just a minute and you can't stay here by yourself."

"Why?"

"Because. You're a kid. It's different when you're just sleeping, but you can't hang out here when you're awake. You'd be lonely."

"I'm not ever, ever only. I can do schoolwork all by myself."

"Della said you can color at one of the tables, okay? And Clancy will make you a waffle." She took a brush to Emaleen's hair, but the snarls at the back of her head were impossible and Emaleen wrestled away from her and tried to crawl back under the bed covers.

"Mommmmyyyy!" Emaleen's voice was an unbearable, nasally whine. "Pleeeease. I will be very good. I won't go outside by myself. I promise."

"That's not it. You're not in trouble. We're just changing things up a bit, and this way, I'll get to have dinner with you and relax at night. That'll be nice, right?"

She picked up Emaleen and stood her by the door so that her feet slipped into her rubber boots as she set her down. The only thing to go as planned this morning. She had Emaleen's knapsack with crayons and papers. Coats on. Lights off. Shoot, Emaleen hadn't brushed her teeth. There was no time.

"Come on, it'll be fun. You can pretend you're at school and do your work while I do my work. And on Friday, you'll stay with Grandma Jo." Birdie opened the door and ushered Emaleen outside.

In a burst, Emaleen was fully awake. "Why can't I go to Grandma Jo's every day? She's silly, and she never ever gets mad and she lets me jump on the couch and run on the stairs and sometimes she . . ."

"Shhh."

"But did you know that Grandma Jo, she says—"

"Shhh! Do you hear that?"

From somewhere close by came a nasally, braying cry that almost sounded like a human infant or a baby goat. *Meh, meh, maaaa. Meh. Meh.*

"I hear it!" Emaleen said in a loud whisper. "What is it?"

Birdie took her hand and led her around the side of the cabin toward the sound. They peeked around the corner. Less than a hundred yards away, at the edge of the trees, was a moose calf. It stood on its long, knobby legs and nibbled at a blade of grass, then raised its head and called again. *Meh, meh, meh.*

"He's soooo cute," Emaleen whispered as she bunched up her hands under her chin, like she was hugging her own face. "But why is he crying? Is he trying to find his mommy?"

Birdie nodded.

"We got to help him."

"No, we should leave him alone," Birdie whispered. "She'll be back."

"Let's show Aunt Della!"

By the time they'd made the short walk to the lodge, though, the calf had already disappeared into the woods.

Within the first hour, Birdie had four tables in the cafe, everybody wanting full breakfasts, and she'd gone through three pots of coffee. As she was taking orders, she heard a clunk behind her. "Uh-oh. Mommy, I spilled my hot cocoa. Ow, it's super hot."

"Hey Birdie, can we get some more hash browns over here?"

"And I'll take a warm-up on my coffee when you get a chance."

"Be right with you guys. Here, Emmie, don't smear it around."

Della was always saying Birdie didn't know how lucky she was to have a kid like Emaleen. So smart and well-behaved. An easy keeper. *Just bring her to work with you and let her color at one of the tables.* All well and good for

Della to say—she wasn't the one trying to keep an eye on a six-year-old while waitressing.

"Why don't you go ask Della if you can watch TV upstairs," Birdie said as she soaked up the hot cocoa with a rag and picked up Emaleen's crayons from under the table. She watched Emaleen run up the stairs beyond the hallway, then spotted the pool of hot cocoa on the floor. Swab it up, run the rag to the kitchen sink, shove the crayons and coloring book behind the counter, slide the ticket for table three into her apron pocket, put in an order for more hash browns, and grab the coffeepot, her mind always two steps ahead.

As she cleared one table and set the coffee maker to brew another pot, Birdie heard the door to the bar open and close and saw someone pass by the unlit hallway.

"We're not open over there yet," she called out, but when there was no response, she crossed over into the bar.

It was shadowy and quiet in contrast to the cafe, and it took a moment for Birdie's eyes to adapt. It was Arthur, sitting in the booth by the woodstove.

"Oh, you know, it's just the cafe until noon."

"I sit here and cause no trouble," he said. "Please, I am having chamomile tea."

Birdie laughed before she knew he was serious. "Slow down, it's early still," she teased. "You want a chaser with that?"

"No, thank you."

"Okay, do you take sugar?"

Birdie waited for the sleazy follow-up, something about dipping one of her body parts into the tea to sweeten it, but he only said, "I favor honey." He didn't look up at her but instead stared down at his large hands clasped on the table in front of him.

"Yeah, sure." She reached past him and flipped a light switch on the nearby wall. She could closely see the rippled crease running down the side of his head and across his cheek, as if the flesh and bone had folded in on itself. And under his coarse blond hair, the small flap of scarred skin where his ear should have been.

"The light can be off."

"Oh?" She tapped the switch back down. "Can I get you something to eat?"

"No, thank you."

It was vaguely annoying. Why go to the hassle of coming into the lodge just to sit alone in the bar with a cup of tea? But in the kitchen, as she poured hot water over the tea bag and the steamy scent of flower petals rose up from the mug, she breathed it in and a calmness poured through her. When Birdie was a little girl and had a stomachache, Grandma Jo would brew a cup of chamomile tea for her.

She brought the mug and a jar of honey back into the cool gloom of the bar and set them on the table in front of Arthur. She had the urge to linger.

"I can't thank you enough, you know, for finding Emaleen and bringing her back like that."

"It's good she is home," he said.

"So you're still around?" she asked.

Arthur looked up with a confused expression but went back to stirring his honey into his tea. He licked the spoon.

"I mean, obviously, right? I just meant, I don't see you much. Your place is up on the North Fork, isn't it?"

He swallowed, as if he hadn't expected to have to talk anymore. "Yes," he said finally. He picked up his mug and took a slow drink. It struck Birdie as funny, this big man with his scars and unkempt beard and chamomile tea.

"Well, let me know if you need more hot water then."

Arthur didn't respond. He was hunched over the table like a man recovering from a hard night.

Chapter 4

"What happened here?" Birdie touched the side of her own face, the place where the scar cut deep from Arthur's ear down across his cheek. "I don't think I ever heard that story."

It was the third or fourth time Arthur had come by the lodge. He always sat alone at the same booth in the bar by the woodstove, but at least he'd started letting her turn on the lights. The cafe was empty today, so when she brought his tea and honey and stack of brown toast, she sat across from him uninvited. Arthur was trying to peel open a plastic packet of blackberry jelly with his large hands. Birdie watched him fumble with it, then she reached across the table and quickly opened three of the packets.

He nodded a thank you, then said, "It is nothing."

"Looks like a bar fight. Like a broken beer bottle?"

"No."

"It didn't happen here?"

"No."

"Is that why you don't drink anymore?"

"I never drink alcohol."

"Really? Never? So you're just a brawler?"

Arthur picked up his mug of tea and sipped. Birdie was reminded of Grandpa Hank, sitting cross-legged in the homestead meadow when she was a little girl and she'd serve up creek water in her tiny porcelain tea set.

Grandpa Hank could barely hold on to the toy cup with his big, work-worn hands but he played the part, tipping out a pinky as he drank the tablespoon of water. That's how Arthur looked with his mug—a giant playing at a tea party.

She realized he was watching her. "Sorry," she said. "I was thinking about something else. About bar fights actually. Did you ever hear what happened, a couple of years back? The community council used to meet here in the bar. So this one night, Burt and Landon Jeffreys got into it. You know those two, right? Like oil and water. I wasn't around, but I guess all hell broke loose, everyone throwing punches and breaking stuff."

A nod. A shrug. A quiet word or two. This is how it went every time Birdie tried to talk with Arthur. Maybe she bored him. But he didn't have to keep coming to the lodge, or he could tell her to shove off if he didn't want to talk. The bigger question was why she kept at it, but he was like a stuck zipper, an annoying knot she couldn't walk away from.

"At one point Landon, he picks up a pool cue, starts swinging it," Birdie said. "And then Burt pulls out a little derringer, like he's going to shoot him. It was Wild West, for real. Della had to wrestle them apart and chase them into the parking lot, tell them all to go home. That's why the council's not allowed to meet here anymore." She was starting to laugh now. "And it was over the community plan, something about how many pigs people are allowed to keep in their yards."

Arthur wasn't laughing with her. He was watching her, steadily. Observing her. It was like that morning at the creek when they'd stumbled on each other in the alders and she hadn't been able to tell what he was thinking. Did he admire her or desire her in some way? But he didn't offer encouragement. His mouth flattened into a line that wasn't a frown or a smile, and the skin crinkled at the corners of his eyes, like he was confounded, and maybe a little sad.

For the first time, Birdie let herself openly meet his gaze. She'd thought there was something peculiar about his eyes. Now she could see: the golden-brown irises were rimmed in black so thick that it swallowed up most of the white. His lashes and the inside edges of his eyelids were nearly black, which didn't seem right with his blond hair. And in the corner of each eye was an amber-colored membrane, as if he had another secret eye-lid that might flicker.

Arthur didn't look away. Birdie could hear the wall clock ticking and water draining out of the kitchen dishwashing sink. She realized she'd stopped breathing. Then Della came down from her office and scowled in their direction.

Birdie wanted one last look at Arthur's eyes, but his head was down. She noticed the time on the clock. "Shoot, I got to get going," she said. "Jo will have had her fill of Emaleen by now."

She pulled on her coat as she walked to the door. Arthur was still at the table with his toast and tea, faced away from her. His head was slightly bowed so that she could see his bare neck. She imagined walking back to him and lightly running the tips of her fingers across his skin and watching goosebumps rise.

Since that night with Roy and the coke, Birdie had spent every day try-ing to prove to Della that she could stay upright and clear-headed and take care of her little girl. Della seemed to be coming around. She had even hinted that she might let Birdie switch back to the night shift at the bar soon, since the waitress she'd hired for the upcoming summer season wasn't going to work out.

But when Birdie walked in the door on Friday morning, she heard—"Hey, we need to have a talk." Della, stern-faced behind the bar, filling the refrigerator case with bottles of MGD and Budweiser.

Birdie grabbed her apron off its hook and kept moving, like she was too busy to slow down and listen. "We're all good," she said over her shoulder. She couldn't stand another lecture. She picked up a cue stick from where it was propped in a corner and replaced it in the rack on the wall, then got a broom from the closet. It was either going to be another "talk" about the perils of her working the night shift, or something to do with Arthur. "What's he still doing around here?" Della had asked the other day. "I've never seen him at the lodge this much." Della had known him since he was a little boy and said he'd always been strange. "Because he's quiet?" Birdie had said. "He doesn't swig beer or pinch me on the ass? I guess I'll take that kind of strange."

This morning, she was going to duck any arguments. She kept her back to Della and started sweeping.

"Just stop that for a minute and come talk to me."

Birdie sighed. "Really, Della—we're doing good. I got Emaleen her school workbooks so she can catch up. She's spending more time at the homestead with Jo. And I've cut back a lot. You see me. Sober Susie."

"Yeah, I see you're trying. It's not about that. It's got to do with Roy. Evelyn called. You know how he's been staying with family since Lois eighty-sixed him." Della's pause was deliberate. Everyone knew. It had gotten back to Lois, about that night with the coke and Birdie. It was stupid, of course—Birdie never had anything with Roy but partying. He was a goofy, scrawny alcoholic who couldn't hold down a job. But she also knew how it looked, their time in the bathroom together, the dancing.

"Well, his sister got sick of his crap and sent him packing, thinking he'd end up at George's or Dwight's place. Six o'clock this morning, her phone rings. Roy's landed in the hospital in Anchorage. He was driving out of town, drunker than a skunk, and slammed into a power pole."

"Oh shit, is he all right?"

"He's pretty messed up, sounds like, broken bones and whatnot. And he's looking at jail time. This isn't his first rodeo."

Birdie rested her cheek on the broom handle, eyes on the floor. It wasn't her fault. Anyone who knew Roy could have seen this coming. But she also knew he'd been a month sober, just smoking a little bud and drinking a ton of coffee, before that weekend with the coke. She should have turned him down. Told him to go home to his wife and kids.

"We'll put the jar out for them. The only money they've got coming in is Roy's unemployment checks, and they're going to have lawyer bills. Hospital bills. And damnation," Della said, "Lois is just done with that hysterectomy. She's hardly getting around. And with all those little ones."

Della pulled the gallon mason jar out from behind the bar, and Birdie tore off the old label. In October, they'd gathered $320, mostly in ones and fives, to help Burt after he injured his back and had to quit the North Slope.

"I'll make a new sign for it," Birdie said. In Della's upstairs office, she got a piece of paper from the desk and some colorful markers. FUND FOR THE STANHOPE FAMILY, she wrote in bubble letters, and she drew stars and flowers around the edges. She taped the label to the jar, took her wallet out of her back pocket, and put in a ten-dollar bill.

It was another quiet day at the lodge, not a single customer all morning, so Birdie was sharing a plate of pancakes with Emaleen.

"Mommy! Look! Uncle Roy, he's riding a bike." Emaleen was kneeling on her chair and craning her neck to look out toward the parking lot.

"Sit down. You're going to tip over and spill your hot cocoa."

"But Mommy, you gotta see!"

"Are you playing a joke on me?"

"No, I promise."

Birdie got up from her chair to look, and there was Roy, his left arm in a sling, a cigarette in the corner of his mouth, pedaling a rickety old ten-speed bicycle down the highway toward the lodge. He nearly toppled over when he hit the gravel parking lot, but he got off the bicycle and walked the rest of the way.

"Morning, Roy. You pedal your sorry ass all the way over here?" Birdie could hear Della call from the bar.

"You know I don't got a car anymore. And it's not so bad. Just a mile. All downhill. But I could use a cold one all right." There was the scrape of a barstool on the plank floor.

"You sure? How about a cup of coffee? I've got a fresh pot on."

"How about you just get me a beer." Roy's voice was hard, but then he added more diplomatically, "I sure do appreciate it, Del." Birdie heard a cap being pried off and a bottle set on the bar top.

"How you holding up?" Della said. "You're looking worse for the wear."

"Mostly just the arm. Broke a couple of ribs too. I guess I'm busted up some."

"I figured they'd still have you down at the pre-trial."

"My hearing's coming up next week. Got out on bail this morning. My sister drove me home."

Birdie was tempted to leave with Emaleen now without saying anything to Roy, but that didn't feel right either.

"Stay here. I'm going to say hi to Roy real quick."

"Can I come too? Can I see his ten-speed?"

"Finish your breakfast, okay? Then we'll go to Grandma Jo's."

"Can I ride my bike? Wait, Mommy, can I get a ten-speed, like Uncle Roy's? Mommy?"

Roy was more pitiable than Birdie had anticipated. His left eye was bruised and swollen nearly shut, and they'd shaved part of his head to stitch his scalp. He was pale and haggard—the weight he'd lost made him look like an old man—and his forehead was slick with sweat. He was lucky he hadn't had a heart attack, riding that bicycle.

"Hey Birdie. Good to see you." He wiped the beer foam from his whiskers and nodded at her.

"You too, Roy. You look like hell."

He drained the last of his beer and gestured toward Della for another, but she didn't move.

"Can't you take it out of the pool there?" Roy said, raising his chin at the mason jar.

"Christ, Roy."

"Nah, I'm just kidding, Del. I'm good for it."

The jar held a handful of crumpled bills and a thin layer of coins on the bottom. Not even fifty dollars yet. The label, with its childish pink flowers and blue and yellow stars that had seemed cheerful when Birdie drew them, now seemed ridiculous. What difference could it make, really?

"So tell me this . . ." Birdie began.

"Yeah, what's that, Birdie." He looked at the empty beer bottle in his hand, tipped it toward the overhead light as if he were reading the label.

"You're just out of jail, headed back in a few days, right? It's ten o'clock in the morning." Her voice was climbing. "Your wife just had major surgery and she's got your three kids at home with her. And where the fuck are you?"

Roy didn't say anything at first, just stared at the beer bottle. When he turned on the stool to face her, he winced and repositioned the broken arm against his side.

"All right, all right." One hand up, like a surrendering fugitive. "But let me ask you something. How old are you, Birdie?"

"Twenty-six."

"Well, give it fifteen years then, and let's see where the fuck you are."

Chapter 5

Birdie's favorite place at the lodge was the picnic table out the back door of the cafe. She'd often go there during her breaks if the weather was good, and she'd sit on top of the table with her feet on the bench, facing the mountains. Tourists thought the Wolverine Lodge was in the middle of nowhere, but it wasn't. Over there, on the far side of the river, away from the highway and the power lines, way up in the mountains where the spruce forests looked more blue than green and the valleys disappeared behind peak after peak, that was the true wilderness. Usually it cleared her head, just letting her eyes wander the creeks and ridges.

But today was different. It was as if her mind had taken a nosedive into every worst memory in her possession. That hungover morning when she thought she'd lost Emaleen. Roy's son walking into the bar the other night just before closing time, a little boy, eight or nine years old, standing brave with his sleeves pushed up and his cheeks red, "Mom wants you to come home," while Lois waited out in the car with her two girls. Then Roy just out of that wreck, stitches in his head, riding a bicycle because it was the only way he could get to the bar. And then it was each and every time Birdie had failed or someone had failed her, like a series of flash cards. What the hell, but her brain went all the way back to that day when they were kids, she and Liz sitting on the couch with *Romper Room* on the television and Grandma Jo slamming around the kitchen. Grandpa Hank, kneeling in front of them. "Your mother's gone on down to Florida for a while."

Birdie wasn't going to be a Lois. She wasn't going to try to wheedle and nag a man into being a better person than he was, and she wouldn't send a child in to fight her battles. But she wasn't like her own mother, Norma. That's one thing she would never be.

She lit a cigarette, blew out a lungful of smoke, and let the river wind carry it away. When the sun was out, it was almost like summer, but today the clouds had moved in and the air had a chill to it. There was fresh snow on the mountaintops.

When she heard a vehicle pull into the parking lot of the lodge, she turned to look.

It was Arthur, driving his father Warren's pickup truck.

"Hey!" she called out as he shut the truck door behind him. "Let me finish this cigarette and I'll go in and get your tea and toast." A pause. "Unless you'd rather come and sit with me for a while."

He started in her direction but stopped. "I don't care for the smoke."

"This?" She gestured with the cigarette. "You don't smoke?" Birdie stubbed it out on the bottom of her sneaker and then waved a hand around as if to clear the air. When she scooted to one side, Arthur sat beside her on top of the picnic table.

"It's a nice view from here, yeah? Isn't your place over there somewhere? Point it out to me."

"It is too far," Arthur said.

"I know, but I mean just the general direction."

"It is through the pass, north of Soapstone Mountain, at the headwaters of the North Fork."

"It must be so beautiful. Quiet."

They sat for a few minutes, both looking toward the mountains. Without a cigarette in her hand, Birdie noticed the damp cold cutting through her thin jeans and old coat. She stuffed her hands into her pockets and huddled into herself, but she didn't want to go inside yet.

"Some of my very best memories are of being out on the tundra with my grandparents," Birdie said. "Up north. They took us caribou hunting when I was a kid. Me and my sister, we'd just run wild around camp. Eating blueberries and fried ptarmigan. That was a long time ago. I was little, like maybe six." The same age as Emaleen, now that she thought of it.

"I always feel like I'm missing something," she went on. "You know like when you're craving an orange and you think maybe your body needs the vitamin C or something. I'm like that all the time, just craving and craving. And I sit here looking across the river and I think that's it. That's what I'm craving."

The breeze shifted, and she could smell Arthur. He looked like a man who would stink of armpit sweat and Deet and charred wood, like a man who lived alone in a cabin and never took a bath. But that wasn't it. He smelled like the forest. Peeled spruce bark and clean moss and fresh air, and another, musty odor, like damp fur.

"Are you happy when you're over there in your cabin?"

"I am."

"Even though you're all by yourself? Don't you ever get lonely?"

Arthur tilted his head to one side, a half shrug.

"Is that why you're still hanging around here?" Birdie leaned to nudge him with her shoulder, flirty, expecting there to be some give, but it was like bumping into a boulder. Arthur sat very still with his hands on his knees.

"You see that ridge way up on the skyline?" she said. "Not the mountain closest to us, but back in that valley and to the left there, where the sun is hitting that cornice of snow? Whenever I'm sitting here, I picture what it'd be like to stand in that spot."

Arthur didn't say anything.

"What? Do you think that's stupid of me?"

"No," he said quietly. "I go there. It is a favorite place."

"You've been up on that ridge? There's no way."

"It is not . . . so difficult."

"You're serious. All this time, I never imagined someone actually did it. What's it like?"

"On the way up, it is a slide . . . of shale crumble. There are Dall sheep trails, but I make my own way. When I cross over the top to the other side, it is . . . wide open. No trees. There is Labrador tea. Mountain sage. Crow-berries are good. I eat many of them."

"Crowberries? They don't taste like much, do they?"

"I like them fine."

"Tell me more, about what it's like to be up there."

It was the most she had ever heard him speak. In his halting, almost for-mal way, he described when the blueberries and soapberries come ripe in the far valley, and the taste of snowmelt as it runs down through the rocks. How when the wind is right, he can catch the salty air from the inlet hun-dreds of miles away and can even smell when the salmon are getting near. He spoke as if at that exact moment he and Birdie were together on that mountain ridge, everything unfolding in front of them. The hoary mar-mots sunning themselves on the rocky outcroppings, the parky squirrels chirping from their tunnels, the small groups of caribou trotting across the skyline—his voice was rumbling and low, like when you put your head on a man's chest and can hear his words resonate from deep within.

Another guy, another day, she would have climbed on top of him, straddled him there on the picnic table, and kissed him. She liked to catch a man off guard, to watch his eyes widen with astonishment.

Instead she only leaned Arthur's way and allowed her legs to fall slightly open so that her knee touched against him. His voice got quieter. After a moment, she felt him relax back into her, a solid, warm pressure that caused Birdie a rush of heat.

She wanted to say, *Take me there. To the far side of the river, up on that moun-tain ridge.* But she was afraid to make any quick movements, or else she might spook him.

"Do you like it here?"

"What, Mommy?"

"Do you like being here?"

"Umm . . . yes!"

They were cuddling together in their bed, Emaleen's head resting in the crook of Birdie's arm, a half-empty bag of microwave popcorn beside them. It was payday, so Birdie had rented a VCR and the movie *Heidi* from the video store in Alpine. Emaleen had begged and begged for them to wear their matching flannel nightgowns, red-and-green Christmas plaid with lacy ruffles at the neck and cuffs, that a friend of Della's had sewn for them. They were hot and the lace itched at Birdie's neck—she usually slept in a T-shirt and underwear—but she'd relented.

"But what do you like about being here?"

"I *love* our nightgowns. They are very, very pretty. And I love . . ." Emaleen raised her head to look around the dim room. "I like the window and the TV . . ." She nodded her head broadly with each item. "And, and, and the teapot and my cup and the . . . and the . . . actually, I don't like the teapot because sometimes it burns."

"But I mean here at the lodge, like us living here and me having this job."

"Ummm, waffles are good. And shaushages. And Della sometimes . . . sometimes Della . . . she puts a lot of whip cream on my hot cocoa. A lot!" Emaleen sat up and put her mouth to Birdie's ear. "But sometimes I don't like Clancy," she whispered loudly.

"Really? How come?"

"He gets mad. One time, 'member, he said, he said it's not allowed to run around. And he looked at me meanly." Then, whispering again, "Don't tell him I said that, okay? I don't want him to have hurt feelings."

"Right. But what if we could live somewhere else? And maybe I didn't have to go to work every day. And we could be outside more?"

"And I want to wear our nightgowns. Can I bring my toys?"

"When I was your age, I wanted to live in a cabin far away in the mountains."

"Like Heidi?"

"Yeah, kind of."

"And did you like to drink hot cocoa with whip cream?"

"Yeah, I probably did."

"And you always wanted to fly like a bird? But you weren't very good at it. Tell that story, about the angel dog? The one who only had three legs."

"You want that story again? But you've heard it a thousand times."

"Please. Pretty please, with cherries on top."

"Well, I was about the same age as you, and I thought that if I roller-skated fast enough, I would somehow fly up into the air, like a kite or some-thing, I don't know. So I put on my roller skates and I got Big Jake's husky."

"Her name was Angel?"

"Yep, and she was missing one of her front legs."

"Why?"

"I don't remember. That's just how she always was."

"Why?"

"Like I said, I don't know."

"Did she bite?"

"Nah. She was a sweet girl. She would follow me around when I was playing in the yard, and it was like she was listening when I talked to her."

"And she had wings?"

"Not for real. But she was a white husky, and she had these marks on her shoulders, gray and brown, that looked like wings—that's why she was called Angel. So I put a harness on her and hooked up a lead that I tied around my waist. Then we went out to the dirt road."

"By Grandma Jo's house? Where I ride my bicycle when the snow's all gone?"

"Yep. And I called out to Angel, 'Hyah! Hyah!' The way Big Jake called out to his dog team. And Angel was real strong, even if she only had three legs, and she pulled me fast."

"And you flew?"

"Nope, I didn't. I fell down and got drug across the rocks and dirt. But I didn't want to give up and so I kept yelling, 'Hyah! Hyah!' And poor Angel, she kept looking back at me and trying to run and drag me, because she thought that's what she was supposed to do. So I guess it wasn't such a great plan after all."

"And you got big cuts?" Emaleen was finding the long, white scar on the palm of Birdie's hand and gently touching it with the tip of her finger.

"Yeah, I did. And Grandma Jo started calling me Birdie. She said all I ever wanted to do was fly, even if I wasn't any good at it."

"And Grandma Jo, she's your grandma, but she's kind of your mom too? Because you don't have a mom like me?"

"Yep, that's true."

That day with Angel was also the day Birdie and Liz learned that their mother had left them behind to go to Florida with a man they'd never met. The girls moved in permanently with Grandma Jo and Grandpa Hank, though the transition was minor. They had been sleeping on their couch most nights anyhow.

Liz was abandoned, sullen and leaden. But Birdie only wanted to fly higher. She didn't want to go to Florida; she didn't want to care about any of that. She just needed to get high enough to see over the trees, for her belly to fill with giddy fear.

How many ways had she tried to fly since? That sunny March day when she was nine, the snow deep enough to bury the sawhorses in Grandma Jo's yard. Birdie hanging on to the rope that swung out over the hill from a birch tree. It was nothing premeditated or tested—at the swing's pinnacle, nearly fifteen feet above the ground, she launched herself into the cold blue sky. She became weightless and crystalline. Hollow-boned. Boundless. Soaring a thin line between terror and bliss.

There were bicycle jumps. Leaps from the shed roof. A running summersault off the dock and into the lake. By the time she was a freshman at Alpine High School, she realized the sensation could be evoked in countless, thrilling ways. Standing in the back of Ben's pickup, holding on to the roof as he gunned it through the hayfields—there was one crest where they were guaranteed to catch air. Arm wrestling the boys and when she lost, volunteering to lift her shirt, their eyes on her bare nipples like a shiver of moving air. Peppermint schnapps. Sunny D screwdrivers. Plugs of Copenhagen chewing tobacco between her cheek and gum. Menthol cigarettes. None of it tasted good. But spinning drunk and high on the floor of Ben's trailer house, the glacial wind howling outside, she was flying all the same.

All that should have stopped when Emaleen was born. Birdie wasn't a teenager anymore, and giving birth held the promise of change. She hoped for it even. She would plant carrots and potatoes in a garden, the baby asleep in a basket in the sun beside her. She would drink herbal tea, learn how to bake whole wheat bread and sew clothes. She would be grounded, weighted, finally content.

There were those first moments, newborn Emaleen bundled against her chest, warm and drowsy together by the woodstove. Jo let them have the spare bedroom. No rent, and she would help with the baby. Maybe it should have been enough for Birdie—an entire separate life yanked bloody and bawling from her womb. Emaleen, six pounds three ounces with her bleary little eyes, needed and wanted only Birdie. It was an intense and startling attachment that consumed them both, sucked the air out of the room and the light out of each day so that the two of them existed alone together in a state of pared-down survival. Breathe, eat, sleep. For a while, it was enough because it was all there could be.

But it couldn't last. Grandma Jo hovered and tch-tched. *You can't eat like that when you're breastfeeding. Hold her like this, or she'll never stop fussing.* Do this. Don't do that. And always, always Grandma Jo kept watch, like she was afraid that abandonment might run through the female line. Over the weeks, her grandmother's house began to smother her. Birdie was re-pulsed by the smell of sour milk and old sweat in her hair, the organic heaviness of her own body. She wanted to feel like herself again. Lithe. Free. Barely tethered to the earth. Motherhood had failed to transform her. She was the same person she'd always been, but now there was this tiny child, and it was as if one had to be sacrificed for the sake of the other.

There was no chance of asking Emaleen's father for help; Birdie wouldn't know how to find him even if she wanted. Rex was a thirty-three-year-old dozer operator from Oklahoma, or maybe it'd been Arkansas, who had only been in Alaska for a few months working on a road construction crew. She hadn't found out she was pregnant until he was already gone, but she'd had no desire to anchor herself to him anyhow.

So she'd left Emaleen with Grandma Jo when she could, and she went back to work at the bar for Della. After a few months, she and Emaleen moved into one of the cabins at the lodge, and once Emaleen was sleeping through the night, Birdie would sometimes leave her alone in her crib while she worked the evening shift, checking on her during her breaks. It wasn't the worst thing. Birdie was making do, the best she could.

"If you go live in a mountain, you have to take me too."

"What? Of course." She kissed Emaleen on top of the head. "Anyways, we're probably not going anywhere. Don't say anything about this to anyone, okay? It's just me daydreaming. Sometimes, I don't know, sometimes I think I could be better. Like a better mom for you."

Emaleen reached over and put her small hand on top of Birdie's, patting it, like an old woman comforting a child.

"You're a very, very good mommy. You're the best mommy in the whole wide world."

Chapter 6

Warren stood at the sink and watched out the kitchen window as Arthur drove the red pickup truck away from the house and down through the field. At dawn, a flock of sandhill cranes had gathered at the snowmelt ponds, and as the truck passed, the slender, gray birds stretched their wings and hopped on their long legs, but they didn't take to the air.

Arthur hadn't asked, just taken the keys from the hook by the front door and left without a goodbye. He would be going to the lodge again, the third time in as many days. For weeks, Warren had been mystified. It wasn't unusual for Arthur to come out for the change of the seasons, a short visit in the spring and fall, but he never stayed more than a week and rarely left the house. It wasn't until Warren ran into Della at the post office in Alpine last Friday that he understood more clearly. "Arthur and Birdie are seeing each other an awful lot. Is he planning to stick around much longer?" As she spoke, she'd sorted through the stack of bills and envelopes in her hands, as casual as if the conversation were about Sunday dinner, but Warren could see that she was concerned.

Della was no gossipmonger. Over the years he had watched her take on the lodge and succeed at the expense of no one but herself. She was level-headed and plain-spoken and smart enough to spot trouble before it arrived, yet she also managed to be remarkably kind to stragglers and misfits, people who found it a challenge to keep their act together. He'd seen how she looked out for Birdie and her little girl.

As for Birdie, Warren didn't know her well, but he'd heard stories. Child protective services had been called twice that he knew of, once when a tourist passing through witnessed some kind of scene at the bar with Birdie drunk and her daughter sick with a fever, and another time a couple of years ago when the child had broken her arm. At the hospital, it came out that the little girl had been climbing up on a dresser, trying to reach a package of instant soup to make her own dinner, when she had fallen. At four years old, she'd been left to fend for herself while her mother worked her shift.

Birdie was no villain. Unlike some lawmen and prosecutors Warren had known over the years, he did not see the world neatly split between perpetrators and victims but rather as a complex interchange of suffering. He had witnessed it again and again, people drawn to the very ones most likely to destroy them.

"You're probably wanting to get back out to your place," he'd said more than once, but Arthur never answered.

The pickup truck passed the snow fences that kept the road from drifting closed in the winter, paused at the end of the road, and pulled out onto the highway. Long after the truck had disappeared and the dust cloud along the driveway had settled, Warren watched. The house was quiet and still, and he noticed himself—how he was standing at the sink wearing Carol's ruffled apron, his hands resting on the edge of the counter, staring out the window. A fretful old man.

He whistled, not just to call the dog, but to dispel the house of its empty silence. The golden retriever galloped in from the living room, spun herself around in a few quick circles, and skidded to a stop at the edge of the linoleum. The pup was all feet and ears, not quite a year old, but she and Warren had already settled into a routine. Spinner sat at attention as Warren scooped dry dog food from the bin and into the dog's bowl. With a hot pad, he picked up the cast-iron skillet from the stove, poured bacon grease over the food, and scraped the last bits in with the spatula. He set the bowl on the floor. Spinner watched him closely. "All right," he said quietly, and she set to gobbling it up.

If wishes were horses. All the same, Warren couldn't help but wish it were different. He wished that his son's homecoming was a reprieve from loneliness, a source of joy rather than apprehension. He wished Arthur might find a good life for himself on this side of the river, maybe settle down with a caring, intelligent woman and bring home a few grandchildren. He wished the house to once again be filled with the happy, boisterous sounds of family.

And then against his greatest will, because this was one hell of a hopeless wish if there ever was one, he found himself wishing that Carol were still alive. She would laugh to see him wearing her apron. I didn't know you could wash the dishes, she would tease. She would bend over and kiss the dog on top of the head, though they'd never met, and then she'd start a pot of coffee. Don't worry, love. We'll sort it out together.

What would she do, if she were still here? She wouldn't allow Arthur to leave the house without a conversation, that was for damned sure. She'd always had a way of drawing the truth out of him. Maybe Arthur would confess that he was in love with the young woman, and Carol would smile and say, How wonderful, this is what we've always hoped for you. At night in bed, maybe Warren and Carol would talk about their son's new life and how pleased they were for him. Remember when we fell in love, Carol would say. That autumn all those years ago at the hospital. Alaska hadn't even earned its statehood yet, and Warren was a young officer with the Territorial Highway Patrol. He'd dislocated his shoulder trying to lasso an unbroken horse running free through downtown Anchorage, and Carol, with her no-nonsense kindness, was the nurse who attended him.

But Arthur, he isn't the same. What about everything that happened before? Isn't it too dangerous? No, no, Carol would answer. Don't you see? This is the beginning of a new life for him. Love is the most powerful force in the world. Warren could imagine Carol speaking those words. Love is powerful. Our son can be happy.

If wishes were horses. When it came to Arthur, Carol always had a sixth sense. She would have stopped Arthur at the door. She would have brought him over to the couch and sat him down beside her. The two of them would have talked in hushed voices, with Warren listening and pacing. Maybe over the hours she'd coax Arthur, so subtly that neither he nor

Warren would realize what was happening. Where are you the happiest, she'd ask him. She would listen and nod and hold Arthur's hand as he spoke, and then she'd say, We love you so much, you know that don't you. Arthur had cried before in these moments, their powerful grown son, lost and torn. But maybe Carol would help him to see that it was pointless to moon over Birdie, that it was time for him to go back to the other side of the river. We know it's lonely for you, but that's where you're able to find some peace, isn't it? Don't you think it's for the best?

At night in bed, instead of talking of love and grandchildren, maybe Carol's voice would be urgent. We have to do something. We can't let this go on. And Warren would feel like a fool for not seeing it sooner. They had talked about it over the years, that at some point it might become untenable. No matter how much they loved their son.

Warren wiped down the kitchen counter with a soapy rag and hung the cast-iron pan back on its hook over the stove. He took off the apron and draped it over the back of the chair by the woodstove to dry, just the way Carol would have.

When he put on his chore coat, Spinner pranced at his side.

"Not just now. You stay," he said quietly. "Be good."

Warren didn't take a hunting rifle or his revolver. He had neighbors, good people up and down the highway, who wouldn't step out their front door without a firearm. He understood the motivation. It was common enough for a black bear to wander through this time of year, scrounging for food, and every once in a while, there was a rash of house burglaries, desperate young people looking for televisions and guns to steal. But Warren was no longer certain he had the desire to choose his life over another's.

As he stepped out onto the porch and closed the front door, the sandhill cranes stirred again in the field. Their reedy bugling echoed through the air. There was a quality to the sound that Warren found both lovely and melancholy, as if their strange voices were filtered through fog, or were coming through the veil between this world and the next.

With his hands in his coat pockets, Warren walked slowly down the dirt road, past the gazebo, and out into the hayfield, toward the airstrip. They'd managed a second cutting late in autumn, and the field had been left a golden stubble. Warren no longer kept any horses, and he made very little money off the alfalfa once he'd paid Boots to cut and bale it, but that wasn't the point. It was the bright scent of mowed hay in the summer, the snowy and wind-blown expanse through the winter, the migratory birds gathering in the fields each spring.

This is why he'd come out here, he told himself. To welcome back the cranes. To acknowledge the tender brevity of the season, for soon the spring ponds would dry up and the fields and trees would be a rush of green and sunshine. Tomorrow, or next week, the cranes would be gone, on their way to their nesting grounds, but for now they stood on their twiglike legs and turned their long necks to watch him, the flare of red across their foreheads. This is what he had come to see.

Rather than turn back toward the house, he walked down the mowed airstrip, away from the cranes, toward the old World War II Quonset hut he used as a workshop. He dialed in the combination on the lock and opened the steel door, peered inside, as if this were his true goal. To check on things. The work benches were uncluttered, if a little dusty. Baby food jars lined a shelf, each filled with their sorted screws, washers, and bolts. Hammers and saws hung in order of size across a pegboard. The concrete floor was swept clean of sawdust and sand. He couldn't remember when he'd last spent any time working in here. It had been different when Carol was alive—it had given them each their own space, Carol piecing together a quilt at the kitchen table, Warren out in the shop changing the oil in the pickup or building a bookshelf.

Warren closed the door and secured the lock, but still he didn't turn toward the house. He walked around the back of the Quonset hut, past his Piper Super Cub airplane where it was tied down to anchors against the wind. In the distance he heard the echoing calls of the cranes. Like sorrow, it occurred to him. A quivering, throaty keening.

His pace quickened as he neared the trees. His stride became purposeful. It was the sensation he'd had as a young officer approaching a scene, that he needed to center himself. Calm and sure. He walked into the forest.

During the last starving days of winter, moose had resorted to eating the bark off the willow and young cottonwoods, and in places the trunks and low branches were stripped bare. Warren reached out and ran an index finger across the grooves of teeth in the wood. A snowshoe hare bounded away, caught between winter and spring with its white fur turning to brown. Farther ahead, through the leafless trees, Warren could see the place.

Years ago, a massive spruce tree had toppled in the wind, its entire root system pulled up from the earth. The wall of dirt and twining roots stood eight feet in the air. At the sides, the roots still clung to the ground, and at the top, the sod hung down so that it looked like the entrance to a small cave.

Warren ducked low and stepped into the earthy hollow. He knew it was here—the dirt at his feet was freshly dug and there was a heap of moss, brush, and dried grass. When Arthur was a little boy, it had been a hole he excavated under the back porch, but he'd grown more secretive over the years. He only came and went when he thought Warren wasn't watching. He'd know, now, that Warren had been here. He would see the tracks in the dirt; he would smell his scent in the air.

Warren lowered himself to his knees and began clearing away the pile—green willow branches, moss, and dead leaves. He hadn't worn gloves, and his fingers snagged on something thorny. Mixed in the heap were the brittle stalks and dusty roots of last year's devil's club plants. He tossed them aside. He'd considered bringing a shovel or trowel but worried he would accidentally pierce the hide. Eventually there was the brush of fur against the palm of his hand. He scraped away dirt and leaves until he could make out the bristly outline. He got to his feet in a crouch, grabbed the edge of the hide and pulled. His knees and lower back, the shoulder he had dislocated years ago, all of it pained him. The bear hide, heavy with blood and life, weighed near to a hundred pounds. He tugged and twisted, and finally was able to wrestle it out of the hole and away from the tree roots. He was lightheaded and out of breath. He reached out a hand to a nearby birch tree and rested against it. When he had regained his composure, he bent and picked up a handful of old, brown leaves. His breathing slowed and, as he rubbed the dirt from his hands, he caught the odor of the place. Wet earth and rotting wood, the smell of both life and death. He considered the plants Arthur had used to bury it. Peat moss, cottonwood boughs, willow leaves, devil's club roots. This place wasn't just about secreting it away. It was the cool and damp, the organic web of plant roots and fungus, the heap of medicinal plants. All to keep the pelt alive.

Warren crouched and put his hands on the bundle of fur and skin. The coat was dense, with a soft grayish underfur and long, brown guard hairs tipped in blond. Warren rolled it over, gently knocking away more of the leaves and dirt, and found himself looking down into the face of his son. Vacant and boneless eye sockets, a black nose at the end of a long, narrow muzzle, the torn ear and the scar line running down through the fur. Warren lifted the skull-less head away from the bundle and unfurled it to let it rest on the ground. His hands trembled.

Since Arthur was a baby, Warren had wondered if he should destroy the thing. He could set it on fire, or sink it in the river, or cut it into pieces and bury it somewhere deep in the woods. He thought of the hide as a curse that bound the boy, and Warren wanted to set him free. But we don't really know, do we? Carol had spoken his deepest fear. Maybe the curse was having to step out of it.

Warren continued to unfold the hide, like unwrapping a rolled-up blanket. He uncurled the empty limbs until he exposed the thick, padded feet, the long claws. He spread the empty body out until it lay wide across the ground, head back, legs outstretched, belly fur to the sky.

A long, jagged rip ran down the center of the chest and belly, the skin on either side thick with rough scar tissue where it had healed and been torn again hundreds, maybe thousands of times over. Every transformation a kind of torment. Years ago, standing on the back deck of the house on an autumn night, Warren had been startled by a tremendous, bellowing moan that resonated through the forest. It had been the animal cry of his son's suffering.

Warren unzipped his canvas chore jacket, took it off, and set it on the ground, and then he unbuttoned the cuff of his shirt and pulled up the sleeve as far as it would go, up to the shoulder. In the bright daylight, he hardly recognized his own arm, thinner and paler and nearly hairless, no longer the arm of a young man. He slid his hand into the opening in the bear skin. The inside was sticky with membrane, fat, and congealing blood, but he reached into the front leg, pushed and pulled up the hide until the fur touched his shoulder and his arm was encased as if in a sleeve.

The bear's skin was moist and cold against his own. He set the padded foot on the ground and pushed the weight of his body down his arm and into the earth, his fingertips touching the hard, rubbery cartilage where the claws began.

The trees were silent, the air still. The cranes didn't call, and no birds sang overhead. Warren knelt alone on the forest floor and tried to imagine how it would feel to walk in those feet, how it would feel to be his son.

Chapter 7

Arthur was shy and clumsy, like a good church boy on a first date. Birdie might have predicted that, but everything else was unexpected. Usually when she had the cabin to herself and brought a man back, it was late at night and they were both tipsy, maybe a little high. There was a sloppy, reckless quality to the sex, any hang-ups or misgivings blunted by the slight numbness.

This was the bold light of day, two in the afternoon. There had been no drawn-out, double-entendre jokes or shared cigarettes, no flattering warm glow of the string of Christmas lights over the bar, no slow dancing or singing together to the jukebox. They were both stone-cold sober.

Arthur had been coming in regularly, always asking for the same tea and toast. On busy afternoons Birdie couldn't stay long, but she'd rest a hand on his shoulder as she set his mug of tea in front of him, or she'd bump him with her hip when she made a joke. When the cafe was quiet, she'd sit across from him and try to draw him out. He was unlike anyone she had ever talked to before. He seemed to listen closely, and he didn't brag or make crude jokes or talk over her, but he never asked her any questions. Mostly he was quiet.

"Do you ever go by Art? Or Archie?" Birdie asked one afternoon.

"No."

"So it's just Arthur, then," she said with mock seriousness, expecting to get a smile off of him.

"Yes. It is the name my second mother gives me."

"Why do you talk like that?"

"What do you mean?"

"I don't know how to explain it." She thought about his words, *the name my second mother gives me.* Not *gave. Gives,* as if it were happening right now.

"You know what it is?" she said. "You don't ever talk in the past, or about something coming up. It's always the present. Do you know what I mean?"

Arthur shook his head, but it seemed to Birdie that he wasn't disagreeing as much as trying to clear his head.

"It is how my brain works."

"What do you mean, the way your brain works?"

"It is as you say. It is always the present."

"Yeah, I guess. But there are things that already happened, and things that might happen tomorrow. Like a timeline, right?"

"When I am young, a teacher says this. Time is a flat line, from here to there, and we mark our place on it. But it is not that simple."

"What is it then?"

Arthur hesitated, like maybe he wasn't sure he wanted to get into such a long conversation, but then he said, "It is more like circles, the many circles spinning, each within another. There is nothing to hold on to."

"What does that mean?"

"Every thing, every time, it is all now," he said. "I talk to you now, but I am also knowing that day we sit on the table and together look at the mountains, and I am also knowing that someday you are with me, there in the mountains."

Birdie nodded, and she was trying hard to understand what he was saying, but the pleasant, deep rumble of his voice was making her lightheaded.

They were both quiet for a moment.

"Wait, what?" Birdie said. "Did you just say that I'm going out to your place?"

"It is possible."

"Are you asking me?"

"No. I say that all times, every possibility, is now."

"Um, okay, I'm not sure I'm following. You and Syd, you guys need to talk. This is the way he likes to go on, about how time and memory don't work the way we think they do. But I don't know, he's stoned half the time."

She had laughed, and when Arthur didn't smile or look at her, she was embarrassed. Did he think she was too stupid to understand his convoluted way of seeing things? For a long moment, neither of them spoke, and her embarrassment was hardening into anger when he said something she couldn't quite hear.

"What?"

"I like the sound of your laugh," he said.

No one had ever told her that before.

Today when he showed up, she knew it was a chance she might not have again for a while. A slow Wednesday, Della gone to Anchorage on a supply run. As long as the cafe stayed empty, Clancy wouldn't notice if she took a longer break than normal. She sat across from Arthur and dared herself to say it—*Would you want to? How about we?*—but the words resisted coming out of her mouth. She fidgeted with the stack of jam packets. She brought him more hot water. The clock ticked on the wall. Finally, she managed it. "I can take my break in a few minutes. Do you . . . would you want to come back to my cabin? No one is there. My little girl is with my grandmother."

He looked directly into her eyes for a long time without smiling, then nodded, finished his tea in a gulp like a man downing a beer, and followed her out the front door of the lodge.

It was pouring rain and there was a chill in Birdie's little cabin. She turned up the baseboard heater. "Come on in. Don't worry about your boots." He was trying to keep on the small rug just inside the door as he undid his laces.

"I need a shower?" he asked.

"What?" Birdie laughed. "God no, we'd never fit in there together."

Arthur stood in his socked feet. He was too tall for Birdie to put her arms around his neck, so she took him by the hand and led him across the room. When she climbed up and stood on the edge of the bed, she was an inch or two taller than him. She turned her head down to kiss him, then ran the tip of her tongue slowly along the soft underside of his upper lip, his beard rough against her chin. He tasted good, like sweet chamomile tea and buttered toast. But he wasn't much of a kisser. He didn't move his lips or tongue at all, and when Birdie looked, she saw his eyes were wide open.

Birdie fell back on the bed and pulled off her jeans and underwear together and tossed them on the floor. She was going to have to take the lead. He was either too shy or too inexperienced, but she didn't mind.

Arthur stood still with his arms at his sides. The rain was pounding on the cabin's metal roof. Birdie couldn't remember ever being so aroused. It was the clarity of it all, daylight peeping around the curtains, her bare skin raised in goosebumps and shudders.

Sitting on the edge of the bed, she pulled off her T-shirt and bra, then reached up and began unbuttoning his jeans. He was so quiet. He didn't moan or speak or even open his mouth. The only sound was each strong, steady breath through his nose.

She was easing down his pants, and kissing the thick blond hair below his belly button, when he lunged and sprawled over the top of her. The bed creaked and groaned under his weight, and he was shoving his face into her neck, into the side of her head, his mouth open like a dog mouthing a toy. Birdie let out a startled laugh. He continued his awkward lurching and shoving. She tried to wiggle and maneuver her way under him, so that they would at least be in a better position, but he was still mouthing the side of her head and she could feel his warm, wet breath against her scalp. She laughed again. "It's not going to work like this," she said.

He stopped and looked down at her, a deep blush spreading across his face, and then that same expression she'd seen before, the lines at the corners of his eyes crinkled like he was sad or confused.

"You didn't hurt me or anything," she said. "You won't." She pulled for him to get on top of her, but the mattress was too soft beneath them and each time he moved, she sank farther in. She squirmed and pushed him away until he was kneeling on the floor beside the bed. He began to button up his pants.

"No, listen," she said. "Lay down, right there."

She wanted to straddle him on the hard floor, his jeans rough against the inside of her thighs, her bare knees rubbing on the old carpet. She could make this work.

"Lay down," she said again.

But he didn't. Still kneeling by the bed, he wrapped his arms around her calves and put his cheek down on her lap, his face turned away from her. She could feel him inhale and exhale against her thigh like he was smelling her skin.

Birdie put a hand on top of his head. His choppy blond hair was softer than it looked. She ran her fingertips along his eyebrow to the edge of the scar. She hesitated and then gently, slowly touched the scar, tracing it down into his beard. The skin was taut and rough. She could see where most of his ear had been cut or ripped away, and the stippled skin healed roughly around the opening, but she wasn't brave enough to touch it. Instead, she leaned over and kissed the side of his face.

"Arthur? It's no big deal. You haven't done it a lot, right? So we'll figure it out. It'll be fun."

But he was standing, buttoning his jeans, stepping into his boots.

"Wait, what?" she said. "We didn't even . . . you didn't . . ."

He walked out without lacing his boots or closing the door behind him.

"What the hell?" Birdie grabbed the bedspread, wrapped it around herself, and followed him outside.

"Arthur?" she yelled after him. "What, so you're just leaving?" His stride was purposeful and unhesitating. As he climbed into the truck and started the engine, she was sure he would look back at her, but he never did.

"Let's have us a chat." Della came around from the bar and patted one of the stools for Birdie to sit.

Just Birdie's luck, Della had returned earlier than expected from Anchorage and pulled up in time to catch Birdie standing barefoot in the muddy parking lot, wrapped in nothing but a bedspread and screaming like a crazy woman as Arthur drove away. Birdie had retreated into her cabin without acknowledging Della. She'd gotten dressed and stretched the minutes as long as she could, but she knew she'd have to face her eventually.

"Fine, stand if you want," Della said after Birdie refused to sit at a bar-stool. "I need to tell you a story I don't think you've heard before. You re-member Sarah? That little blond gal who waitressed for me a couple of summers ago? Did I ever tell you about her run-in with Arthur?"

"No, but it doesn't—"

"So that summer," Della talked over her, "Warren and Carol hired her to house-sit. Carol had to go down to Seattle with the cancer. One night, Sarah is alone at their place, and Arthur shows up. Naked as a loon, crouched on the back porch. That old German shepherd they used to have, he's barking and growling at him, like he's a stranger."

"Okay."

"Sarah said he looked half-starved, hollowed out and scratched up like he'd been running through the brush for days. He wouldn't stand up straight, and when he talked, he wasn't making any sense. She was scared, but she was also worried about him. She tried to coax him inside, and he wouldn't budge, so she went to get a bathrobe. When she came back, he was gone. She tried to phone Warren and Carol, but she couldn't get through to them."

"All right." Birdie was impatient with the conversation. "Did he come back or something?"

"No, not that she could see."

"So, that's it?"

"What do you mean, that's it? A man shows up stark raving in the mid-dle of the night, and you say, 'That's it'? Sarah said it was one of the most upsetting things she'd ever seen."

Birdie was silent.

"And you know all about that kid at his cabin," Della went on. "What happened to him."

"Everyone's heard that story. But I don't see how you can blame Arthur for that."

"Maybe, maybe not. But seems to me, you and Emaleen don't need any more craziness in your life."

"Any more craziness? What the hell is that supposed to mean?"

"I'm not . . . I don't mean anything by it. I see you trying to make some-thing for yourself and Emaleen. I do. But Arthur, he's not the way."

"What, because he doesn't fit in around here? Did you ever consider maybe that's a good thing? That maybe that's what Emaleen and I need, something different than this place?"

Birdie didn't think she'd see Arthur at the lodge anytime soon. She'd run the scene through her head again and again, how she'd been the one pushing it all. She'd asked him back to the cabin, she'd kissed him and unbuttoned his pants, she'd made every move. But was she supposed to be ashamed? If he was looking for some timid mouse of a woman, then he hadn't understood her at all.

As the days passed, though, Birdie thought of the way he had sprawled on top of her, clumsy and open-mouthed, and that sudden blush across his face. She thought of his breath on the inside of her thigh and his tight grasp on her calves, like he was trying to keep from falling.

It was ridiculous, being so distracted that she knocked a lemon meringue pie to the floor, kept counting back the wrong change, and even sliced her thumb on a butcher knife. *Get a grip,* she thought. Every time she heard a truck pull up outside, she refused to look out the cafe windows. She tried not to listen for the sound of the bar door opening and closing. She pretended not to notice the days, the weeks, since she'd last seen him. Della was right, he was strange and awkward and didn't know how to interact with people in the right way. He was probably better off alone in the mountains.

It still knocked the wind out of her when Della told her the news.

"Arthur's finally gone on back to his place on the North Fork." She said it kindly, like she was breaking it to Birdie.

"Oh? I hadn't heard." Birdie continued to set the plastic bottles of ketchup and mustard at each table and take away the stacks of jelly. It was almost lunchtime.

Della gave her a sideways hug. "Hey, I know you took a liking to him. But it's all for the best . . . You okay then?"

"Fine, Del. Just getting the work done."

* * *

When it came to Arthur, the only smart thing she'd done was keep Emaleen away. Emaleen had no fear or caution when it came to loving people—she wanted them all to be part of some big, happy family, and she called most everybody "Uncle" or "Aunt." They spun her around on the barstools and gave her maraschino cherries from their drinks. Some of them even remembered her birthday and gave her a five-dollar bill or a stuffed animal. It was harmless enough. Last summer, though, Emaleen started calling Pete Anderson "Daddy." He'd put her up to it, Birdie was sure—just one more way he'd tried to pin her down. He also showed up at the bar nearly every night, making comments about how Birdie dressed or how friendly she was with her customers. He said the lodge was no place for a woman to raise a child. One night, he invited them to his house for a spaghetti dinner. She was wary as soon as she saw the white tablecloth and bouquet of roses in a vase. Several times during the evening, Pete corrected Emaleen about her table manners and her grammar, and then he asked, a look in Birdie's direction, if she wouldn't like to live in a real house like his where she could have her own bedroom and maybe get a puppy.

Birdie didn't have any trouble walking away from him. But for Emaleen, it wasn't as easy. "I want him to be my dad," she'd begged. "And I want a puppy. Please, Mommy. Please." It was weeks before Emaleen got over it, and Birdie told herself she'd never make that mistake again. Her relationships were her own, and there was no reason to break Emaleen's heart every time a man turned out to be a son of a bitch.

Chapter 8

Birdie was sitting cross-legged on the bed while she sewed a patch into the armpit of her favorite button-up shirt, and Emaleen was at the card table, drawing with crayons on a notepad, when the knock came. Della always knocked once, then charged in without waiting to be asked, so Birdie wondered why she bothered at all. But this time there was a long silence, and then louder pounding at the door. Birdie left her sewing on the bed, went to the window, and pulled back the curtain. It was Arthur, solemnly waiting at the door with no notice toward the window. In one hand he held what looked like a chunk of sod.

"Mommy, what's that sound?"

"Hello?" Arthur called through the door. He'd heard Emaleen. There was no hiding out and pretending they weren't home.

"You are not at the lodge," he said when Birdie opened the door.

"No, it's my day off. What are you doing here?"

"I have . . ." He held the clump out toward her. "This is for you."

It was tundra, like he had ripped the moss and plants out of the ground with his bare hands. The roots hung down through his fingers.

"What is it?"

"It grows where you like."

Birdie didn't understand. Arthur set the ball of dirt and plants into her hands. It was lighter than she expected, like holding a burlap pillow.

"It is from the place you point to," he said.

"Wait. You're saying you went to that spot up on the mountain and brought this all the way back for me?"

"It is winter after, and the flowers grow."

"Flowers? I want to see the flowers! Can I see?" Emaleen said, but when Birdie set the clump of tundra on the card table, Emaleen frowned. "That's not flowers," she said as she went back to her coloring.

"Look closely," Arthur said from the doorway. His voice was neutral, with none of the impatience or cheerful reassurance adults tended to use with children.

"Why?" Emaleen asked.

"The flowers, they are small."

Emaleen stood up from the chair, put her nose within inches of the tundra, and gasped with surprise. "Oh, oh, I see them!"

"What do you see?" Arthur asked.

"I see teensy-weensy baby flowers. They're like tiny little bells, kind of pink and kind of white, all together."

"*Arctostaphylos uva-ursi*," Arthur said.

"That's a weird word," Emaleen said. "Why did you say that?"

"That is one of its names. It is also called kinnikinnick."

"Kinnikinnik-innik-innik," Emaleen repeated, still inspecting the tundra, and then she looked up at Arthur.

"I can write my letters. Do you want to see?" she asked.

As Emaleen chattered on about her numbers and letters, Birdie reached down and touched one of the flowers, smaller than the tip of her finger. Also in the mossy clump, several little mushrooms had survived the upheaval, as well as a scattering of grayish-white caribou lichen. It was easy to think tundra was nothing, like rolled out greenish-brown carpet, but up close it was a hundred miniature lives in a square foot, intertwined and delicate. A peculiar and beautiful gift.

But Birdie wasn't going to throw herself off that cliff again. He'd left her standing out in the parking lot like a jackass.

"Emaleen, I need to talk with Arthur for a minute." Birdie motioned for him to step outside with her. "So," she said as she closed the door behind herself. "What do you want?"

"To see you."

Birdie let out a hard laugh. "Really? So. You run off, disappear for weeks, and then show back up here like we're on a date or something?"

"Mommy?" Emaleen had opened the door. "Can we go to the river and look for more flowers? And can he come with us?"

"Emaleen, just give us a minute, okay? And maybe Arthur doesn't want to go with us."

"I do," Arthur said quietly.

"Yippee! He's going too! Mommy. Mommy, where are my boots? My pretty boots with the rainbows?"

Birdie's head felt like an overcrowded, noisy room. Maybe on a walk, Emaleen would stop talking for two seconds and Birdie would be able to think coherently. "Yeah, I guess we can go. Your boots are right there. Stay close to us though, okay? And get a sweater."

"But I don't want a sweater. 'Cause it's summertime." Emaleen pushed her way past them and into the empty parking lot.

"Where's your dad's truck?" Birdie asked Arthur.

"I come on foot."

"All the way from your dad's place? That's like what, four or five miles?"

"Hurry, hurry, hurry," Emaleen said, running back and pulling on Birdie's hand, then sprinting ahead again. She ran across the grass behind the lodge until she reached the spruce forest, where she stopped and waited for them.

"Look at my water boots," Emaleen said, kicking each foot out as she walked beside Arthur. "See! Do you see? And they have rainbows. They can go in the mud. And the puddles. And when it's raining. Do you have water boots ..."

She turned to Birdie and in a loud whisper said, "What's his name? I forgetted."

"Arthur. His name is Arthur."

"Arthur, so you want to go to the river with us? But you've got to be very careful. You can't go very close. Okay? Because you can get drownded."

The path became too narrow for them all to walk side by side, so Birdie followed behind the two of them.

"If you don't know how to go there, that's okay," Emaleen was saying to Arthur. "Did you know there's a baby moose? He has a big nose and long legs, and his ears are so cute." She reached up with both hands and touched her head where the ears would have been if she were a moose. "Did you know he was kind of red and brown? Kind of red and orange, maybe, together so that it's brown. That's not my favorite color. I love purple. Maybe we can look for purple flowers. Do you love purple?"

Emaleen reached high above her head and grabbed on to Arthur's hand so that he had to stoop to walk beside her. Then she spotted something on the ground.

"Look, Arthur! Come here! They're so pretty!"

Emaleen squatted next to a cluster of small pink orchids growing up from the moss.

"I think those are fairy slippers," Birdie called to her. "Don't pick them, okay?" But she could see that Emaleen had already plucked one and was hiding it behind her back.

"Why?"

"It's all right. You're not in trouble. It's just those flowers are different. Grandma Jo says when you pick it, for some reason the whole plant dies, and there aren't a lot of them. But just that one. No more, okay?"

Emaleen held up the small flower to Arthur.

"Look. See—this is a pretty flower," she said. "It's for you."

"Thank you," he said, letting her drop it into the palm of his hand. "*Calypso bulbosa.* But I am not eating it."

"No way!" Emaleen said. "Who wants to eat flowers?"

Arthur pointed a thumb at his own chest.

"You do? Nun-uh, I don't think so. Is he pulling my leg, Mommy?"

Birdie shrugged and raised an eyebrow at Arthur. "You know, are you teasing her? Or maybe, by some chance, do you eat a lot of flowers?"

"Most are good. Even this." He held up the fairy slipper. "The flower is not so much. But the bulbs, the roots underground, are very good."

"Ewww. I don't think soooo," Emaleen said in a singsong voice.

They had returned to the path and Emaleen led the way toward the river. The floor of the spruce forest was carpeted in moss and dwarf dogwoods with their leaves deep green and their bracts just turning white.

"Do you eat these ones, Arthur?"

"Yes."

"And how about those yucky brown ones?" she asked, pointing to some late-coming horsetail sprouts.

"They are tasty. I eat them and eat them and eat them until my belly is full." Arthur patted his middle, and Emaleen laughed.

"You're so silly," she said, and Arthur laughed too. It was a big, rumbling, joyful laugh that Birdie had never heard before. She was losing control of the situation.

The rest of the way to the river, the back-and-forth game continued. Emaleen dashing from one place to another, can you eat this, and how about that. Arthur answering yes or no and often saying some kind of scientific-sounding name. Birdie didn't know all the plants so well, but she wasn't sure about eating any of them. Later, she would need to sit down with Emaleen and tell her that despite anything he'd said, she should treat all wild plants as if they were poisonous. A handful of baneberries or a few purple-black monkshood flowers could kill a little girl.

At the Wolverine River, the last of the ice was gone and the water had risen to a fast, silty gray. Arthur and Emaleen were several strides ahead and disappeared into a cluster of willows. When Birdie stepped into the next clearing, she couldn't see or hear either of them.

Every year or two, somewhere along the river, a dog or a child or a fisherman drowned. Just last summer, Della's nephew overturned a canoe near the mouth of Quartz Creek and survived only because she'd insisted he wear a lifejacket. It wasn't the depth of the water alone. It was the fast current, the glacial cold, and the fine, silty mud that clung to you and weighted you down.

"Emaleen? Arthur?" she called out. "Where are you guys?"

"We're right here, Mommy!"

Just upstream, on the other side of a large boulder, Arthur and Emaleen were next to a small, spring-fed pool that was only a foot or two deep and surrounded by a sandy, dried-out river channel. Emaleen was picking up pebbles and throwing them into the water. The sun had come out from behind the clouds, and the clear water sparkled.

"Now you try it," Emaleen ordered. She handed Arthur a round, flat rock, and it made a small *ploonk* when he threw it into the center of the pool.

"That one's too little. Let's get a bigger one," she said. Emaleen found a large piece of granite sticking out of the gray sand. When she pulled at it and it didn't move, she let out a dramatic "Ugggh."

"This one is way, way too big." Then looking up to Arthur, she said, "You try."

Arthur pushed at the rock with his boot, then bent over, pried it up with his fingertips, and pulled it out. It left behind a deep hole in the sand. The boulder was the size of three basketballs, and Arthur held it in his arms as if not sure what to do next.

"Mommy, look! It's super big. Let's throw it, Arthur!"

Arthur heaved the rock into the center of the pool, and in a magnificent sun-streaked *sploosh*, water flew in all directions, splashing Arthur's legs and raining water down on Emaleen's head. She sputtered and spit out water as she wiped her face with her hands, and then came her surprised laughter. "Did you see that, Mommy?" Arthur laughed too, that great, deep rumble.

"Again! Let's go again!" Emaleen shouted.

The three of them searched for rocks of all sizes and took turns throwing them into the pool. Birdie tried to teach Emaleen how to skip the small, flat stones. The sun rose high above the mountains, the chill left the air, and it was as if in that moment, summer arrived. Emaleen took off her boots and socks to wade in the water. Birdie sat on a gray driftwood log not far away and stretched her legs in front of her and let her eyes close. The sun was warm on her face and the fragrance of sticky new cottonwood leaves strong in the air. She didn't hear Arthur approach, but she felt him sit beside her on the log. For a moment, it was quiet except for the call of a chickadee from a nearby branch, Emaleen's bare feet smacking in the mud, and Arthur's slow, steady breaths. With her eyes closed, Birdie heard the smallest sounds, noticed the reddened glow of the sun on her eyelids and the light breeze that came through the cottonwood branches. It was the kind of afternoon that usually made her drowsy and lazy, but Arthur was like an electric charge in the air around her. She kept her eyes closed and listened to him breathe, the hairs on her arms prickling. She'd never felt this way just sitting quietly next to a man, and she didn't understand it now, but it was a sensation she'd always loved—that narrow slip between excitement and fear.

When Arthur cleared his throat, Birdie startled as if falling in her sleep.

"I want to say. After your question, I am thinking about it."

"Oh," she said. "What question?"

"Am I lonely."

"Yeah?"

"It is true. Maybe always."

"I don't get it, why did you leave then? Why didn't you say goodbye or tell me what was wrong?"

He cleared his throat again and began to methodically rub his knees.

"I am troubled here. I try, but it is no good." He looked to the other side of the river. "I am better when I am away, over there. When I am young, I think this is what I want. To be away from here. But when I am older, I am one way, another, back again."

Several times, he started to say something but then stopped, as if he couldn't find the words. Birdie thought of the foreign tourists who occasionally came through the lodge; Arthur didn't have an accent, but like them, his sentences were halting and broken. He knew what he wanted to say—he wasn't thick-headed the way Della made him out to be—but it was like he was working to translate it from a different first language. And the harder he tried, the more he struggled.

"Here or there, why I am not content," he said. "It is a . . . a fight. With myself."

Neither of them spoke for a while.

"I know what you mean," Birdie said. "We're just barely scraping by, you know. Me and Emaleen. It's like it takes everything I've got to get through the week. Every day is the same. Do this, don't do that, get this done, and there's never enough money, never enough time. Just everyone telling me I'm screwing up, that I should be doing it all better. You're never really free. But I don't know, what does that even mean—*free*? And then I look at you. You're not caught up in it. When we were out on the picnic table, you said that you make your own way. Maybe that's what I should be doing. Maybe I need to get out of here and make my own way."

For a long time he didn't say anything, and she wondered if they didn't really understand each other. She watched Emaleen push handfuls of sand and small rocks into the hole where Arthur had pulled out the boulder.

Arthur cleared his throat again and stood up, and the log rebounded from his weight.

"Yeah, we should be getting back," Birdie said. "Emaleen hasn't had lunch yet and . . ."

As she started to stand up, Arthur bent down and put his lips to the crown of her head. He didn't kiss her, only breathed in and out through her hair. She thought about turning her face up to him so they could kiss, but instead she sat very still, a pleasant shudder down the back of her neck.

When he finally pulled away, Birdie stood and picked up Emaleen's boots and shook out her socks.

"Hey Arthur, I was thinking . . ." But when she looked over her shoulder, he had disappeared into the willows without following any trail.

"Where did he go?" Emaleen asked.

"I don't know, I guess he's going home."

It was like that morning at the creek, the exhilaration when the rainbow trout hit the lure and leapt and splashed. For just a moment they were joined, Birdie and that dancing, pulsing shimmer of life, and the cool creek water, she could feel it flowing through her veins.

That's how it was with Arthur. Getting close to him, feeling his eyes on her—like touching something dark and wild, and then watching it dart away.

Late that night, Birdie heard him outside of her cabin. She was watching Johnny Carson on the television with the volume turned low, Emaleen asleep in the bed beside her, when the noise came. Not a pounding or even a light knock, just the faintest rustle of movement from the other side of the door.

She took a flashlight from the drawer in the bedside table, unlocked the door and eased it open, but she didn't need the light. A three-quarter moon had risen in the clear sky above the mountains, and he was just a few feet from the door, crouched on the ground with his back to her.

"Arthur?" she whispered. "What are you doing here?"

He stood and faced her. "I am thinking about you," he said. "All the time." His voice was low and hoarse, like he'd injured his vocal cords from yelling.

"I've been thinking about you too," she said.

Birdie looked into the cabin, to Emaleen sleeping on their bed. If she left the television on, with the volume low, she probably wouldn't wake up.

"Just give me a second," Birdie whispered. She went to the closet and as quietly as she could, took a spare blanket from the top shelf. By the door, she crammed one foot into a sneaker and reached for the other.

"You can leave them," he said.

"My shoes? Yeah?" She hesitated, then laughed, and kicked off the sneaker and stepped outside. "Come on," she said, taking Arthur's hand and leading him toward the woods behind the cabin. She was wearing only the underwear and T-shirt she slept in, and the air was cold against her naked arms and legs, the ground damp and prickly against her bare feet. She was trying not to laugh out loud. She felt like a teenager, sneaking out in the middle of the night. She led him away from the cabin and into the spruce trees, the thick bed of fallen needles cushioning her steps. The roar of the Wolverine River grew closer, but she could still see the cabin through the trees. She touched the ground—it seemed dry enough, so she shook the blanket and spread it out. When she straightened up, Arthur was so close that she bumped into him. One side of his face was lit by the bright moon, the other darkened by the shadows of the trees. He bent his head down and put his lips to hers. It was like he had been thinking about how to do it better because he left his lips slightly open and tilted his head down to meet hers. His facial hair bristled against her lips. Birdie shivered as they kissed.

"You are cold."

"Not really," she said. "I'm just . . . excited." She reached for his hands to pull him down toward the blanket. At the same time, he tried to put his arms around her, so that they were working at odds to each other. Birdie laughed and let go, and he grabbed her around the waist. She spun around, slipped out of his grasp, and still laughing, ran a few steps away. Arthur lunged at her and caught hold of the hem of her T-shirt, but she pulled it off over her head and broke away. She sprinted around the other side of a spruce tree. She could hear him coming closer to her, and she ran again. The moonlight flashing through the branches, his hard breaths just behind her—it made her want to run all the more. She slipped off her underwear and dropped them on the ground. She was naked now, sprinting through the moonlight and cold night air, adrenaline making her light on her feet even as she worked to catch her breath. A scream was rising at the back of her throat. Something was going to startle her. It just hadn't come yet. She ran faster. The branches scratched at her arms and legs, and her toes bumped into roots and bushes. She tripped and fell to her knees, and then he was on top of her, his weight pressing the bare skin of her breasts and belly and thighs into the rough earth. Heat radiated off his entire body. His exhalations were each a quiet moan, and he was mouthing the back of her neck, her shoulders. He had her pinned to the ground, and she was panting and laughing under him. He slid his hand around her waist and pulled her up onto her hands and knees, and she heard him unbuttoning his jeans.

All the awkward hesitation was gone, and there was only impulse. At first he was behind her, grabbing hard on to her hips, then they tumbled and wrestled, and she straddled him with her bare feet flat on the ground, dirt and leaves and spruce needles clinging to them both. He was quiet and intensely focused, as if nothing existed beyond the touch of their skin and tongues and teeth, and Birdie, looking up through the branches and into the moon-filled night sky, had become wild and powerful, soaring naked through the trees, a woman who had truly broken free.

Chapter 9

Something big, and maybe exciting or sad, was happening, and Emaleen was trying very hard to figure it out.

"... down in the alders ... nothing but scraps left."

"... haven't seen the cow at all."

"Any other sign?"

"... pile of scat the size of a fucking dinner plate ..."

Emaleen was pretending to play, reaching up to the pool table and rolling the balls around, but really she was listening to the grown-ups. She wasn't sure why she was allowed to be in the bar today, but maybe it was because something so big had happened that the grown-ups forgot about the rule. They weren't laughing and hollering like they normally did in the bar. Whatever they were talking about was interesting and serious. It sounded like Uncle Syd had found something in the woods.

"... probably sometime yesterday."

"That calf was around here again just the other day. What was that, Della? Like Saturday? Emaleen was watching it out the window."

At the sound of her name, Emaleen took her chance. "Mommy, what's happening?"

Her mom didn't want to say, Emaleen could see. All the grown-ups were quiet and looking down at Emaleen, which made her nervous. "Okay, so you know that baby moose that's been coming around," her mom said.

"A grizzly bear killed it. Syd found where it happened not far from his place."

It took a second for Emaleen to understand what her mom was saying, and then she thought maybe she was going to cry, or was she supposed to cry? She wasn't sure. "But why? Why did the bear do that?"

"Just hustling up his dinner," Uncle Syd said, but he said it nicely. "He's got to eat, just like us. But when there's a grizzly around, we've got to mind our p's and q's."

"So don't you dare run off to play in the woods like that again," Aunt Della said. "You hear? This is serious business."

Emaleen nodded obediently, but she didn't like it when Aunt Della talked to her like that. She wanted to say that she wasn't a baby, she hadn't been playing in the woods that day, and she knew all about the scary things out in the world. She'd only gone because she'd had no choice.

Emaleen kept thinking about it all day even though she didn't want to. It wouldn't be good if a bear missed his dinner and got all skinny and died. But it was even more horrible about the baby moose. At Grandma Jo's house, she used crayons to color a picture of the moose calf the best she could remember him, and she thought about the rainbow trout she and her mom had eaten, and Della's dog that got stompled by a moose, and the red-backed vole Clancy killed in a trap because it was eating the cabbages. Grandma Jo said dying was like going to sleep, but that didn't seem right. Sleeping was cuddly and quiet, but getting all eaten up or caught in a trap wasn't like that at all.

Emaleen used to think that Norma had died. Norma was her mom's mom, except nobody called her Mom or Grandma. Nobody talked about her at all, and if Emaleen got brave enough to ask about her, her mom would go quiet and Grandma Jo would get angry and say, "She's as good as dead to me."

"How come she died?" Emaleen asked one time, and her mom explained that Norma wasn't really dead, she'd just left when she and Aunt Liz were little girls and gone to a place called Florida where it was hot and sunny and there was lots of sand and lots and lots of people.

Now that she was a big kid, Emaleen understood all of it, that people and animals sometimes died and moms sometimes left. It seemed impossible and horrifying, but also important to know. Once she understood, Emaleen started watching her mom carefully. Sometimes, when her mom stood on the front step of their cabin and smoked her cigarettes and looked into the woods, Emaleen was sure she wanted to go far away and leave Emaleen behind.

That was the secret. The one she didn't tell anyone, not even Thimblina. Because it either meant her mom was a bad person who might leave her daughter behind, or Emaleen was a bad person for thinking of it.

Chapter 10

Birdie had planned for them to be gone to Arthur's cabin on the other side of the Wolverine by now, but this one night she was glad they hadn't left yet. It was summer solstice—more than twenty hours of sunlight in a single day and never a true darkness to the sky, and then, just as summer arrived, the days would begin to dim. Tomorrow would be just a bit shorter, winter a little closer. A celebration and a mourning.

Della wouldn't leave anybody out in the cold on a holiday, so Thanksgiving, Christmas, New Year's, Easter, the lodge was open through dinnertime. Summer solstice was the one exception. Della shut everything down and invited everyone to a potluck dinner and bonfire. For days, she and Syd had gathered broken pallets and heaps of junk wood for the fire. This morning Birdie had helped them set up folding tables and lawn chairs and, in case the weather turned bad, stretch a tarp out from the eaves of the lodge so people could get out of the rain. They pulled the old volleyball net tight, and Clancy mowed the tall grass so it'd be easier to play. By early afternoon, people began to trickle in, from Alpine and Rocky Lake, some from as far as Anchorage, Homer, and Fairbanks. They set up their tents and camper trailers along the edge of the forest. No one would be driving home.

As the people came, the tables filled up with food—casseroles and stews and Cathy's ptarmigan jalapeño enchiladas, bags of potato chips, trays of smoked salmon, moose sausage, cheese and crackers, a leafy salad in a giant carved wooden bowl, and an entire table devoted to dessert—Jell-O and fruit concoctions, cakes and cookies, Boots's currant and brandy pie, and Syd's brownies. Syd had brought two batches, one for the kid-friendly table and another "magic" batch for the grown-ups that was kept on a high shelf by the back door of the lodge.

Clancy was slow-cooking a front quarter of a caribou in the fifty-gallon oil drum he'd converted into a smoker. He had also cut a dozen or so willow branches for hot dog sticks for the kids. By six in the evening, there was a good crowd, and it looked like the tarp would be unnecessary—the sun was shining over the mountains and there wasn't a cloud in sight. Della tapped the kegs, and with a splash of gasoline and a tossed match, lit the bonfire. People set up their lawn chairs around the yard and started gathering at the tables to fill their paper plates with food.

Birdie helped Emaleen put ketchup on her hot dog, which looked like it had been charred in the flames, as well as dropped on the ground a few times. Before she could get her a plate with some carrots and chips, Emaleen was off and running with a pack of kids.

Warren was coming in from the parking lot, carrying a box of store-bought cookies. Carol had been the baker in their house, and this would be the first time he'd come to a potluck since she'd passed away. He had always seemed out of place at these gatherings, at least a decade older and more formally dressed than everyone else. His khaki slacks ironed, his short-sleeved dress shirt tucked in and buttoned to the neck, his black leather shoes polished, the Alaska State Trooper never entirely retired. But he had slowed down since Carol's death. He seemed more fragile and a little lost, like he had just gotten over a long illness and wasn't quite himself yet.

"Hi," Birdie called out to him with a wave. "The weather's looking good, isn't it?"

Warren made a small sound of agreement.

"I hope it stays this way," she said. "For when you fly us out."

He stopped and looked at her closely.

"We can't wait. Both of us, me and Emaleen. I think Arthur too."

Warren said nothing, and Birdie knew. Arthur hadn't told him. Warren's eyes went to Birdie's neck—her sweater had slipped to the side and uncovered a half-circle bruise. It was one of several places where Arthur had bitten her, that night in the forest. Birdie quickly pulled the sweater up to cover it, but Warren was already walking away.

It doesn't hurt, she'd told Arthur when he'd seen the bite marks. He didn't apologize or say he didn't mean it. She liked that better. It made her sick when a man fawned or groveled or made excuses for something he'd done.

Warren made his way to the food tables, and watching him, Birdie realized it didn't matter. She would get there one way or another. She was light on her feet, light in her chest, and as she moved through the crowd, she was slightly detached from everyone around her. She talked to people, even Lois and Roy. She offered to hold their youngest so Lois could get plates of food for the older children. When Boots jostled into her, Birdie teased him about dipping too far into the brandy bottle while he was making his pie. She brought Clancy a plastic cup of beer and told him the caribou was smelling delicious. From the outside, she probably seemed like the same old Birdie, joking and flirting and having a good time, but she knew otherwise. Within days she and Emaleen would be gone. She thought of the teeth marks hidden under the edge of her sweater. She might even be falling in love.

These people knew none of that. For the first time in her life, she was like a mysterious visitor, someone passing through the lodge on her way to something better. She took a sip of beer. She wouldn't drink too much tonight, and she'd skip Syd's brownies. She was on the brink of a different life. Soon enough there'd be no beer or cigarettes or magic brownies, and she needed to learn to do without.

"Mommy, Mommy." Emaleen's cheeks were smeared with ketchup and dirt. "Can I have cake now? Aunt Bonnie has rhubarb cake. With frosting and flowers and everything. It's the most pretty ever. Please. Please."

Birdie pulled her up onto her lap. "Not yet," she said. "I don't think people are ready for dessert. Syd hasn't even cut up the caribou. You want some of that, don't you?"

"I want cake, cake, cake," she said.

"Pretty soon, okay?" Birdie hugged Emaleen and pressed her cheek against hers. "Ooooh, you're cold." Even though it was now officially sum-

er and the sun was still above the mountains, the evening was cool.
Boots threw a large cottonwood log onto the fire and a blaze of sparks
burst into the sky. Birdie opened her jacket and tried to pull Emaleen in
closer. She wanted to whisper in her ear—"We're going to the mountains.
You and me. We're leaving this place for something better, something we
don't even know yet."

"I'm not cold." Emaleen squirmed to be let down. "Can I go on the
swing?"

"What swing?"

Emaleen pointed to the rope hammock that Della and Syd had tied between two spruce trees at the edge of the forest.

"It's not really a swing. It's to take a nap in."

"But I don't want to take a nap. I want to swing," Emaleen said, already
running away.

It was just after midnight and Birdie refilled her plastic cup one last time
from the keg and found an empty chair by the fire. While she sat staring
into the flames, Syd unfolded a lawn chair next to her. He was wearing a
floppy leather cowboy hat, his long hair in a thick braid down his back. His
beard wasn't trimmed but it was brushed, and he wore a faded but clean
pair of jeans and a handsewn cotton shirt in a paisley print.

Birdie gave an admiring whistle. "Look at you," she said. "You clean up
good."

Syd bowed slightly and swept off his hat, like a gentleman gnome, and
then he put the hat on Birdie's head. When he sat down beside her, he
folded his hands over his belly and tipped his head back to let it rest on the
lawn chair.

"Hmmm. Parrish blue," he said. "Lovely."

Birdie looked up, and as the hat began to slip off, she tightened the
stampede string under her chin. "What kind of blue?"

"You know, *The Dinky Bird* and *The Lute Players*? *Daybreak* and *Ecstasy*? He
was neoclassical. Turn of the century. But from what I've read he thought
of himself more like a mechanic. Loved knowing how things worked, the
printing process. The lighting. *Arabian Nights*—one of my favorite books

growing up. You know, though, I don't think it was the one Richard Burton did. Not Elizabeth Taylor's Burton. *Sir Richard Francis Burton.*" He pronounced the name with an exaggerated British accent. "The one who went looking for the source of the Nile. And you know what I just found out? Not the same Burton that wrote the *Melancholy* book. Did you know that? I had those two conflated in my mind, but totally the wrong century. That was, like, 1600 something instead of the nineteenth century. For that matter, the wrong first name. Robert Burton, not Richard. No relation, at least that I know of. Just learned that a while back. At this bookshop down on the coast. He's got old books stacked all around on chairs and the floor, the shelves bowing under all the weight, but not a fleck of dust, and no rhyme or reason to it, but he could put his hand on any book in the shop, just name it." Syd began to chuckle and his hands jumped up and down on his belly. "Here's the best part. Do you know his name—the owner's name, of the bookstore . . ." His laughter turned high-pitched and hiccupy. "You know what his name was? Robert! At least I think that's what it was. Shit, maybe it was Richard." He laughed and snorted like a kid trying to keep from giggling in class. When he stopped, he wiped at his eyes and sat up slightly in the lawn chair. "How'd we get way over here? Where were we?"

"Blue, I think."

"Parrish blue! Right, that's right. Maxfield Parrish. I've never much cared for the people in his paintings. Gloomy eyes, kind of sickly. Like ghosts, or sculptures of ghosts, without any bones and barely alive and it makes you queasy. But those skies. Christ almighty. Cobalt oxide. The clouds, the cool shadows in the trees. Everything in this golden blue. Like the beginning of the end. Dawn or sunset, that moment just before it's gone." With his head still rested on the back of the chair, he shouted into the night sky, "Whoo-whee." A high giggle. "That's a good batch of brownies, if I may say so myself. I've been playing around with some Maui Wowie and Matanuska Thunder Fuck this year, and I've got wacky tobacky coming out my ears." He sighed contentedly, turned his head toward Birdie, and held up his plastic cup of beer. "Happy midsummer night," he said. She touched her cup to his and they both drank.

Most of the time, she had no idea what Syd was talking about. He was probably the smartest person she'd ever known. People said he had an advanced degree from Back East, something to do with rocks or chemistry, and that he could make a killing up on the oil fields as an engineer if he wanted, but Syd never talked about it. For as long as Birdie had known him, he'd been a packer on Jim Mahoney's hunts, leading horses into the mountains and carrying in supplies, setting up camps, tracking sheep and moose, caribou and bears, and when the clients shot them, skinning off their hides and hauling out the trophies. Hard, hard work, and making just enough money so he could hole up for the winter and read piles of books about everything under the sun. Birdie wondered if that was why he talked ninety miles an hour, jumping from one thing to the next, remembering something as he forgot a half dozen others. It was all that time spent alone reading. Or maybe it was his magic brownies.

Syd tipped his head back on his lawn chair again and stared up at the night sky. He inhaled slowly and deeply through his nostrils. "Now are the woods all black, but still the sky is blue. May you always see a blue sky overhead, my young friend."

Birdie could tell he was using his narration voice. "What's that from?"

"Fucking Proust. Yeah, yeah, still mucking around with that," he said, as if she knew the book he was talking about. "On and off for too many years, and about the time I'm ready to give him the heave-ho, right out the window, I come across a line like that. It's not his, he's quoting someone else, I think."

"It's pretty," she said. She tilted her head back so that she could almost see the entirety of the sky, a giant pale-blue dome overhead, its edges trimmed in mountain ranges, jagged treetops, and the brim of Syd's hat. She watched a few sparks from the bonfire rise higher and higher until they extinguished in the cold blue. The moon was a thin, translucent sliver just above the trees, and out of the corner of her eye she thought she saw a star but when she looked at it directly, it vanished. Tonight, it would never get dark enough to see more than a handful of stars.

"So, fess up," Syd said.

"What?"

"Come on," he said. "You haven't opened a single one of them, have you? Not even McMurtry, God love him."

It was the books that he was talking about.

"Or *True Grit*? That slip of a thing would take you a day if you put your mind to it," he said. "*Lost Horizon*? Shangri-La! Come on, kid. Just a few pages, you won't be able to set it down. But that poetry collection. The Canadians? Cohen. Margaret Atwood. The greats. There's a line in there, something about 'In this country . . . in this country the animals have the faces of people.' Something like that. It'll take hold of you, Birdie. But you've got to give it a chance."

"I will," she lied. "I really will."

At some point during their friendship, she had admitted that while she'd done all right in high school and graduated a semester early, she had never liked to read. Syd was appalled, heartbroken. But then he had taken it on as a mission. Eventually, he said, he would find the book to make her fall in love.

"So." Syd sat up and crossed one leg over the other, leaning conspiratorially toward her. "You are"—he put his two thumbs together and flapped his hands like butterfly wings—"off and away."

It took her a second to realize that this time he was talking about her move to the other side of the Wolverine. Della must have told him.

"Yeah, I think me and Emaleen, we need a change. We're going to stay with Arthur, at his cabin on the North Fork. You've been out there, haven't you? To Arthur's place?"

"Sure. Here's the thing, though—nobody says his real name. They're all euphemisms. Did you know that? Barefoot wanderer. Four-legged man. Golden friend. Honey-eater. A dark thing. No one wants to call him up with his true name, you see. No one wants to summon him. Scares the shit out of us. Not just here. All over the world, all down through the ages, we've come up with these secret names."

Syd sat up straight. "Or say he's here, right? Standing in front of us, and he's blocking our path." He gestured toward some unseen thing between them and the bonfire. "We've got to keep our eyes down and ask him nicely, please move along. Maybe we call him our gentle cousin. Gentle cousin." Syd's laughter was high-pitched and giggly, and it always made Birdie smile even when she didn't understand what was so funny. "Please spare us, because we're your kin," he said in a mocking high voice, and then in his regular voice: "We don't want him to fucking eat us, right? I know. I know what you're thinking. In English, it's *bear*. You know what that means? Brown one. Just—the brown one." He laughed and tipped precariously in the lawn chair so that Birdie thought he might topple backward, but then he came safely back down. "If we ever knew his true name, it's long forgotten."

"There are a lot of bears on the other side, yeah?" Birdie said, trying to follow his zigzagging train of thought. "But Arthur, he's lived over there a long time. We'll be fine."

Syd didn't say anything, only stared into the fire.

"I know Della, she thinks it's a bad idea," Birdie continued. "She's probably told you that."

Syd was looking at her now, his intensely blue eyes catching the light of the fire. "Have you ever seen one skinned out before?" he asked.

"What? Oh . . . a bear? Yeah, years ago. A black bear. When I was a kid. Grandpa Hank shot it on the homestead."

"You remember what it looked like?"

She did, even after all these years—when she'd first caught sight of the bloody, gutted, and skinned animal on her grandparents' back porch, she'd thought someone had been murdered.

"Like a person," she said.

"Exactly. The hands, the feet, the muscles in the legs and chest, you peel back that hide and it could be your brother under it all."

She expected him to say more, but he stared as if lost or mesmerized or too stoned to remember what he had been talking about.

"Is that why you don't do many bear hunts for Jim?" she asked.

"Couple years back, I read this article about a group of people in Siberia," Syd said.

Birdie didn't interrupt. Syd usually answered a question from so far afield you couldn't see it coming, but then again, sometimes he got lost along the way and forgot the original question.

"They believe it's a sin to kill a bear," he continued. "Because he's divine. A child of the moon and the Ursa Major constellation. His eyes are stars and his front paws are hands, and his back paws, they call those his boots. And they don't say that he has a hide or a pelt—it's his cloak. But even with all of that, they're compelled to kill him. It's part of how they perceive their own survival. Hunting the bear. Sometimes they eat the meat, but in their eyes it's more like cannibalism. Who wants to fucking eat their brother? It's this outrageous transgression, and they've got to reconcile it somehow, right? So how do they go about that? Same as we humans always have done—rituals. They prop up the bear's disembodied head. They offer him food and drink and honor. It's about fear. Reverence. Awe. But maybe shame too. Hell of a beautiful mess."

As Syd talked, Birdie watched Warren pick up his box of uneaten, store-bought cookies from the table and head toward his truck. He'd stayed later than she would have expected. Syd had stopped talking and was looking at Warren too.

"You know Carol, she saw it from the start," he said. "Right when they found him and brought him home. It's Warren who's always had a hard time coming to terms with it."

"What do you—"

"Hey Syd!" Della called from the volleyball net. "Syd, hustle up, we're short one." It was tradition on summer solstice to play at least one game after midnight. They had four on one side of the net, only three on the other, and Syd was known for his ace serves.

"Yep, yep," he called back. "I'm coming."

Syd stood up from his chair, bowed a little and took Birdie's hand again, patting it as he talked.

"Here's the thing, Birdie—nobody can tell us who to love. Or where we're allowed to go searching for happiness. People will try, they always do, but it's a waste of breath. I was younger than you when I said to my family, TTFN, I'm headed north. To live by some river I found on a map. On a fucking map. I had absolutely no idea what I was getting into. No job, no friends, no place to stay, no plans at all. My old man, he said it was reckless, selfish, and I'd probably end up dead. But we can't listen to that. We've got to follow that stronger compass inside of us." He thumped his fist against his chest, as if indicating a compass somewhere next to his heart. "The one that tells us where we belong. We've got to be witness to the mystery. Explorers. Fearless in the face of adventure and love." This last bit he said in his recitation voice, his fist still on his chest and his chin raised, like it was a proclamation.

"Okay, Syd, whatever you say," Birdie said with half a smile. She took off his hat and held it up to him. "Hey, don't forget this."

"Suits you better." He set it back on her head and tapped it down so that it nearly covered her eyes. "It'll keep the sun and mosquitoes off your head when you're on the other side of the river."

Chapter 11

The heat from the bonfire made Emaleen's cheeks all warm and roasty. She poked her willow stick deep into the red coals and counted, and counted, and waited. When the tip of the stick finally burst into flames, she held it up in the air.

"Whoa, careful with that," she heard a grown-up say, but she was already off and running. She held the stick over her head as she went. The flame blew out fast, but the end kept on glowing red and throwing off sparks. She ran around the picnic table and then around the hammock, waving the burning stick over her head, and then in bigger and bigger circles she ran until she reached the spruce trees. She stopped and looked into the dark woods.

She liked standing there, right at the edge. The air from the forest was quiet and shivery, but behind her, she could hear the voices of the grown-ups, and when she looked back, she could see the flames of the bonfire.

It was a magical night. Uncle Syd said so. He'd tucked a dandelion behind Emaleen's ear and told her to dance with the fairies before they all disappeared, and she couldn't tell if he was joking or not. But Emaleen knew this—it was the best night ever. They were all together, just the way she liked it. Her mom and Uncle Syd and Aunt Della and Uncle Roy and Aunt Bonnie, and lots and lots of other grown-ups and children and dogs, some Emaleen knew, and some she didn't. All the guest cabins were full, and some people had tents and campers, and some people only rolled out their sleeping bags in the grass and said they hoped it didn't rain.

The grown-ups were laughing a lot and dancing silly and playing volleyball, and nobody said, "No running!" or "No getting dirty!" Everyone was too happy to care whether children followed rules or not. Emaleen had eaten two chocolate cookies before dinner, and when she didn't want to finish her hot dog, she fed the last bites to a little gray dog named Popper. She tried to pet him, and the dog snapped like he was going to bite her. Emaleen looked around because maybe she and the dog would both be in trouble, but nobody noticed, so she stuck her tongue out at the dog and went back for more of Aunt Bonnie's pretty cake. Later, an older boy she didn't know told her she had frosting on her face, but Emaleen didn't care because he had frosting on his face too.

For a while, Emaleen made friends with a girl who was five years old and kind of bossy. Emaleen had taught her how to hold a dandelion under her chin to see if she liked butter, and the girl showed her the truck camper where she was going to sleep with her family that night. Later they played tag with Uncle Roy's kids. Then the girl had fallen and skinned her knees and cried like she was a baby, so the game was over.

Emaleen also got to push the button on the keg to fill plastic cups with beer for the grown-ups, and Uncle Roy showed her how to tip the cup and make the beer run down the inside, that way it wouldn't be too foamy. She thought the foam looked delicious. When no one was looking, she'd squirted beer in her mouth, but it was disgusting and tasted like the smell of moldy bread. So she'd gone back to the hammock to swing some more. The pretty blue sky and the moon that looked like a witch's silver fingernail and the birch branches went back and forth, back and forth over her head, and she'd thought of Thimblina. She hadn't talked to her all day, but Emaleen had imagined she was flying all around the party, dipping her toes in the frosting and spraying beer in her mouth, because she was a grown-up and thought it tasted good.

Emaleen had been standing at the edge of the dark forest for a long time now, and she thought her willow stick had gone out. When she blew on the tip, though, the gray black started to burn red again. She held it up in the air and waved it all around, so the sparks would go up and be stars. That's when she saw one star, all alone next to the moon.

Star light, star bright, first star I see tonight. I wish I may, I wish I might have this wish I wish tonight. You were only allowed one wish, but if you were smart, you could make a list inside of a wish. Like you could wish for everything frightening in the woods—the wild animals and witches and devil's clubs—to vanish, all together. You had to think very carefully when you made wishes, though, because they might come true and be a trick that actually made you sad. Emaleen thought hard. What if there wasn't a single wild or scary thing in the woods? Maybe it wouldn't be so much fun to stand at the edge of the trees. As long as she could hear her mom laughing nearby and she could see the bonfire, she liked to think that a witch might be up in those tall branches looking back at her with golden eyes, or that a bear might be walking through the shadows on his quiet, clawed feet. Emaleen swirled the burning stick over her head, around and around, the end glowing like her mom's cigarette at night time, and she wished only that she could be with her mom forever and ever.

A loud cheer went up from the grown-ups by the bonfire. They hooted like owls and howled like wolves. Somebody said it was after midnight, the days were already shorter and it might as well be winter. Some people booed and some people laughed.

Emaleen didn't drop her willow stick because you had to be careful and not set the forest on fire. She ran back to the bonfire and threw the willow stick into it.

Parents were saying it was bed time and they were making their children go away for the night, and Emaleen was worried her mom would say the same. Now that she wasn't little, she was smarter and knew that if you were very quiet and very still, the grown-ups sometimes forgot you were there and didn't make you go to bed. So she sat in a plastic lawn chair, hugging her knees and looking into the fire as the willow stick curled and burned into a red-hot snake. She didn't want this night to ever, ever end, but she was getting cold and maybe, just a tiny bit, sleepy. She could bring a warm blanket from the cabin, but if her mom saw, then she would say it was time to go to bed anyways.

She was the only child left at the fire, all the others were gone, and the grown-ups were getting wild. Aunt Della tripped and fell down, and when people tried to help her stand up, she laughed and said she was fine, just three sheets to the wind, and Uncle Roy dusted off her big bottom and everyone laughed.

Some men Emaleen didn't know started putting lots of logs and branches onto the fire. When they tried to drag the picnic table over to burn it too, Uncle Syd called them "fuckin' heathens" and told them to put it down. Then he helped them get more and more logs from the forest. When they got the fire really, really big, the men started playing a game where they had to run and jump over it without catching on fire. *Jack be nimble, Jack be quick.* One of the strangers had a giant knife in a leather sheath at his belt, and another was wearing a shoulder holster with a pistol in it. The fire was getting bigger and bigger, and the men's faces looked like fiery masks. It was exciting, but also maybe scary. Emaleen looked around for her mom. She was sitting on the picnic table, maybe to keep it from getting thrown onto the fire.

"Hey sweetie," she said when Emaleen went to her. "Should we call it a night?"

"But I'm not tired."

"No, of course not," she said. "Did you have fun?" Her mom kissed her on the cheek, and her breath was sweet like Aunt Bonnie's cake and her long, silky hair smelled like woodsmoke.

"Lots and lots!"

Inside the cabin, her mom turned up the electric heater and they both ran around fast, giggling and shivering while they got on their pajamas.

"Brrrrr," her mom said as they snuggled under the covers together. When Emaleen put her cold feet on her mom's warm belly, her mom shrieked and called her popsicle toes, and then she rubbed Emaleen's feet with her hands so they would warm up.

Emaleen was just beginning to fall asleep when her mom said, "Guess what?"

"What?"

"We're going to the mountains. You're going to love it there."

"Really? Are you just pretending?"

"No, we're going for real. Maybe tomorrow."

"And I get to go with you?"

"Of course."

"And we're going to live on the mountains forever?"

"We'll see."

PART TWO

DEVIL'S CLUB
Oplopanax horridus

Chapter 12

As they climbed into the sky from the airstrip near the Wolverine Lodge, Warren banked the Super Cub and turned up the steep-sided valley. A few fluffy clouds gathered across the mountaintops. The air was steady and calm.

"You two doing all right back there?" Warren said through the headset. A pause and crackle, then he heard Birdie's voice. "We're all good." Birdie was harnessed into the rear seat, with the little girl on her lap and their belongings stuffed into the far back of the small airplane.

"That's the North Fork straight below us," he said, dipping the left wing so they'd be able to look down. Below them was a tumble of creeks, mountain cliffs, and dense alder thickets. With the weather so fine, he could have flown directly across the mountains and been at the cabin in fifteen minutes, but he was following the creeks and valleys so Birdie could see the terrain. She needed to know—it was at least twenty miles and several days of hard travel if she and the child had to hike out for help.

Warren had tried to put her off as long as he could, but every day she was calling the house. "The weather looks good today, right? I'll pay you back for the fuel. I don't want to put you out. Do you think we could go soon?"

He could have refused. He could have told her it wasn't safe. No telephone lines, no way to contact anyone. No neighbors or roads, only miles and miles of mountain wilderness. But Birdie knew Alaska as well as anyone, and he suspected she was the kind of woman who riled at a challenge. He had no authority over her. It was, as the young people liked to say, a free country, and he was by no means the only person with a bush plane capable of flying into that valley. It would cost her something, but if Birdie were determined, she would find a way, and a rushed pilot-for-hire might not give her the room to change her mind. She and the child would be set down at the landing strip, their bags piled at their feet, and the plane might be gone before they had put eyes on the cabin.

Warren rarely flew out here anymore, and when he did, he never walked all the way to the old place. It made him sad to see it. This time, though, he would. He'd follow the trail up from the creek bed and through the spruce forest, and at the cabin he would wait, give her time to take it all in. God willing, she would come to the right conclusion on her own.

The narrow sandbar along the unnamed creek was a landing strip only by Alaska standards. No asphalt, no markers. Just a stretch of sand and gravel barely long enough for a Super Cub to land and take off. As Warren circled the plane to face upwind, he was pleased to see that Arthur had clipped back the bushes, rolled a few boulders out of the way, and hung a piece of surveyor's tape from a willow branch at the far end so Warren would be able to judge wind direction. As he brought the plane in closer, he could see that Arthur had even shoveled and raked over the rough spots. All those times Warren had asked him to clean up the landing strip, and he'd finally done it.

When the Super Cub touched down, it bounced on its oversized tundra tires, and Warren pulled it up just short of the rocky creek bed. He pivoted the airplane to turn the nose to face back down the landing strip, the propeller kicking up a cloud of glacial silt around them, and then he pulled back the throttle, cut the power, removed his headset and hung it overhead. As he was unbuckling his harness, he saw Arthur step out from the willows. He was as scruffy as ever—feet bare, blue chamois shirt unbuttoned and flapping in the breeze, hair and beard looking like they'd never known a comb—but he was waving at them, and smiling. Warren couldn't recall seeing such a thing.

As soon as Warren lifted the child out of the plane and set her on the ground, she was running to Arthur. "Arthur! Did you see us? We were just like ea-gulls. Up in the sky! Your dad, he flew us all the way in his airplane. And I wasn't scared except my stomach rolled over, but I didn't throw up. Not one time. And my mom, she didn't throw up either."

The little girl had grabbed on to his hand and was hopping up and down as he walked toward the plane. "And did you know what? We saw sheep. On the mountain. I don't know. Why they don't fall off? But I couldn't see them very good. My mom. Her name is Birdie. Do you 'member? She saw them. We had to yell because your dad's airplane is loud! She said they looked like snow, the sheep looked like snow, but I don't think I saw them."

Birdie jogged up to Arthur, threw her arms around his chest, and let out a whoop. "I can't believe it. We're here!" Arthur leaned down and kissed her on the lips, the little girl chattering and hopping up and down beside them all the while.

If only Carol could see. Arthur was in love.

Arthur went down on one knee. "You are climbing on, little one," he said, and the girl jumped onto his shoulders. "Mommy, look, look!" she shouted as he stood up. "I'm super tall. Even taller than Arthur."

Arthur walked to the plane and picked up several of the heaviest bags.

"You are holding on so you do not fall," he said to the child.

Birdie shouldered a backpack and grabbed a milk crate filled with canned and boxed food. Warren was left only with a duffel bag and the .375 rifle he had tied into the scabbard on the airplane wing.

The three of them were nearly out of sight in the willow shrubs as Warren closed up the plane and began to follow. He could hear the young woman and Arthur talking, and he saw the child pat Arthur on the head and lean down to say something into his good ear. Warren could only catch bits and pieces of their conversation, Birdie telling Arthur about what she'd brought with her, the child asking if they would see "snow sheep" again.

It was bittersweet to be back here. The meadow was sprinkled with wildflowers, the log cabin set back in the trees. The open-fronted shed was full of wood Warren had bucked up and stacked many years ago. Not far behind the cabin, there was the old outhouse, the crescent moon and star carved into the door above the caribou-antler handle. Deeper into the woods, beyond the woodshed, the cache stood tall, like a miniature log cabin on stilts, with a ladder leading up to its small door.

"What's this one's name?" The little girl was holding a cluster of blue flowers up to Arthur.

"*Mertensia paniculata*," Arthur said.

Warren hadn't thought of it in years, but this was where Carol had first begun to teach the boy. *Delphinium glaucum. Mertensia paniculata.* Larkspur and bluebell. In this very meadow, sitting in the grass with Arthur, Carol would point to one flower and then another, sounding out the Latin slowly as she read from the botany book. She would say which were edible and which were poisonous, and Arthur would put the plant to his nose or his tongue. In school, Arthur had been silent, withdrawn, and often refused to go altogether, so that eventually they would turn to correspondence study. But here, with only his mother and the wild plants, he had excelled.

"No, no," the little girl said. "What's its other name?"

"Bluebell. Or you say 'lungwort.'"

"Lung wart? Yuck! That's horrible. Blue bells sounds prettier."

"That one, even you like to eat it."

"Nuh-uh. No way."

Arthur pulled the small flower from its stem and held it out to the child.

"Are you sure?" she said. "It's not poison? Because my mom, she says I'm not allowed to eat flowers because they can make me sick and die. I don't want to be sick and die."

"It is fine to eat. Here, this part, the white bottom of the bell."

"Hmm, it is good! Like sweet purple."

All the way across the meadow, the child picked bluebells, asking Arthur to make sure each one was safe for her to eat.

Up close, the cabin seemed smaller than Warren remembered. The sod roof was alive and well, with tall green grass, sprays of foxtails, and even an Arctic rose bush that bloomed near the stovepipe. The two windows were still boarded up. They had been a luxury Carol insisted upon, real glass windows. Warren had suggested bringing out replacements, but Arthur expressed no interest. "It's his doing," Carol had said. "It's time he learned to fix the things he breaks." And so the windows had remained boarded.

There were other lapses in the upkeep. The stairs up to the porch had begun to rot and the entire cabin needed to be resealed with log oil. Many of the logs were scratched and gouged by claw marks, and here and there, tufts of blond grizzly bear fur had snagged on the graying wood.

Warren and Carol had spent their youthful years building this place, flying out on weekends and any vacations they could spare. Their daughters had been small, Wendy a toddler and Theresa still a baby, when they'd staked the land and started felling the spruce trees for the cabin. Carol had peeled the logs with a drawknife, and Warren had notched and scribe-fit the logs with a chainsaw. The cabin was sixteen feet by twenty and not even a loft. They realized too late that it wasn't big enough for all of them, but it didn't matter. They built a bunk bed for the children, and the cache for extra storage. Most often, Warren came alone for hunting season. As a family, they visited a few weeks each summer, one or two Christmases, and then, overnight it seemed, the girls were grown and moved away. Anymore he thought of it as Arthur's home, and it was like he'd surrendered it back to the wilderness.

When they reached the front steps, Warren didn't follow them to the door.

"It's way too dark in here," he heard the little girl say. "Let's turn on a light."

"There's no electricity. But I've got a flashlight. And some candles."

Give Birdie time, Warren told himself. Maybe not right away, but eventually this adventure would lose its shine. She would learn the truth of life out here—the quiet turns to loneliness and boredom. No jukebox or beer on tap. No hot showers or washing machine.

She was a strong-willed individual, though. Warren could see that. His hands in his pockets and his eyes on the ground, he walked away from the cabin and beyond the woodshed. What choice did he have but to leave them here? He would come back tomorrow or the next day, weather permitting, and at some point, he would insist Birdie and the little girl leave with him.

Carol would have insisted already. She would have spoken plainly but kindly to Birdie, tried to make her see sense. When all else failed, she would've said, Let the child come stay with us until you're settled in. Warren was in no position to make such an offer even if he was so disposed. He thought of Arthur, leaning down to kiss the woman, walking through the trees with the little girl riding on his shoulders. Love is powerful. Our son can be happy. Carol might have spoken those words.

Distracted by his thoughts, Warren didn't notice where he was walking until he stopped and looked up.

All sign of the mound was gone now—the fireweed and wild grass had grown in—but he was certain. It'd been three years, come September. The boy was just eighteen years old, graduated from high school in Anchorage, the grandson of an old family friend. Danny was a good kid, smart and wide-eyed, hardly able to grow a mustache but keen on becoming the next Jeremiah Johnson. He wanted Arthur to teach him how to hunt moose and caribou. Carol's apprehension was drowned out by Danny's enthusiasm and Warren's cautious optimism. It would be good for Arthur to have a friend. He flew Danny out to the cabin but couldn't stay; Carol had medical appointments the next day in Anchorage.

The morning Warren returned, the day had started out foul, sleet and wind coming sideways as he flew through the mountain pass, but by the time he'd landed, the sun had broken out and it had turned warm and pleasant. Warren had no premonition, no sense that anything was wrong. It was the silence that struck him first. Nothing but the buzz of black flies. And then the odor of putrefaction. He expected to find meat hanging in the shed, maybe a pair of antlers by the woodpile, but there was nothing to account for the smell.

"Hello? Anyone about?" Warren called out their names. No one answered. He'd started toward the cabin when something caught his attention out beyond the edge of the meadow. A camp robber had flown up and roosted in a spruce tree, chattering noisily. Warren didn't have a clear view, but it looked as if the ground at the base of the tree had been disturbed. As he walked closer, the smell of rotting meat grew stronger. Maybe the boys had been lucky enough to shoot a bull so close by.

"Mr. Neilsen! Is that you?"

Danny's voice had come from the cabin. Even from a distance, Warren could see that the boy was injured. He was leaning inside the doorframe as if his legs couldn't support him and he was cradling one arm. Up close, it was even more concerning. His clothes were bloody and torn, his skin was washed-out, and he was taking in quick, shallow breaths.

"What happened? Here, sit down. Careful, son. Careful."

While Warren inspected his wounds and pulled down the first aid kit from a shelf, Danny told of how he'd shot a bull moose within view of the cabin. It'd been near nightfall, but with Arthur's help, he'd managed to get it field dressed before they lost all light. Danny had wanted to get the quarters and backstrap hung in the trees, out of the reach of animals, but Arthur had said to leave it until the morning.

The next day when Danny woke, Arthur was gone, maybe up the hillside to look for another moose they'd spotted earlier. Anxious to get the meat taken care of, Danny didn't want to wait around. He approached the kill site with an armload of game bags, knives, and a small hatchet.

"I was so stupid. I should have had my rifle," Danny said.

The boy was confused when he got to where he'd shot the moose. The entire area had changed, like a bulldozer had come through and pushed up a huge pile. It was only at the last minute that he realized a grizzly bear was lying on top of the mound, spread out and facing away from him, maybe even asleep. Before he could process what was happening, the bear spun around and charged at him. Danny turned to run, but the bear knocked him to the ground and tore into his back. The bear clamped down on his thigh and began dragging him toward the mound. As Danny tried to crawl away, he was able to reach his hatchet, and he hacked at the bear's head. It only seemed to provoke the animal. Danny curled into a ball, his hands at the back of his head to protect it. The bear bit at him once or twice, swiped at him with its paw, then returned to the mound.

Danny lay there pretending to be dead for what seemed like hours but was maybe only minutes, and then the bear returned to him.

"I thought that was it. I was done for. The bear was pushing at me with its nose and then it started raking all this stuff on me, like he was burying me. I tried to stay still. I was holding my breath and praying, just praying to God."

Finally, the bear seemed to lose interest and wandered off, and Danny was able to make his way to the cabin.

"We need to get you to the hospital," Warren said. The boy had several deep lacerations to his thigh that had narrowly missed his femoral artery, as well as claw and teeth wounds to his upper back and shoulders.

"But Arthur . . . the bear must have gotten him."

"Carol will drive you to the hospital, and I'll come back out here to look for him."

There wasn't enough room in the two-seater plane for all three of them, but also Warren wasn't sure what he would find when he went looking for Arthur. It was best to do it alone.

When Warren returned later that same day, Arthur was sitting on the steps to the cabin, naked, his head in his hands. Blood was smeared across his arms and legs, and when he looked up, there were hatchet wounds to the side of his head. Neither of them spoke as Warren helped Arthur into pants and a shirt, like he was a child, and pulled his hiking boots over his bare feet and loosely tied the laces. Warren had put his son's arm over his shoulders and together they hobbled down the long trail to the airplane. They wouldn't be going to the hospital. Carol would do her best to patch him up.

The child's voice came through the trees like birdsong, high and cheerful. "Arthur! Can you see me? Arthur? I'm up here." She had climbed up a spruce tree and was calling from the branches with her hands at the side of her mouth. "Up here! Up here!"

At the cabin, the young woman had already dragged all their bags onto the porch and was sorting through them.

"Hey, do you know if that woodstove works anymore?" she asked. "It doesn't look like it's been used in a long time, and I don't want to burn the place down."

"You're thinking to stay?"

"Of course," Birdie said.

Warren put a hand to the side of the cabin, touching the logs where Carol had peeled away the bark all those years ago.

"Maybe . . ." he said. "Maybe it's not for the best, you and your daughter being out here."

"We'll be fine."

"Things can turn on you. You could be putting yourself at some risk. Endangering your child."

Birdie looked up, her eyes narrowed at him. "What?"

Warren hadn't considered the loaded connotation of his words, and he regretted them. "I don't speak as a trooper anymore, Birdie. I'm just asking you to consider what's best for all of you."

"And I'm pretty sure that's none of your business."

The little girl was talking to Arthur out near the cache, and for a while, Warren tried to hear what they were saying. Birdie had gone back to her work.

"Can I help you carry your belongings into the cabin then?" he asked.

"I'll manage," she said, keeping her back to him.

Birdie had a .30-06 rifle on one of the duffel bags. "You know how to use that?" he asked.

"I shot my first caribou with it. Grandpa Hank gave it to me."

A .375 H&H or a .45-70 might be better protection from a bear, but Warren also knew that being comfortable with a weapon was almost as important as the caliber.

"Nothing wrong with keeping it handy," he said. "Even when you're just working around the place. As soon as you leave it behind, that's when you'll need it. And inside, on a rack by the door, there should be a 12-gauge shotgun. The ammunition is in the cupboard. Make sure the little one can't reach any of it. But keep them handy."

"I'm not an idiot, Warren."

It was troubling, everything he wasn't saying. How Arthur had come into their lives as a foundling cub with two skins, half in this world and half in another. How a boy had been mauled not three hundred yards from these steps. How Arthur's scars had come from a hatchet, and that hadn't been enough to stop him.

The circumstances were entirely different now, though. Danny had been a near stranger, and there'd been the dead moose. It's rare for a boar grizzly to attack a human, but when he does, it's almost always about food. Survival. A perceived threat. None of that was at play here.

After Danny, Carol had been resolute. *Of course we care about our son, but we must be honest with ourselves. We have to remember who he is.*

But he's young still, Warren contended. Someday, maybe, he'll fall in love. That can change a man, give him the strength to set his course, even if it means leaving some part of himself behind.

Carol hadn't disagreed, only smiled a little, as if his words were sweet but foolish. But if she could be here to see Arthur now. The way he'd leaned down to kiss Birdie. The way the child held on to his hand. The three of them together like a little family. Maybe his son could have the life they'd always hoped for him.

Love is the most powerful force in the world. If you couldn't put your hope in that, what was the point of anything.

Chapter 13

When she first stepped through the door of Arthur's cabin, Birdie had a strange sensation. It wasn't fear, or shock, or disgust. It was a cool shudder around her heart, as if a gust of night air had blown through her ribcage. She walked slowly, cautiously into the near darkness. The sounds from outside—the hum of bumblebees and flies, Arthur and Emaleen's voices—became muffled and distant. The floor was cushioned, and when she faced toward the light of the doorway, she saw that it wasn't carpet under her feet, but dirt embedded with moss, leaves, and twigs. A small, silver-blue butterfly flickered in the doorway, passing back and forth between daylight and shade.

When she turned back into the room and her eyes adjusted, she saw where dried alder leaves had collected in the corners and dusty cobwebs hung from the log rafters. There wasn't the usual smell of a bachelor cabin—woodsmoke, leftover bacon and beans, sweaty work shirts—but instead the musky, nearly pleasant odor of moss and earth and wood. Small, white mushrooms sprouted along the edges of the log walls. The counter and few cupboards that served as a kitchen were coated in dust. The woodstove hadn't been used in so long that a line of yellow-orange lichen had grown along the top of the cast-iron door, and when Birdie reached out to touch it, a daddy longlegs scurried away from her hand. She jumped, let out a small yelp, and then laughed at herself.

That's when Birdie remembered when she'd last felt this way. She'd been a teenager, she and Grandma Jo on a drive down to the coast, and they'd stopped at an old log church Jo knew from her childhood. The building had been abandoned for years. A portion of the roof had collapsed, and most of the windowpanes were shattered or missing, but there was still a cross on top of the weathered log steeple. Inside, the church was a long, narrow room with rows of wooden pews, some of them buckled and cracked, others overturned by vandals. A small altar and an old upright piano had been left at the far end. A few rays of sunlight streamed through broken glass, but mostly the church was dim. In the middle of the main aisle rising through the decaying floor was a cottonwood tree, its leafy branches reaching up through the hole in the roof.

"I wouldn't trust that floor," Grandma Jo had warned, but Birdie ignored her and walked down the center aisle, the boards flexing under her weight, until she reached the cottonwood tree. To go around, she climbed and stepped over the empty pews. She went up to the altar and stood behind it, as if she were the preacher. The old church was quiet and spooky. She put her hands on either side of the lectern, and because she couldn't think of anything better to say, she had shouted "Ha!"

"Christ's sake," Grandma Jo had called from the doorway. "Don't you have any respect?" And it made Birdie laugh.

It was the same here, inside Arthur's cabin—the thrill of stepping across a threshold, of trespassing into a shadowy place you're not sure you belong.

Birdie sat on the edge of Arthur's bed. It was a simple platform built from a piece of plywood on a frame of spruce poles. No blankets or mattress, only a dusty, plaid sleeping bag shoved into a corner and a pillow that was torn open on one end. It looked as if a squirrel or some other little animal had stolen half the stuffing for a nest.

It made sense that this was Arthur's home. Of course he wouldn't cook or clean, wash his sheets or dust off the furniture. He lived closer to the bone. She could too. She wondered what that would mean. How would they survive? Berries and mushrooms and fish from the creek? It wasn't so far-fetched. She'd brought her fishing rod. She'd teach Emaleen how to build a campfire and how to wrap a trout in foil to bake in the coals. And later, in the twilight of summer nights, they'd pile logs and spruce branches so tall that the flames would brighten the forest around them. When they got tired, they would sleep wherever they lay down, and as they slept, ermine and red-backed voles would scurry past and owls would fly low through the trees. She and Emaleen would wake up with the sun or the moon or whenever they wished, and like Arthur, they would go barefoot and carefree. They would bathe in the creek when it suited them, and they would never look at a clock or a mirror or care what day it was. It would be like those days at hunting camp with her sister, Liz, when they were children and hadn't yet learned to be suspicious of the world. But this time it would be her and her daughter, running free in the woods, their cheeks freckled by afternoons in the sunshine, their hair long and uncombed. It was as close to pure joy as she'd ever imagined for the two of them.

And then she heard Warren's plane, flying low over the cabin. He was checking on them one last time, probably hoping to see Birdie standing in the yard with both arms raised in the air. He didn't like them being out here. Warren, with his worried frown, his pressed khakis, his "child endangerment." He would be back, and retired or not, he'd hinted at the reality—he could have Emaleen taken from her.

For a time, at least, she would have to live by the old rules.

She began with the floor. The cabin was built on log posts off the ground, so there had to be solid planks under the dirt. A broom, the straw worn to nubs, was wedged between the cupboard and the wall, but it wouldn't be enough. She needed a rake or a shovel. After some searching, she found tools hanging on the back side of the woodshed, including a handsaw, hammers, a rake, and several shovels.

Emaleen was playing in front of the cabin, where she had stomped down the grass in a circle and arranged bluebells and spruce cones on a giant cow parsnip leaf.

"Me and Thimblina, we're having a pic-i-nic," Emaleen said. "What are you doing?"

"Cleaning up the cabin. Where's Arthur?"

Emaleen shrugged. "Can I help?"

Birdie told her to go inside and get a washcloth or towel to start wiping away all the dust.

"But it's scary dark in there."

"That's why I've got this," Birdie said, holding up a hammer.

Standing on a chair she'd brought out from the cabin, she still couldn't reach high enough to pull the nails out at the top of the window, so she'd emptied one of the milk crates and balanced it on top of the chair.

"Be careful, Mommy."

Using the claw side of the hammer, Birdie began to yank and pry at the boards that covered the window opening, each nail screeching as she pulled it out.

"But I don't know," Emaleen said. "Maybe Arthur, maybe he likes his house like this."

"Yeah, maybe, but if we're going to stay here, we've got to clean it up, okay?"

She wondered where Arthur had disappeared to. She considered taking a cigarette break, since he wasn't around, but she needed to parcel them out as slowly as possible. She'd brought three packs, and a single bottle of whiskey, only so she wouldn't have to go cold turkey.

With the boards gone, the glassless windows let in daylight as well as a cross-current of fresh air, but in the light, she could see now how much work there was to do in the cabin. It was as if nothing but mice and spiders had been living there. Cleaning up the floor alone seemed nearly impossible, but once she scraped away a small section, she discovered she could catch the edge of the spade shovel under the layers of dirt, push it along the floor, and pry up crumbling sections of dried mud and leaves. She carried it by the shovelful and heaved it into the yard.

"That's a lot of dirt!" Emaleen said. "Why's it so furry?"

"Furry? What are you talking about?"

"See?" Emaleen held up a handful of grayish fluff and longer golden-brown strands. "Why is it furry?"

"I have no idea."

"Maybe Arthur has a puppy?"

"No, I don't think so."

"But why is it like that?"

"Stop playing in the dirt," Birdie said as she went back into the cabin. She was close to having the floor down to the wood. She could try to scrub it, but decided she'd leave the last bit of dirt to dry to dust and then she could sweep it away.

"I don't think it's working too good," Emaleen said as she rubbed at the front of the woodstove with an old dishrag she'd found.

They needed hot water, but that wasn't as simple as turning on a faucet. There was a five-gallon bucket with a wooden lid by the kitchen counter that looked like it had been used for drinking water. "Come on, Emmie."

"Where are we going?"

"To get water."

As they walked past the pile of their belongings in the yard, she supposed Warren was right about one thing. She picked up her rifle, loaded five bullets into the magazine and left the chamber empty.

It was a long walk down to the landing strip and the creek, and it wouldn't be easy hauling a five-gallon bucket of water back to the cabin. Emaleen wasn't strong enough to be of any help. Birdie wished she'd thought to look for another bucket—it was almost easier with one in each hand to balance yourself. Not far down the trail, though, as the cabin went out of sight, Birdie heard water running nearby. She stepped off the trail and pushed through the alder bushes toward the sound.

"Emmie? Stay close, okay."

Far into the alder thicket, she found the small, trickling stream, but there were no pools or deeper sections that would allow her to dip the bucket. Uphill, she spotted a place where the stream ran down through ferns and boulders and rushed clear and fast in a miniature waterfall.

"Step on the rocks so you don't get your feet wet," she told Emaleen as they hiked along the edge of the stream. "Shit."

"What's the matter? Mommy, what is it?"

The fresh track was set perfectly in a patch of mud. Birdie crouched and set her hand in the middle of it, and even with her fingers splayed, she couldn't reach across.

"What is it?" Emaleen whispered.

"Has to be a grizzly. A big mother . . ."

"Is it a bad bear?"

Birdie stood and shouted, "Hey bear! Hey bear!"

"Mommy, don't call her," Emaleen whispered. "We don't want her to come. Do we?"

"It's not to call the bears," she said, purposefully talking louder than normal. "It's so they know we're here and can GO AWAY. Bears are smart. They'll leave us alone as long as we give them a chance." Birdie clapped her hands. "Hey bear!" she called again and again as she reached the waterfall.

"Sing a song and clap your hands, real loud," she told Emaleen as she held the bucket in the water. "Make lots of noise."

"OKAY!" Emaleen yelled. "Like that?"

"Yep, keep going. Sing a song as loud as you can."

"LONDON BRIDGE IS FALLING DOWN, FALLING DOWN. MY FAIR LAAAAADDDYY." Emaleen hopped up and down and clapped her hands.

Small, aggressive mosquitoes began to dart around their faces. Birdie felt a smack on top of her head.

"HE WAS GONNA BITE YOU!" Emaleen shouted.

"A mosquito? Did you get it?"

"He was way too fast." Emaleen was slapping at her bare arms. "LON-DON BRIDGE. LONDON BRIDGE."

As Birdie pulled the nearly full bucket from the stream, out of the corner of her eye, she saw something moving through the brush on the other side of the stream. A figure disappeared into the foliage, but the tops of the bushes continued to jostle slightly. She slid the rifle strap off of her shoulder and, using the bolt action, chambered a bullet.

"ARTHUR!" Emaleen shouted. "Hi, Arthur! Did you hear us? I was singing a song REAL LOUD. 'Cause there's a bear. Did you know that? My mom said it's a big mother. 'Cause maybe she has lots and lots of babies."

Arthur was standing just downstream from them, his feet bare, his shirt still unbuttoned and exposing his broad chest, the hems of his blue jeans frayed and muddy.

"We're getting water," Emaleen said. "Because you don't have a faucet. Did you know that? And I'm sooooo thirsty. 'Cause I was singing and singing." Emaleen did an exaggerated slump, as if she were going to faint from the thirst. "I should've brung a cup."

"Here, little one," Arthur said as he approached them, and he got down on his hands and knees at the edge of the stream, put his lip to the waterfall and slurped. When he stopped, water was dripping from his beard and hair, and he shook his head like a dog.

Emaleen laughed and got on her hands and knees beside him on the moss, but when she tried to lean into the stream, she couldn't reach. Arthur grabbed the back of her shirt and pants and held her out in the air so she could put her face into the small waterfall and drink and drink. She screeched and laughed as the water splashed her.

"You have some, Mommy!" she said when Arthur set her back down. "Please, please, please. It's the best!"

"All right, all right." Birdie dipped water with her cupped hands and brought it up to her mouth, trying to drink it quickly before it ran out between her fingers. The water was so cold it ached in her teeth. There was the taste of granite and green leaves, but it was sweet too, sweeter than any water she'd ever drank. She scooped another handful, slurped it up, and then patted some on the back of her neck.

"You showed up in the nick of time," she said to Arthur. "You can carry that bucket for me. I'm going to heat it up on the woodstove, as long as I can get the fire started."

"My mom is cleaning your house. Is that okay, Arthur? Because it was kind of dirty, but don't be sad because it's going to be lots more pretty."

Arthur said nothing as he picked up the bucket and began walking up the stream, across the mossy rocks and through the water. Birdie went the other way, leading Emaleen back toward the trail.

"Why can't we go with him?"

"Our shoes will get all wet."

"But what about the bear?"

"I guess we'll sing lots of songs."

When they reached the cabin, Birdie expected Arthur to be splitting wood or starting the fire. Surely, he'd have something to say about what she was doing to his cabin. But he had set the water bucket on the steps and then sprawled at the base of a birch tree, his head resting on a root and his hands folded across his belly. He looked like he was already asleep.

"Is he taking a nap?" Emaleen asked.

"Yeah, I guess so."

It put her at ease. Arthur knew this place better than she did. Bears probably passed through now and then and it was something you got used to. She'd follow Warren's advice and carry the rifle when she went to the creek, but there was no point getting worked up about it.

"You see that tree where Arthur is sleeping?" she said to Emaleen. "Why don't you go and peel off some of the bark."

"How come?"

"It'll help us light the fire."

"But I don't know how."

"It's easy. It's like paper. Just find a loose part and pull it off. Then put it inside by the woodstove."

The wood in the shed, stacked in even rows, was dry and solid, and while the splitting maul was rusted, the edge of the blade was sharp enough. Birdie set one of the largest rounds of wood to use as a chopping block, balanced a piece of spruce on top, and swung the maul down as hard as she could. She overshot, the handle of the maul slammed on wood, and the spruce round toppled off the block. She swore, then glanced in Arthur's direction.

She'd never known a man who didn't step in. Grandpa Hank would've offered a few gentle tips, and then he'd have hauled armloads of wood into the cabin for her. A guy like Pete would've swaggered up and insisted on splitting the kindling himself, to show her how it was supposed to be done. Arthur only swatted away a mosquito without opening his eyes.

Birdie liked it this way. Nobody watching over her shoulder, criticizing her every move. Nobody waiting for her to screw up. *Leave me to it,* she thought. It'd been a while, but she knew how to chop kindling. She set the piece of wood back up on the chopping block and swung again, this time landing the maul on the spruce but only splitting partway through a large knot. She lifted the maul with the wood stuck to the blade and brought it down again and again, eventually breaking it into messy, splintery halves.

The next piece she made sure was straight with no obvious knots or warps. When she brought the maul down on it, there was a satisfying crack, and with the second strike, it cleaved into two perfect sections. She grabbed the maul handle up closer to the head, carefully held one of the halves upright on the block with the edge of her palm, and with a short, one-handed swing, split it again and again, thin pieces of wood falling to the ground. Within minutes she had a pile of kindling.

"I put the bark inside," Emaleen said.

"Good job. You get the little pieces of wood," Birdie said, "and I'll get the rest of this."

Without a whine or grumble, Emaleen cradled the kindling in her arms and ran ahead to the cabin. Della was right. She was a good kid. And they were going to be happier out here, the two of them together, the fresh air, working hard for no one but themselves. Like how she'd first imagined being a mother.

The birch bark caught easily in the woodstove, and the fire was instant and crackling, but smoke started pouring into the cabin. Birdie shut the stove door, and the smoke puffed out the seams and from around the stovepipe.

Emaleen coughed and pulled her shirt up over her nose. "Are we on fire?" she asked.

"No. Some reason there's not a good draft."

"Grandma Jo, when I'm at her house sometimes, Grandma Jo says, 'God damn it' and she turns that thing," Emaleen said, pointing to the damper on the stovepipe.

"Right, right. I forgot the magic words." Birdie was laughing and coughing as she said, "God damn it," and turned the damper up and down so that the air could draw up the chimney. The fire flared up and the smoke dissipated.

Birdie filled a stainless-steel pot with creek water and set it on the stove. It would take a while for the water to get hot, so she and Emaleen took the time to fill the box next to the woodstove with several armloads of wood. Birdie wadded up the old sleeping bag and pillow and tossed them out onto the porch. She swept the dust and leaves off the platform bed.

"Is that where we're going to sleep?" Emaleen asked.

"That's for me and Arthur."

"But what about me? Where's my bed?"

Birdie pointed to the narrow beds built in a stack along the wall.

"That's not a bed. That's a shelf."

"Arthur used to sleep there when he was little, and before that his sisters. We've just got to clear off the junk."

Slowly, the cabin was coming into shape. The floor was down to bare wood, the cobwebs and dust swept away, the boxes and cans of food organized on the kitchen shelves. The air was steamy from the boiling water, and they had wiped down all the surfaces with warm, wet rags. She'd piled their belongings on Arthur's bed.

Next, Birdie wanted to wash the pots and pans that hung from nails along the wall and the enamel dishes stacked on the shelves—they were coated with grime and dust. She found another five-gallon bucket under the cabin, and asked Arthur to haul water from the stream.

For hours, Birdie worked without stop in the small, hot cabin. She wouldn't claim to love housework, but she could get this way sometimes, caught up in a manic binge, staying up all night to scrub the bathroom or organize a closet. The sun had shifted enough that there was no direct light coming through the windows and the cabin was dim again. The mosquitoes had worsened, buzzing constantly around her head. Emaleen complained that they were biting her arms, so Birdie told her to put on a sweatshirt. Then Emaleen was whining that she was hungry; have some graham crackers, Birdie said—they'd eat dinner later. If only Emaleen would stop hassling her, she could lose herself in the work. She liked that feeling.

The heat of the woodstove had dried the last of the dirt on the floor, and clouds of dust rose up from the boards as Birdie swept vigorously out the open door. Standing on the porch, she saw that Arthur was gone. The sun had dipped behind the mountains and while it wouldn't get truly dark, several stars glinted in the pale sky. She wondered what time it was, but then remembered that it didn't matter here. They were free from all that.

Birdie had let the fire go out. It was getting dim enough that she couldn't see well inside the cabin, so she looked through their bags until she found the flashlight. Emaleen had been quiet for a long time, and when Birdie turned on the flashlight, she saw that she'd fallen asleep on the bottom bunk, squeezed between coffee cans and a wooden ammunition box. Her coat was bundled into a pillow under her head, and the box of graham crackers was open next to her.

It was too late to cook dinner now anyhow. She took Emaleen's blanket from one of the duffel bags and laid it over her. She'd brought two sleeping bags as well, but she hadn't thought of pillows.

There was no dresser or closet in the cabin to store their clothes if she unpacked them. For now, she could shove the duffel bags and backpack under Arthur's bed, if there was room. Birdie got on her hands and knees and shined the flashlight along the floor. There were only a couple of cardboard boxes, and she could push them to the side. But then, in the far corner, she noticed a pile of slender, white shapes, like sticks, and there was a faint odor, not rancid exactly, but like the smell of old lard. Curious, she lay down on the floor and felt blindly under the bed as far as she could, but she couldn't reach. She got the broom and used it to slowly drag something out.

It was a bone, the size and shape of a child's arm or leg bone. Birdie tried to think what kind of animal it could have belonged to. It wasn't bloody, but there were still stringy bits of dried tendon at the joint.

Birdie set the flashlight on the floor so that it shone under the bed, and again she used the broom to slide out another bone, then another and another. Mostly there were shards and pieces, but also a short section of backbone with the vertebrae still held together by tendon, and a little scapula so thin at the edge that the light shone through it. There were clumps of fur and a stiff piece of animal hide with a soft, reddish-brown fur. Then a ball joint, smaller than a child's fist, with a rough, hollow end where something had sucked out the marrow. Finally, a slender leg bone with a tiny hoof still attached. This one she recognized—it had come from a moose calf.

She carried the bones outside and put them in a pile.

"Arthur?" she called. "Arthur? Are you out there?"

Tomorrow she would bury the bones in the woods somewhere, so they wouldn't attract animals. The smell clung to her dirty hands. She wished she could take a shower, or at least that there was hot water left over to wash herself. Instead, she went to her backpack. The cigarettes and whiskey were hidden among her clothes in the main pouch. She took a gulp from the bottle, but it was too easy to lose track that way. She found an empty jelly jar and poured two fingers, then two more, and she lit a cigarette.

She stood in the doorway, looking out into the blue-black twilight, the end of her cigarette glowing with each inhale. The threshold had reversed. The cabin at her back had been turned warm and tame, and out there was the cold, endless forest, Arthur gone into the night.

Chapter 14

Birdie couldn't remember sleeping at all, only the mosquitoes tormenting her, buzzing around her head and leaving itchy welts on her neck and arms. She'd been too hot inside the sleeping bag, but any skin left uncovered became prey for the insects. She'd slapped and batted at them, and then it had occurred to her that without boards over the windows, it wasn't just the bugs that could get inside. She had lain awake, eyes wide, listening for any sound of movement outside the cabin.

She didn't know what time it was now. It had to be ungodly early—the air was chilly and the sun hadn't come through the windows yet—but a few mosquitoes continued to whine in her ears and tickle her face. She might as well give up on sleep. When she sat up, she saw that Arthur was asleep on the floor beside the bed. She must have drifted off at some point in the night because she didn't remember him coming home.

"Arthur? What are you doing down there? Arthur?"

His snoring continued uninterrupted. On the bottom bunk, Emaleen had escaped the mosquitoes by covering her head with a blanket.

Birdie would make a good breakfast for them all. She'd brought Krusteaz pancake mix, several sticks of butter, and a bottle of Mrs. Butterworth's syrup. It was too early in the summer for ripe berries, and there was no bacon or sausage because she'd worried it would go bad too quickly without refrigeration. But she'd make coffee for herself, tea for Arthur, and hot cocoa for Emaleen.

Grandma Jo had wanted her to bring the camp stove from the old homestead; it ran on white gas and had two burners that lit with the flick of a lighter, but it had seemed like an encumbrance, another way of binding herself to that complicated, unsatisfying life. Now, she almost regretted leaving it behind. Just to heat water and cook pancakes, she'd have to build another fire in the woodstove and wait for the stovetop to heat up.

She shouldered the rifle and picked up the empty water buckets. A cool mist lay along the valley, but the sun was breaking through the trees and directly overhead the sky was blue. All the way to the stream, she called out "Hey Bear!" and whacked the buckets loudly against each other, but even that pulse of adrenaline only made her feel more alive. By the time she'd hauled water back to the cabin, split kindling, started the fire, mixed up the batter, and fried pancakes, she was buzzing with excitement.

"Rise and shine. The pancakes are coming out of the pan! Come on, Emmie, while they're still hot."

When Birdie tried to wake her, Emaleen squeaked unhappily and pulled the blanket back over her head.

"I made hot cocoa for you."

Emaleen peeked from under the blanket. "And whip cream?"

"No, but it's got those little marshmallows you like. And look, you don't even have to get dressed. You already are."

Emaleen looked down at herself, confused, then grinned and hopped off the bunk.

"Oh, Mommy, what happened?" She pointed to Birdie's face, and Birdie touched along her brow and cheek where there were small bits of crusted blood.

"Damned bugs." The mosquitoes she'd killed in the night had been plump full of blood. "We'll wash up after breakfast."

The fire was crackling, and the cabin smelled of woodsmoke, melted butter, fried pancakes, and hot coffee. There were only two kitchen chairs, so Birdie had brought in a large round of spruce from the woodshed that when placed on end was nearly as high as a chair. She'd set the small table with the blue enamel camp plates and mugs she'd found in the cabin. Emaleen's bouquet of bluebells, purple geraniums, and Arctic roses was arranged in a mason jar filled with creek water—the flowers had wilted some in the night, but still, it was a cheerful scene.

"Arthur! Come on! My mommy made us pancakes. And hot cocoa!" Emaleen put her hand on his shoulder, then leaned down by his face and patted his cheek. "Arthur, it's morning time," she whispered. "Rise and shine." Arthur didn't stir, and Emaleen used her fingers to pry open one of his eyes and she put her face close to his. "Arthur? Are you awake?"

"God, careful, Emmie. Don't poke him in the eye."

"Yes, yes, I am awake now," Arthur said and yawned and stretched his arms over his head.

For such a big man, he ate very little and was almost dainty about it. He cut the pancake with the edge of his fork and brought each small bite carefully to his mouth. He blew on his hot tea and sipped it.

"How come you don't wear any shoes?" Emaleen was looking down at his large, dirty feet.

"I am more comfortable this way," he said.

"But you'll get owies on your feet."

"No," he said, and drank more of his tea.

"Are you sure you don't want more?" Birdie said when Arthur stood up from the table. "There's a whole stack of pancakes up on the counter there."

"No, thank you."

Birdie wanted to ask where he'd been but thought better of it. She gathered up the plates. "I'll see if I can do something about the bugs," she said. "They were awful. Are there any old sheets or pieces of fabric anywhere around here? I was thinking I could cover the windows. It'd let in some light but keep the mosquitoes out."

"In the cache," Arthur said from the doorway. "My second mother, she keeps many things up there."

As he left, Birdie remembered the bones.

"Hey—I found those," she called to him. "Maybe a moose calf?"

But he was walking away from the cabin and didn't answer.

She'd thought about it during the night when she couldn't sleep. It must have been a bear, or maybe a wolverine. Something with jaws strong enough to crack the bones. It was odd that they were under the bed, though. Bears and wolverines were intelligent, wary animals, and she couldn't imagine them dragging their prey into a cabin.

The cache was like a treasure attic on stilts. Birdie discovered several large jars of honey, bags of rice, dried beans, oats, flour and sugar, canisters of black pepper, salt, and baking powder. She wasn't sure how long the food had been there and the honey had crystallized, but everything was dry and unopened, so she hoped it would still be good to eat.

"Why is it like this?" Emaleen called from below. She was pointing to the tin wrapped around the base of each leg of the cache.

"It's so voles and shrews can't climb up the pole and get inside."

"Because it's too slippery for them to hold on?"

"Yep. Watch out, I'm going to throw some things down."

Inside plastic garbage bags, Birdie found wool blankets, several pillows, and then, at the bottom of one, a roll of mosquito netting. "Jackpot!" she hollered. She tossed the bag to the ground and carried one of the jars of honey as she climbed down the ladder.

"Can I see up there?" Emaleen begged. "Please, please."

The ladder was made of spruce saplings, the rungs lashed to the sides with rope.

"Where are your shoes?" Birdie asked.

"But Arthur doesn't wear them."

"You're going to get a splinter."

"No, I have tough feet. Just like Arthur."

Birdie followed her to the top of the ladder and helped her climb into the cache.

"Ooooh, it's like a little house," Emaleen said. "Can I sleep here?"

"Nah, I don't think so."

"Why is it way up high?"

"That way bears and weasels and mice can't get in there and eat up all the food. I think in the old days, they used to keep smoked fish and meat in these kinds of caches."

When they'd climbed back down, Birdie laid the ladder on the ground and gathered up the bags and honey. In the woodshed by the tools, there was a coffee can full of different-sized nails. Birdie picked out a handful of roofing tacks. The mosquito netting was designed to hang in a canopy over a cot, but she used her pocketknife to cut and rip it into two large squares that she nailed across the window openings. It reduced the daylight some, but it would keep the bugs out. Come winter, if they didn't bring out glass windows, they'd have to board them up again.

She cleaned up breakfast, and Emaleen took one of the leftover pancakes. "I want to find a squirrel and make friends with him," Emaleen said as she ran outside with it. "Squirrels like pancakes, right?"

"Put some shoes on!" Birdie called.

Emaleen had decided she'd like to have the top bunk, so Birdie cleared it off and unrolled her small sleeping bag onto it. The pillows and blankets from the cache were in good enough shape, but they smelled musty, so Birdie spread them on the porch to air out.

"Hey Emmie, where are you?"

"I'm looking for the squirrel," she answered from near the woodshed.

"Don't go too far, okay? Stay where you can see the cabin."

The day was quickly heating up. There was no clock or thermometer, but Birdie guessed it was late morning and already in the seventies. It was cooler inside the cabin, and Birdie closed the door and heard the whine of a mosquito. She couldn't spot it in the dim light, so she turned on the flashlight. When one flew toward the ceiling, she climbed the bunk bed and swatted at it with the broom. "You little suckers," she said as she squished one that was so fat with blood that it left a smear on the log wall. It was doubtful that she'd gotten them all, but maybe tonight she'd be able to sleep.

"Close the door, quick. Or you'll let the mosquitoes in," Birdie said as Emaleen came inside. When she looked at her daughter, though, she could see that her dirty cheeks were streaked from tears and her bottom lip was trembling.

"What's wrong?"

Emaleen sat on the lower bunk without answering.

"Did you step on a sticker bush or something? I told you to put your shoes on."

Emaleen shook her head and wiped her nose with her forearm. Birdie smacked another mosquito and went looking for more, but then she heard Emaleen sniffling again.

"For Pete's sake, if you're going to pout all day, just spit it out."

Emaleen sucked in a hiccupy breath, the way kids do when they've been crying hard.

"Arthur . . ." Another shuddering breath. "Arthur got mad at me."

"How come?"

"I was looking for the squirrel. So he can eat some pancake. And there was a hole. Like a place where you dig, but I didn't dig. I promise. I just looked at it. And he . . . he got mad and said I'm not allowed there."

"I'm sure he had his reasons. This is his place, right? So we've got to respect what he says. If he doesn't want us to do something or go someplace."

"But he . . ." Emaleen had begun to cry again. "He doesn't like me anymore. He's going to make us go home."

"Oh come on, that's not true. I'm sure he likes you fine. Just listen to what he tells you. Let's go back outside. It's too nice of a day to be cooped up in here."

Chapter 15

The wedding cakes were almost done. Emaleen put her face down by the three flat, round stones, and then pretended to shut the oven door. She was going to stack them together like layers and decorate it with all the flowers she'd picked. It was like they were hidden before, the wildflowers, but now that Arthur had taught her their names, they jumped out of the meadow at her. Bluebell. Geranium. Arctic rose. Star flower. When she picked one and said its name and looked at it closely, it was like a spell. The colors brightened and the smallest details came into focus, like the dark purple veins in the thin petals, or the tiny stems at the center that were dusted in gold.

Emaleen wished she had something white to use as frosting when she stacked the layers of cake, but she mixed water and dirt in a jelly jar, stirring it with a twig until it was a frothy muddy color. Then she sprinkled in some spruce needles, just to make it extra special.

She loved everything about being at Arthur's cabin. She got to be with her mom all day and all night, and nobody was ever frustrated with them. Arthur was nice and silly, even though he got mad at her that one time, and she was allowed to use the whole woodshed as a playhouse. She'd always wished for a playhouse. She thought the tall cache would be even more better, but her mom had said no, it's too dangerous. Even in the shed she had to be careful. She wasn't allowed to climb too high on the stacks of wood because her mom said they might fall down on her, and she had to always stay where she could see the cabin, but otherwise she could do whatever she pleased. Sometimes the woodshed was an orphanage for lost baby gnomes that Thimblina found in the forest. Emaleen had learned about gnomes from a big book that Uncle Syd had in his library, and when she had asked him if they were for real or only make-believe, Uncle Syd had winked and smiled.

In the cracks between the logs, Emaleen had made beds for the gnomes, with leaves for blankets and pebbles for pillows, and she fed the gnomes red berries that she found. Her mom said red berries are sometimes poisonous to children, so she didn't even pretend to eat them, but they were good for gnomes.

Today she was pretending a different story. She was baking a wedding cake for her friend, a snow queen who was going to marry Santa Claus.

One time, a long time ago, she was playing kitchen at the picnic table behind the lodge, and a man she didn't know asked what she was doing. She didn't want to say, but he wouldn't leave. Finally, just so he'd go away, she'd said, "I'm baking cookies." The man had looked down at the row of speckled rocks and the branch she used as a spatula. "You must have one heck of an imagination," he'd said, and he laughed and shook his head. He was making fun of her. He thought it was dumb to pretend a rock was a cookie. Emaleen was still furious when she thought about it, and sometimes she imagined throwing a rock-cookie at the man.

But out here, she didn't have to talk to strangers or be embarrassed about playing make-believe. Arthur was gone lots, and when he was home, he never made her explain herself. And her mom understood the way most grown-ups didn't. Sometimes she came out to the woodshed, and she'd say, "I've got some clean blankets for the gnomes," and she'd hold out her empty hand, or she'd say, "I'll have a piece of cake when it's done, but not too much frosting."

The woodshed was made out of skinny logs and only had three walls, with the front open. She liked it that way because she didn't want to be very alone or in the dark while she played. It was best right now, when the sunshine came into the woodshed and she could see her mom sitting out on the cabin porch. It was just the right amount of being alone and being together.

There were big ants that crawled around on the wood and the shed, and when Emaleen looked at their crooked legs and their shiny, hard armor, it gave her the shivers. She didn't want to hurt the ants, and there were way too many to move them all out of the shed. Anyways, they were here first. So she decided to pretend they were the gnomes' pets, like their puppies and kittens, and even though she didn't want the ants to ever, ever crawl on her skin, she didn't mind them so much.

Just now she was watching an ant climb up the back wall of the wood-shed. It looked like it was on an important mission, and Emaleen was curious to see where it would go. She watched as it climbed up each rounded log, one after another, like it was going over lots of hills. Then, partway up the wall, it went through a hole between the logs and disappeared. The hole was in the shape of an eye. Emaleen stood on a piece of wood like a stool and put her eye to the hole and looked in. It wasn't working, but when she covered her other eye with her hand, then she could see. The ant was gone, but she could look all the way out into the woods behind the shed. She was like a pirate with a spyglass, and the woodshed was a big ship out on the ocean. She watched through the hole for a long time, until she remembered the wedding cakes in the oven—she didn't want to burn them. Every so often, though, she returned to the spyglass and peeked through it like she was a pirate.

After lunch, Emaleen was sleepy and bored. She looked at some of the picture books Uncle Syd had given her, and she colored for a while, but none of it was any fun. She wished she had a friend to play with. She was too bored to imagine Thimblina, and her mom only liked to play for a short time, and then she always had some grown-up thing to do, like clean dishes, or take a nap. But then Emaleen remembered about the hole in the back of the woodshed. Being a pirate was interesting. "I need to cover my eye, like this," she said to her mom as she held her hand over her left eye.

"Why? Did you hurt it?"

"No. Because I'm a pirate. And that way I can see out my ship."

"Oh, like an eye patch?" Her mom found a yellow dishcloth and a piece of string, and she put it over Emaleen's eye and tied the string at the back of her head.

"It's supposed to be black," Emaleen said.

"It doesn't matter. You can't see what it looks like when you're wearing it. Just pretend."

"Can I have this?" Emaleen asked as she took a wooden spoon from the countertop.

"What for?"

"It's my sword, see?" and Emaleen tucked it through a belt loop on her pants.

"All right, sure. But bring it back, okay?"

Pirates didn't wear shoes, just like Arthur. But the chips of wood in the shed were poky, and she definitely did not want to step on a creepy ant with her bare feet, so she put on her shoes and ran outside.

All she needed now was a tattoo, because that's what pirates had. She got in trouble if she wrote on her skin with markers or pens. But there was the campfire ring. There hadn't been a fire there for a very long time, and grass and plants were growing inside the circle of rocks. When she dug around, though, she found what she was looking for—a burned-up stick that was crumbly like coal. She used it to draw dusty black circles on both of her arms and her forehead, and then she ran to the woodshed. "Yo-ho-ho!" she sang. She would draw pirate flags on pieces of wood too. First, though, she climbed up on the step-stool log and looked through the spyglass. She was going to make believe there were bad guy ships out on the grassy ocean, and she would yell "Bombs ahoy!" and jab her sword-spoon in the air.

But when she peeked through the hole in the wall, she saw an animal. It was big and furry, and it wasn't a moose or a dog or a porcupine. It was a big bear with golden-brown fur. It was walking closer, closer, and then it stopped.

Emaleen looked back over her shoulder, but her mom wasn't on the cabin porch. She put her eye to the spyglass again. The bear was standing up on its back legs now, and it was tall, as tall as a giant, and looking at it made Emaleen's arms and legs go all weeble-wobbly. The bear had its back to her, so she couldn't see what it was doing, but she thought it was clawing at itself, at its belly and its face. It wasn't very loud, but the bear was making sounds like growls or grunts.

This one time, when Emaleen was little, she saw a baby goat being born. She couldn't remember where, or why she'd been there. But she did remember that she was excited because she thought the baby would be fuzzy and adorable and the mom would be so happy. It wasn't like that at all. The mom goat had a hard time breathing and made horrible coughing sounds like she was hurting, and there was all this watery yuck. The baby came out in a slimy, weird bag that had blood on it, and at first Emaleen thought the baby was dead. Later, when the mom licked the baby goat and it tried to stand up, it was kind of better. But still, Emaleen wished she had never seen any of it.

That was something like what she was watching right now. Like a bear was giving birth to a man. A man was crawling out of the bear, and he was all bloody and yucky like the baby goat. He was trying to pull the fur-skin off of him, but it must have been stuck and maybe it hurt to pull it off. First he used the big paws to push and claw the skin off his shoulders and his arms and hands, and then he used his hands to pull the fur off the back of his head, and the man groaned and panted like he was running. When he stood up and turned so Emaleen could see his face, she held her breath, because it was Arthur. His hair was wet and his skin was covered in something goopy and white like Crisco, and he was all naked so that Emaleen saw his funny penis hanging down. She'd seen boy parts before, when a baby was getting his diaper changed at the lodge, and she'd only been mildly curious. It was different to see Arthur like this. It was the biggest feeling of fear and shame that she'd ever known, and it was as if she were frozen, she couldn't move or look away or call for her mom.

While she watched, naked Arthur bent over and rolled up the bear's skin like it was a sleeping bag, except maybe it was much heavier. He folded and rolled, and all the time he was very careful. Then he went to the hole in the ground, the one Emaleen had seen before when he got mad at her. He took out some clothes and he used clumps of moss to wipe away the blood and goopy white stuff off his skin, and he got dressed. When he was done, he rolled the bear skin into the hole. He did it slowly and carefully, like he didn't want to hurt it, and then he put dirt and leaves and branches on top, gentle, like he was tucking it into bed.

Some secrets when you didn't tell them, it was the right thing to do, but with others, it was bad. Mostly Emaleen knew the difference. Like when she broke her mom's golden bracelet on accident when she was playing with it, and she hid it in a shoe in the back of the closet. She knew it was a bad secret because she was sick to her stomach all the time and couldn't go to sleep until she told her mom the truth. But this other time, she heard Clancy call her mom a swear word when he thought no one could hear, and she didn't tell her mom because she knew it would make her sad and mad. Emaleen never, ever told her mom about that, and she didn't feel guilty about it one bit, except she didn't act nice to Clancy anymore.

About Arthur and the bear, she didn't know. Was it a good secret or a bad secret? If she told, maybe her mom would be scared and upset, and then they would have to leave. That would be awful. Emaleen and her mom would both be sad, and Arthur would be left all alone. Also, if Emaleen told her mom, maybe she would be angry because it would ruin everything.

But what if she didn't tell? What would happen then? This was all she could think about while she kept very still on her shelf bed. It was night time. Her mom and Arthur were outside together, and she was supposed to be going to sleep. She wished she could, because the cabin was lonely-feeling and she didn't want to be thinking, thinking anymore, but her thoughts were running around so fast.

Grizzly bears had very sharp teeth and giant claws, and they ate up moose calves even as they were still alive and crying for their moms. She'd heard the grown-ups talking about it. But she also knew that sometimes bears just ate leaves and berries and ran away when you saw them. *We've got to mind our p's and q's.* That's what Uncle Syd said. There was no way Arthur wanted to hurt people. He was careful and nice and laughed sometimes, and even that day when he was mad at her, he didn't spank her. But a grizzly bear was something else.

It was like that day in the woods, when she didn't know if she should stay on the path or go down into the witches' forest to look for her mom. She'd tried very hard that day, but she had made a wrong choice. She didn't want to make a wrong choice again.

Chapter 16

An uneasiness had settled over Warren, worsening each day, so that tonight rather than going to bed like he should, he was sitting up in the recliner after eleven. He had turned into a soppy fool. Ever since he'd lost Carol, he teared up over the smallest things—the pup's soft lick on his hand, the sight of Carol's coffee mug in the kitchen cabinet, the calls of the cranes out in the field. He'd had to hang up quickly during a phone conversation with his daughter Theresa the other day because he'd been overcome with emotion. She'd only been telling him about a trip to the farmer's market where she was living in upstate New York, but she'd sounded so irretrievably far away, and he'd recalled when she and Wendy were little girls, how vulnerable and treasured they'd been. His heart had trembled weakly in his chest, and he'd wondered if he was having some kind of attack.

You have a blind spot when it comes to Arthur, Carol would say. Let's go to bed. We'll take care of it in the morning.

Tomorrow, as soon as light permitted, he would fly out there, and God forgive him if anything had happened. Birdie was a grown woman. She made her own choices, for good or for bad. But someone had to think of the little girl.

Warren pushed the chair back into its reclining position and stared up at the ceiling. The house was quiet and the only light came from the fixture above the kitchen stove. The dog slept on the floor beside him, occasionally kicking her feet in her dreams. Warren ran his thumb back and forth along the underside of his gold wedding band. Over the years his fingers had thickened and aged so that the ring sat in a deep groove. In all that time, he'd removed it only once, when a nurse rolling him into an operating room for an emergency appendectomy said those were the rules. He had never considered himself superstitious, but as he handed the gold band to Carol, he was certain he'd broken some blessing on his life and that he would die in surgery. Next thing, he was coming to in the recovery room and Carol had already slipped the ring back onto his finger.

They'd been so young when they started out. A mortgage signed, careers begun, both daughters born, before either of them was thirty, and the next twenty years rushing by like the hours of a hectic, joyful day. Warren looked once, then twice, and both Wendy and Theresa were off at college, and he and Carol were on their own. No more worries about money or young children. It would be just the two of them, with the luxury of time. They would finish some of their projects around the house. Maybe even travel to Europe. And when Warren eventually retired, Carol wanted to spend more time at the cabin on the North Fork. She had plans for a garden, a root cellar, and a generator so they could keep a freezer full of meat.

"What are we going to do out there all day long, just the two of us?" he asked, sincerely puzzled.

"I can think of a few things." She'd smiled and arched an eyebrow at him.

But life rarely goes the way a man expects.

Sometime in the night, Warren had fallen asleep in the recliner. When he woke it was late morning and the dog was prancing by the door to be let out. By the time he'd fried bacon and eggs, fed the dog, showered and shaved, fueled the airplane and gone through all the checks, noon was well gone. He should have known he wouldn't make it out of the house by six in the morning. He'd never been one to rush, and it had gotten worse over the years. Dawdling, Carol used to say. Methodical was the word he preferred. Best to be prepared for every possibility.

Today, though, the weather was calm and clear, and as he flew through the pass and along the North Fork, he spotted a few clusters of Dall sheep on the high mountain ridges and a solitary bull moose down along the river. And then he descended slightly—there was an unnatural block of color along the hillside that he was trying to make out. It had to be a tent or some man-made object, but Jim Mahoney was the only one who hunted this side of the river, and the season was more than a month away.

As he drew closer, the colorful block turned into three figures in white, brown, and purple, the purple one smaller than the other two. Warren was nearly past them when he realized it was Arthur, Birdie, and the child. He craned his neck to look, and the scene had a slow-motion, dreamlike quality to it as he flew by. The three of them were waving up at him cheerfully, and surely he was only imagining it, but Warren thought he could see Arthur's face with a grin and the child hopping up and down in excitement. As he continued along the valley toward the cabin, Warren rocked the airplane side to side, waggling the wings in a pilot's hello.

He couldn't remember when the cabin ever looked so good. The porch was swept clean, and firewood was stacked neatly beside the door. The boards had been removed from the windows, and instead they were covered with white mosquito netting. He hesitated at the door, thinking maybe he was being too intrusive, but he opened it. Inside, the transformation was even more noticeable. The platform bed was made up with pillows and blankets. All the dust and cobwebs and dried leaves were gone, the floor was scrubbed clean, and there was the fragrance of dish soap, pancakes, and honey.

Warren stepped into the cabin slowly, as if it were a mirage that might ripple. By the woodstove, the pots and pans were tidy, the shelves lined with food and supplies. The top bunk had been cleared of clutter and there was a child-sized heap of blankets, picture books, and a baby doll wrapped in a pink blanket. A cross-breeze came through the windows so that the mosquito netting billowed slightly in the sunshine. Warren turned to the small kitchen table and saw a coloring book, crayons, and a mason jar with a bouquet of wildflowers.

He closed the door behind him as he stepped out onto the porch. It was a long hike up to the mountainside where he'd spotted Arthur and the girls, but it would be a quicker trip down, and they might have started hiking home when they saw his plane. As good as everything seemed, he wanted to put eyes on them, talk to them, before he left.

Warren sat on the bottom porch step. The sun blazed down on him, and he began to wish for shade. He took an old handkerchief from his back pocket and wiped his brow. There were water buckets inside the cabin, and he wondered if they were full and if the water was cool. He would sit a while longer, then go in for a drink. He was picking a stem of wild grass when he noticed a rope tied to the porch post by his feet. Without thinking, he reached down and felt his way through the matted grass and leaves.

The rough texture of the rope in his palm, that's what jolted his memory, and he wondered that he could have ever forgotten. He fed the rope through his hands, expecting to find the blue, padded collar at the end, but it was lost to the years.

September 19. That was the day they came to celebrate as Arthur's birthday, because it was all they had. It was the first hunting season he and Carol spent alone out at the North Fork, with both daughters off at college. Warren had been in his forties, still ambitious and strong enough to hike up into caribou country and back again with an entire animal, the meat cut from the bones and in game bags in his backpack, all in one long day. At the cabin, Carol would start to worry as night came on, so he'd walked as quickly as he could, bent under the weight of his pack, with his eyes on his feet so as not to trip over the boulders on the riverbed. He'd followed the North Fork down toward the airstrip.

As the sun sank behind the mountains, there was only a drab light to see by. He was bone-tired and all he could hear were his own huffs and groans, but then came another sound, distant and squalling. As he continued down the valley, the rhythmic cries sharpened. It sounded like "Mama, mama," but that couldn't be right. A stranded moose calf perhaps, or a lynx. They'd been known to make surprising, humanlike cries. After he dropped the meat at the cabin, he might be curious enough to go looking for the source of the sound.

He frequently stopped to rest, bent over with his elbows on his knees and the hundred-pound pack pressing down on him. This time when he straightened up, he saw something farther down the riverbed. It looked like an animal with light-colored fur. He unhooked the rifle from where it hung from his pack frame. As he walked closer, he was stunned to see that it was a small child, not much more than a baby, with chubby arms and legs and an animal pelt across its back.

"Hello there?" he'd called out.

Startled by Warren's voice, the toddler stood and scampered toward the water's edge, looking back and forth from Warren to the far bank. "No, no. I won't hurt you," Warren called.

The child seemed equally terrified of him as of the river. Warren lowered his pack and rifle to the ground, took a few slow steps forward. The little boy waded deeper, deeper so that the current began to lift him off his feet and pull him downstream.

Warren sprinted toward him.

"No! Don't go out there. It's dangerous. I'm not going to hurt you," he called again.

The child was crying "Ma ma ma," as he struggled to keep his face out of the water. Warren was knee-high in the river, reaching for the boy, when a grizzly bear charged out of the willow bushes on the other side. It caught sight or scent of Warren, stopped, and stood up on its hind legs with its front paws by its chest and its ears perked forward. A small cub emerged from the brush behind her.

Warren grabbed up the boy. He hadn't expected the child to fight him, to wail and screech and writhe in his arms, and the racket seemed to provoke the sow bear. She dropped back onto all four feet and clacked her jaws.

"Go on!" Warren shouted at her. "Get!"

The sow lunged forward and blew out her cheeks with rushes of air. Warren backed out of the water and ran toward his rifle, hardly managing to hold on to the child as he bit and scratched at him. He didn't dare set him down, so with one hand he picked up his rifle and shoved the safety off. For the first time, he wished he had a semi-automatic that wouldn't require him to work the sliding bolt, but at least he'd kept a bullet in the chamber as he hiked off the mountain.

The bear was coming down the bank, and then it plunged into the river. There was no time to think, only decide, and with the rifle stock lodged under his arm, Warren fired into the water in front of the bear. He'd hate to orphan a cub, but if she kept coming, he would be lucky to get off another shot and it would have to count. Once she was on top of him, there would be little chance of saving himself or the child.

At the gunshot, the grizzly bear spun around and crashed away through the water, up the far bank and back to her cub. Warren went to one knee, trying to keep hold of the struggling child as he slid the rifle bolt. The sow bear had not gone far—she was pacing on the bank, huffing and popping her jaws, long threads of saliva dripping from her mouth. Warren sprinted in the general direction of the cabin. The boy continued to thrash and howl in his arms. When Warren looked back, the sow bear was coming down the bank again. Her huffs had turned to loud, undulating growls, but she moved slowly, warily. He shot again in her direction, mentally noting the four bullets that remained in the rifle even as he ran with the boy into the woods.

Warren kicked at the cabin door for Carol to unlatch it from the inside as the child screeched in his arms.

"What on earth?" Carol said. He staggered inside and leaned back against the cabin door to close it.

"What . . . where . . ." Carol started.

"By the river." He was out of breath and his legs felt weak as the adrenaline drained away.

"All alone?"

They had to talk loudly to be heard over the child.

"I don't know. I didn't have any time to look around. There was a grizzly with a cub."

Carol reached for the boy. "Careful, he's a wild one," Warren said, and as he spoke the boy fought his way free of Carol's grasp and ran to the door. He clawed at the wood, as if trying to find a way to open it, and made wordless, angry vocalizations. When Warren stepped toward him, the child faced him and growled like an animal and made a popping sound with his teeth and cheeks.

"Shhh. Shhh. It's all right," Carol said. She took a wool blanket from the bed and scooped up the child, quickly swaddling him so his arms and legs were immobilized. She sat on the edge of the bed and rocked and cooed at him.

"My pack's down there," Warren said. "The bears will get into the meat."

"You should wait until morning, when there's light."

They took turns holding the child wrapped in the blanket. They worried he would hurt himself or escape the cabin if they set him down. After several hours of fighting and crying, the boy fell asleep in Carol's arms. She eased down the blanket to look at him.

"What is this, that he's wearing?"

"A fur of some sort," he said.

"It's . . . stuck to him."

Warren reached down and tugged at it, and when the fur didn't come away, he pulled harder. The child whimpered in his sleep and blood beaded up where the skin and fur came together.

"Oh don't, you'll hurt him," Carol said.

They unwrapped more of the blanket and found that it wasn't just a scrap of hide. It was a complete pelt, four legs dangling with padded, clawed feet, and at the back of the boy's neck, the skull-less, eyeless head of a bear cub hung like the hood of a sweatshirt. Wherever the animal skin touched the boy's, it was adhered as if by glue or flesh.

"I don't understand," Carol said as she looked down at the sleeping toddler.

The next morning, after a long and sleepless night, Warren stoked the fire in the woodstove and picked up his rifle.

"I don't want to leave you alone like this, but I should . . ."

"Of course," Carol said. "Maybe there's a hunting camp? Or a plane crash?"

"Maybe."

"Could he be Althea's baby?"

"After all this time? I don't see how."

When Warren opened the door, the sow grizzly was at the edge of the meadow, her eyes on the cabin. It was dangerous, perplexing behavior—he would have expected her to take her cub far from any sign of humans.

"Carol," he said. "We might have to shoot her."

Failure to thrive. The words haunted Warren all these years. During the first weeks, the toddler who'd been plump and feisty when Warren first found him at the river's edge became emaciated and hollow-eyed. After they'd flown back to their house with the child and notified authorities, Warren had returned to search the hillsides and valleys near the cabin, but he found no camps or wrecked airplanes, only game trails. Carol stayed with the boy. After numerous baths and applications of warm compresses, she was able, painstakingly and little by little, to peel the bear hide away from his skin, but he didn't eat, didn't speak or communicate in any way except bouts of screeching and scratching and biting.

At Carol's urging, they tried to track down Althea. She was a solitary young woman who'd lived in an abandoned cabin across the Wolverine River from the lodge. Everyone had assumed she was a relative of the property owner, but later it was determined that she'd been a squatter, and no one knew anything more of her than her first name. She came and went by a hand-pulled cart that crossed the river by a cable. After a year or so, though she avoided interactions of any kind, people began to notice that she was visibly pregnant. Carol worried over the girl, and every week or so, she climbed into the cable cart and crossed the river with a bundle of food and vitamins and hopes of offering help. Althea never came to the door. Undeterred, Carol left behind supplies and pamphlets on prenatal care. Months went by, and then Althea was seen around town again, hitchhiking and begging groceries from the store. She was no longer pregnant, but there was no infant either. Warren was the contract officer in Alpine at the time, and when he went across the river to do a welfare check, Althea allowed him into the cabin. Was she well? Had she delivered a baby, and if so, did she need assistance? There were no indications that she was caring for a child, and she denied ever being pregnant. Within days of his interview, Althea disappeared. Someone said they saw her hitchhiking north of town. Someone else said she was spotted in Fairbanks that winter.

Two years had passed, and all they had was a first name and a physical description, but Carol wrote to the owner of the cabin where she'd lived, and Warren put word out among police officers and friends around the state. No one knew or had seen the young woman. It didn't make sense to Warren anyhow. Even as the crow flew, it was more than ten miles of mountains between Althea's cabin on the Wolverine and the North Fork. How would an infant survive alone in those woods all that time?

They were unable to identify any of the boy's relatives, and Warren and Carol were assigned as temporary foster parents. Carol made the long drive to Anchorage every week, sometimes every day, to take the child to pediatricians and specialists who proposed only more tests and theories but never any solutions. She told them about the bear skin, how he'd been dressed in nothing else and it had fused to his skin, but that he had seemed otherwise healthy. Now, under their care, the child wouldn't eat and was growing weaker. Even as he starved, he found the strength to kick and shriek anytime doctors examined him. Carol would sit on the tiled floors or the edge of exam tables and hug the boy tightly so that eventually he fell asleep in her arms, his face flushed and rimmed in sweat.

During one of the last trips to Anchorage, the pediatrician was rushed and impatient and didn't seem to listen to anything Carol tried to tell him. There was nothing more he could offer. Though the tests had all been inconclusive, it was clear the child suffered from some kind of severe developmental and behavioral disorder. They could hospitalize the boy, sedate him, and install a feeding tube, he said nonchalantly, but the only long-term solution would be to send the child away to be institutionalized. It would be different if he was your own son, the doctor added.

Carol came home enraged. "Never," she said. "We will never let that happen."

With their daughters, Carol had been an attentive and gentle mother, but with Arthur her love was fierce and guarded. They didn't know it at the time, didn't understand the full repercussions of their choices, but all other plans would be pushed aside. There would be no vacations abroad, no leisurely days together at the cabin. When the time came, Warren postponed retirement, concerned that if someday they were forced to put the child in a facility, they wouldn't be able to afford someplace acceptable. And Carol became entirely devoted to the boy's well-being, determined that he should thrive.

It was well into evening now, and still there was no sign of Arthur and the girls. Warren had filled the buckets in the cabin with fresh water from the creek and drank several cupfuls. He'd walked around the property, the memories wearing on him. It was time to go. Before he left, though, he took out his pocketknife and cut away the rope where it was tied to the porch post.

Chapter 17

The sun was already hot enough to chase the mosquitoes into the shade, and the day stretched out ahead of Birdie like when she was a child on summer break; the lazy, peaceful boredom of not knowing what you'll do now, or in an hour, or an hour after that. She lay back on the cabin porch and rested her head on one of the musty pillows she'd found in the cache. Emaleen played under the porch beneath her, talking to her imaginary friend, and Birdie drifted in and out of sleep, occasionally brushing away a fly or answering Emaleen with a drowsy "Hmm-mmm."

"Mommy? Mommy, it is soooo hot."

"Hmm-mmm."

Emaleen was standing over her, blocking the sun. "Can we have ice cream? Please?"

"You're kidding, right?" Birdie said without opening her eyes. "Where would we get ice cream out here?"

"I don't know. Maybe, Arthur . . . maybe he has a freezer. Like Della?"

Birdie laughed. "Sorry, Em. No ice cream. No freezers. You can get a cup of water out of the bucket."

"Can I pour it on my head?"

"Sure. Why not." And she heard Emaleen's feet thumping across the porch, the cabin door opening. "Not inside though, right? Bring the water out here."

Birdie drowsed again as Emaleen ran in and out of the cabin with cups of water.

"It is a warm day," she heard Arthur say. "I think we are going to a place you like." Birdie squinted into the bright sky and saw the dark outlines of Emaleen standing on the porch and Arthur on the steps.

"Me?" Emaleen stepped closer to Birdie.

"Yes, and your mother too."

"Oh, okay, like right now?" Birdie said. "How far is it?"

"Maybe . . . one day," Arthur said.

"A day? So we'll be back tonight?"

"Yes, maybe."

Birdie helped Emaleen put on long pants, socks, sneakers, and a ball cap, even as Emaleen complained that she didn't want to go.

"I hate these pants," Emaleen said. "I can't run fast."

"I don't know what you're talking about."

"See," and Emaleen took several exaggerated, stiff steps across the cabin floor as if the blue jeans were as heavy as steel.

"Oh come on, it's not that bad. You want your legs scratched to hell by the brush?"

Birdie put their coats and winter hats into the backpack—the weather could change quickly in the mountains—along with a canteen of creek water, a package of graham crackers, and the rest of the pancakes wrapped in foil. She put on her backpack and rifle and grabbed Syd's cowboy hat from the hook by the door.

"All right, think we're ready."

Arthur hadn't moved from where he sat on the porch steps.

"You don't need that," he said, nodding toward the rifle.

"What? You sure? Your dad said—"

"It is not necessary," Arthur said, so she left the rifle in the cabin, shut the door, and followed him into the forest.

For the first mile or so, they were down in the thick of the woods, climbing over fallen spruce trees and breaking through alder bushes. Arthur covered the ground silently, effortlessly. His strides weren't particularly long or graceful, but he moved at a speed that required Birdie to jog at times to keep him in sight.

Emaleen seemed out of sorts. She walked slowly with her eyes on her feet, and she was unusually quiet.

"Come on, Emmie. Buck up. This'll be fun."

Emaleen nodded, but her face was serious.

"Hey, see that log up there," Birdie said. "I'll race you, okay? Are you ready? Set?"

Emaleen sprinted ahead, laughing, as Birdie called out, "Cheater, cheater, pumpkin eater."

After that, Emaleen ran and leapt and chattered along as if she could hike all day, but Birdie knew it would be short-lived. Less than a half hour later, Emaleen fell back behind Birdie and complained that she was hot and tired and thirsty. There were ways to keep a child going—sing songs, play animal vegetable or mineral, tell knock-knock jokes—but sometimes it wore on Birdie, the constant drain of it. She just wanted to walk and be with her own thoughts.

"Can I eat this flower? How 'bout this one?" "But I don't want to ask Arthur." "I'm hot. My tummy hurts. Can we go home now?" Mommy, Mommy, Mommy.

"Shhhh, Emaleen. Please. Maybe we'll see a baby quieter."

"That's not real. Grandma Jo says it's just a trick. For babies."

Birdie laughed. "Turncoat."

"What's that mean?"

"It means Grandma Jo calls it a trick now, but she used it on me all the time when I was a kid. Sometimes I really thought I saw them."

"What did they look like?"

"Like fat, cute little babies."

"All by themselves, in the woods? Like gnomes?"

"Yeah, I guess."

"I want to see them!"

Birdie held a finger up to her lips. "You have to be very quiet then, so you don't scare them away."

Emaleen squinted skeptically, but then looked out into the trees.

* * *

Where was he taking them? Into the middle of a stinking muskeg? They'd been walking for more than an hour and the day had only turned hotter. The air was heavy and smelled like swamp gas. Birdie, sweating and cursing, tried to balance atop the hummocks of tall, yellow grass and keep out of the murky water, but Emaleen wasn't making it easy. She pulled on Birdie's arm and whined that her feet were wet and that the mosquitoes were biting her. Overhead, some kind of speckled brown bird swooped and screeched at them relentlessly.

Arthur had already reached the small, black spruce trees on the other side of the marsh, oblivious to Birdie and Emaleen. For the first time, it irritated Birdie.

"Arthur! Hey, Arthur!" she shouted as loudly as she could and waved an arm. "We could use a hand here!"

Within minutes, he'd made his way back to them. He crouched and gestured for Emaleen to get onto his back. Emaleen looked to Birdie and, almost imperceptibly, shook her head.

"What's wrong? Go on, he doesn't mind."

"No thank you," Emaleen whispered.

"It's not a choice." Birdie picked her up and set her on Arthur's shoulders. Emaleen must be coming down with something—she definitely wasn't her usual cheery self. Before Birdie stepped away, Emaleen said quietly, "Can we go home now? I don't like it here."

"We are not there yet, little one," Arthur said. He stood and adjusted her weight on his shoulders. It was the same tone he always used with Emaleen, no exasperation, no talking down to her, just stating a fact. He started back across the marsh with Emaleen, and Birdie followed, hopping from one hummock to the next, trying to keep out of the deepest water. The next time she looked up, Arthur was disappearing beyond the black spruce with Emaleen.

She hoped that when she made it that far, she'd be done with the marsh, but when she reached the stunted, twisted little trees, the land beyond opened into a long, narrow bog, stretching much farther side to side than across. There were no winding streams of open water, no mounds of yellow grass to stand on. Instead it looked like a perfectly flat meadow of dense green moss and small white flowers, like a short, pleasant walk across a mowed lawn, but Birdie knew better. She couldn't see Arthur, or where he had crossed. He'd left no tracks in the bog, but he couldn't have gone around in either direction—it would take hours to skirt the edges. Balancing on the roots of one of the spruce trees, she reached a foot out to the moss and pushed on it, and it was like a soaked sponge. Grandpa Hank had called these jelly bogs. He'd told a story of losing one of his favorite packhorses in a place like this. Something had startled the string of horses, and the last one had broken free and dashed into the middle of the bog. It had broken through and was wallowing in the black, watery mud that formed a suction the more the animal struggled. The horse became so submerged that only its muzzle and wild eyes remained in sight, and the men couldn't pull it free. Grandpa Hank had shot the horse in the head rather than leave it to suffer a slow death.

Birdie caught sight of Arthur as he emerged from the brush in the distance, Emaleen still on his back.

"Arthur!" Birdie cupped her hands on either side of her mouth and shouted, "Arthur! Is this where you crossed?"

He was steadily walking up the far hill. He probably couldn't hear her, with Emaleen chattering away in his ear, but he didn't look back to check on her. He didn't give her any thought. Or, maybe, he'd listened that afternoon when the three of them had walked together from the lodge down to the river and she'd said she wanted to make her own way.

She eased all of her weight onto the boggy moss, and it rippled under her feet like a waterbed. She held her breath high in her chest, as if somehow she could will herself lighter, and she began to walk quickly straight across the bog. When she hesitated, or tested the next step to be sure the surface was firm enough to hold her, she began to sink into the squelchy moss. Would Arthur hear if she shouted for help, and would he be able to pull her out if she sank too far? As she neared the middle of the bog, the moss got thinner and wetter, and in her peripheral vision she could see open water far to the left. Her right foot broke through and plunged into cold, black water, but she kept her balance, yanked her foot out, and kept going in a kind of tiptoeing trot. Syd's hat slid off her head so that it hung at her back by its string across her neck. She was nearly there. Just ahead was a grassy rise and a group of bushes that promised solid ground. With only a couple of yards to go, she ran more quickly and first her right foot, then her left, went through the moss and into black mud, and she fell forward and grabbed on to the grassy bank. Each foot came out of the mud with a disgusting, sucking sound, and she felt her left shoe being pulled off her foot. Her lightweight tennis shoes had seemed like a good idea, but now she wished she'd worn her hiking boots.

"God damn it." She climbed on hands and knees onto the solid ground, then reached down into the mud to pull out her shoe. When she rolled over into a sitting position, the damp soaked into her jeans. Her tennis shoes and jeans below the knees were coated in black mud, as well as her right arm up past the elbow. She set Syd's hat on a nearby bush and slid the backpack off her shoulders. She wiped sweat and splattered mud from her forehead with the back of her clean arm. There was only Arthur, Emmie, and the great wide open, and she was wearing a bra. She pulled off her T-shirt and held her arms in the air, hoping for even a smidge of a breeze to cool her skin, but there was only the hot sun. She wadded up the T-shirt and stuffed it into the pack.

Fuck it. She unzipped the side pouch on the backpack and fished out a lighter and a pack of cigarettes. She lit one and took a long, deep drag as she sat and looked back over the jelly bog. When a swarm of no-see-um gnats formed a cloud around her head, she waved the burning cigarette at them with her muddy hand, hoping the smoke would chase them off. She wondered how far away Arthur and Emaleen had gone.

They'd left the marsh and trees behind and were climbing, climbing. Birdie could tell they were ascending the base of a mountain, but she couldn't see the top. There was always another hill, another rise. Sweat dripped down the side of her face and the small of her back, and her leg muscles ached. She hadn't known she was so out of shape. The dwarf birch, Labrador tea, and blueberry bushes were tall enough, and the game trail worn so deep into the tundra, that Birdie couldn't see far in any direction. "Hey bear!" she called out. "Hey bear!" She hoped Arthur was right and that she didn't need a gun. When she crested a rise, she would sometimes see him, Emaleen riding on his back, but they were drawing farther and farther away. The terrain became steeper, so that Birdie had to rest more frequently, and when she faced down the mountainside, she saw the valley far below—the yellow-brown marsh and the strip of green bog, and beyond that the spruce forest rolling down into the creek valley and up the other side into the foothills and then, in the distance, the tall mountain peaks. There wasn't a single cloud in the blue sky, and it was as hot as any summer day in Alaska, well into the seventies. Without her T-shirt, her shoulders were getting scorched by the sun. She tipped Syd's hat off her head and a small breeze came down the valley and stirred her hair, and it was as good as a cold drink of water.

When she continued on, the brush dwindled until she was in alpine tundra—club moss and lowbush cranberries and boulders covered in lichen. She thought she could hear voices farther up the trail, and when she reached the top of the steepest climb yet, there was Emaleen peering down at her with her hands on her little hips.

"Mommy, Mommy, here I am! How come you're so slow? Why are you naked?"

"I took my shirt off because . . ." Birdie was sucking in air and her lungs burned with every breath. "Because I'm sweating . . . like a pig."

With a hand on each knee, pushing with her arms for a boost of strength, Birdie took the last few steps to get to the top of the rise. Arthur was sprawled on his back on the tundra, his hands behind his head, snoring. Birdie let her backpack fall to the ground and she collapsed next to him, the lichen and moss prickly against her bare skin. She pulled on her T-shirt and lay back again.

"You see this, Mommy?" Emaleen crouched beside her and held a wildflower an inch away from Birdie's eye. "Can you see it? It's my favorite purple! And even the green leaves, see, see, they're kind of purple. They look poky, but they don't hurt, see." She brushed a spiky leaf against Birdie's cheek. "And you know what? It doesn't have a name. Arthur says. Nobody ever ever did give it a name. Isn't that weird? I want to, but Arthur says it won't be its real name. Somebody else has to do it. But I don't know why. And you know what? Arthur . . . Arthur . . . he counted a hundred different ones. He says he never counted them before, but I asked him to do it. He knows all their names. While we were walking. They're all different and he knows every one."

"Hmm-mmm," Birdie said, letting her eyes close. She could fall asleep here on the ground. But then she heard Arthur getting up.

"No, no. Not yet." Birdie held her arm over her eyes to block the sun as she looked up at them. "Can't we rest a little longer?"

"How come you're so tired, Mommy? I'm not tired one bit."

Cleary Emaleen was feeling better. Birdie shut her eyes and listened to Emaleen and Arthur talking as they walked away from her.

"Did you make this? This is a good trail."

"We all make the trail," Arthur answered.

"Who helped you?"

"The black bears and moose and caribou. Sometimes the sheep come down from the mountains to cross the valley."

Their voices were getting more distant.

"And you all walk here?"

"Yes."

"That's very smart, because it's way better to go on a trail. That way you don't get lost."

As their voices faded, Birdie heard another sound, a low buzzing that at first she thought was a bumblebee or some other insect. It grew louder, though, and she could tell that it was larger and mechanical. She stood, dusted off her jeans, put on her backpack, and followed Arthur and Emaleen's path up the mountain. They had stopped and were looking at something, and by the time Birdie caught up, she could see the plane flying along the valley.

"Look, Mommy, look! We're up taller than an airplane!"

"Is that your dad?" Birdie asked.

Arthur nodded.

"Hi, Mr. Warren!" Emaleen shouted and waved both her arms in the air. The airplane flew closer to their side of the valley and tipped its wing in their direction, as if Warren were trying to get a better look at them.

"Don't do that, Em," Birdie said. "Don't wave both your arms."

"How come?"

"Because that means we need help. Just wave with one arm to say hello."

Emaleen waved one arm back and forth over her head. "Hi, Mr. Warren! Hi, Mr. Warren! We're on top of a mountain!"

As they watched, the airplane went out of sight around the next ridge, toward Arthur's cabin.

All that time, she hadn't realized where he was taking them, even as they climbed the shale slope, the crumbling dark shards of rock sliding out from their feet and the sun beating down on them. All she could think is that she wished she'd brought more water. But then they reached the top of the ridge and the land opened up in front of her.

"You know this place," Arthur said.

"Are we . . . is that where we are?"

He pointed. "Della's lodge, you can see it?"

From this height, the impressive Wolverine River looked like a small creek, and on the other side she saw the barest glints of metal that had to be the roofs of the lodge and cabins. She couldn't make out the picnic table, it was much too far, but she knew it was there, and she had the sensation of slipping outside of herself, of inhabiting both places at once—sitting on the picnic table and imagining what it would be like to stand on this mountain ridge, and also standing here and looking down at her old life, and it was as if she soared, breathless and thrilled, in the blue sky between the two.

"Mommy, look, it's snow! Can we go down there?"

The rocky slope below leveled off into a small alpine bowl with a carpet of green moss and berry bushes and delicate white flowers that waved in the breeze on their thin green stems. On the other side of the bowl was a north-facing incline that held a last drift of glistening white snow. Arthur was already striding down toward it, and Emaleen followed without waiting for Birdie to answer.

Birdie wanted to run with them, to race across the alpine tundra, but her legs were worn out and her right knee hurt, so she walked more slowly. By the time she reached the drift, Arthur had climbed halfway up it, and Emaleen was grabbing snow and throwing it into the air. Birdie scooped some up in her hand, took a mouthful and let the watery coolness run down her throat. Grandma Jo had called this sugar snow, when it melts and freezes until the individual flakes disappear and instead become tiny, rounded grains of ice.

At the top of the snowy slope, Arthur sat and slid down on his back, and as he gained speed, he stuck his hands and feet into the air. Partway down, he did several summersaults and came up grinning, his shirt and hair wet with snow.

"I want to sled too! Can I sled?" and Emaleen took Arthur's hand as if to pull him back up the drift.

Arthur reached out to Birdie, and the three of them, hand in hand, hiked up the drift. The granular snow seeped into Birdie's shoes and dampened the cuffs of her jeans, but it was a relief after being so hot all day. When Emaleen slipped or struggled, they gently lifted her and swung her forward up the hill, and it became a game. "Again, again!" Emaleen cheered as they swung her like she was on a trapeze.

Arthur slid the fastest down the drift, maybe because of his weight. Birdie scooted, trying to use her hands and feet to propel herself. Emaleen gave up quickly and began rolling down the hill, laughing and screeching in delight.

For hours, they played in the snow and threw snowballs at each other and drank from the nearby snowmelt creek, and the hot sun and mountain wind dried their clothes. All the colors were brilliant and sparkling, white and blue and green, the sun shimmering off the snowcapped mountains. Emaleen picked wildflowers and winter-sweetened lowbush cranberries, and Arthur and Birdie napped on the mossy tundra. With her head rested in the warm crook of Arthur's arm and her daughter playing nearby, Birdie knew—this was the life she had dreamed for them.

Chapter 18

Birdie was losing her sense of time, or at least it was changing into something else. When they first moved to Arthur's cabin, she often jumped awake in the morning—she was late for something. What day was it? She hadn't set the alarm, she'd overslept and missed work, forgotten some responsibility.

That didn't happen anymore. Occasionally, she lazed in bed until a full bladder forced her outside, but more often, she woke early and gently, not always certain what had roused her—a robin's whistling song from a nearby tree, Emaleen playing one of her imaginary games, or Arthur snoring next to her in bed. Those were the rare and best mornings, when she woke to Arthur sleeping beside her.

She didn't know how many days or weeks had passed. She kept no calendar or watch. Instead there was sunrise and sunset, the ends of each day shaved almost imperceptibly by the approaching winter, the moon fattening night by night into a perfect luminous globe before shrinking piece by piece into the dark blue. Near the meadow, the white petals on the tall cranberry bushes yellowed and fell away, leaving in their place hard, green berries. On the forest floor, puffball mushrooms sprouted and grew and grew, then dried into leathery pockets that burst underfoot, their spores rising like brown smoke. Down along the riverbed, the dryas waved their shaggy seed heads in the wind, the silverberry willows lost their fragrant blossoms, and Birdie thought of Arthur's circles—the earth spinning through the days and seasons and years, the sun and moon and stars traveling across the sky on a loop, all of time existing at once.

She couldn't always tell one day from the next. The tasks were the same. Split kindling. Haul water. Make meals. Color with Emaleen. Read books to Emaleen. Start a fire. Cook dinner. Heat water. Wash the dishes. Sweep the floor. Sometimes she missed the excitement of strangers and friends coming and going from the bar, the jokes and gossip and flirtations, the first gulp of a cold beer. She missed days off, the mindless indulgence of watching television from bed and eating microwave popcorn. The luxury, too, of hot showers, clean clothes, fresh sheets.

One afternoon, she smoked her last cigarette down to the filter. The next days she was short-tempered and agitated. She nearly broke down and made a mountain-man cigarette out of whatever leaves she could stuff into a dried cow parsnip cane, like when she was a kid. Instead, she ate more—bannock fried in Crisco, salted jerky, chocolate bars, Sailor Boy Pilot Bread smeared with syrup—and she could feel her waist thickening, her thighs growing stouter, and under the layers of fat, her muscles were hardening. More than forty pounds of water in every bucket carried up the hill from the creek, the swing of the maul overhead and down onto each log, the armloads of wood brought into the cabin. There was no turning up the heat or turning on the faucet. Even the most basic comforts required work.

But then Birdie would remember how it had been at the lodge—the hangovers and bounced checks and other stupid screwups, her hours and days set by Della, everyone side-eyeing her choices—and she would feel a rush. It wasn't the manic, head-spinning high she'd always chased. Instead, it was like she'd been kept in a small box without any holes to let in the light or air, but now she'd climbed out and could fill her lungs with the fresh mountain breeze.

And there were perfect moments. The stormy evening she'd taught Arthur and Emaleen how to play blackjack; the three of them had pulled the kitchen table up close to the warmth of the woodstove and shuffled cards by candlelight, betting with chocolate chips and raisins. Through the netted windows, they'd listened to the wind rushing across the tops of the trees and the rain on the leaves, but inside it was cozy and dry. They drank mugs of chamomile tea with honey, and Birdie slipped a shot of whiskey into her own.

Another day, after the fog and rain lifted, Arthur had led them through the wet trees to look for boletes. He showed them how to spot the mushroom's golden cap among the moss and leaves, and how the underside had no gills but instead was more like the texture of a sponge. Once Emaleen got the hang of it, she ran and gleefully pointed, "Here, and here, and over there!" Arthur brought each one up to his nose and sniffed and licked it, to make sure it was good, he said, and the three of them filled a paper sack. That night, Arthur was gone, but Birdie sliced and salted the wild mushrooms, fried them in Crisco, and served them over spaghetti noodles. Emaleen said it was the best thing she'd eaten in her whole life.

There were other surprises. One afternoon, a pair of white swans flew so close and low along the river valley that they were almost at eye level, and Birdie could hear the slow *fwpt-fwpt* of their giant white wings. In the cool mornings, as Birdie and Emaleen stood outside in their bare feet to brush their teeth and spit in the dirt, they sometimes watched a moose or porcupine or a snowshoe hare pass by the cabin. A short-tailed weasel often darted in and out of the woodshed, and Emaleen had made Birdie laugh when she said he looked like he'd unzipped his brown coat so you could see his furry, white long underwear along his belly and chest. A brazen magpie got so accustomed to dinner scraps that he squawked and danced on the porch in the evenings. They named the magpie Old Mags, the weasel Mister Huey.

Some nights, when the cabin wasn't too hot, Arthur stayed. He and Birdie would lie side by side on the bed. They kept their voices soft so they wouldn't wake Emaleen, and they didn't look directly at each other but up at the log ceiling. In these moments, they talked more openly than at any other time. It felt like another kind of lovemaking. She told about her mother leaving them when they were young, how she and her sister had been raised by their grandparents. She described the few times as children that she and Liz had visited Norma in Florida. They'd gone swimming in an outdoor, chlorinated swimming pool and caught lizards along the side of the condo.

"Tell me something about when you were a kid," Birdie said.

"It is not easy," Arthur said.

"Did you have a hard time?"

"It's not easy because it is different from the words you use."

They were silent for a long time, and she didn't expect more. But then he started again, like he'd been considering how to tell her. "There are places I go where I am seeing her and I am smelling her. Places where I put a foot down and her feet are stepping there too, and I am with her. There are places where we eat blueberries together, and places where we catch fish, and I am with her but she is gone."

"Are you talking about your real mother? What was her name?"

"My first mother, yes. But her name . . . I don't know. It is a smell and a taste. It is the sense of being near to her."

"Is that because you were so little? You don't remember her name?"

She felt Arthur stiffen next to her, as if annoyed or frustrated.

"Warren, he found you out here, didn't he? Down by the North Fork?" *Careful,* she told herself. *Don't push too hard.*

"Yes."

"But what happened to your real family?"

A long time passed and he didn't answer, but she couldn't help herself. "I mean, didn't you ever want to find them?"

He never once shouted or swore or slammed things on his way out. He just slowly got up from the bed, opened the cabin door, and stepped out into the night.

Even when they didn't argue, Birdie had the bed to herself most nights. Arthur wandered away in the evenings and was gone for hours, sometimes even days. When he came back to the cabin in the early morning and lay down beside her, he smelled like the forest and mountains and his mouth tasted oddly metallic, like iron or blood.

"Where do you go?" she asked him once. "Maybe sometime we could go with you. Me and Emaleen."

"No," he said, and then as if foreseeing some intention on her part, he added, "You aren't following me."

"Seriously? What are you talking about?"

"Please. I am asking nothing else of you, just let me be."

There was the sting of rejection, but Birdie also knew it was true—he didn't demand anything of her. If she didn't cook dinner or straighten up the cabin or wash their clothes, he didn't care. Emaleen could run and giggle and try to do cartwheels inside the cabin, and none of it bothered him. If Birdie stayed in bed all afternoon, or napped in the sunshine for hours, he didn't berate her for wasting the day.

But now that he had drawn this line, she couldn't help but be curious. Whenever he left, he didn't take a tent or rifle or fishing pole, so he must have another cabin somewhere in the valley, the way fur trappers did. She was tempted to follow him and see for herself, but then she would think of how strained his voice had been. "Let me be."

She learned not to wait for him. When the evenings were calm and fair, she took Emaleen to the creek to fish for grayling, or to the pond to watch the beaver haul his sticks across the water. She didn't leave a note for Arthur. It was strange, no one knowing where they were in that immense wilderness. Like free-falling.

Birdie wanted to be at ease in her own skin. She wanted to be content. All those afternoons, she'd sat on that picnic table behind the lodge and daydreamed about taking Emaleen away, across the Wolverine River, up into the mountains. Now they were here, and she should be entirely happy. But the hours were circling and meandering and bleeding into each other, and it was like the wilderness had the pull of a dangerous eddy.

"Mommy, Mommy! Come on, let's go!" Emaleen had come to know the sound of Warren's airplane approaching through the mountain pass. As soon as she heard the distant engine, she wanted to run down to the airstrip to watch him land. She was well-mannered and didn't ask out loud, but they all knew that she was waiting to see what treats Warren had brought from town. Once there was a Tupperware container full of frosted cinnamon rolls that Della had baked, another time a bag of assorted chocolate bars.

This afternoon, Warren had a pair of binoculars for them to borrow. "So you can watch for those snow sheep," he said to Emaleen. He helped her bring the eyepieces closer together so she could look through them. Birdie hesitated—what if they got lost or broken? But he insisted that he had several pairs at home and he never used these.

He'd also brought a package of moose burger, so Birdie fried patties in a cast-iron pan on the woodstove and served them with rice and onion-powder gravy. The four of them sat on the porch with the enamel camp plates balanced on their laps. Birdie watched Arthur. He would take a few small bites, then move the food around to look as if he'd eaten more. She finished hers quickly so she could take away his plate before Warren noticed. When Warren looked in her direction, she said, "We had a huge breakfast this morning." She didn't know why she lied. More than once, she'd asked Arthur if there was something about her cooking that he didn't like. He shrugged it off, saying he wasn't a big eater. It didn't matter. He looked healthy. If anything, he'd gained weight since she and Emaleen had arrived.

Either Warren didn't see, or he didn't care. In fact, it was the most Birdie had ever enjoyed the man's company. He listened with quiet interest as Emaleen talked about Old Mags and how the bird liked leftovers, and Warren said that magpies are so smart, they can be taught to say words and do tricks. "I want to do that!" Emaleen said. After they ate, Warren and Birdie talked and laughed about all the people they knew in common, and he told stories about Grandpa Hank and Grandma Jo, some that she'd heard and others she hadn't.

Before he left, Warren offered to get them supplies. As Birdie made out a list, she resisted the urge to write "3 cartons of Marlboros & a couple of fifths of Jim Beam," but she did include menstrual pads along with toilet paper, bread, rice, and canned ham.

"It's kind of embarrassing," she said as she handed it to him along with two twenty-dollar bills. "You sure you don't mind?"

Warren looked over the list. "You have to remember, Carol and I raised two girls. I've shopped for my share of Tampax and mascara."

"Oh, and we really, really need ice cream," Emaleen said. "Please. Write that too. And milkshakes." Warren chuckled, and Emaleen said, "But it's true. I *need* it."

"I'm afraid it would all melt before I got it to you," Warren said.

"Oh," Emaleen said quietly. But she was cheered up when Warren talked about how his dog liked to lick the last bit of ice cream out of his bowl.

"She likes ice cream, just like me? What's her name? What color is she? Is she big or little?" Emaleen said she was going to color a picture of Spinner.

As Warren was leaving later that evening, Birdie heard him say to Arthur, "What you're doing here, I'm proud of you, son." Arthur was expressionless, almost as if he hadn't heard.

Birdie had been thinking about the coming winter and everything that needed to be done. She would have to enroll Emaleen in correspondence school and buy her a new winter coat and boots. They should stockpile more food for when the weather kept Warren from flying in. And there was always the worry about money.

"How much do you think the glass would cost for those two windows?" she asked Arthur. "A couple hundred bucks, at least, don't you think? But I don't want to board them up again . . . Arthur? Are you listening?"

He stood up from the stump where he'd been sitting in the yard and turned his back to her. Just like every other time he'd left, he didn't seem annoyed, only that he had someplace better to be. And as always, he didn't say goodbye or explain where he was going, or when he would be back, or how much the goddamned windows would cost.

"So we're not having this conversation, then? You decide, and we're just done?" she called. He was walking toward the woodshed, and she ran after him.

"Hey, where are you going?" She reached out to grab his arm, and he turned on her with such quick ferocity that she stumbled backward.

"What the—" She wanted to yell at him, but it was intimidating when he stepped toward her. He was more than a foot taller, and nearly twice her weight, and there was aggression in the way he lowered his head and raised his shoulders. "I am telling you," he said in a low voice. "Let me be."

She ran to the cabin, shut the door, and latched it, more out of anger than fear. He wouldn't follow her.

As evening approached and he still didn't turn up, she cleaned the cabin in a hot fury, dragging the table across the floor to sweep where she never usually swept, throwing dirty pots and pans into the washtub in a clanging racket, wanting something to break. She rifled through all their belongings in case somewhere there was a stray cigarette, and when she didn't find one, she drank the last swallows of whiskey without pouring it into a glass. If she'd been alone, she would have shattered the empty bottle against the wall.

"What's the matter, Mommy?"

"Nothing," she said, because she honestly didn't know. It was a burning, ravenous greed, but for what?

"Do I hurt you?" Arthur said into the darkness. They were at the base of a big spruce tree not far from the cabin, where they came to be alone in the night. It was cloudy and the moon had yet to rise so the darkness was nearly absolute. She was straddling him with a wool blanket wrapped around her naked shoulders.

"No, it was great. It feels good, doesn't it?"

The sex had gotten better over time. He'd grown more curious, both more tender and at times more dominant, and she was teaching him how her body worked, where she liked to be touched and licked. Sometimes she made them start slowly, teasingly. She would ask, "Do you like it when I do this?" or she would stop and say, "No, you have to tell me what to do next." Other times, like tonight, the sex was quick and aggressive. Neither of them spoke, but her moans rose up from deep within her body and ended as open-mouthed, high-pitched sighs. She liked it when she could feel that his lust was so intense that he was having to hold himself back.

"But do I hurt you?" Arthur said again.

"You don't have to keep asking me that. Trust me, if you hurt me, you'll know it."

"What is it then?"

"Do you even want us here?"

"Why are you saying that?" he said.

"Because most of the time you're not around, and you won't talk to me about it. So it makes me wonder, maybe you'd be happier if we left you alone."

"No." His tone was subdued. "Please, I am wanting you here. Both of you."

"Okay, you say that. But tonight? You'll leave again, right? I know. I'm not supposed to ask. But I don't know where you go or what you do. And maybe I'll see you tomorrow or two days from now. Whenever you decide to show up."

"You are lonely?"

"No, that's not it. I'm not lonely." She slid off him and sat on the ground, wrapped even more tightly in the wool blanket. "I don't want you to change. Or feel like you're trapped here with me. You go, and you're sleeping out under a tree or hiking up a mountain or whatever you do, and . . ." She was embarrassed to admit the truth. "Okay fine, maybe I'm jealous. Maybe I wish I could do that, just wander off whenever, wherever. You don't have to answer to anybody else. It's not . . . I don't know. I love Emaleen so much. I would do anything for her. She makes me laugh and she's, I know it sounds crazy, but she's like a friend, you know? We have fun together. Something I didn't have with my mom. And I don't want to be like her, like my mom. The way she left us. She was so goddamned selfish. I could never do that to Emaleen. But sometimes, I miss . . . myself. Just being me. By myself."

"We all go where we please."

"No, that's not true. Because I've got to think of her. You don't know what that's like. It's all on me. Just me. I had no clue before I had her. That I would never get a break. Not from her really, but from having to think about her, worry about her. Sometimes I wish I could . . . walk away, just for a little while. You disappear and I have no idea where you go, and I'm not even supposed to ask? But when you decide to come back, you don't have to wonder where I am, right? Because where else would I be?"

He wasn't listening. Or he'd fallen asleep. She brushed the spruce needles and dirt off her bare skin, got dressed, and crawled out from under the tree.

"I'm going in," she said. He wouldn't come after her, and that was all the more infuriating. She turned on the flashlight and wadded up the blanket under her arm. "Good night." She didn't wait for him to answer.

Chapter 19

"Birdie. Birdie." Arthur was sitting on the edge of the bed with his hand on her hip, jostling her. "Are you waking up?" he whispered. "You are going now."

"What? Going?" Birdie lifted her head to look around, confused. It felt earlier than she normally woke up.

"You are going now," he said.

"Where?"

"Wherever you want."

Birdie sat up. "What are you talking about?"

"You say you want to go for a long walk?"

She blinked her eyes hard and yawned. "Yeah, okay."

"So, you are going." He stood up, took her hands and pulled her to her feet.

"You mean right now?"

"Yes. You go, and you come back when you want." He was gently pushing her toward the door.

"Wait. I can't leave like this. I need my pants and my shoes at least," Birdie said with a laugh, and then she looked over at sleeping Emaleen. "But what about her?" she whispered.

"I am staying with her."

"Do you know how to take care of her?" She was getting dressed while she talked. "Like, you've got to make lunch for her. And make sure she is safe."

"Yes, I am making peanut-butter sandwiches."

He had thought it out, and it made Birdie smile. "Actually, she'd like that. But you can't leave her alone. You have to stay with her all day."

"I am staying with her always, as long as you are gone."

He was offering this to her. Like that odd clump of tundra he'd brought down from the mountain. A gift no one else had ever given her.

"But where would I go?" Birdie went out onto the porch and looked around. The forest made it difficult to see anything except the very tops of the mountains in all directions, but her mind was opening up to the idea. She could hike up the ridge to that snowdrift where they'd played. It would have melted away by now, though, and it seemed like the safe, easy choice, to go somewhere she'd already been.

She looked down the creek valley and out to the North Fork. Summer was fading, and along the alpine slopes, the green was turning to gold and rust. She could walk up into those mountains, someplace she'd never gone before, and she'd probably be able to keep the cabin in sight. Back inside, she filled her canteen and put the binoculars, warm clothes, and a few snacks in her backpack. Then she loaded the rifle and got Syd's hat from the hook by the door.

"Maybe I'll hike across the North Fork. Just to see someplace new. I'll be back before dark."

"You are coming and going as you please," he said.

"Yeah, but what if something happens to me? You've got to come look for me."

"I am finding you if you need me. But you aren't."

"How long do you think it will take, for me to get over there and up on the mountainside?"

"It depends."

"Well sure, but do you think I can do it?"

"Of course," he said.

"But seriously—" Emaleen stirred on her bunk, and Birdie lowered her voice. "I don't want to break my ankle and be laying out there for days. If I'm not back tonight, it means something is wrong."

"You are not coming back today. Tomorrow, maybe."

"There's no way I'm spending the night out there by myself. I don't have a tent or sleeping bag."

"It's not necessary."

"Maybe not for you." She went back out onto the porch and looked through the binoculars. "Here, come out here. I'm going to try to get up to those rocks. It looks like cliffs, kind of. Up that slope. Do you see where I'm talking about?"

He didn't take the binoculars when she held them out. "Yes," he said.

"Have you ever been there?"

"Yes," he said, and his smile seemed a little distant and sad.

Birdie trotted down the trail. She wanted to leave quickly, before she second-guessed herself, before Emaleen woke up and wanted to know where she was going.

She crossed the airstrip, then followed the creek down to where it flowed into the North Fork of the Wolverine. The river's blue-gray glacial water was deeper and faster than she'd expected. She walked up and down the bank, looking for a better place to cross. Arthur would give her a piggyback ride to the other side if she went back to ask him, but she didn't want to.

She hadn't brought a change of clothes, so she stripped to the nude, stuffed everything into her pack, and put her boots back on her bare feet. The water was unbelievably cold, and she sucked in a breath and sputtered as she stepped into the current. When it neared her crotch, she didn't think she could do it, but she plunged ahead. "Ho- Hol- Holy . . . Hol- Holy . . . Fuh . . ." She couldn't finish the words and the sound came out as wheezes. "Hol—Fuh, fuh."

She wanted to go faster, get it over with as quickly as possible, but the current was swift. Each time she lifted a foot to step forward, the river threatened to sweep her away, and when she hesitated in one place, the current pulled the sandy gravel out from under her boots. Her feet and legs were in agony from the cold, and every muscle in her body was clenched against it.

When she got out on the other side, she would have dried off and brushed the wet sand off her feet and legs, but she didn't have a towel and she was so cold. She swore and her teeth chattered as she pulled her clothes over her damp, gritty skin. She needed to get moving to warm up. Looking up the valley, she could see that the rock formation was farther upstream than she'd realized. She stayed down along the river and walked in her wet boots across the gravel and sandbars, keeping her eyes on that place in the mountains.

As a little girl, she'd spent a lot of time in the woods, mostly at the old homestead within sight of her grandparents' house. Grandpa Hank had taken her hunting after school for snowshoe hare or spruce grouse, a few times on longer trips into the mountains for caribou and moose. But he'd always been there, just a few strides ahead. She remembered watching the backs of his legs and trying to step where he had stepped.

This was different. No one was going to tell her which direction to go, and she would have to find her own way home. She looked back down the river. The airstrip and cabin were out of sight already, and she couldn't see the mouth of the creek where it flowed into the North Fork.

When she was directly below the rock formation, she left the river's edge and hiked up through a patch of spruce trees, then through alders and devil's club and across a small stream and into more alders that had grown so thickly together that she wasn't sure she would be able to find her way through them. She took the rifle off her shoulder and held it with both hands, ready to shoot if necessary. "Hey! Hey there!" As she shoved her way through the brush with no clear view in any direction, she considered turning back—this was going to take too long. But eventually she broke free and could see up the mountainside. The peculiar rock formation looked like a row of giant teeth rising gray and crooked out of a crumbling slide. If she approached it directly, the climb would become nearly vertical, but to the south there was a gentle slope that looked like it would lead her up and around the back side of the rocks.

The hike up was steeper than it had looked, but it got easier the farther she went. The bushes dwindled and she passed one last, stunted and windbent spruce tree, and then she was in the alpine tundra—moss and lichen growing over rocky ground. Thin game trails crisscrossed the hillside, and following them, Birdie stepped over caribou tracks and Dall sheep dung.

As she crested a ridge, the land opened into an immense panorama of reddish-gold hillsides, rocky valleys, folding and buckling ribbons of limestone, and layered in all directions, slate-gray mountain peaks. A ravine cut deep into the mountainside, hundreds of feet down, and ended in a narrow slot of jagged, dark rocks. Standing at the precipice, Birdie was intensely aware of her own body. A small life, beating inside a paper-thin skin. At the end of that long fall, her bones would splinter like toothpicks, the rocks would rip and gouge her flesh. She became conscious of the muscles of her heart pumping and her lungs drawing in the thin air. She drew her eyes out of the ravine and up toward the nearest mountain peak, and it was as if willpower alone kept her bound to the earth. Like that day when she was a little girl and she'd launched herself off the swing—the gulp of air, the sudden clarity. The ground tilting under her.

It was the altitude, or a touch of vertigo. She backed away from the ravine and sat on a hump of moss, drank several long gulps of water from her canteen, and the dizziness subsided. She ate a couple of bites of jerky, drank some more water, and then took the binoculars out of her pack and looked down and across the North Fork. From this vantage point, she could see the airstrip again—a long, straight clearing along the creek. She couldn't locate the cabin; the forest was too thick, and the sod roof would camouflage it. She pictured Emaleen playing outside, talking with her imaginary friend, and occasionally looking toward the mountains. Birdie's heart ached pleasantly, as if a string ran the distance between her and her daughter and it was being pulled taut.

With her elbows resting on her bent knees to steady the binoculars, she slowly swung her gaze back across the valley to the near mountainside and up to the top of the ridge. On a far slope, she saw a smudge of white, and then lost sight of it. She thought it had moved, but it might have only been her unsteady hands on the binoculars.

A cool wind blew across the ridge, and clouds had condensed in a charcoal strip along the horizon. Rain, maybe even snow, could be coming her way. She dug a sweater out of her pack and was glad to see she'd remembered her raincoat as well. Half the day was gone. She needed to pick up her pace. She continued her climb up the ridge, and the land flattened so that she could see back into a wide, rocky bowl more than a mile across, cradled in the mountains, and at the very top of the bowl, the fingers of a blue-white glacier reached down among the rocks. The air was noticeably colder, and the wind blew harder.

Birdie was getting a knit hat and gloves out of the front pouch of her pack when, in her peripheral vision, she glimpsed what looked like ragged, bloody branches marching across the tundra. She quickly put on her pack and stooped low so as to be less visible. She crept closer, then dropped to her belly and crawled like a soldier until she could see, less than a hundred yards away, four bull caribou walking in a line. Their antlers reached three or four feet into the air above their heads. The largest bull led the way, the thick white fur along his chest rippling in the wind, and several times, he tossed his head. He was beginning to lose the velvety fur that grew on the antlers in the summer, so the brown strips hung and drooped from the many points, and where the bone was exposed, the antlers were blood red.

Birdie stayed prone on the ground. The wind was in her favor, and the caribou ignored her. They weren't running, but they seemed to travel with a purpose, and quickly they crossed the hillside and turned away from her and back into the mountain bowl. For a while, she could see their white rear ends and their antlers, but then, one after the other, they disappeared into a fold in the land and were gone.

Did you hear that, Emmie? The clicking sound the tendons in their feet make as they walk? And did you see their antlers?

Emaleen would have whined and complained the entire way, and maybe she wasn't even strong enough to make the journey. But if she'd been here, Birdie would have said *shhhh*, and gestured for her to stay low, and Emaleen would have minded. And when the caribou passed by, her eyes would have grown wide. *Mommy, I see them! I see them! They're just like Santa's reindeer.*

It was impossible, what Birdie wanted. To go alone, to experience the world on her own terms. But also, to share it all with Emaleen.

* * *

She was above the rock formation now, and what from the valley had looked like a row of teeth, now appeared as a massive plateau that had been cracked in half, leaving a winding green path between two walls of solid rock. The hillside leading down to the formation was gradual. She heard the high chirp of parky squirrels as they alerted each other, and she spotted one of the chubby rodents standing up on its hind legs, watching her, while another squeaked and raced from one hole to another.

When she found a game trail to follow down, she let gravity pull her into a run, her pack thumping against her back. Her legs had never been so strong, her feet so sure. It was as if she could run forever, on and on over ridges and valleys, and when she jumped up onto a large rock and leapt off the other side, she let out a whoop.

As she neared the rock formation, the mountainside steepened and she found she was taking long strides to step down, left foot, then right, on what seemed like off-centered stairs set into the tundra. This wasn't a thin, switchback game trail made by caribou or sheep. These were giant, plodding footsteps, left then right, and then it struck Birdie—it was a bear trail. She could picture a grizzly easing itself down headfirst, lumbering side to side. No leaves grew at the center of each large track, and in places dirt was visible through the thick moss and springy shrubs where it had been disturbed frequently and recently. This trail hadn't been formed by a single bear over the course of one summer. Each indentation was set into the tundra at least six inches, and the land itself seemed to conform to each footstep. Bears had worn this path into the earth over the course of decades, maybe hundreds or thousands of years.

The trail continued down and between two rock walls that were so close together it was like descending a narrow stairwell. Birdie reached out to the cold stone to steady herself. She couldn't see far ahead, and she wondered why bears would follow this path time and time again. There were cliffs and rockslides up and down the valley, so maybe this was one of the easiest routes to the river.

"Hey bear!" she called down through the rocks. "Hey bear!"

After a short distance, the land flattened into a plateau, the rock walls spread farther apart, and the game trail led across a mossy clearing. All around, the rocks stood upright, craggy and gray, almost like photos of Stonehenge in Grandpa Hank's *National Geographic* magazines, and they were much taller than they'd seemed from a distance, close to twenty feet. Some of the massive rocks leaned into each other, and others had toppled and cracked, but it must have happened long ago because moss and grass had grown over the rubble.

The rock faces were marked in what looked like graffiti—dots and circles, some as small as a dime, others as large as a platter with open centers, spirals and twists and bull's-eyes. Like prehistoric paintings, peeling and faded in shades of orange and white against the gray stone, but when Birdie looked more closely and touched them, there was the scaly, crusty growth of lichen under her fingertips.

The stillness, the absolute silence of the place was eerie. There was no wind, no parky squirrels or alpine sparrows. Even Birdie's steps were hushed by the turf under her feet. As she turned back toward the center of the clearing, she nearly stepped on a group of delicate, beige mushrooms that grew out of the tundra in a perfect circle nearly six feet in diameter. "Fairy ring!" Birdie whispered in surprise.

Don't you dare go blundering into it. That's what Grandma Jo would say. Witches and fairies danced in a circle here on moonlit nights, the mushrooms sprouting up where their feet touched. If you trespassed inside the circle, they would punish you. You might be forced to dance away the rest of your life inside the ring, or, if you escaped, the curse would follow you back home and weave mischief and sorrow through your days. *Are you joking?* Birdie had asked when she was a little girl. No, this was no joke, and Grandma Jo had told of some distant cousin back in New Hampshire who had stomped on a fairy ring out of pure contrariness. What happened to him? Birdie had wanted to know. All kinds of nonsense, Grandma Jo answered.

Birdie paused and then, careful not to crush any of the mushrooms, stepped into the circle. It was something like that day in the derelict church when she'd stood at the altar and shouted a laugh into the sanctuary—the peculiar thrill of transgressing. A smile tugged at the corners of her lips. She slid her pack off her shoulders, sat down cross-legged in the middle of the fairy ring, and took out her lunch.

Chapter 20

Emaleen opened her eyes and the cabin wasn't right. The fire wasn't going and she didn't smell pancakes or oatmeal, and she didn't hear her mom moving around. Arthur was sitting on a chair, and he was looking at her.

"Where's my mom?" she asked.

"She is gone," he said.

"Did she go to the outhouse?"

"No. She is farther now."

Emaleen was thinking about this, and she wanted to ask Arthur if her mom was filling the water buckets at the creek. But then she remembered something scary. Last night, she'd woken up and it had been very quiet and very dark, except for a little bit of red that seeped and flickered out the edges of the door of the woodstove when the fire was burning. "Mommy?" she'd whispered, but no one answered. She wasn't going to be afraid, though. There was a little shelf by her bed where she put Thimblina each night, and she reached out in the dark and found the thimble and put it on her thumb.

That's when she'd heard something outside. It didn't sound like an owl or a coyote or anything like that. It sounded like a woman crying and moaning, like something was hurting her. Emaleen tried to look out the window, but it was too dark to see. She heard the cries again and again, and they didn't seem far away, like maybe just out by the big spruce tree. After a while, the noise stopped and Emaleen listened very, very hard, and she thought she could hear voices. There weren't any words, and the sounds turned into whatever she imagined—her mom and Arthur talking back and forth, trees groaning in the wind, a forest witch murmuring to herself. Emaleen would have climbed out of bed, turned on a flashlight, and gone to look for her mom, but she knew she would get in trouble. She wasn't allowed to be up in the middle of the night, except if she really, really had to go to the outhouse and then her mom would take her. So she'd kept still for a long time, and the voices were like waves going up and down, louder and quieter, louder and quieter, and as Emaleen tried to make out the words that the trees were speaking, she'd fallen asleep.

But now, her mom was gone. She thought about the crying sound that had woken her, and she thought of the bear hide buried behind the woodshed and how Arthur had looked when he was inside of it. She thought of the moose calf, all eaten up, and the bones her mom had found under the bed. Arthur was still watching her from the chair. He wasn't smiling or laughing. Emaleen stayed under her blanket, and she didn't move a muscle.

"You are getting out of bed," he said. The way Arthur talked, sometimes Emaleen didn't know if he was asking her or telling her.

"But I have to get dressed," she said quietly.

"Oh. Yes." Arthur seemed kind of embarrassed, and he went outside. Emaleen jumped down from her bunk and quickly put on her shirt and her pants over her underwear, all the time thinking, thinking. *Running only makes bears want to chase you.* Her ribs were getting tighter and tighter so that it was like her insides were being pushed up and she could feel her heart beating by her tonsils. What if the bear had hurt her mom, and she was outside needing help? *We've got to mind our p's and q's.* She found her shoes, and she put them on, and she was very glad she had learned to tie them all by herself.

His voice made her jump. "You are ready?" he called from the other side of the door.

"Yes," she said, because she couldn't think fast enough to tell a lie. She climbed back up on the top bunk and sat cross-legged, all the while trying not to show any expression on her face. Arthur's footsteps were very quiet on the cabin floor because of his bare feet.

Emaleen had never seen him do anything inside the cabin, except some-times sleep on the bed beside her mother or eat a little bit of food her mom cooked. But he was taking things off the shelves and setting them on the table, and then he was picking up a butter knife.

"What are you doing?" she asked.

"I am making a peanut-butter sandwich for you."

"Oh," she said, and then thought to add, "Thank you."

"You are welcome."

When he turned back to the table and opened the peanut-butter jar, Emaleen very slowly slid down from her bed.

"Umm, I have to go to the bathroom," she said. "I can go by myself. My mom lets me."

When she reached up to unlatch the door, though, she saw that her mom's boots weren't there, and neither was the backpack or her coat that usually hung from a nail by the door. And up on the hook, her mother's rifle was gone too.

Outside, Emaleen looked all around, by the woodshed and the big spruce tree, and she called for her mom in a loud whisper so that her mom would be able to hear, but not Arthur. Nobody answered. It was quiet ex-cept for the birds that sang *chicka-dee-dee-dee*. Emaleen went to the out-house, because she really did have to go pee, and she sat on the wooden bench with her bottom hanging down into the cold, dark hole. She watched as a spider let itself down on its invisible string from a top corner, and it was coming closer and closer to her. Usually, Emaleen would have screeched for her mom to get rid of it. Instead, as the spider got closer and closer, she blew softly on it, and it went back up its spider string.

"Emaleen?"

She pulled up her pants and left the outhouse. Arthur was on the cabin porch. "Your breakfast is ready."

At the table, he had put a sandwich on one of the pretty blue plates, and he gave her a cup of water. The bites of bread and peanut butter were sticky and dry in her mouth, and the water tasted lukewarm and old. Arthur sat across from her, watching her.

She swallowed hard. "Where is my mom?"

"She is walking into the mountains."

Emaleen nodded. The bear hadn't hurt her mom. It was the other thing, the terrible thing. Her mom had gone away and left her behind. Emaleen's eyes were stinging, and she kept them wide open so that the tears wouldn't squeeze out onto her cheeks.

Arthur frowned. "Why are you crying?"

It was very hard to keep the tears in and make the words come out. "Why . . . why didn't she take me with her?"

"It is good, to be alone sometimes."

"No, it's not." She was crying now.

"Yes, yes, I am like that too." He smiled, as if thinking of something for the first time. "When I'm young, I am sad to be away from my first mother."

Emaleen sniffled to try to stop crying. "How many moms do you have?"

"My first and my second."

"Where are they?"

"They are both gone now."

Emaleen nodded solemnly and wiped the tears with her sleeves. Maybe his moms had died, or they'd gone away to the mountains, or to Florida.

"Do you miss them?" she asked.

"Yes, I do. My first mother, for a long time, I still see her and I want to be with her."

"What if my mom doesn't come home?"

"She is coming back to you."

Emaleen wanted to believe him.

"Do you like your sandwich?" he asked.

Even though a peanut-butter sandwich was a weird thing to eat for breakfast, and she wasn't hungry at all, she nodded politely and took another bite.

It was the longest day ever, and mostly Emaleen sat on the steps of the porch and waited and watched for her mom. Sometimes Arthur sat next to her, and he didn't say anything. When he got up and walked around, she wondered if he was going to leave, because that's what he always did, and she tried to imagine what it would be like to live here all by herself. She thought of the boy lost in the wilderness with his marshmallows, and she thought about listening for Warren's airplane. But Arthur didn't leave, and he always stayed where he could see her.

At lunchtime, it was another peanut-butter sandwich, and she ate it on the porch steps. She didn't want to play in the woodshed or read books or color. It was windy and cloudy and cold. She wanted her mom to come home and start a fire in the woodstove and cook warm noodles or rice for dinner. She wanted to breathe in the smoky smell of her mom's long hair and be hugged up in her arms, and she wanted to put her head in that place between her mom's chin and her collarbone, the place where Emaleen's head fit perfectly.

When it started raining, she went inside and made her bed as neatly as she could and put away her books and toys and wiped off her plate from lunch, and she tried her best to sweep with the big broom. She didn't want the house to be messy for when her mom came home.

Arthur didn't seem to care that it was a cold, cloudy day and the lantern wasn't lit and the fire wasn't going. Emaleen put on her water boots and went out to the woodshed. The splitting maul was way too heavy. She could barely lift it off the ground. She couldn't cut up kindling like her mom did, so she made a little basket out of the bottom of her sweatshirt and picked up as many wood chips and slivers as she could find on the ground inside the shed. She carried them to the cabin and put them into the woodstove, and she went outside and peeled bark off the birch tree and put that into the woodstove too. Then she found a lighter on the kitchen counter and held it up to Arthur.

"You have to do it," she said. "I'm not allowed."

He hesitated, but he took the lighter and flipped it with his thumb. He wasn't very good at it, and it took lots of times for him to make it work. He lit the bark, and for a little while, the flames got big and crackling. When all the wood chips were almost burned up, Emaleen pushed a log into the stove, and the fire went out. She wasn't going to cry, though. No matter what.

* * *

It was almost night time, and it was raining outside, and still her mother wasn't home. Arthur was making another peanut-butter sandwich. Emaleen had never eaten the exact same thing for breakfast, lunch, and dinner.

"Can there be honey on it too?" she asked. "Please."

Arthur dribbled lots of honey over the peanut butter. He gave her another cup of lukewarm water from the bucket. It was very, very quiet in the cabin so that her mouth smacked loudly even when she tried not to. She drank some water.

"Aren't you going to eat dinner?" she asked.

"No." He was sitting across the table from her, but she couldn't see his face very well because it was getting darker now.

"You know, sometimes." Emaleen was going to be brave and say what she'd been thinking about a lot. "Sometimes bears . . . they eat fish and berries and mushrooms. And they don't even have to eat baby animals or anybody 'cause there's so much other good stuff to eat. And peanut-butter sandwiches, they're very good. You should try it."

He didn't say anything, and Emaleen wondered if his face was looking happy or mad. She could hear him breathing deeply through his nose.

"I think a bear likes peanut butter. And honey and bread," she said. "And then he doesn't have to hurt anybody."

"It is none of your concern what a bear eats." His voice was angry now, like that day when she saw the hole in the ground.

"Arthur?"

"Yes."

"Are you still here?"

"Yes."

It was dark night and Emaleen couldn't see him because there wasn't a lamp or a fire, but it sounded like he was sitting at the table. She was in her bed, under all of her covers because it was cold. She was also wearing all her clothes, even her shoes. In case she had to run fast.

"Are you going away?" she asked Arthur.

"No. I am staying here with you."

"Okay."

Her mom had been gone all day, and still she wasn't home. Emaleen decided it was best if Arthur stayed. If he left, he might go put on his bear skin. And also she would be all alone in the dark cabin. She didn't want to be all alone.

A long, long time went by, and she heard Arthur move over to the bed and lie down. She waited awhile, and then she said, "Arthur?"

"Yes."

"Are you still here?"

"Yes."

"Are you cold?"

"No."

"Okay . . . Are you having a hard time going to sleep too?"

"Yes."

"I can tell you a story. If you want. That way we can fall asleep."

"Okay."

Chapter 21

It was the blueberries that misled her. They pulled Birdie away from the fairy ring and the tall rocks, down into a ravine where the bushes grew low and thick along the ground. Some of the branches were so laden she could pick four or five berries in a single handful, and they were so ripe and full of sweet-tart juice that they burst when she pressed them between her tongue and the roof of her mouth. The only container she had was her canteen, so she gulped the last of the water and began to fill it with berries. She daydreamed about bringing them back to Arthur and Emáleen, cooking the berries into pancakes, sprinkling them over oatmeal, drizzling them with honey for dessert. Crouching by the bushes and walking on her knees, lured on and on, she ate berries and filled the canteen at the same time even as the rain drizzled down on her. Periodically, she brought her head up and looked all around and, even though she didn't see anything, shouted, "Hey bear!" Her back grew stiff, her fingertips stained purple-blue, her jeans soggy, but the canteen was nearly full. Just a little farther, just a few more berries.

As she crawled across the wet tundra, she caught a strong fragrance. She picked leaves and sniffed at them. Maybe it was the Labrador tea, or the blueberry bushes. She also came across a small plant with silver, lacy leaves and an herbal scent like a cross of camphor and sage.

It was all of it together. The wild smell of the tundra. She grabbed clumps of wet moss and all the different leaves, and she crushed them between her hands and rubbed them across the back of her neck and along her throat. It was the smell of longing and hunger. It was the smell that drew Arthur away from her, and the smell he brought back with him into the cabin. Birdie wanted it in her and on her, a part of her skin and her hair and her breath. That way, he wouldn't be able to leave her.

It had been cloudy all day, but now the gray seemed to wash across the mountains and down through the valley. It wasn't just the weather. Daylight was fading. All that time while Birdie followed the blueberry bushes down into the valley, the hours had turned and twisted and dwindled away. She looked back up toward the rock formation and realized how far she'd ranged as she picked berries. If she hiked up the hill to retrace her path across the mountain, she would run out of light. The more direct route was straight down. Down led to the river, and the river led home. She had maybe an hour or two before it would be too dark.

She scampered downhill as fast as she dared, her boots slipping on loose rocks. In the steepest places, she slid on her butt and grabbed at shrubs to slow her momentum. She thought about night coming and Emaleen waiting for her back at the cabin, and a fluttery panic set in. Once she reached the river, it would take maybe an hour to follow it down to the airstrip, and then another half an hour to cross and make her way to the cabin. She wouldn't stop until she was home.

At the bottom of the ravine, though, she didn't find the spruce forest or river willows she expected, but instead a vast boulder field that stretched in a fan shape toward the river. It was as if an entire mountainside had shattered and tumbled down. The angular pieces of limestone were immense, many of them the size of small cars, piled on top of each other, and their edges looked sharp and new. Back up, to the north of the ravine, Birdie could see where they had broken away from the face of the mountain.

It wouldn't be easy crossing the rock field, but if she backtracked, there was no doubt she would have to spend the night out here. She began the slow climb over and through the rocks. She'd assumed they were in a single layer across the ground, but as she made her way among them, she realized that the pieces of limestone were layered so thickly that in some places she could look down between them ten or fifteen feet and still not see the bottom. At times, she could hear water running under the rocks. If she fell into one of those crevasses, she might not be able to get herself out again. She focused on each step in front of her. *Don't think about tripping. Don't think about falling.* She climbed carefully from one boulder to the next, and when she had to, gathered her nerve to leap across a gap.

It'd been a mistake, coming this way, but it was too late to turn back. She could hear the river in the distance, and she had a flashlight in her backpack. As darkness set in, though, she found it was too difficult to climb over the boulders and carry the flashlight at the same time, and even when she could, it was disorienting trying to navigate within that narrow tunnel of light. She was afraid of losing her bearings and meandering in the wrong direction.

When she reached a flat slab of rock the size of a pickup bed, which was protected by several larger rocks towering around it, she stopped. It was a miserable place—no cushiony tundra to sleep on, no branches or grass to light a fire, no trees to shelter her from the weather—but it would have to do. She ate the last few crackers and strips of salty jerky from her pack, and then remembered that she didn't have any water, only a canteen full of blueberries. At least the juice moistened her dry mouth. She took off her raincoat to put on a sweater underneath, then snugged Syd's hat down on top of her knit hat. When the rain quickened, Birdie lowered her head so that the icy water dripped off the brim in front of her nose.

At some point, the rain stopped, and she curled up on her side with her head on her pack. When she closed her eyes, she saw blueberries and blueberry branches and more blueberries, as if they had imprinted on the backs of her eyelids. She was drifting, floating. The berries turned to circles of lichen, orange and gray, that spiraled across a black void. She was dreaming, maybe, of fairy rings. *It is like circles, many circles spinning within one another. There is nothing to hold on to.* She watched a blue-black silhouette of herself run along mountain ridges, the rocky earth slowly rotating and grinding under her feet as if her steps did the turning, and the stars in all their constellations traveled at the same slow, steady pace across the sky above her.

A giant creature, so immense that maybe it was the entire earth itself, breathed in and breathed out, and the icy exhalation came down through the rocks and wrapped itself around her body. She was so cold.

She changed positions again and again. The slab of limestone was unforgiving under her soft body, and she searched for any bit of warmth, her hands clasped between her legs, her shoulders hunched up to her ears, but the cold was sinking deeper into her core. When she stood up to do jumping jacks and hop in place, she noticed that the clouds had lifted. The stars were out. Not just a few, but millions upon millions. Some glittered, and others burned steadily in shades of orange and blue. She searched for the only two constellations she knew—the Big Dipper and Orion's Belt. She found them eventually, but they didn't stand out like most nights. The stars were so numerous and dense that they created a hazy ribbon across the sky. It didn't seem possible that they could give off enough light, but Birdie could make out the colorless angles of the rocks around her, then even the shadowy outlines of spruce trees on the other side of the valley and, in the farthest distance, the rise and fall of the black mountains against the blue-black sky.

She couldn't stop shivering. Night went on and on. She sat huddled in a tight ball, rubbing at her arms and legs with her hands. She wiggled her toes against the cold. Her pant legs and feet were damp. Grandpa Hank had taught her to carry spare wool socks, but she'd forgotten. She wondered if frostbite was possible when it was above freezing. She took off her shoes and knit hat and wrapped her feet inside the hat, but it didn't do any good. Would she know if she was hypothermic?

She didn't wait for the sun to appear. As soon as there was the gray-light beginnings of dawn and she could see well enough, she resumed her climb over the rocks. For a long time, she continued to shiver and shudder, but after a while, she started to warm up and the exhaustion hit her. It was as if her shoes were made of iron, her legs too heavy to lift.

When she was in labor with Emaleen, after about eight hours she'd told the doctor, "I can't do it anymore." She'd had nothing left to give, no strength, no coherent thought. The doctor had coached her, Come on, just a few more pushes, you can do this. *I can't. I can't. I'm not strong enough.* You couldn't let yourself think about how far you had to go or all you'd been through. Just this step, and this step, and one more after that.

And then the first rays of the sun broke through the mountains. The heat radiated across Birdie's skin, through her clothing and into her sore muscles. Eventually she was able to take off her coat and knit hat, and she even began to sweat some. She thought she heard an airplane, but she searched the sky and couldn't see it.

It was hours before she reached the end of the rockslide and stepped onto soft ground. The sun was high in the sky now, and there was a summerlike heat to it. When she found a trickle of fresh water running out of the rocks, she got on her hands and knees to slurp it up.

Nothing looked familiar. As Birdie followed the river downstream, she strained to recognize some landmark—the mouth of the creek or the airstrip. Had she already passed it, or mistakenly come down into some other valley? Was she walking farther away from the cabin with each step? If she got lost, how would Arthur know where to look for her?

When she finally spotted her own tracks across a sandbar from the day before, she hollered, "Yes!" Around the next bend in the valley, she saw the mouth of the creek and the place where she'd crossed the North Fork. She didn't stop to take off her clothes before she stepped into the river. It was as if her mind had left her body and was several strides ahead, pulling her forward, across the river, along the creek, through the airstrip, up the familiar path to the cabin, her legs and feet numb with fatigue.

"Emaleen! Arthur! I'm home." She stopped between the woodshed and the cabin, waiting for Emaleen to run out from somewhere. But there was no answer. "Emaleen? I brought you a surprise." She climbed the stairs to the porch, but when she opened the door, the cabin was empty.

Several cardboard boxes were stacked by the bed—it must have been Warren's plane she had heard earlier. And there was a note on the table, written in crayon block letters. "EMALEEN SAYS I SHOULD WRITE THIS SO YOU ARE NOT AFRAID AND ARE KNOWING WHERE WE ARE. WE ARE AT THE BEAVER POND." Below that, Emaleen had written, "I love you Mommy" in her childish lettering.

Birdie kicked off her dirty, wet boots, stripped off her damp clothes, and rolled herself up in a blanket on the bed. She wanted everything at once—to start a fire, to sleep for days, to stuff herself with food and guzzle a gallon of water, and to find Emaleen and Arthur and tell them everything. She didn't have the energy for any of it. For a long time, she just lay there, overwhelmed with relief to be back at the cabin. Finally, she got up, still wrapped in the blanket, and drank several cups of water, then opened a can of Spam and forked the cold, gelatinous meat into her mouth, laughing quietly to herself because it tasted like the best thing she'd ever eaten. Between bites she found clean clothes, and then she sat on the bed. Her feet were puckered, clammy, and aching. As she pulled on dry wool socks, she moaned out loud, it felt so good. Once she was dressed, she finished the can of Spam, ate a few blueberries from the canteen, and drank more water.

The pillow was soft, the blankets warm and comforting. Arthur and Emaleen would come back soon enough. She would rest here for a while.

When she tried to sleep, though, her brain hummed. The circles on the rocks, did Arthur know the names of the lichen? The fairy ring, the caribou, the parky squirrels, and the canteen full of blueberries, the night she'd spent alone under the stars with a rock for a bed. Birdie wanted to tell them all about it.

She sat up and put her wet boots back on over her wool socks.

She could hear Emaleen's squeals and Arthur's deep laughter in the distance. The pond lay in a depression surrounded on all sides by mossy spruce forest. In some places, the edges of the pond were marshy, but at the far side, there was a lookout where the bank was steep with moss-covered rocks. She spotted Emaleen in the middle of the pond in her wet underwear and T-shirt, climbing out of the water and onto the beaver house. Nearby, Arthur slowly treaded water with only the top of his head and his nose visible. Birdie waited until Emaleen was safely on top of the beaver house before she shouted, "Emaleen!"

Emaleen brought her head up and looked all around.

"Over here! I'm over here!" Birdie waved, and Emaleen finally saw her.

"Mommy! Mommy! You're home! Arthur, look, it's my mom!"

Arthur lifted his head out of the water and grinned up at Birdie, like he was pleased but not surprised.

"Mommy, watch this! Are you watching?" Emaleen took a small step backward and then leapt off a log and into the water with a splash, and for a moment she was completely submerged. When she bobbed up, Arthur was right next to her.

"The rocket, the rocket," she yelled to Arthur. "Let's do the rocket! Are you watching, Mommy? Watch me." And she grabbed on to Arthur's neck and put her feet up on his hands so he could launch her backward and up into the air as she screeched with delight. She landed with another splash, and when she came up again, she paddled in Birdie's direction like a little puppy.

"Did you see? Did you see me?" Emaleen stammered with cold and excitement as she climbed up on the bank.

"Yeah, but you don't know how to swim."

"Yes, yes I do! Arthur, he taught me and and, he says . . . He says you don't have to think and think. You just do . . . do it. And he taught me how to swim like a bear."

Birdie picked her up. "Ooo, you're all wet."

Emaleen wrapped her cold, skinny arms around Birdie's neck and hugged her desperately. "I am missing you and missing you and missing you," Emaleen said, and Birdie thought her daughter was nearly in tears.

"I know. I missed you so much too. Guess what I saw? Caribou. Four big bulls."

"I want to see them!"

"And I brought back some blueberries. They're really good. Did you hear that, Arthur? Blueberries!"

He was still treading water out in the pond. "I am happy to see you," he called out.

"Yeah, me too. I've got so much to tell you."

"Come swim with us, Mommy." Emaleen pulled on her hand. "Please, please."

"God, no. I'm finally warm and dry. I want to stay this way."

"Please, pretty please. Oh wait, Mommy." Emaleen was running back down the bank. "Watch this. Watch what he does. It's so funny."

The beaver had emerged from his house and was swimming across the pond. Emaleen waded out and smacked her hand flat on the surface of the water. The beaver popped its head up to look in their direction, then slapped its tail and disappeared under the water.

As the sun moved across the valley, Emaleen and Arthur swam around the pond and eventually convinced Birdie to take off her boots, roll her pant legs up to her knees, and wade in. The water was lukewarm compared to the icy river, but she didn't like the way her feet squished into the deep mud at the bottom.

"Make sure you're not getting any of that water in your mouth," she called to Emaleen. "You don't want to get beaver fever."

Back on the mossy bank, Birdie found a dry place to lie in the sun. She pulled Syd's hat down over her face, and for the first time in two days, slept soundly.

She woke to Emaleen rubbing her hand up and down one of Birdie's bare shins.

"You're like a furry witch," Emaleen said.

Birdie laughed and took the hat off her face. "What did you call me? A furry witch?" It was true that the hair on her legs and armpits had grown long and silky, and there were even a couple of wiry hairs on her chin. There wasn't any point in shaving and plucking out here. Arthur didn't care, and there was no one else to worry about. "I thought witches were green and ugly."

"No," Emaleen said in a serious voice. "Forest witches are furry and pretty and they have long, scratchy hair and it gets caught in the trees when they fly."

"But my hair isn't scratchy."

"That's because you're not all the way a witch yet." Emaleen crouched and put her face close to Birdie's. Her breath smelled like peanut butter. "And forest witches, they have . . . They have golden eyes."

"All right, then, see—I'm not a witch. My eyes are brown."

"But, you . . . you know what?" Emaleen put one eye right up next to Birdie's so that their eyelashes touched. "There are little tiny pieces of gold in there too. I can see them."

"Really? Huh. I didn't know that."

"First, your eyes got to get all the way golden. Then, your hair will be all long and scratchy."

"So is it good or bad? Being a forest witch?"

"I don't know," Emaleen said with an exaggerated shrug with one shoulder up to her ear. "We'll see," and the tone mimicked Birdie's, when she didn't want to answer one of Emaleen's questions. *We'll see.*

Birdie laughed again, but it was slightly unnerving. How did Emaleen come up with this stuff? Was it the storybooks she read, or just her own wild imagination? Birdie had been so different when she was that age— too shy to speak around adults, but easily provoked. Grandpa Hank just had to say, "I bet you can't do it," and Birdie would lunge at a challenge. Driving three-wheelers, climbing ladders, shooting guns. But she'd hated schoolwork. Emaleen was the opposite. She would talk to anyone who would listen. She adored her books and her crayons, her elaborate stories and make-believe friends. And if an older kid taunted her or she failed at some physical challenge, Emaleen shrugged it off, like she had more interesting things to think about.

It was amazing, really. When Birdie was pregnant, she'd imagined raising a miniature version of herself, but instead she'd given birth to a stranger she was just beginning to get to know.

It was nearing evening when the three of them began the walk back to the cabin.

"Where are your shoes?" Birdie asked Emaleen.

"I don't need them. See." She was following right behind Arthur and taking big strides to try to step exactly where he'd stepped. "My feet are tough, just like Arthur's. You should do it, Mommy. It's super fun."

"Nah, that's okay. My feet are sore enough already."

Even after napping all afternoon, Birdie was worn-out, and she lagged farther and farther behind the two of them, then finally sat on a fallen tree to rest. She didn't expect Arthur to notice, but he turned back and found her. He went down on one knee and gestured for Birdie to climb on.

"Oh god, I've gained like fifteen pounds out here. I'd break your back."

Arthur smiled. "No, you are not breaking my back."

"Wait, I want a ride!" Emaleen said as she ran up to them. "Can I have a ride?"

"It is your mother's turn."

Emaleen dramatically slumped her shoulders. "But I'm super-duper tired."

Arthur continued to look at Birdie expectantly.

"You're really serious?" she said. "Okay, but you're going to regret it." Birdie climbed onto his back and Arthur stood up, hooking his arms under her knees. She kissed the side of his head. "Are you sure it's not too much?" she asked, but he walked on as if she weighed no more than Emaleen.

When they got back to the cabin, Emaleen struggled to keep her eyes open while Birdie got her a plate of jerky, crackers, and blueberries. "I'm too tired to cook tonight," Birdie said, "but in the morning, I'll make blue-berry pancakes. You should have seen them all. It was unbelievable. I could have filled buckets. Hey, that tickles." Arthur had come up behind her, wrapped his arms around her waist, and was snuffling at the back of her neck.

"You smell good," he said. His breath in her ear made her go light-headed.

She expected him to leave as soon as they got back to the cabin—he'd been stuck here for two days with Emaleen. And that would have been fine with Birdie, because more than anything, she wanted sleep. But Arthur stayed. He followed her around the cabin, touching her hips and the backs of her thighs, brushing her hair away from her neck so he could kiss her again and again, his eyes always on her.

As soon as she'd finished eating, Emaleen climbed up on the top bunk and was asleep within minutes. Arthur started to pull Birdie toward the door. "Oh, okay," Birdie said, surprised. "Let me get a blanket."

For the first time, Arthur did everything—pulled her shirt off over her head, eased her down onto the blanket, unzipped her jeans, slid his hand down into her pants—and it was exciting to let him. He got on top of her and kissed her fully on the mouth again and again, then licked her earlobes and the underside of her chin. "The way you taste," he said. "The way you smell. I am wanting all of it."

Birdie laughed. "So it worked."

"What?"

"Nothing."

They'd barely finished and rested for a few minutes when Arthur began kissing her and moving for her to get on top of him.

"Again?" Birdie said.

"Hmm-mmm," he said. "I am loving you."

It didn't strike her at first, the way he said it. Was he talking about the sex, or something else?

"Are you saying you love me?"

"Yes."

"Say it again."

"I am loving you."

I am loving you. As if love, once it came into existence, radiated backward and forward, encompassing all of time.

Birdie had always been quick to tell people she loved them—family and friends, the men she'd slept with—and every time, she meant it, if not always in the same way. Arthur's words were different. They felt like a binding pledge.

"I love you too," she said.

Chapter 22

"Mommy, Mommy? What's this word?"

Birdie rolled onto her side, the platform bed hard under her hips and shoulder. She hurt everywhere—her lower back, both of her knees, the bones in her feet, the sunburned skin on her shoulders, even her lips were parched and sore. Emaleen was holding something so close to her face that she couldn't make it out through her squinted, bleary eyes.

"Mommy? I'm sorry, but you have to wake up. It's important. What's this one called?"

"What?"

"What's this one called?"

"Go back to sleep, Emmie."

"I'm too excited. Will you read it to me? Uncle Syd, he sent lots and lots of books."

"Later. Let me wake up, okay?"

Birdie had never been more physically drained, and it was like a month had passed in two days. The hike down from the mountain, the hours at the pond, Arthur saying that he loved her, that had all been yesterday. He'd even come back to the cabin with her afterward and lain down on the bed beside her, and she'd wrapped an arm across his chest and fallen asleep instantly. The few times she woke briefly, she could tell Arthur was awake, motionless and breathing quietly, as if he didn't want to disturb her. This morning, he was gone.

"See, these are for me 'cause they have pictures and not too many big words," Emaleen was saying. Emaleen had opened one of the boxes and arranged stacks of books on the table. "And these are for you, 'cause they're growed-up books."

"Syd doesn't give up, does he?" Birdie mumbled.

"But this one, this one looks inter-sting, so maybe you can tell me about it."

"Later, okay? Let me have some coffee." She stretched her arms over her head and then sniffed at an armpit. "Whew, I stink. We need a bath."

"I don't," Emaleen said. "I'm all clean."

Birdie raised an eyebrow. "Really?" She picked a piece of gray lichen from Emaleen's matted blond hair and tried to rub away a streak of dried mud across Emaleen's forehead.

By early afternoon, Birdie had heated enough water on the woodstove to fill several pots and buckets. She and Emaleen stood naked in the grass outside the cabin and dumped ladles of warm water over their bodies. It was the perfect day for an outdoor wash, sunshiny with an occasional breeze to keep the mosquitoes away. Syd had sent out a bottle of liquid peppermint soap with a note that said it could wash anything—skin, hair, clothes. The scent was refreshing, and the soap tingled on their skin, but it left their hair as brittle as straw.

After they were washed and rinsed, both of them still naked, Birdie began dunking their clothes into the bucket of soapy water and scrubbing at them with her hands.

"Come and help. We've got to pretend like we're a washing machine."

"No, I want to run around naked," Emaleen said.

"Watch out, those ones bite," Birdie said as a fat horsefly buzzed over Emaleen's head. Emaleen flapped a hand at it but kept running and spinning, and she reminded Birdie of a long-legged foal.

Birdie plunged the clothes in and out of the soapy water and began rinsing them in a bucket of cold, clean water. She glanced up occasionally as she worked, to be sure that Emaleen didn't stray too far. And then she looked up and, at the edge of the meadow, a bear stepped out of the shadows.

It was moving slowly, snuffling at the ground, the sun blazing across the blond tips of his fur. It seemed oblivious to them. Birdie slowly straightened, letting the wet clothes slide quietly back into the bucket. At the same moment, Emaleen squealed and hopped, and the bear stopped and raised his head in their direction. Birdie could see now that one of his ears drooped and a deep scar ran along the side of his head and down his muzzle.

"Emaleen, shhh!"

"But it's biting me! That horse's fly is trying to get me!" Emaleen shrieked again, and the bear stood up on its hind legs.

"Jesus," Birdie whispered. Then, as loudly and as deeply as she could manage, she yelled, "HEY BEAR! GO ON, BEAR!"

Emaleen ran to her side. The bear had dropped back down onto all four feet and was moving toward them.

"Emmie. Do not scream. You hear me? Don't run. Just back up. Slowly. HEY BEAR! GO ON, BEAR!"

The bear was continuing in their direction, meandering in a slow zigzag.

"Go on! HEY BEAR!" Birdie yelled again. She pushed Emaleen up the stairs to the cabin.

The bear stopped. It was less than fifty yards away now, and its small, dark eyes followed Emaleen as she ran to the door.

"Just GO ON! Get!" Birdie yelled as she backed through the door and shut it. She was securing the latch, thinking about putting something heavy up against the door, when she remembered the mosquito netting in the open windows. "Fuck." Still naked and dripping water, she picked up her rifle.

"Get on the chair and look out the window," she told Emaleen as she fed bullets into the magazine. "Can you see it?"

"I can't see."

Birdie went to the window and looked through the netting.

"There he is!" Emaleen said.

The bear was walking sideways to the cabin, like it might go back into the forest, but then it continued around the corner of the cabin and out of sight. Birdie went to the other window with the rifle in her hands.

"But Mommy, you can't shoot him!" Emaleen was crying.

Birdie needed to be sure of her aim, because wounding a grizzly bear could make it more dangerous. But when she looked through the window, the bear wasn't in sight.

Birdie quickly pulled on a pair of jeans and a T-shirt over her wet skin, wrapped Emaleen in a blanket, and placed a chair with its back to the woodstove, where she would be able to see both windows and the door. She gathered Emaleen on her lap and sat with the rifle against her side.

She had no idea how long they'd been sitting there. Water dripped off the ends of her hair and down her back. She listened, and mostly it was quiet outside the cabin but occasionally she thought she could hear movement. Emaleen stopped shivering and leaned her head against Birdie's chest. Birdie's eyes followed a repeating path as she sat and listened—to the window, the door, then the side window. The next time she looked to the side window, the outline of the bear's head was visible through the white mosquito netting. It was standing with its front paws on the windowsill, and when it pushed its muzzle into the mosquito netting, it breathed deeply in and out like it was smelling them.

Birdie raised the rifle and slowly slid back the bolt. The sound wasn't loud, but distinct and metallic. Before she could finish chambering the bullet and pull the trigger, the bear's head had disappeared and she heard a soft huff as its front paws hit the ground. Birdie nudged Emaleen off her lap and ran to the window. The way the sun was coming directly through the mosquito netting blinded her. She pulled a corner of the netting away and looked out in time to watch the bear lope across the meadow and into the forest.

Birdie was standing on an upside-down bucket set carefully on top of a chair outside the cabin as she nailed boards back over the windows. The rifle was slung over her shoulder. She was trying to hammer as fast as possible while balancing and keeping an eye out for the bear.

"Are you watching?" she asked Emaleen.

"I'm looking and looking. I don't see him."

"Hand me another board."

Back inside, the cabin was gloomy with the sun blotted out. The mantles on the Coleman lantern had burned out, but Warren had brought her a new package. Birdie changed them out, filled the lantern with gas, and worked the thumb pump over and over again until it was pressurized. When she lit the mantles, they glowed brightly beneath the glass and the cabin was brighter than it had been even in the peak of daylight. She hung the lantern in the center of the room by its steel handle. The log walls and ceiling glowed a golden brown, and the lantern hissed quietly. It felt safer somehow, but she wished Arthur would come home.

With the windows boarded up, it was impossible to tell time inside the cabin. Occasionally, Birdie opened the door to look out. She wanted to start a fire, but she wasn't going to walk out to the woodshed to split kindling.

They had cold, leftover blueberry pancakes for dinner, and afterward, Emaleen occupied herself with the books. Birdie paced around the cabin, but finally sat at the table across from Emaleen and picked up a few of the books, flipping them over to read their back covers.

"See, Mommy, this is the one about Grover. 'Member, it's funny. He's scared and scared, but the monster is just him. Silly Grover." Emaleen pushed aside the stack of Little Golden Books with their foil spines. "But those are baby books. I want to read this one. It's about a pirate and a little boy. See. How come there aren't more pictures? What's it called? Please, Mommy, can you read it to me?"

Birdie was irritable and distracted, but maybe if they cuddled under the blankets and she read to her for a little while, Emaleen would drift off to sleep.

"Okay, bring it over here. Let's see. It's called *Treasure Island*."

After only a few pages, Emaleen put her hand on the book and pushed to close it. "It's way too boring."

"I don't know, let's read a little more. Look, there's a picture of the pirate ship."

Birdie continued reading out loud, and when she realized Emaleen was asleep against her, she kissed the top of her head and read the rest of the chapter.

The next day, Birdie kept Emaleen inside with the door latched, except when they needed to use the outhouse. Any time they stepped outside, Birdie carried the loaded rifle and watched over her shoulders, but there was no sign that the bear had returned.

There was nothing to do but nap and drink cold coffee and stare at the walls. She would tell Syd, next time she saw him—the books were a life-saver. Emaleen was pretending she was Miss Gwin, the librarian at the Alpine children's hour where Grandma Jo had taken her on Tuesday afternoons. She sorted and resorted the books on the table and scribbled on little pieces of paper, pretending to check them out, and then, slowly sounding out the words, she read them aloud to her imaginary friend.

"And now," cried Max, "let the wild . . . rum- rum- rum-pus"—"Mommy, what's a rumpus?"

Frog walked into the house. It was dark. All the shutters were closed. "It's like us, with the windows all closed up."

It is cold. See the snow. See the snow come down.

Later, when the cabin grew too quiet and the day too long, Birdie read out loud again from *Treasure Island,* the chapter where the boy first meets Long John Silver in person, but Emaleen complained from the top bunk, "I don't want to hear that story anymore." So Birdie silently read the next few chapters to herself.

They couldn't live like this forever, cowering inside the cabin. In the morning, when Arthur was still gone and the bear hadn't returned, Birdie decided enough was enough. She went to the shed and split a pile of kindling, filled the woodbox by the stove, then hauled several buckets of water from the creek. With the chores done, she sat on the porch and read more of the book while Emaleen played in the grass and wildflowers. She didn't let Emaleen out of her sight, and she always kept her rifle within reach.

"Mommy, do you think maybe sometimes bears can be nice?"

"I don't know," Birdie said without looking up from the page she was on. It occurred to her that Syd had finally gotten her hooked.

"Because maybe some bears, they're bad and eat baby moose and people, but maybe a bear is nice and doesn't want to hurt you."

"Mmm-hmm." But Birdie wasn't really listening.

The next morning was cool, and dark clouds had gathered along the mountains. By midday, it was raining, and it continued all afternoon. Birdie started a fire in the woodstove and brewed fresh coffee, and when the cabin got too warm, she propped the door open to let in the fresh air and the sound of the rain. Emaleen was coloring at the table and Birdie was reading the last chapter of *Treasure Island* when Emaleen said something.

"Mommy, Mommy, did you hear me?" and it was like Birdie was being woken in the middle of a dream. She reluctantly set the book down.

"Look! It's Arthur." Emaleen was standing in the doorway, and beyond her, Birdie saw Arthur walking through the rain and toward the cabin. When he came in, he shook the water from his head and warmed himself by the woodstove. He was in a good mood. He'd spent the past few days fishing for Dolly Varden and grayling near a beaver dam, he said.

"That's really good, Arthur. Because fish are yummy and very very healfy," Emaleen said.

"You should have brought some home," Birdie said. "I could have fried them up for dinner—"

"Yes! Yes! Can we get fish for dinner?" Emaleen interrupted. "'Cause my mom, she has a fishing pole and everything—"

"I don't know, with that bear around," Birdie said, then looked to Arthur. "So yeah, that's our news. I almost shot a grizzly. Looked like a scrapper—one ear was nearly torn off and its head was all scarred up. The damned thing chased us into the cabin and wanted to come right through the window at us. When I chambered a bullet, it startled and ran."

She'd expected Arthur to be impressed with how well she'd dealt with it, but instead he looked stricken. "It's all right," she said. "You don't have to worry. That's why I boarded the windows up again. It was just a little excitement. But it's all good now."

"It is not happening again," he said.

"What, you mean the bear? It's hard to say if it will come back. But it's part of the deal, living out here. I can handle it."

Arthur was shaking his head slowly.

"But Mommy, maybe he's not a bad bear," Emaleen was chattering on. "Maybe he's a bear who eats fish and berries and . . ."

"What are you . . . shhh."

"But if he's a nice bear, maybe he can live here too. Right, Arthur? And that means he won't hurt us and he can be our friend."

"Emaleen, listen to me," Birdie said. "It's very dangerous, and if it keeps coming around here, we might have to shoot it. You've got to stay close and mind me. No matter what, okay?"

Emaleen was nodding her head, but she looked like she was going to cry.

"No," Arthur said. "No, I am taking care of this. I am not leaving."

He sat on the edge of the bed and pulled Emaleen up onto his knee. "I am staying here, with you and your mother, and you are not worrying anymore. Yes?"

Chapter 23

For a while, it was the best. Arthur stayed home and he wasn't tired or sick or anything, and Emaleen's mom was happy all the time. Even though winter was coming and the pond was colder, they went swimming with the beaver, all three of them, and Arthur even did the rocket with her mom and then they came home and got dried off and warmed up by the woodstove. At night, both her mom and Arthur slept together on the big bed and it was cozy inside the cabin. A long time ago, Emaleen sometimes wished that they were back at the lodge, where she could eat cheeseburgers and french fries and ice cream, and she could ride the bus to go to first grade in Alpine when the summer was over. But not now. Now, she wanted to live here forever with Arthur and her mom. Even when she was a grown-up, she wanted to live here with them.

She was also thinking that maybe when she grew up she would like to be a bear. Except like Arthur, so that sometimes she could be a little girl, and other times a bear. She would sleep on the tundra and not even be cold because of her warm fur, and she would be so strong she could swim in the big river and walk a long, long ways without any shoes and she would never get tired.

"Did you ever go on that mountain?" She pointed over Arthur's shoulder. He was giving her a piggyback ride up the hill to the blueberries, but he seemed more tired than usual, and he took such slow steps that Emaleen's mom had gone past them. "Did you?" she asked again.

"Hmm-mmm."

"And did it take you lots and lots of days?"

"No. Only one day."

"And that one over there? Do you see it? It is super far away."

"Yes, that one too."

"But you didn't even look. See? That one!"

"Every mountain, all of them that you see, I walk across."

When her mom was nearby, they didn't talk about the bear. It was a secret, just between her and Arthur, and Emaleen had decided that maybe it was a good secret. As she held on to the back of his shirt, she imagined she was holding on to his fur as he galloped across all the mountains.

"Maybe sometime," she said quietly into his ear, "maybe one time, I can be with you when you're a bear and you can give me a ride."

"No," Arthur said.

"But how come? It'll be fun!"

"I am telling you, no," he said, and he slid her off his back and set her on the tundra in front of him. He didn't seem angry, but he was looking down at her with a very serious expression. "It is important, yes? When I am like that, you are keeping away from me."

"Okay," Emaleen said, but she was only kind of listening because the tundra moss was so deep and bouncy and she was jumping up and down and pretending she was a snow rabbit, hop, hop, hop.

They picked berries all afternoon, except mostly it was her mom who filled up the coffee cans. Emaleen was getting lots and lots of berries, but then her mom said, no, those are just crowberries.

"But Arthur, he said they're good to eat."

"Don't worry about it. They'll be fine mixed in," her mom said. "Why don't you go get some lunch out of the pack?"

Emaleen found some crackers and she took them to where Arthur was lying on the tundra. She sat beside him.

"Do you want one?" she asked. "I have lots."

"No."

"How come you don't eat with us?"

"It is no good," he said without opening his eyes.

"You don't think our food is good?"

"It is not the same. I am not tasting it and it is not making me fat."

"You silly. You want to be fat?"

"Yes." And he smiled and patted his belly, which didn't look very fat at all to Emaleen.

"But when you're a . . ." Emaleen looked around, but her mom was picking berries on the other side of a big rock all covered in moss. She leaned over and put her mouth to Arthur's ear. "When you're a bear," she whispered, "the food tastes yummy and you can eat lots and get fat."

He nodded.

While she ate her crackers, Emaleen watched Arthur sleep. The scar on his face was interesting because it made him look sad-frowny even when his eyes were happy. She didn't like to look at the place where his ear should have been, though, because it was horrible. But Arthur wasn't even embarrassed. Actually, he wasn't ever worried or embarrassed. He didn't care if his hair was messy or his clothes were old or his feet were tough and dirty.

When Emaleen finished her crackers, she took off her shoes and socks and wiggled her toes around in the tundra and it was nice and scratchy on the bottoms of her feet. She wanted her feet to be just as tough as Arthur's.

"Arthur? Are you awake now?"

"Hmmm."

"So, do you like being a bear?"

Arthur was quiet for so long that Emaleen thought he was asleep again. She started picking the small red-purple leaves off a blueberry bush. Each one was perfect and tiny, smaller than her fingernail. Before, she had thought the mountains turned all purple-red in the fall because of the berries, but Arthur told her it was the leaves on all the tundra bushes and plants, and he'd shown her the blueberry leaves, how small and bright they were. She was arranging the leaves in a pattern on Arthur's knee, the purple-red against his blue jeans, so that it looked like a flower with lots and lots of petals.

"It is hard to remember. Everything is different," Arthur said. "The colors and the light, the smells. For a short time, I am almost remembering, but then it goes away and I am not remembering anymore. I am thinking, this is a dream. Or maybe the other is a dream."

"Is it a good dream, or is it a bad dream?" Emaleen asked.

"I am not sure."

And then Emaleen gasped. "Arthur! Look, look!"

Arthur sat up fast and was looking all around the mountainside. "What is it?"

"No, right here. Look!" Emaleen pointed to a plant.

It was the flower that didn't have a name, except the flowers were gone and instead there were fluffy puffs like miniature, purple dandelions in a cluster.

"See?" She picked one. "I know it because the leaves are all poky and green and purple."

Arthur began to laugh. "You are right. It is our little no-name flower. The sound you are making, I am thinking it is something big and important." He was laughing harder, and it made Emaleen laugh too.

"But it's sad because it doesn't have a name," Emaleen said. "Let's name it. Umm . . . purple fuzzy wuzzy. That's its name." She blew on one of the seed heads, then blew harder and harder until finally some of the fluff came free and floated in the air.

"Fuzzy wuzzy was a bear," she said and shook the plant hard, trying to get the last of the seeds free. "Fuzzy wuzzy had no hair. Fuzzy wuzzy wasn't very fuzzy, was he?"

Arthur and Emaleen laughed and laughed, and each time they stopped, Emaleen would say, "Fuzzy wuzzy," and they would start laughing again.

"No, no, I can't laugh more," Emaleen said. "My belly hurts."

That was the last happy day. After that, Arthur was getting more and more tired, and even when Emaleen said, "Fuzzy wuzzy," he didn't laugh even a little bit. They stopped going to the beaver pond, and they didn't walk barefoot through the forest or climb high up in the mountains to play in the snow or pick berries or look for their no-name flower. There wasn't any sunshine. It rained and rained and rained, and it was cold, like summertime was gone for good. The three of them stayed in the cabin all day and all night, but it wasn't cozy or fun. Emaleen's mom didn't laugh or smile, not even the little smiles when she was sad but wanted Emaleen to think she was happy. If Emaleen asked if they could play tic-tac-toe or blackjack, her mom said, "Not now," in a way that said to not ask again.

One night, Emaleen woke up and her mom and Arthur were sitting at the table and it was very dark except for one candle between them. Arthur's elbows were on the table and he was rubbing his forehead with his hands, and Emaleen thought maybe he was crying, which seemed like a terrible thing. He was giant and strong and had a big laugh, so if he could be sad and cry, then anybody could be sad and cry. Emaleen pretended to be asleep, but she was listening. Maybe Arthur was going to tell the truth, about the bear.

"I didn't ask you to stick around here all the time." Her mom's voice was hushed, but she sounded angry. "I keep telling you, we're fine. I can take care of myself, and Emaleen. What do you think I did before I met you?"

"No. What you are saying isn't right. I am wanting this."

"Yeah, okay. You look really fucking happy right now. I was stupid, thinking we could come out here and live with you and have some kind of normal . . . Like a family, you know. Della tried to tell me . . . When your dad comes back, I don't know, maybe we should leave. Me and Emaleen. Go back to the lodge or something. I don't know."

"No. Please, Birdie." Arthur was definitely crying now. "Please, you are not leaving me. I am doing this. I am making it right so we can be together. The three of us."

"I wish I could believe that." Maybe her mom was crying, too, except that her mom never cried.

It was hard, but Emaleen tried to be quiet inside the cabin. She colored and read books and tiptoed across the floor so it wouldn't creak. Arthur lay on the bed all day and all night and all day, and mostly he was asleep.

When he was awake, he was different. He turned his face toward the wall and he didn't talk, and he never, ever ate one single thing. Her mom tried cooking lots of different foods and bringing them to Arthur in bowls and plates and holding up a bite on a fork, like he was a baby. This morning, her mom had gotten mad and slammed the blue metal plate on the counter and said bad words, like *why the hell would you starve yourself like that for fuck's sake*. Then her mom went outside, like she was going on another long walk into the mountains without Emaleen, but when Emaleen peeked out the door, her mom was just standing under the eaves of the cabin and watching the rain fall. "Go back inside," she said, so Emaleen closed the door.

Emaleen had to drag a chair over to the shelves to reach the jar of peanut butter and the honey and bread.

"Arthur?" she whispered. "I am making you a sandwich." When it was ready, she licked the honey off the palms of her hands, wrapped the sandwich in a paper towel, and brought it over to the bed. "There's honey too. Just like the one you made me. When my mom was gone. Remember? It tastes good. I promise. Arthur?"

He didn't answer, and she couldn't tell if he was awake. She climbed up on the bed and leaned over his head to hold the sandwich up to his face, but his eyes were closed.

"Arthur? Don't you want some? It'll make you better. Even . . . I think . . ." she whispered more quietly, "even a bear likes it."

"NO!" He turned his head fast at her, like that dog Popper when he almost bit her, and his voice was so deep and angry that it startled Emaleen and she almost fell off the bed.

"Emaleen!" her mom said from the doorway. "What are you doing? Just leave him alone."

"I . . . I was . . . I . . ."

"You don't need to be climbing all over him. Can't you tell he's sick?"

"I know, Mommy. I just . . ."

"There's no way your dad is flying in here." Her mom was talking to Arthur, and she sounded tired. "I mean the mountains are so socked in I can't even see across the valley. But you need to get to a doctor or something."

"I am doing this," Arthur said.

"Doing what? Starving yourself to death?" Then she looked over at Emaleen. "Go outside and play, okay?"

It was foggy and rainy and her mom had said it was snowing up in the mountains. Emaleen went to the woodshed, but she just sat on a log and kicked her feet. She couldn't imagine her interesting games. She had the thimble in her pocket, but Thimblina wouldn't come out because of all the yelling from the cabin. The sound of it made Emaleen jumpy, like she wanted to march inside and tell them to stop, but she would get in trouble, or she wanted to run far away into the woods where she couldn't hear the yelling anymore, but that was too scary. She put her hands over her ears and kicked her feet in the wood chips and tried not to be sad. Sometimes, when you play outside after dinner, and the last of the yellow sunshine goes away, everything turns gray and cold and lonely. That's how it was now.

And there was that bad smell too. Emaleen smelled it yesterday, but it was even worse today. It was like the time at the lodge when her mom and Della had to throw out a bunch of rotten meat from a refrigerator that had stopped working. It was such a bad smell that even when you tried to breathe through your mouth instead, you could taste it on the back of your tongue and it made you gag a little bit.

Emaleen was pretty sure it was coming from the forest behind the woodshed. She climbed up on the log she used as a step stool, and she looked through the eyehole in the back wall.

"Mommy, I have to tell you something. But please don't be mad, okay?"

"What?" Her mom's voice was flat.

"You have to promise, though," Emaleen said. "Cross your heart, hope to die, you can't be mad at me."

"I can't do this right now."

"And you have to promise, you won't get mad at Arthur either."

"What?" Her mom's voice had turned sharp, and she was looking right at Emaleen. "Did he hurt you? Did he do something to you?"

"No," Emaleen said, "but no matter what, you can't shoot him, okay?"

"Emaleen, what the hell are you talking about?"

"You have to come with me," and she pulled on her mom's hand. "Please."

It wasn't really raining except there was still water dripping off the spruce branches and the ground was all wet and squishy, so that's why Emaleen wore her rainbow water boots. She wasn't sleepy or bored anymore. Her heartbeat was going fast. She wasn't going to keep this bad secret anymore.

"Come on, Mommy. We're almost there."

Even though it wasn't summertime anymore, her mom wasn't wearing a coat, only a T-shirt, and she pulled her hand away from Emaleen and folded her arms up tight across her chest like she was cold and mad. When they were past the woodshed, her mom wrinkled up her nose and squinted her eyes. "What's that smell?"

"We're almost there."

"I don't think we should go any farther," her mom said.

"We have to." It was like Emaleen was the grown-up, and her mom was the little kid. "It'll be okay."

Arthur had moved the hole after Emaleen saw it that one day. But when she'd spied out of the hole in the woodshed and watched him take off the bear skin, she'd seen the new place where he buried it. She was pretty sure she could find it. They walked between two spruce trees and through some tall cranberry bushes that had lots of red, sour berries, and then Emaleen saw the mound of branches.

"Leave it alone, Emmie. It's just something dead and rotten."

"No, it's not. It's Arthur." Emaleen was on her hands and knees, pulling away the moss and dirt and branches. "See, look."

"God, stop it. We're going now."

"Mommy, you have to listen to me. This is how come he's sick. He has to put his fur back on."

"Is this one of your pretend games? You need to stop it, right now."

"No, no it's not. Remember, Mommy. Remember the bear when he came, and we hid inside the cabin and you had the gun? That was Arthur."

"Knock it off. We're going back inside." Her mom yanked her by the arm, and it did hurt, but mostly Emaleen was crying because her mom wasn't listening.

"It's true, Mommy. I promise. I'm not telling a lie."

"I'm not saying . . . Jesus, Emaleen. You have this imagination. But this. This is too much."

Chapter 24

Warren had searched through his daughters' rooms, digging through the closets and pulling out boxes from under the beds, with no luck. It'd been years since they were both grown and gone, but he could picture the dollhouse clearly—not much bigger than a wooden ammunition box, cheerful yellow with green trim and pretend shingles painted on the roof. It swung open on hinges to reveal two rooms on both sides, an upstairs and a downstairs. As he recalled, he and Carol had barely finished it in time for Christmas that year. He'd spent hours out in the Quonset hut, painting the details, building little cupboards and chairs, even putting down scrap pieces of carpet and linoleum in the rooms. Carol bought a miniature doll family made of some kind of molded plastic, and she'd miraculously sewn tiny clothes for them. On Christmas Eve, they'd set it up under the tree without wrapping it, and the next morning, the look of pure awe and joy on their daughters' faces had made it worth every minute. Wendy would have been six that Christmas, the same age as little Emaleen.

When he phoned Wendy, an expensive long-distance call in the middle of a weekday, she sounded alarmed when she answered. "Dad? What's wrong?"

"No, no. Everything is fine. I've just been looking for that old dollhouse. You remember, the one Mom and I made for you two?"

Once she seemed to get over her shock and confusion, she said of course she remembered it, but no, she didn't think she or Theresa had ever taken it from the house. "What do you want with it anyhow?"

Arthur was a topic they'd long avoided. Wendy and Theresa believed it had been a mistake for Warren and Carol to adopt the little boy, with his strange illnesses and developmental problems. Over the years, whenever it came out that there'd been some incident with Arthur, their resentments bubbled to the surface. Carol was a patient, kind woman, but the disagreement had sparked in her a rare vehemence. How could their daughters, who'd enjoyed such idyllic childhoods, be so selfish? They'd both moved thousands of miles away from Alaska and had their own lives, as was their prerogative, but it was none of their business how she and Warren chose to spend their time.

They weren't a fighting family, so as time passed, neither sister asked about Arthur, and Warren and Carol didn't volunteer anything.

"Birdie's little girl, over at the lodge," he said to Wendy. "She's about the same age you were. She might enjoy it."

"Oh, that's a nice thought," she said. "Did you look in the attic?"

He hadn't been up there for years. All his tools and outdoor gear, the tents, rifles, and fishing rods, were out in the workshop. The attic had been more Carol's domain, where she stored holiday decorations and keepsakes, bags of old clothes, sheets and towels, pieces of fabric that might be of use someday.

As soon as he hung up the phone with Wendy, he climbed the ladder and opened the hatch into the attic. He pulled the string to turn on the bare lightbulb, and there was the dollhouse, sitting on a side table against the far wall, as if waiting all this time for another little girl. Hunched over to avoid hitting his head on the rafters, he carried it to the open hatch, then returned to the side table to look for the dolls and furniture. He was thinking of giving it to Emaleen as a Christmas present. Of course, that was months off yet. Why not let her have it sooner? He was smiling to himself as he imagined flying out there with the dollhouse tucked into the back of the airplane.

The conversation with Wendy had ended the way it often did. "You should really come down for a visit, Dad. We'd love to have you, and the boys miss you." Warren made a half-hearted excuse as to why it was an inconvenient time. Six hours on one of those sardine-can commercial jets. Urban sprawl, then suburbs so flat and featureless that Warren had gotten lost more than once just driving to the grocery store. Truth be told, as much as Wendy tried to guide the two men into conversation, Warren didn't particularly care for his son-in-law, who earned his living off questionable real estate deals and talked endlessly without listening. And the grandsons, they had no use for Warren.

He loved them, they were family after all, and he wished them happiness, but that wasn't the same as enjoying their company. When Carol was alive, she'd insisted they travel to visit each daughter at least once a year. Warren grumbled about it, but he'd gone along. Without Carol, it seemed he was on course to becoming a lonely, miserable recluse. Where had it all gone, his capacity for affection, happiness . . . anticipation? Sure, the young dog brought some comfort, but most days stretched so long and thin that sleep was a mercy.

Over the course of the summer, though, he'd started keeping a list on a legal pad in the kitchen, just small things to bring out for Birdie and Emaleen, like candy bars or mantles for the Coleman lantern or the binoculars. He watched the weather with renewed interest, and when it was good, he sometimes made the quick flight over the mountains for no other reason than to say hello. Each time he came in for the landing along the creek, he watched for the little girl, who usually came running down the trail to greet him.

On his last visit, Emaleen had presented him with a crayon drawing of Spinner, and it was one of the most whimsical, delightful pieces of art he'd ever seen. She'd given the dog green and orange swirling stripes and a humanlike grin. "The likeness is uncanny," he'd told Emaleen. And the two of them proceeded to have a long, interesting discussion about how some dogs were gentle and others were dangerous. The drawing of Spinner now hung by a magnet on Warren's refrigerator.

It wasn't just the child, though. Wendy and Theresa, despite how they'd been raised, showed no interest in the cabin or the tough work it required. Birdie, on the other hand, had taken to it like a fish to water, and it had done her good. There had always been a lean hardness to her face, a defensive wariness in her interactions, but she'd softened. She had the healthy glow of someone who spent her days working outdoors, and she laughed easily and openly around Warren, even asked for advice. She wanted to restock the woodshed before winter—this pleased Warren on several fronts—and she asked if he could teach her how to run a chainsaw. The two of them had talked about which trees to bring down and how the standing dead would be ready to burn sooner than the living trees. Much to his surprise, he saw in Birdie a tenacity of spirit that reminded him of Carol.

As he rummaged through bags and boxes in the attic, still looking for the dolls, Warren had a thought. What if he invited Arthur, Birdie, and Emaleen to the house, just for a short visit? There were the two spare bedrooms and the extra bathroom. The girls would appreciate being able to soak in the big tub, and Arthur might help him align the TV antenna on the roof so they could watch a football game. He'd been wanting to show Birdie the photo album from when he and Carol had built the cabin. And Spinner and Emaleen, they were bound to become fast friends.

The thought of all that laughter and warmth back in the house—Warren felt a wave of emotion.

Don't get carried away, you old fool. It wasn't Carol's voice in his head, though. She would never have been so unkind as to call him a fool.

Next to the table where he'd found the dollhouse was a stack of shoeboxes. The top few were full of eight-track tapes, but farther down was a box with "Wendy" written across the top in Carol's neat cursive and, inside, an assortment of keepsakes: Wendy's baby footprints in ink on card stock, a dried flower corsage from some high school dance, a set of marbles, other odds and ends. Theresa's box held the knit hat she'd worn home as a newborn from the Anchorage maternity ward, a charm bracelet, and several ribbons and medals from spelling bees.

Then he came to a box marked "Arthur." What could Carol have possibly saved from his childhood? He pulled back the cardboard lid, and there it was. The padded blue collar.

I know it's hard to see, love. This time, it was Carol's voice. But that's the truth right there.

No birth certificate or spelling bee ribbons, no prom boutonniere. Just a collar stained with dirt and smelling of wild animal. A bear cub tied to the back porch by a rope, like a dog on a lead.

Don't be angry. It was the only way.

Warren recalled the first time he saw the collar. It was a few weeks after they'd brought the boy home from the North Fork, and Warren had come home early from work to find a grizzly cub wrestling around in the yard at the end of a rope. Carol stepped out the back door, startled. "I didn't hear you pull up."

"What is this?"

"It's the only thing that comforts him," she'd said.

Warren had been dumbfounded. What was Carol talking about, and where had this bear cub come from?

"It's just to keep him safe, Warren. I know it's dreadful, to tie him up like that. But watch. Just see this." And she'd gone to the kitchen and come out with a dog bowl full of leftover moose stew. When she set it in the grass, the cub loped across the lawn toward them.

"It gets easier each time," Carol said. "He doesn't cry so much now when I peel away the hide."

The cub had its front paws on either side of the bowl and was slurping and gobbling noisily, bits of food clinging to the fur of its muzzle.

"Good Lord," Warren said weakly, and a cold surge of nausea passed through him.

"At first, I didn't understand," Carol said. "But now I know how we can help him."

He would admit it to no one, but he blamed Carol. He'd wanted to throw out the bear hide from the beginning. Instead, she had coddled Arthur and given in to his worst leanings. When the boy recoiled from playing with other children, she stopped taking him to birthday parties, and when he struggled in the classroom, she'd switched him to correspondence school at home. Rather than forcing him to adapt, she'd allowed him to live like a wild thing. And what had Warren done? He'd turned his head, looked away. He'd left the burden to Carol.

The nightmares didn't spare him, though. A bear cub suckling noisily at a woman's breast, drops of blood against her creamy skin. Fur growing like mold across the tender cheeks of a child. The boy, crouched in a dark corner, gnawing on something small and whimpering.

Over the years, the nightmares had faded, and Warren didn't think of them much anymore. This summer, though, the worst had returned. He is standing in the forest with a hunting knife in his hand. He has shot a bear and needs to field dress it, but it is getting too dark to see. He strikes a match, holds up the hissing lantern. Sprawled on the ground at his feet isn't a bear carcass. It is his son that he has shot and killed.

Grizzly bears were mysterious animals. Intelligent, Warren had no doubt, and at times, nearly humanlike in their behavior. Young bears would run and slide down snowy mountainsides with as much glee as any child. A sow grizzly appeared to care for her cubs with the same tender exasperation and amusement as a human mother, and when threatened by a bear twice her size, she wouldn't hesitate to put herself between the attacker and her offspring. She was the most formidable animal in all of the Alaska wilderness, a sow defending her cub.

It was tempting, then, to draw a direct line from us to them, to forget the unfathomable void between a man's moral judgment and a bear's wild mind.

"Want to know the quickest way to bring in a big grizzly?" Jim Mahoney had asked years ago. The guide had stopped by the house one morning to have a cup of coffee with Warren and Carol, and sitting at the kitchen table, he'd taken a predator call out of his shirt pocket. When he blew on it, the sound was a grating, high-pitched mewl. "But you better be ready, because the last thing you want to do is make a bad shot," Mahoney said with a chuckle. He didn't need to say more because any Alaskan knew—pursuing a wounded grizzly bear was taking your life into your own hands.

"What is it supposed to be, that sound?" Carol had asked.

"A cub in distress," Mahoney said.

"Oh, that's sad. It thinks you're hurting the cub, and it's trying to rescue it?"

"No, ma'am. I'm sorry to say, but a boar is looking to kill the cub. That's why they come in hard and fast. They're hunting."

Carol had been aghast. It made no sense. Why would an animal kill the helpless infants of its own kind? Mahoney said there was some speculation that male grizzly bears killed cubs in order to make the female, abruptly without offspring, come into estrus and want to breed again, but he was of the opinion that it was simply the powerful hunt instinct of a bear to chase down and eat smaller animals, even cubs.

Down on the Alaskan coast, where there was a bounty of salmon, brown bears had their fill and grew immensely fat. But the North Fork of the Wolverine River was lean country. The rocky, glacial stream didn't support a large salmon run, and no caribou herds calved in the region, so bears ate what they could find—wild grasses and berries, ground squirrels, beaver, moose calves. Occasionally one would manage to bring down a full-grown moose, but it was a slow and harrowing battle.

That same morning, Mahoney had told them about a spring hunt on the North Fork when he and his hunter spotted a large boar grizzly mating with a sow on a south-facing slope. After they'd bred, the two bears lay together, face-to-face in what looked like a lovers' embrace. The hunter had joked that he wasn't sure he could bring himself to shoot an animal capable of such tenderness. But the next morning, the scene had changed. The boar was hunched over something, and the ground was torn up in a wide swath. Through the powerful lens of his spotting scope, Mahoney was able to see blood splattered across the snow, the exposed ribcage and outthrown paws of a dead and half-eaten bear. The boar was ripping away and eating hunks of the flesh.

There was no way to be certain what had happened. Maybe a younger boar had tried to move in and had been killed and cannibalized, but Mahoney hadn't spotted any other grizzlies. It seemed more likely that the dead bear was the sow. In the midst of breeding, something had turned in the boar. His appetites had shifted. She'd become his prey.

Warren could not believe that his son, at his deepest core, was such a creature. The little boy who'd picked bouquets of dandelions for Carol. The child who had walked the fields with Warren, naming the birds as they flew up out of the grass. When Carol was in her final days of hospice care, Arthur had come home from the woods and sat at her bedside. His tears had been just as real as any of theirs. Arthur was capable of profound love, Warren was certain. And just as he had always hoped and predicted, it was love that had granted Arthur the strength to leave his other skin behind.

Chapter 25

Birdie didn't understand what was happening. She'd done everything she could think of to pull Arthur out of whatever illness or depression was consuming him, and for days, she had slept badly and eaten very little. It left her in a weary stupor, and nothing Emaleen and Arthur were saying made sense.

"Arthur, you have to tell my mom about your fur," Emaleen said. "Tell her, okay? And then we can help you, and you won't be sick anymore."

"Yes, it is true," Arthur said, but when he tried to stand up from the bed, he was so weak that his legs trembled and Birdie saw how far this all had gone. His face was gaunt, and his eyes had a glassy, unfocused sheen.

"You'll see, Mommy." Emaleen took Arthur's hand and put it on her own small shoulder, as if she were strong enough to support his weight. And then the three of them were walking out the cabin door, down the steps, and out into the icy rain, and it was like Birdie was in a trance. Arthur shuffled over the rough ground, one arm around Birdie's shoulders, his other hand on Emaleen. Every few steps, he had to pull up the waistband of his blue jeans to keep them from slipping off his hips.

Out among the spruce trees, beyond the woodshed, Arthur and Emaleen started dragging dirt and vegetation away from a mound. "Come on, Mommy. We have to dig it out for him."

The gag-inducing stench, Arthur's ragged breaths, the wet fur slowly being unearthed—the details were so weird and crystal-sharp that Birdie felt high.

"We are not strong enough," Arthur said to Emaleen. "Unroll it where it is."

Birdie could only stare down at the half-buried thing, but Emaleen must have understood because she began to tug at a corner of the pelt, digging her hands deep into the fur until she was able to pull something free and slowly unfold it. It was like an empty pant leg, but made of brown fur and skin, and at the end, there was a padded foot and long claws.

Arthur staggered to his feet and grabbed on to the paw, leaned back and dragged the entire, immense pelt out of the hole. It took all of his weight and strength, and when he let go, he lurched backward.

While Birdie looked on, he and Emaleen stretched out each foot and the head until the hide was spread flat on the ground, chest up to the sky. There was a large, jagged tear down the throat and front of the bear skin, and Emaleen opened it up, like a sleeping bag for someone to crawl into, and then she turned her back to Arthur and put her hands over her eyes.

"You have to help him, Mommy," she said. "Help him get naked and get inside."

"What...I don't..."

"Please. Birdie." It was Arthur, saying her name. He bent over and held his hands up so she could pull the T-shirt off him. There was no need to unbutton his pants, they were so loose, and then Arthur was naked, sitting on top of the hide and pushing his feet into the rip. He eased himself onto one side until he was lying in the mud and wet leaves as he tried to slide into the bear's skin. It was such a pathetic sight that Birdie began to sob.

"Leave me," he said hoarsely.

"I can't."

"Go."

Emaleen was pulling on her hand. "He's okay, Mommy. You'll see. I promise."

* * *

For a long time, Birdie sat in the cabin, staring at nothing. Emaleen asked over and over again for her to make a warm fire and cook dinner. "Not now," Birdie said.

"Why? What are you doing?"

"Thinking."

She couldn't leave Arthur out there all night. But she was afraid—of Arthur's naked and weak body, the rotting bear hide. And it would be dark in the woods now.

"I want to go too," Emaleen said when she saw Birdie getting the flashlight.

"No, stay here. I'm just going to check on him. Latch the door behind me. I'll be right back, okay?"

She wore Syd's hat and her raincoat and the rifle at her shoulder. It was still raining, but the autumn air smelled like snow. As she walked across the damp yard and past the woodshed, she was thinking about Warren, how even if the weather improved, it could be another week or two before he flew out. She could attempt the hike out to get help, but she remembered the flight in with Warren as they followed the river and valleys—it would take days, and some of those canyons might be impassable. And what would she do with Emaleen?

Arthur would be in worse condition since he'd been lying out in the rain and cold. He needed to come inside and get cleaned up and at least drink some hot tea, and she would care for him the best she could until Warren returned. Then she would take Emaleen and they would leave, and they would never come back.

When she got to the place in the woods, though, everything was gone—Arthur, the bear hide. Birdie swept the light across the ground. The vegetation was trampled, and she saw the heap of branches and moss, the empty hole in the ground.

"Arthur?" she called into the trees. "Arthur? Where are you?"

Sitting on the tundra, Birdie found him again through the binoculars. For a while, he had disappeared behind a knoll, but he reemerged now on the other side and ambled slowly across the mountainside, his head low to the ground.

"What's he doing, Mommy? Can you see him?"

"He's eating berries, I think."

He. Not *it.* Because Birdie knew. It wasn't just the scar across the bear's muzzle or the damaged ear, or even the place in the forest where Arthur and the bear hide should have been. Perhaps she'd always known. She might not have understood the gruesome particulars, but her subconscious had caught here and there—the calf bones under the bed, the days he disappeared into the woods without a pack or tent, the smell of his skin and the taste of his mouth.

Solstice night, talking to Syd, he had known too. Barefoot wanderer. Four-legged man. Golden friend. Honey-eater. A dark thing. *Carol, she saw it from the start.* The fur like a cloak, and beneath it, the muscles and bones, the hands and feet of a man. *Nobody can tell us who to love.* Syd thumping his fist against his chest.

When she'd gone back last night to look for Arthur, she had been afraid, and when she returned to the cabin, as she lay awake all night, the fear intensified. This morning, she found vague impressions of what might have been bear tracks on the forest floor, but she couldn't be sure. She'd searched through the trees and brush around the cabin, and she'd called his name again and again. That's when she decided that she and Emaleen needed to climb to higher ground where she could glass with the binoculars.

Throughout the cold morning, they'd sat on the hillside behind the cabin, looking up and down the valley, studying all the mountain slopes. Birdie began to doubt herself—Arthur could be down in the trees, out of sight, or he could have returned to the cabin, and they would have no way to know.

Emaleen had spotted him first. "What's that?" she'd said, pointing to a brown form on a nearby slope.

Birdie had looked through the binoculars. "It's him," she'd whispered, and she wasn't afraid anymore.

All she wanted now was to get closer. She led Emaleen through the dwarf birch and low willow shrubs. A gust of wind occasionally rose from the valley floor, so Birdie was climbing higher, above the knoll, where the air current wouldn't carry their scent to him.

"I'm tired, tired, tired, tired," Emaleen said, her words in rhythm with her steps. "Why can't we go home?"

Birdie held a finger up to shush her. As they gained elevation, she expected the bear to come into view a long distance away, but she ducked and pulled Emaleen to the ground with her.

"What?" Emaleen asked. "What's the matter?"

In exaggerated, silent syllables, Birdie mouthed, *He's right there.* She gestured for Emaleen to quietly follow as they crept down the hill and to the edge of the knoll.

The bear was about two hundred yards below them, stripping berries and leaves off bushes with his mouth. Sometimes he would hold a branch to the ground with one huge paw as he plucked the berries carefully with tongue and teeth. He was emaciated. His legs looked proportionally too long, his hide was draped loosely over his frame, and the outlines of his ribs and his spine were visible. He brought his head up and sniffed at the wind, but he didn't seem to have any idea that they were there watching him, and he lowered his head back down to the tundra, moving slowly as he ate.

Birdie sat and watched him through the binoculars. She was faintly aware of Emaleen putting her head on her lap, of the wind swirling across the mountainside and the sun glowing like a haloed orb through the overcast gray. Parky squirrels darted in and out of the rocks, a hawk flew low over the tundra as it hunted, Birdie shifted to ease some ache in her back or hips, and as her arms tired, she wedged her elbows against her sides to keep the binoculars stable. But all of that was peripheral. In her center, there was only the bear. She could see him clearly with the naked eye, but the binoculars closed the distance, brought her right up next to him, as if she could reach out and stroke the blond-tipped fur across his back, put her lips to his muzzle. She could live here, suspended in this moment.

The bear abruptly lifted his head and disappeared in a dark blur. Birdie lowered the binoculars and saw the bear charging toward them across the tundra. She jumped to her feet with her rifle in her hands, and he stopped almost directly below them. He wasn't looking up in her direction. His head was down, and he was digging into the earth with his front paws. Birdie could hear his claws raking through the bushes and dirt and over-turning rocks as he dug faster and faster. He stopped and was still, as if listening intently, and then he lunged forward to slam his front paws again and again into the ground.

"What's he doing?" Emaleen whispered. Birdie shook her head, *No talk-ing*, then pointed two fingers from her own eyes down to the bear, *Watch*.

The bear thumped the ground several more times with his front paws, stood motionless for a few seconds, and started digging again, feverishly, dirt flying up from his paws. He shoved his muzzle into the hole and, when he withdrew his head and sat back on his haunches, a small, furry animal writhed in his mouth. The parky squirrel squeaked as the bear chomped and bit down, and then he swallowed the entire thing.

Birdie watched without reaction. The bear was on the move again, sniff-ing at the ground and occasionally lapping up a mouthful of berries. There was a kind of swagger to his walk as his huge front shoulders rolled under his fur. He went around the side of the knoll and out of sight. Birdie crept quietly closer, and there he was, his head to the ground as he ate berries and leaves, and he was steadily coming in her direction. Thirty yards, twenty yards.

"Arthur," she said.

At the sound of her voice, the bear brought his head up. He was looking at her now. He opened his mouth slightly and his nostrils flared, and Birdie could hear him sniff the air deeply.

"Arthur, it's me. It's Birdie."

Something registered—the human scent, the human voice—and he wheeled around. His first strides were back the way he'd come, as if he would continue down the knoll and toward the creek, but then he veered uphill.

"Come on!" Birdie grabbed Emaleen's hand to pull her along.

The bear wasn't sprinting, just loping steadily away, at times looking back at Birdie, but he was covering distance at an incredible speed. She would never keep up if she had Emaleen with her. She dropped her daugh-ter's hand. "Stay here."

"I can go fast, I promise," Emaleen said, but Birdie was already running

up the mountainside and away from Emaleen. She could hear her cries—
"Mommy! Don't leave me all alone! Mommy!"

"Just wait there," she shouted without looking back.

The bear had left the mossy tundra and was up among the rocks. Birdie paused long enough to find him through the binoculars—he was climbing up a nearly vertical slide and loose shale crumbled away from his paws with each step.

For a while, Birdie tried to run uphill after him, but as the terrain grew steeper and rockier, she was quickly winded. She slowed to a walk and kept her eyes down to watch her footing. The next time she looked, he was gone. She scanned the mountainside through the binoculars and finally saw him at the very top of the mountain ridge, his silhouette against the gray skyline.

"Arthur!" she shouted, though she knew it was too far. "I love you. Do you hear me? You can come home now!"

The bear might have hesitated, and he might have looked back at her, Birdie couldn't be sure. And then he vanished over the top of the ridge.

She would go after him. She would follow him over the tundra, up and down the mountain valleys, across rivers and streams. She would leave everything behind to be with him.

She turned to face down into the valley. The knoll was far, far below—she'd hiked much farther up the mountain than she'd realized, and she couldn't see Emaleen. Maybe she was taking a nap on the tundra, or there was a dip in the terrain that obscured Birdie's view. Birdie looked to the vacant skyline, and then she began her descent.

"Emaleen!" she called again and again as she made her way down. It wasn't until she stood at the edge of the knoll that she saw Emaleen farther down the hillside, walking away.

"Where are you going? Wait!" Birdie quickened her pace, scrambling down the hill and jogging along a game trail until she caught up with Emaleen and grabbed her arm. "Didn't you hear me? I told you to wait."

Emaleen jerked from Birdie's grasp and marched away. "You left me, Mommy," she said. "You left me."

Emaleen began running down the mountainside at a surprisingly quick

pace. She tripped and fell, but she got up and kept on, seemingly determined not to look at or speak to Birdie.

"We need to go more that way," Birdie said, pointing toward the North
Fork. Finally, Emaleen allowed her to lead the way.

"Do you want a drink of water?" Birdie offered her the canteen, but Emaleen shook her head. "Don't be silly. Just because you're mad at me, that's
no reason." Emaleen took the canteen and drank for a long time. When
she handed it back, she didn't make eye contact with Birdie or say thank
you, but faced straight ahead with a steely expression. It was the most
grown-up her little girl had ever seemed.

Once they'd made it down into the forest, they stopped to sit on a log.
Emaleen was obviously cold and worn-out—she was shivering and her
chin trembled—but when Birdie tried to put her arms around her, she
pulled away. Birdie took off her coat and bundled up Emaleen inside of it;
her daughter's body relaxed and slumped into her side. Emaleen was crying quietly, but it would pass.

Birdie could only think about Arthur. At last, she had seen his true self.
He'd tried to hide it, had starved himself, all to protect Birdie and Emaleen.

She wondered where he was now. With ease, he had crossed over an
entire mountain and into a different valley. He could be miles away by
now. What were Syd's words, about love and fear and bravery? No one can
tell us where to find happiness.

Hours later, the evening sky darkening, they finally reached the cabin.

"Leave the door open," she told Emaleen.

"But Mommy . . ."

"I said leave it."

She wouldn't start a fire or latch the door, and she wouldn't sleep with
the rifle in her bed. She wanted Arthur to come home. He loved her. And
he loved Emaleen. He would never hurt them.

Chapter 26

Inside and outside were the same now. The cabin floor was all dirty with leaves and grass and twigs and mud that got tracked in on their feet, and in the morning there was sparkly frost on everything, even the blankets. Emaleen didn't brush her teeth or wash her face or change her clothes. It was cold, almost like winter time, but her mom didn't start a fire in the woodstove. When Emaleen asked how come, her mom said Arthur didn't like the smoke and flames, and she said they had to leave the door open all the time so he could come home whenever he was ready. It was too cold for mosquitoes and flies, but the black beetles and daddy longlegs went in and out, in and out.

Even when she was inside, coloring at the table, Emaleen wore lots of clothes—two pairs of socks and her water boots with the rainbows, her warmest pants and sweatshirt and purple coat, and sometimes she put socks on her hands because she didn't have any mittens, but she was still shivery.

All the time, her mom watched for the bear with the binoculars. Once, she said she saw him far away on a hill. Emaleen wanted to see, too, but her mom said it was too late. He was gone just that fast.

Emaleen wondered if maybe the bear was going away for the winter. She knew that bears dug holes in the mountains and climbed in and slept under the snow, and it was almost winter. It was snowy on the mountains. Down by the river all the leaves on the trees had turned yellowy orange, and when they went to the creek to get water, there was ice along the edges.

When they got back with the water buckets, though, the bear was inside the cabin. Through the open door, Emaleen saw the big mess he'd made. The pots and pans and plates and blankets were all over the place, and the shelves were knocked down. Lots of jars were broken, and the flour and honey and rice were spilled all over. The bear was licking it up. He was giant, lots and lots and lots bigger than he was up on the mountain, so there was no more room for anything else in the cabin except him.

"Arthur." Her mom said it quiet and nice, but the bear turned around so fast that he flipped over the table. Emaleen hid behind the doorframe, but her mom didn't move. The bear's head was going side to side, side to side, and he was breathing loud.

"You're home," her mom said to the bear.

The bear put his head down low and he huffed, like the big bad wolf. Slimy drool hung off his black lips and bits of rice were stuck to his black nose, and Emaleen could see his sharp white teeth inside of his mouth.

Her mom walked through the doorway, closer to the bear.

"Mommy, don't." Emaleen meant to say it loud, but it came out soft because she didn't have any air inside of her. Her mom took another step and another until she was all the way inside the cabin. That's when the bear pulled back and lifted up his front paws, like he was going to stand, and for a second, Emaleen thought—he's too tall, he'll hit his head on the ceiling. But he didn't stand. Instead, he lunged forward and hit her mom with his great big paw. He hit her so hard that it knocked her to the floor. Emaleen couldn't yell or move or do anything because the bear was charging through the doorway and off the porch, and it happened so fast that Emaleen didn't really see it, only felt the wind and fur going past her.

When her mom got up from the floor, there was blood on the side of her face. But her mom didn't cry. She never cried. She took down the box with Band-Aids and bandages, and she asked Emaleen to get a washcloth wet in the water bucket and bring it to her.

Emaleen didn't want to look, but she saw it—a piece of her mom's cheek was peeling off her face, and Emaleen could see the meat underneath it.

"It's all right. I'll be fine." Her mom sounded like she had marbles in her mouth when she talked. "He didn't mean it. His claws just caught me."

She put a big bandage on the side of her face, and Emaleen handed her pieces of doctor's tape. There was another cut somewhere on her mom's head underneath her hair, and it kept bleeding and bleeding. Her mom said your head bleeds lots, but it doesn't mean anything. She held the wash-cloth on it for a long time, and then a bandage. The tape wouldn't work on hair, though, so she put on Uncle Syd's hat to keep the bandage from fall-ing off.

Her mom rinsed the washcloth in a bowl of water, and ribbons of her blood swirled around and around until the water turned all pink and the only sound was the pink water dripping into the bowl when her mom squeezed the washcloth. The cabin had gone very quiet and calm. Emaleen wanted to be quiet and calm, too, but her whole body trembled. She wanted her mom to hug her tight so the shaking would stop, but her mom was getting her rifle down from its hook, and she was putting bullets into it.

"What's happening?" Emaleen asked.

"He'll be himself again," her mom said. "Once he gets enough to eat." She said he was too skinny to be ready for winter, but he was eating berries and parky squirrels, and pretty soon a few silver salmon would make it this far into the mountains, and then everything would be good again.

Most of the yummy food in the cabin—the bread and honey and pea-nut butter and crackers—was all gone. There was still food in cans, though, because the bear couldn't open them. Emaleen helped her mom pick up the cans. The bear had poked holes all over them with his big teeth. Her mom opened a bit-up can of creamed corn and a can of Spam and put it on two plates. Emaleen didn't want it, but she ate the cold goop because oth-erwise she'd be in trouble.

When it was time to go to sleep, Emaleen went to close the door, but her mom said, "Don't be scared. Leave the door open. This is his home."

It didn't seem right. Now that they were inside and the bear was outside, why didn't they shut the door fast and lock it up?

* * *

That night, Emaleen had a dream. At least she thought it was a dream, but it was very real. Like the night she dreamed about the woman crying and the trees whispering. But in this dream, the light from the big moon came into the cabin. Her mom was walking out onto the porch, and she was all the way naked and she wasn't even wearing any shoes. Past her, outside the cabin, was the big shadow of the bear.

In the dream, her mom looked back to Emaleen and said, "It's okay." The bandage on her face was gleaming white. "Go back to sleep."

Emaleen didn't want to eat the Dolly Varden. You were supposed to cook fish and put salt and pepper on it, but her mom said it was good to eat just like that, the pieces of orangey-whitish meat all cold and wet and slippery in her mom's fingers. Right there, on the other side of the creek, the bear was fishing, too, but he was catching the rotten old salmon. Emaleen didn't know why her mom called them silver salmon, because they were dark, dark red and blackish green. The bear chased them through the water and when he caught them, he ripped out their guts with his teeth and bit their heads, and sometimes he splashed across the water toward Emaleen and her mom, and Emaleen's heart wanted to jump out of her mouth.

We have to mind our p's and q's. Emaleen understood what that meant now. It meant you had to move very slowly and very quietly, and you couldn't screech or squeal because then the bear's eyes would go to you fast. And no matter what, you couldn't run. Up on the mountain, she'd seen how he could chase a parky squirrel and grab it with his teeth and eat it up. Just like that. Because that's all the bear wanted to do, is eat and eat and eat, like he wanted to gobble up everything in the whole world. It was good that Thimblina was invisible because if she wasn't, the bear would snap her right out of the air.

"Keep still," her mom whispered. "You can't ever run from him, do you hear me?"

Emaleen told her legs to stop shaking and she told Thimblina, *It's okay. You're safe in my pocket. Just be very, very, very quiet.*

Her mom caught another fish with her fishing pole and pulled it up on the bank. She said this one was called a grayling, and it was so pretty and shiny that Emaleen wanted to watch it swim away. But her mom stabbed it with her knife to kill it, and then she slid the knife along the side of the fish to cut off the skin and the meat. "Here," she said, and her fingers were covered with fish blood and shimmery scales. Her mom would be angry if she didn't eat it, so Emaleen took the smallest piece of fish from her mom's hand and slurped it down without chewing it or tasting it, but she still gagged a little bit.

The sun was falling behind the mountains and the woods along the creek were cold and shadowy. More than anything, Emaleen wanted to be back in the cabin. She wanted to be warm by the woodstove and drink hot cocoa and not be scared of the bear, but her mom said there wasn't any reason to leave the creek. When Emaleen said she was hungry for something else besides raw fish, her mom told her to pick cranberries off the tall bushes where the leaves were turning purple. But the berries tasted like sour and stinky socks and each one had a big seed inside of it that she spit out, and still her tummy was rumbly.

It was getting colder and darker. Her mom and the bear kept fishing. Emaleen curled up on a grassy part of the bank. She didn't think this was a good place for a little girl to sleep, and her hands and feet were cold, but when she asked her mom if they could go home, she said. "I already said no. This is where the fish are."

A while later, Emaleen woke to the sound of splashing. It was night, but she wasn't cold anymore. Her mom was cuddled up against her, and she had put her big coat over both of them. Emaleen could hear her mom breathing deep and slow, the way she did when she was sleeping.

The bear, though, was still fishing. He was on this side of the creek now, very, very close to Emaleen and her mom. When he walked, Emaleen could hear the boulders in the creek rolling and grinding under his paws, and when he ran after a fish, there was the sound of the fish swishing its tail fast, trying to get away, and the big *sploosh, sploosh,* as the bear chased after it, and then crunching and slurping as he ate it up.

Emaleen stayed very still and very quiet, but her eyes were wide open. In the night sky, she saw four stars like a square. Her mom said it was called the Big Dipper because it was the shape of a cup for scooping up water. Emaleen picked out the brightest star and kept her eyes on it without blinking for so long that the night air made a few tears dribble down the sides of her face. But she didn't blink or wipe them away until she was done, because this was a very important wish.

She wished for Mr. Warren or Aunt Della or Uncle Syd to come and help them. Her mom knew how to do lots of things. She knew how to find blueberries and catch fish and shoot a gun, but Emaleen was worried that she didn't know how to keep them safe.

Chapter 27

Birdie loved him for his hunger. The single-minded force of it. He gorged himself, licked the mountainsides, plunged his head into the roaring water and swallowed life in great mouthfuls.

For as long as she could remember, Birdie had craved something without being able to name it. There had been brief moments, at the crest of a high, just before the fall, when she'd nearly tasted it, but all along, her desperation had only taken her further and further away.

Because what she craved was life itself. The grayling that swam in the clear waters, the wild berries and mushrooms and roots—when you brought them to your mouth fully alive and bit into their flesh, with every mouthful you swallowed, it was like concentrated light flooding your veins.

Along the creek, Birdie found his prints, sharp-edged in the wet sand. She took off her boots and socks and stepped into the tracks, felt the cold curve of his paws beneath the arches of her feet. *I am exactly where I want to be.* When had she ever been this sure?

It was dangerous, she knew, the way he watched Emaleen. But there had been danger in the old life as well—invisible, insidious, a slow and steady erosion. Comfort was an illusion, and the more you had of it, the less you became; you could eat and eat and drink and drink, and all the while, the self was diminishing.

It was easy to let her thoughts drag her back to the shame of the past and fear of tomorrow, to other people's expectations and the ticking of a clock, but she caught herself. She wouldn't live that way ever again. Time was nothing to hold on to.

There was only this mouthful and the next, the earth slowly turning beneath her feet.

Chapter 28

It was a happy day. Emaleen and her mom were at the cabin, and the bear wasn't. He was fishing at the creek. Her mom said there weren't very many salmon and they were hard to catch, but he would probably stay there all day and all night. Emaleen was glad. She missed Arthur, but she wished the bear would stay gone forever.

Her mom was cheerful and even lit a fire in the woodstove when Emaleen asked please over and over again. The hot cocoa powder and marshmallows and pancake mix had been eaten up by the bear. But her mom found a can of condensed milk, and she cooked the sweet milk with water and blueberries from the mountain, and it was delicious and warmed up Emaleen's belly.

Emaleen didn't really like being inside the cabin anymore because it was so dirty and gloomy. Outside, it was cold, but the sun was shining. Her mom was lying on the porch with Uncle Syd's hat down over her eyes.

"Can I run around?"

"Just here, close by."

"Can I go fast and be loud?"

"I suppose. But don't go too far. You hear me?"

Emaleen had an idea. She was going to take her pony for a ride. She didn't have a name for it yet, because she'd only just thought of having a pony.

"Giddyup!" Emaleen shouted as she trotted across the meadow, past the woodshed and past the cabin, around and around. Thimblina darted here and there above Emaleen's head, and the pony tossed her mane. The pony was the most beautiful purple, and her mane and tail were pink like cotton candy.

Emaleen clicked her tongue against the roof of her mouth and shook pretend reins until they were galloping. They ran around the meadow again and again. She got so tired and sweaty that she stopped at the cabin to get a drink of water from the bucket, and she left her coat and sweatshirt on the bed and wore just her T-shirt. It wasn't summer anymore, and when she went back outside, her arms were cold. That made her happy too, the warm sunshine on her hair and the cold air blowing across her skin. She was getting ready to jump off the porch and onto her pony, just like a cowboy, when she heard a sound.

"Mommy! Do you hear that? It's Mr. Warren. I can hear his plane."

Her mom sat up on the porch, frowning and quiet for a long time, but then she said, "I don't think so. Sounds like a big jet way up high. Come here and take a nap with me."

"No thank you." Emaleen hopped off the porch. "This is way more funner!"

Cowboys could whistle for their horses, but Emaleen had tried and tried ever since she was four years old and she couldn't learn how to do it. Instead, she rounded her lips and called, "Whoo, whoo, whoo" in a very high pitch that almost sounded like a whistle. When her pony didn't come, Emaleen walked into the meadow and pretend whistled. She picked handfuls of yellow grass and red foxtails. Grandma Jo said horses shouldn't eat foxtails because it makes them sick, but her pony was magic, so it was okay. She also picked some tall brown flowers that were sort of pretty and had a strong smell. Arthur had taught her the name, but she couldn't remember it now. When he took off his bear skin, she would ask him.

Finally, behind the woodshed, she found her make-believe pony. Emaleen clicked her tongue and pretend whistled and held out the bouquet of dried flowers and grass. "It's okay, girl. Come on, girl." And when she got close enough, she quick lassoed the pony with an invisible rope and jumped on her back.

"Giddyup!" she shouted again.

They were going even faster this time, so fast that the breeze lifted Emaleen's hair from her face and stirred the pony's silky pink mane. Emaleen leapt into the air to touch Thimblina's wings, but she was flying all the way up by the sky because she was so happy too.

"Lou, Lou, skip to my Lou." Emaleen sang in rhythm to the pony's hoofbeats. Lou-Lou—that would be her pony's name. "Lou-Lou, skip to my Lou! Flies in the buttermilk, shoo fly shoo!"

"Emaleen!"

"Skip to the Lou my darlin'."

"Emaleen!"

Her mom was probably saying she had to go inside, or that it was time to walk back to the creek to catch more fish. But Lou-Lou wasn't listening, just going faster and faster. *Bu-dump, bu-dump, bu-dump,* down the trail from the outhouse, faster and faster.

"Skip, skip, skip to my Lou!" She was nearly to the birch tree where Arthur liked to take naps.

"Emaleen! Stop! Now! He's right there."

Emaleen looked up. Her mom was standing on the cabin porch with something in her hands.

And then, before Emaleen could understand what was happening, she was face-to-face with the bear. There was the floppy ear that hung off one side of his head, and there was the big, ugly scar on his muzzle. Far away, she could hear her mom yelling, but she couldn't make out the words anymore. Everything had gone blurry and hushed. Everything except Emaleen and the bear.

She didn't mean to run. You weren't supposed to run. But it was like her legs had come to life and were making their own decisions, and they were running, running, as fast as they could go. And she was supposed to be quiet, but her mouth had a life of its own too, and it was shouting, "Mommy! Mommy!" Out of the side of her eyes, Emaleen saw the bear lower his head and lunge at her, just the way he chased the salmon in the stream.

A deafening bang startled Emaleen, and she tripped and fell onto her hands and knees. The bear was huffing and roaring, and whipping around in a circle, and it looked like he was trying to bite himself in the side. And then he was running away, into the forest.

"Are you all right?" Her mom was out of breath, her eyes were wide and she had a gun in her hands. She crouched beside Emaleen. "You're okay, you're okay," she said as she squeezed Emaleen's arms and legs and ran her hands down her head and back. "You're fine. I have to go. I think I hit him. I have to see if . . . Stay right here. Do you hear me?"

That was when Emaleen understood. Her mom had shot him with the gun. She had shot Arthur.

"Mommy. Mommy, I'm sorry. I'm sorry I'm sorry I'm sorry." She was trying to catch up, but her mom was running to the woods, the same direction that he'd gone. "Just stay there," her mom said again without looking back.

Maybe Arthur was only a little hurt. Her mom knew how to clean up cuts and put on bandages. She would make him better. But when Emaleen got to the other side of the meadow, her mom and the bear were gone. She made herself wait there at the edge of the trees even though she was scared and her arms were goosebumpy and cold. She listened to her heartbeats, and she counted to ten and twenty and thirty and fifty, and then she started over again.

Her mom would come back. Any minute now. All those times, she always came back. Forty-five, forty-six, forty-seven . . .

A strange sound came from the forest. It was a roar and a growl, but also a whistle or a song or a scream, and it sounded kind of far away, but not that far. It wasn't like anything she'd ever heard before, and then, quick, it stopped. Everything got quiet. She listened and listened so hard that her ears were full, like the quiet was pooling inside of them, and sometimes she thought she could hear the creek far away, and then there was a bird close by, *chicka-dee-dee-dee,* and then a squirrel, *chirk chirk chirk.* If Emaleen let herself, she could imagine the growly screaming cry. She wanted to hear it again, but she also wished she'd never heard it at all.

* * *

Emaleen didn't know what time it was, but the sun was going away. Pretty soon it would be dark. She went inside and put on warmer socks and her sweatshirt and coat. She used a spoon to eat the last bit of sweet milk and blueberries from the pot on the stove, even though it wasn't warm and yummy anymore. The fire had gone out.

Her mom would come home before night time. She had to. Emaleen wasn't allowed to close the door to the cabin, and she didn't know how to start a fire by herself. She didn't know how to use the can opener, and there was nothing else to eat. Her worry got bigger and bigger, until it was like a helium balloon inside of her and she was floating away.

"Mommy!" she yelled from the cabin door. She called for her mom again and again. It was getting darkish so that she couldn't see if her mom was coming out of the trees. Inside the cabin, it was even darker. She found her mom's flashlight and turned it on, but somehow it was scarier because she could only see where the flashlight was pointed.

Come on, she said to Thimblina. No way did she want to be in the cabin anymore, with the corners all black and the door wide open.

Outside, she could see a little bit. She turned off the flashlight because you could use up all the batteries if you weren't careful. She wanted to go to the edge of the forest and call for her mom one more time, but the thought of standing out there alone made her worry even more.

The ladder was leaned up against the front of the cache. She had to be careful not to fall—she didn't have her mom behind her to catch her—but she knew she had to be brave. She climbed up each rung and when she got to the top, she unlatched the door and ducked as she swung it open over the top of her head. When she climbed inside, she turned on the flashlight and shined it all around. She crawled around, opening boxes and bags. In one bag, she found a brown sleeping bag, so that was good to keep her warm. She also saw some boxes of salt and pepper, and some snowshoes and a chainsaw, but there wasn't any food.

She pulled the sleeping bag next to the door of the cache and sat cross-legged on top of it so she could look out. It was all the way night time now and the air was getting colder and colder. There wasn't any moon, but some stars were coming out. Why wasn't her mom home yet?

It was so quiet, not even the chickadees or squirrels were singing their songs.

She thought about closing the door to the cache, but when her mom came home, she wouldn't know where to find her. It'd be safer, though, if the ladder was gone. That way no animals could climb up in the night.

Emaleen looked off the edge. There wasn't enough light to see the ground anymore, but she knew it was a long ways down. Her mom could put the ladder back for her. Emaleen put her feet on the top rung and pushed hard. The ladder thumped right back against the cache. She kicked even harder, and this time the ladder didn't come back. She heard it crash into the bushes below.

Deep down in the warm sleeping bag, Emaleen slept for a while, but she woke up with a tummy ache. Maybe it was because she didn't have any dinner, or lunch before that. But when she thought about food, even french fries and milkshakes, her stomach turned and turned until it was like a mushy pretzel. It was the same feeling as when she'd broken her mom's golden bracelet and hidden it away, like she'd done something bad and it was making her sick.

She wasn't supposed to run from him. Ever, ever. Her mom had yelled, "Stop!" and she hadn't listened. She'd run and run. It was all her fault.

I didn't mean it, I didn't mean it, she told Thimblina over and over again. *I didn't mean it.*

She cried for a long time, so long that it made her tired. She was crying and almost falling asleep when a giant shadow soared by in a black whoosh. It was a lot bigger than a chickadee or a magpie. The cache was way up from the ground. Only birds and witches could fly this high in the air, and Emaleen was pretty sure birds didn't fly around at night. She thought about the witch's long, scratchy hair catching on the branches, and she listened for the screeches and laughter. She turned on the flashlight and, careful not to fall out, pulled the door of the cache closed. It wasn't like the cabin—there was no way to latch the door from the inside— but at least the witch couldn't fly right in.

* * *

Tap, tap, tap. Tap. Tap, tap, tap.

Something was knocking. It was morning time, sunlight was coming from somewhere, and for a second, Emaleen was confused about why her bed looked so different. But then she remembered. She was in the cache and the light was coming from the door that wasn't closed all the way. *Tap, tap-tap-tap.*

"Mommy!"

Tap. Tap.

"Mommy! Is that you?"

When Emaleen pushed the door open, a bird flew away from the side of the cache. The ladder was still on the ground, and the tapping had stopped.

"Mommy!" she shouted.

Her mom had probably come home in the night and was asleep in the cabin. She just didn't know where to find Emaleen.

It had been a bad idea to make the ladder fall, because now the only way to get down was to jump, and it was a long ways. It would hurt to fall on the ladder, so she crouched and jumped to the side. She landed straight down on her feet so hard that a jolt of pain sprung up through her ankles and her knees buckled, but she hopped right up again and ran to the cabin. Maybe Arthur was home too, the way he used to be, and they were cuddled in bed together. Her mom would wake up and say, *Let's make pancakes,* and Emaleen would climb up on the bed and hug Arthur and she wouldn't have to say she was sorry because he wasn't hurt at all.

But when she got there, the cabin was empty. No one was sleeping in the bed, the woodstove was cold, and everything was still a big mess. Emaleen went out on the porch and looked across the meadow toward the forest.

All night, her mom hadn't come home.

Emaleen kept looking back to be sure she could still see the cabin through the trees. She remembered what had happened before, at the lodge, when she'd gone looking for her mom and had lost her way.

No matter what, her mom would be angry. She had told Emaleen to stay. But she'd waited a long time, for a whole day and a whole night. Maybe her mom was taking care of Arthur and Emaleen could help, or maybe she'd gotten lost and Emaleen could find her and show her the way home.

You were supposed to sing and clap when you walked through the woods, so the bears would run away, but without her mom, Emaleen wasn't brave enough. She was more like a little rabbit or a vole, quiet, quiet, hide and scurry. But as long as she could still see the cabin, she would go a little farther and a little farther. "Mommy," she whispered into the trees. "Mommy, where are you?"

The devil's clubs with their big leaves and long spines got taller and taller until they were over the top of her head and it was like walking through a scary tunnel. When she looked back, she couldn't see the cabin anymore. She couldn't see anything but the giant leaves with thorns all over. But the wild animals had made a trail and maybe if she followed it, she would be able to find her way home again. Every few steps she stopped and listened and whispered for her mom.

After a while, the trail led up a hill with more devil's clubs and dark-green bushes, and when Emaleen climbed partway up, she could see the cabin again. It was far away, but she wasn't lost.

At the top of the hill, a tree had fallen across the trail. All around were prickly bushes. She didn't want to leave the trail, but the log wasn't all the way on the ground, and it was too high for her to climb over. She got on her hands and knees and crawled under it.

When she stood up, she saw her. Her mom. She was at the bottom of the hill. She was lying on her belly in the middle of devil's clubs and grass. Emaleen couldn't see her head, but those were her boots with the red laces and that was her blue plaid shirt, but it was ripped up and muddy. Her mom's arms and legs didn't look right, like they were bent in ways that they shouldn't be.

"Mommy?" she said quietly. She began walking slowly down the hill and her mom's head came into view. Her dark hair looked wet and messy. "Mommy!" she said again. It felt wrong, the way she was lying so still and not answering or making any sounds. Emaleen took another step, and her left boot slipped. She looked at the ground and saw that she was standing in a bear track. It was smeared in the mud and leaves, but those were the giant pads and those were the sharp slices of the claws.

When she brought her eyes up, she saw something deep, deep in the alder bushes beyond her mom. A big shadow. A dark thing. Emaleen held her breath and squinted, trying to make out its shape. Maybe it was a tree stump, or a giant boulder. But then she began to see a head and ears and fur and two shiny eyes staring back at her.

In the center of her chest, a ball of heat swirled and swelled. No matter what, she had to stay quiet. She had to keep that boiling ball of tears and shouts and fists wrapped up tight inside of her.

Emaleen stepped backward, one, two, three, back up the hill until she reached the log. The dried grass and branches crunched and snapped when she got on her hands and knees. She crawled under the log, and she was nearly out from under it when her coat snagged. She was stuck. She pushed harder, and the nylon ripped loudly. Emaleen froze. She imagined the bear's eyes going up the hill toward her. She stayed very still for a long time, waiting, but everything was quiet. She scooted out from under the log and stood up. Quiet, quiet, holding her breath to be so quiet. One step and another, and then she ran, down the game trail, toward the cabin. *I have to help my mom. I have to help her.* Her eyes were blurry with tears so she could hardly see where she was going, and she chanted the words silently to herself. *I have to help my mom.*

Inside the cabin, she looked all around. There was a gun up on a hook. But it was much too big for her to shoot, and she didn't know how to put the bullets into it. There was the splitting maul, out by the woodshed, but she wasn't strong enough to lift it up. There were kitchen knives on the shelves, but she was too scared. A little girl all by herself can't fight a bear.

This one time, Arthur had told her that all the creeks in the world flow into all the rivers of the world, and those flow into all the oceans of the world. You can follow water backward, to get to the mountaintops, or you can follow water downhill, to get to the ocean. She didn't need to go all the way to the ocean. She thought of that day when they played in the snow and they looked out and saw the lodge on the far side of the big river. She didn't know how she would get across the river once she got there, but she was going to follow the water until she got to Aunt Della and Mr. Warren.

It could take a long time. She might have to sleep under a tree. She wouldn't have any marshmallows, or any food at all, but she got her mom's canteen and filled it from the bucket. She got her mom's backpack from under the bed and inside she put the canteen, the flashlight, and a blanket. The backpack was way too big for Emaleen, but she put it on anyways.

When she left the cabin, she didn't shut the door. She looked across the meadow toward the woods where she'd seen her mom and the bear, but no one was coming. She turned away from the cabin, away from the meadow and the cache and the woodshed, and she followed the trail toward the creek.

I have to help my mom. I have to help my mom.

Chapter 29

Standing on the front porch in his leather slippers and old bathrobe, Warren drank his first cup of coffee, his breath rising with the steam from the mug, the redpolls and nuthatches darting about the bird feeder. The dog rolled happily in the grass. After weeks of rain and clouds, the weather had finally turned. The morning sun streamed across the Wolverine Valley, and the mountains were crowned with fresh snow. Below the snow line, the alpine tundra had turned a deep burgundy, and in the foothills, the cottonwoods and birches were beginning to shed their autumn leaves.

The dollhouse was ready. He'd repainted most of it, and Della had given him a few squares of carpet that he'd cut to size and traded out for the old. After finally locating the original dolls in a box in the attic, he'd decided they were too worn to give to Emaleen. The details of their eyes and mouths had faded so that their faces looked ghastly, and the clothes were stained and ratty. The day before yesterday, though, Anne at the five-and-dime in town had called to say she'd found a replacement set.

Arthur and the girls would be getting low on provisions. After a shower and breakfast, he loaded the airplane with groceries he'd picked up in town—several loaves of bread, two dozen eggs, a variety of canned goods, a nice ham, and a few other treats. Moose season had opened more than a week ago, so he also threw in his hunting pack and rifle. He put the dollhouse on the back seat.

By midday, he was through the mountain pass, and he flew low along the North Fork to keep watch out the side windows. This time of year, the moose would be gathering for the rut, the bulls competing with each other to mate with cows. It was illegal to hunt the same day you'd flown an area, but if he spotted a bull, he'd spend the night at the cabin so that he and Arthur could go after it in the morning.

In a wide section of the river valley, a dark shape stood out against the light gray sand. It was too small to be a moose, but he was fairly certain he'd seen it move. He circled back around, descended, and tipped the wings to the side for a better look. It was only a large porcupine, shuffling across an open stretch of sand and gravel. Warren pulled back on the control stick to gain elevation, then banked the plane in a slow loop and continued his path along the North Fork.

He expected to find the little girl waiting for him, the way she so often did. He smiled to himself as he thought about taking the dollhouse from the back seat and presenting it to her. Even after he'd landed, though, no one appeared. He carried a box of groceries up the trail, and as he neared the cabin, he called out a hello.

The windows had been boarded up since he was last here. It was probably getting cold enough at night to necessitate it. He thought it odd, though, that the door was standing open, yet no one seemed to be about. The neat stack of firewood on the porch was gone, and as he climbed the stairs, through the doorway, he saw a water bucket lying on its side beside the bed.

"Hello, Birdie?"

Warren's unease deepened as he entered the cabin. The floor was littered with dried mud and twigs and leaves, and then he saw the broken jars and ripped-up food boxes. The kitchen shelves were empty, and one hung askew as if it had nearly been torn from its nails. Warren picked up a can of Campbell's tomato soup, and thick red liquid dripped down the sides. The steel was riddled with punctures.

A cold sweat prickled Warren's neck and back. He'd gotten careless and left his rifle at the airplane. He took the shotgun down from the wall and found a box of ammunition in the cupboard. After he loaded it, he filled his pockets with extra shells.

The bright sun blinded him as he stepped out of the cabin with the firearm drawn.

"Birdie! Emaleen! Can you hear me?"

He needed to find the calm center. Stay alert. Keep focused. Take note of the small details. No one at the woodshed. The outhouse empty. At the cache, the door open and the ladder lying in the grass.

"Birdie?" he called again and again.

Partway across the meadow, he nearly stepped in a splotch in the grass. He crouched and touched it with the tips of his fingers. Coagulated blood. Not bucketsful, but enough to indicate a significant injury. He stood and scanned the immediate area. The grass was crushed, as if something large had thrashed around. A few feet away, there was a smaller spattering of dark-red blood. Judging by its consistency and color, it wasn't immediately fresh, but he doubted it was older than a day.

He searched as he walked, moving from one blood spatter to the next. By the time he reached the far edge of the meadow, the blood trail had become sparse. His eyes were attuned to the autumn patterns of browns and yellow, though, and he was able to find the spots of dark red, sometimes nothing more than a single drip across a blade of yellowing grass. His eyes darted from the ground to the surrounding forest and back again, and he held the shotgun in a low ready position, his finger on the trigger.

The thinning drops of blood led him to a well-traveled game trail that cut through the trees and across a grassy clearing, through a thicket of devil's club then up a small rise. Set into the damp earth, he saw bear tracks and, on top of them, the small boot prints of a child. At the top, a fallen birch tree blocked the trail. He sat on it and was swinging a leg over when he noticed several strands of long, blond hair, snagged on the underside of the log. They were Emaleen's. Little Emaleen. Anguish threatened to close in on him like a thick curtain, but Warren shoved it back. He needed all his faculties in this moment, here and now. He worked his way over the log, stood on the other side, and looked down into the ravine.

There, among the alder bushes and devil's club, was Birdie. She was lying face down, motionless, with her arms at odd angles to her body, and the hair on the back of her head was matted with blood.

"Birdie! Birdie? Can you hear me?"

He made quick note of the mess of tracks along the trail—Birdie, Emaleen, bear. "Hey!" Warren barked. "Hey!" Even as he approached Birdie, watching for any signs of life, he was scanning the nearby forest, the shotgun barrel following his line of vision.

He strained to register each observation as just information. Lower leg cold to touch, lacerations to face and scalp, perforation of skull near eye orbit. No carotid pulse. Slowly, gently, he rolled her onto her back, but there would be no resuscitating her. Birdie was dead.

He walked around the body, pushing the devil's club stalks out of the way with the barrel of the shotgun, brushing the tall grass back with his boots, peering into the alder thicket. He was disturbing a crime scene, but he needed to be sure. The child wasn't here.

"Emaleen!" he hollered into the forest. "Emaleen!"

Warren was shaky and drenched with sweat by the time he reached the airplane. For more than two hours he had searched the woods in wider and wider circles around Birdie's body, then around the cabin and outbuildings, but he'd found neither his son nor Emaleen. He needed to be levelheaded. He could continue to search on foot, or he could try to spot them from the air. He weighed going for help, but an hour or more would be lost to the round-trip flight out of the mountains.

He flew as low as he dared over the cabin, craning his neck to see in all directions. He traveled up the creek a mile or two, but not wanting to get boxed into the valley, turned, and followed it back down. He circled the cabin again and again. So much of the area was thick forest. How much distance could a little girl cover in the course of a day or two? Doubt niggled at the edges of his thoughts. Emaleen was dead. But it was a truth he wasn't prepared to accept. Not yet.

He looked at his watch. Four hours until sunset, but he only had two hours of gas. Enough time to fly out, alert the troopers, fuel up, and fly back with Syd. Syd was the best tracker Warren could think of, and he knew bears.

He was planning to take the most direct route toward the mountain pass, cutting the corner off the mouth of the creek, but decided at the last minute to search a little longer on his way out. He followed the creek the short distance down to the North Fork, then banked and flew low along the riverbed.

Almost immediately, a glimpse of her bright purple coat passed beneath the plane. He looped around and saw that the child was on her feet and waving both her arms over her head as she ran across a gravel bar to the river's edge. Thank dear God. Thank dear God. He needed a place to land—about a hundred yards of even ground without ditches or logs. He scanned the riverbed as he pulled back on the control stick and climbed higher. Downriver a half mile or so there appeared to be a dry sandbar that might work, but he wasn't sure. He passed over, circled around, and buzzed it again. The poor child would be frantic, thinking that he was leaving her behind.

The landing was rough and short, but he was able to bring the plane to a stop just shy of a clump of willow bushes. Before the propeller had stopped spinning, Warren was out of the plane.

He met the girl in the willow thicket. The backpack she wore was nearly as large as her body and she hobbled on stiff legs, as if in pain.

"Are you hurt?"

"We have to help my mommy."

"Are you all right?"

The child marched past him and toward the plane. "Hurry, hurry," she said. "I was coming to get you. We have to hurry."

"Wait," he said, and he took the backpack off her and carefully picked her up. When he got to the airplane, he sat her on the tire. "Show me where you're hurt."

"We have to go help her. Please, Mr. Warren. Right now."

Her face was dirty and streaked with tears, and her lips were cracked, but he couldn't see any obvious injuries. As he started to pull one of her rubber boots off, she flinched and tried to wrestle out of his grasp and off the tire. "My mommy."

"Hold on. Just let me have a look, okay?"

Her sock was filthy, and as he peeled it off, he saw that it was crusty with dirt and blood. A large blister on her heel had burst and left an open, oozing wound.

"All right. We can get that fixed up. Are you hurt anywhere else?"

"No. Please. We gotta go."

"I know, I know. I'm going to help your mother. But first we're going to take you someplace safe." He eased the sock back onto her foot to keep the wound protected. The child was sobbing and trying to say something at the same time, but he couldn't understand her.

"Shhh," he said. "It's going to be all right."

He lifted her off the tire and put her into the back seat of the airplane.

"I'm ... I'm ... I'm ..." The child couldn't get the words out between her hiccupping gasps for air.

"All right, it's all right." He was trying to secure her in the seat, but the harness straps weren't set for a child.

"I'm ... I'm ... I'm sorry."

"What's that?"

"I'm sorry, Mr. Warren. 'Cause ... 'cause ... I was running around ... I didn't listen ... and ... I'm sorry I'm sorry I'm sorry ..."

"No. Whatever happened, you are not to blame. You hear me? None of this is your fault. But we're going to get some help." He was looking directly into her eyes, and he ran his thumb softly across the side of her cheek. "Everything's going to be all right."

The child nodded.

It was a bald-faced lie. Nothing was all right, and it never would be again. Her mother was dead. There was blame to be had, and none of it was hers.

She was alive, though. Thank God for that.

PART THREE

KINNIKINNICK
Arctostaphylos uva-ursi

Chapter 30

The place had lived inside Emaleen like a trailing-off dream, something half-forgotten. It was shadowy and hidden, cloaked in dark-green alder boughs. When she was a child, without trying, she'd been able to find her way to the patches of sunlight, the wild bluebells and Arctic roses, the cheerful trickle of creek water down through the mossy boulders. But maybe she had only imagined those details to make the memories sweeter, the place less terrifying. Mostly it was shaded and cool, with large paw prints in the mud and the sharp fragrance of devil's club. Sometimes she found herself there just as she fell asleep. Sometimes her mind drifted to the place before she could stop it. And sometimes she went intentionally, sought it out, because it might be home.

Growing up with her mother's sister in Bellingham, Washington, Emaleen had checked out every library book that she could find about Alaska. She'd saved newspaper clippings, photographs from magazines, and the postcards Della King sent from the Wolverine Lodge, and she pasted them into secret scrapbooks. When she was twelve, she devised a plot to sneak money out of her aunt's savings account and purchase an airline ticket to Anchorage. Later, she imagined hitchhiking north out of Washington State and through Canada to the Alaska border. Pages of the old scrapbooks were filled with hand-drawn maps and elaborate itineraries. It wasn't a matter of running away from something, but instead a sense that she might have left something behind.

She hadn't gone through with any of it. Even if she'd come up with a feasible plan, the thought of disappointing or distressing anyone, especially her Aunt Liz, held her back.

The spring after she turned fourteen, she'd received a letter from Della, asking if she wanted to spend a few weeks of summer vacation at the lodge. When she'd handed the letter to Aunt Liz, she expected an immediate, resolute, "No, not under any circumstances." Instead, her aunt had quietly asked, "You wouldn't want to go back, would you? After everything?"

Emaleen had studied her aunt's face and then said, "No, sure. I guess not."

If Liz had left the smallest window open for Emaleen to express her wishes, she might have found the courage to say, *Yes, please, I want to go. I've always wanted to go.* They were only memories of memories now, but she knew that as a little girl she had been acutely homesick for Alaska. When she encountered the fragrance of cottonwood buds opening along the Nooksack River or the *tap-tap* of a woodpecker in the forest of Sehome Hill, the bittersweet ache would return. Walking home from class at the university, she'd often take the path along the arboretum and wonder what it would be like to spend the night out there, under the cover of the hemlocks and cedars. This strange longing for Alaska was a direct betrayal of everything her aunt had done for her. Liz had left home as soon as she was old enough, worked her way through community college, started her own accounting business, and built a new life for herself in Bellingham. In all the years since, she'd returned to Alaska just once—to settle her dead sister's affairs and bring six-year-old Emaleen back to Washington State with her.

Emaleen didn't remember everything about the tumultuous time when she came to live with her aunt, but she did remember Liz's warm acceptance and love. She remembered her aunt's house being like a beautiful castle, with plush blue carpeting in her very own bedroom, cushioned window seats in the turret where she could sit and read books, and the backyard garden lush with tall ferns and mossy bricks. At the time, Liz was renting the small Victorian house that overlooked Bellingham Bay, but later she purchased and renovated it, with Emaleen helping to paint the walls and choose the new dining room set. From the beginning, everything had been clean and orderly and safe. Aunt Liz enrolled Emaleen in the nearby elementary school and, for a time, took her to a therapist to help her with her nightmares and grief.

Emaleen was a smart, obedient child, and she adapted quickly. She learned that it wasn't acceptable to pee in the front yard because the neighbors might see, and that she didn't have to squirrel away food in her room because her aunt would always make sure there was enough to eat. She learned that the nearest grizzly bears were hundreds of miles away, and as far as Aunt Liz knew, no one in Bellingham had ever been killed by a bear. Every day, Emaleen could have warm bubble baths and clean clothes. And there never came a night when her aunt said they were going to sleep outside in the forest.

Emaleen also learned to distrust memory. It can be difficult for children to separate imagination from reality, and no matter how true a memory seems, it might be better left unspoken.

"You're going to call me every day." Aunt Liz was standing in the driveway, the hood of her raincoat pulled up over her head.

"I'll try." Emaleen closed the trunk of her car.

"Promise?"

"I promise, I promise. But don't worry if I don't call for some reason. I'm not sure the cellular phone will work everywhere, and it might be hard to find a pay phone."

Liz looked at her watch. "It's getting late. Why don't you wait and leave in the morning? The weather might get better too."

Emaleen smiled reassuringly at her aunt and hugged her. "I promise— I'll call you tomorrow, as soon as I get the chance, okay?"

"You know, I think this is good. I really do." Liz's eyes were wet with tears. "I'm so, so proud of you."

As Emaleen gave a last wave from the car and backed down the steep driveway, she wondered what her aunt had meant. *Proud.* It wasn't a word Liz threw around carelessly. Emaleen had graduated with honors from the university, but that hadn't been a surprise to either of them. Instead, was it possible that Liz was referring to this specific moment of her packing her car and driving away from the house, the first time Emaleen had asserted her independence? A month ago, she hadn't asked for Liz's permission, but instead announced it as breezily as she could—after graduation, she was going on a road trip to Alaska. When Grandma Jo died a few years ago, a developer had bought the original family homestead where Liz and Birdie grew up. Emaleen wanted to see it before it was subdivided, she explained, and this would be one last adventure before she became a full-fledged adult with a career and responsibilities.

But maybe Liz understood that it meant something more. A reckoning with memory.

Emaleen had imagined this June day differently—the weather would be hot and sunny, she'd wear shorts and Birkenstock sandals, and she would crank open the sunroof of her old Volvo to let in the fresh air. She should have known better. Rain splattered on the windshield as the wipers scraped back and forth, and she had to turn on the heat to keep the windows from fogging up.

It wasn't until she passed through customs at the Canadian border and saw the signs welcoming her to British Columbia that she felt the enormity of it. After all these years, she was finally returning.

By the time she spotted the campground, it was well after sunset. She turned off the highway and drove slowly along the gravel lane that wove through evergreen trees. There was something so clean and wholesome about this part of Canada, everything green and orderly and litter-free. It made her think of the *Ranger Rick* magazine she'd loved as a child.

Near the entrance, she passed the campground hosts, their motor home decked out with flowerpots and U.S. and Canada flags and a warm light glowing through the curtains in their windows. Her headlights flashed through the campsites, each with a picnic table and a metal ring for a fire, and each one occupied by a tent or motor home. Emaleen hadn't considered that the campgrounds might get crowded. She drove the entire loop again more slowly, and finally saw a small site with just enough room for a single tent.

The camping gear had been a gift from her aunt, and Emaleen had understood the implication. Without so many words, Liz was saying, *I don't understand, and I worry about you, but go with my love.*

Emaleen pulled the tent from its nylon bag and shook it out onto the ground in front of the car's headlights. When she and Liz had practiced setting it up in the middle of the living room floor, it had been like a Three Stooges act as they accidentally poked each other with the long poles and nearly knocked over a lamp. The directions made no sense and the two of them had broken down in giggles at the lopsided first attempt. Eventually they'd figured it out, and Liz timed Emaleen as she put it together as quickly as she could. *On your mark, get set, go!* It'd been a silly game, but alone now in the chilly night air, Emaleen was grateful. Within minutes, the tent was up, including the rainfly. The camping mattress, on the other hand, required an unreasonable amount of time to inflate, and she grew more and more lightheaded with each breath. Once it was fully inflated, she turned on a flashlight, unrolled her sleeping bag on top of the mattress, and climbed in without undressing. Even in June, she'd read, temperatures in British Columbia could drop into the forties at night. The sleeping bag was supposed to be good down to ten degrees, but she was skeptical. She grabbed a sweatshirt out of her bag and pulled that on too.

Inside of her sleeping bag, she wrestled around to roll onto her stomach. The flashlight lit up the tent like a lampshade and she could imagine how visible it must be from the other campsites, but for just a few minutes she wanted to look at the *Milepost* she'd brought. For the past few months, ever since she'd found the courage to tell Aunt Liz about her desire to drive to Alaska after graduation, Emaleen had been planning the trip. She'd read about the rivers she would cross and towns she'd drive through, the campgrounds where she might spend the night.

Emaleen unfolded the oversized map included in the book and laid it out on the tent floor beside her. With her finger, she traced the inches of progress she'd made so far, and then she followed the rest of the route with her finger, up through the Fraser Valley, along the Cassiar Mountains, north into Yukon Territory, and finally across the western border into the interior of Alaska. Using the mileage graphs, she calculated how far she still had to go. Two thousand eleven miles. About four days of driving, if everything went according to plan, until she'd be at the Wolverine Lodge.

After she put away *The Milepost* and turned off the flashlight, she lay on her back. She'd never slept in a tent before. It wasn't the warm, comfortable darkness of being in a bedroom at night with the curtains closed. In the dim gray, she could see the outline of the thin poles crossing overhead, and the wind caused the nylon walls to billow and ripple noisily. As the minutes passed, the chill seemed to seep into her body from the air around her and the ground below her. With a shiver of excitement, she snuggled down more deeply into the sleeping bag. She was alone in a way that she hadn't been in a very long time.

"Hi, Della? Yeah, it's me. Emaleen. No, I'm on my way. I left yesterday afternoon. I'm calling from a pay phone . . . someplace called Smithers? Do you know it? Yeah, I'm thinking I'll be there by Sunday. No, you're right. There's no hurry. I know, I can't wait to see you too."

Every year, without fail, Della had sent Emaleen Christmas and birthday packages from the Wolverine Lodge. There would be a toy or some candy, and a book inscribed to Emaleen from "Uncle Syd." There was always a note, too, in Della's neat, block print, where she would share a story or two from the lodge—the orphan baby beaver that a tourist had found beside the highway and brought to the lodge, or the windstorm that knocked the power out for a solid week.

In some ways, Della was like family. But this was only Emaleen's second phone conversation with her, and there was the stilted awkwardness of talking to a stranger. Emaleen squeezed in closer to the pay phone to let a boisterous family pass through the entryway of the diner.

"Oh, Della? Hey, really quick before we hang up, I wanted to ask you something. Does Mr. Neilsen still have his airplane?"

"Warren? Sure, sure he does." Her voice sounded far away.

"And he still flies? I mean, he's getting kind of . . . elderly, isn't he?"

"Well, he's no spring chicken. But old Doc Milner keeps passing him on his flight physicals. Those two have known each other, gosh, fifty years or more."

"Because I was thinking, I mean, if he didn't mind, do you think he could take me out to the cabin?"

"The cabin?"

"Yeah, uh—Arthur's place?"

There was a long silence on the other end of the line.

"Della? Are you there?"

"Yes, honey. I'm here."

"You know, the cabin where I lived that summer with my mom? It's still there, isn't it?"

"I just . . . I'm . . . I'm not sure."

"I mean, it doesn't matter about the cabin that much. Maybe it seems weird, but I'd like to go back. It's hard . . . with my mom and everything . . ." Emaleen was surprised to find herself choking up. "But there are good memories too. I just think, I'd like to see it again."

"Oh."

"Could Mr. Neilsen take me? Could you ask him?"

"I don't . . . It might not be a good idea."

"Oh. Okay. Sure. I didn't mean to put you on the spot. I can talk to him when I get there. And if he can't do it, there's probably someone else, right? Who could fly me out there?"

"Oh . . . maybe. I guess. But I don't know, honey."

As she neared the Yukon Territory, the change was vast. Until now, the highways had been smooth and wide, and Emaleen passed through small towns and picturesque farmland. But not long after she turned onto the Cassiar Highway, the road narrowed to barely two lanes and turned to a hybrid of gravel and asphalt, then eventually just gravel. The miles went by, and Emaleen passed fewer and fewer homes, businesses, or structures of any kind. She couldn't let her mind drift because there were surprises— a one-lane bridge, bulldozers, muddy detours. The road twisted and turned. Semi-trailer trucks with towering stacks of logs barreled past at speeds that didn't seem safe, for them or for her. Around a bend, she came up on a motor home going twenty-five miles per hour. For a while, she followed at a safe distance, but finally she gathered her nerves to pass. The Volvo hit a pothole at fifty miles per hour and she was certain she'd damaged the wheel or axle, but the car continued to drive normally. Wary, she sat up straight and watched the roadway directly in front of her, and then she was rising, rising, until she crested a hill and the vista opened up to great, steely blue mountains and rolling green forest; in every direction that's all there was. Emaleen felt triumphant, but also kind of small and vulnerable in her little car.

The gas gauge was just shy of a quarter of a tank. She'd never driven anywhere she needed to worry about running out of gas before the next service station. She tried to think when she'd last seen a mile marker along the highway. There had been no cellular reception for the past hour or so, and it occurred to her that if something went wrong all she could do is stand alone at the side of the road.

On a long, straight stretch of highway, Emaleen spotted two black animals that seemed to be moving down a grassy slope. They looked like overgrown Labrador retrievers, but rounder and shaggier. Emaleen slowed and ducked her head to look out all the windows. There had to be a house nearby, or the dogs' owners or another vehicle, but as far as she could see, the highway was empty.

As the animals got closer, Emaleen saw that they weren't puppies— they were black bears. She turned off the music and drove so slowly she could hear the rocks turning under her tires. Any minute now, surely the animals would startle and sprint away, but they didn't. They continued down the slope and onto the road. She looked in the rearview mirror, but there were still no other vehicles on the highway. Emaleen braked to a complete stop.

One of the bears seemed more cautious and hesitated, but the other walked brazenly up to the driver's side, stood up on its hind legs, and put its front paws against the car. As it peered through the window at her, it looked nothing like a puppy. The black fur was long and thick and matted with dried mud. The muzzle was brown and narrow, the ears upright and too big for the head, and the eyes so dark they were nearly black.

Emaleen's heart beat faster. Logically, she knew she was safe inside of her car. She took a slow, deep breath and put the palm of her hand against the window.

What would compel a wild animal to approach a car like this? The bear raised its nose in the air and turned its head, as if trying to smell something. *Hunger,* she thought. *It's looking for something to eat.*

One of Emaleen's earliest, most trustworthy memories was of being in the toy aisle of a grocery store and politely asking Aunt Liz to buy her a cowboy cap pistol. Her aunt had taken the toy in its cardboard and plastic box from her hands, but paused before she put it into the grocery cart. "It's just pretend," Emaleen had said, to reassure her aunt. "For fun." It was only years later, reflecting on the memory, that Emaleen understood Liz hadn't been concerned about the toy, but about her niece.

The cap pistol was brilliantly silver, and suspiciously light. Even at six years old, she'd known that the white handle was plastic and the metal wasn't the same as an actual gun. But the paper ribbon of caps smelled like gunpowder and when you pulled the trigger, it snapped and sent a whiff of smoke like a firecracker. In her room, she'd practiced fanning the hammer, flipping it back again and again with the palm of her left hand so she could shoot as quickly as possible, just like Rooster Cogburn. She wasn't stupid. She knew a cap gun wouldn't kill a bear, but it might scare it away.

At night, she'd kept the pistol loaded under her pillow, along with a butter knife. And she knew one thing—next time, she wouldn't run.

Those first years, the fear had been external and tangible. This was no imaginary polka-dotted monster under the bed or sheeted ghost outside the window, because everyone agreed—bears existed. But as real as the fear was, it was also cagey. A looming shadow behind the pantry door that dissolved into the corner. A dark mass behind the living room curtains that evaporated when Aunt Liz drew them back. When Emaleen lay on her side in bed, trying to fall asleep, she sensed it breathing and waiting behind her, and when she quickly rolled over to face it, it poured under her bed like a wave and rose, fur and breath, at her back again.

Around that same time, she'd woken in the middle of the night and wandered downstairs and saw the bear crawling through the hall window, his front paws on the floor, his massive shoulders jammed through the window frame. She could see every detail—the damp shine to his black nose, the deep scar across his muzzle, the ragged ear hanging off the side of his head. Each of his long, sharp claws cut into the linoleum like a knife blade. Emaleen had screamed and screamed until her aunt had stumbled down the stairs in her nightie and wrapped her arms around her. "Wake up, Emmie. You're sleepwalking. It's okay, Emmie. You're safe."

The road signs had taken on a menacing quality. THIS IS YOUR LAST CHANCE, CHECK YOUR FUEL. NEXT SERVICE 100 KM. Around the next bend in the road, Emaleen saw a gas station that looked more like a shabby house with a gas pump in the yard. There was another sign, this one claiming it to be the VERY LAST CHANCE. She turned off the highway and pulled up next to the pump. She would fill her tank, and she'd also wash the windshield, the headlights, and the taillights. She would check her oil and inspect each of the tires. It would make Aunt Liz happy.

When she stepped out of the car and closed the driver's door she saw where the bear had left its paw prints in the dirt on the side of the car. She reached out a finger, wanting to touch the tracks, but pulled away. The plump front pads, the tiny nick of each small claw, every detail was clearly laid down in the dust except for one track that was smeared to the side and almost looked like the handprint of a child.

Chapter 31

Emaleen didn't want to camp in the tent again. It wasn't just her encounter with the black bears, though the idea of sleeping with only a translucent sheet of nylon between her and any wild animal was unsettling. As she'd driven farther north, the landscape continued to shift from one of verdant trees and pristine park trails to something more lonesome and rugged. She went miles at a time without passing another vehicle or seeing a human structure, and when she got out of the car, the air was bracing. There were motels in the few towns she passed through, but they seemed nearly as unwelcoming as sleeping in the tent on the side of the highway. *The Milepost* told her that the Port Alcan border crossing into Alaska was open twenty-four hours. She would drive straight through, day and night. At a gas station, she filled her thermos with acrid coffee and a dozen packets of sugar, and whenever she got drowsy she rolled down the windows or turned up the music.

At two in the morning, unable to keep her eyes open any longer, she parked in an empty gravel pull-off along the highway, peed beside the car, then climbed into the back seat and locked the doors. Hours later, she woke groggy and disoriented to the sound of a truck driving by and the late-morning sunshine blazing through the windshield.

As she sat on the hood of the car, drinking the last of the cold coffee and eating one of the raspberry cookies Liz had sent with her, she heard the rumble of a creek or river nearby. It would be nice to wash up a bit. On the other side of the highway, a trail led into the brush. She finished her cookie and crossed the highway.

A small waterfall spilled down a rock face and, farther up the mountainside, Emaleen could see a shadowy ravine where a bank of last winter's snow and ice remained. She cupped her hands below the waterfall and splashed the water on her face and the back of her neck, and on a whim, plunged her head into the cascade for as long as she could stand the cold. Then she pulled off her sweatshirt and used it to wipe her face and roughly dry her hair.

Up on the rocks, a small flash of violet-blue caught her attention. Mountain harebell, perhaps. She set her sweatshirt on a boulder and began climbing up the steep hillside. Beautiful Jacob's ladder. Juniper. Twinflower. Lowbush cranberry. She adored the common names, with their regional idiosyncrasies and easy cadence. But the Latin was like an incantation, each plant's true and powerful name. *Polemonium pulcherrimum. Juniperus communis. Linnaea borealis. Vaccinium vitis-idaea.*

She didn't yet know how she would earn a living, but she knew this was how she found happiness. Uninterested eyes saw only a uniform green forest, a field, a scraggly rock face, but once you learned the patterns of leaves, the varying shades of green, the blooms and berries, it was as if you were truly present in a way you hadn't been before. The meditative focus was simultaneously exhilarating and peaceful.

There, on a mossy ledge within arm's reach, Emaleen noticed a low evergreen plant. She leaned in, brought her eyes closer. The delicate, bell-shaped flowers were tiny and pale pink.

Arctostaphylos uva-ursi. Kinnikinnick.

Look closely. The flowers, they are small.

All that remained of her mother were a few small details. Her long dark hair, how it smelled of woodsmoke and was silky against Emaleen's cheeks. Her hands, cool and chapped, with slender rims of dirt beneath the nails and blueberry stains on the fingertips. The threadbare knees of her denim jeans. The red laces on her hiking boots, and the greasy mink oil she'd worked into the leather. But there was so much Emaleen couldn't remember. Her mother's smile, or her laugh. How it had felt to be held in her arms, to be hugged or kissed by her.

When she'd first come to live with her aunt, Emaleen had insisted that it didn't matter that she was only six, she could stay home by herself while Liz went to work. Her aunt had been firm but kind in her response. "That's not how we're going to do things. I'm going to keep you safe, because I love you." Emaleen's young brain had been adept at decoding the contrast— her mother had left her alone.

After Grandma Jo died, someone had shipped all the family albums to Liz, but she never unpacked them, and they were stored in cardboard boxes in the garage. Emaleen's favorite photograph was of her mother, sitting cross-legged on a cottonwood log like a beautiful woodland elf but with a cigarette and a brown Michelob bottle in the same hand. Her straight dark hair was pulled around to one shoulder and was shining in the sun, and she had a sardonic, half smile, like she was embarrassed or annoyed at having her picture taken. "Stone Creek, May 30" was written in ink beneath the photograph.

Emaleen had searched every album and found the few pictures that showed them together—Birdie carrying baby Emaleen in a backpack, Emaleen sitting on her mom's lap on Grandma Jo's porch, Birdie pushing Emaleen on a swing set. There was one photograph, though, that troubled her. No one would recognize her mother, except for the words written in pen beneath the photograph: "Birdie and Emaleen, Christmas at the homestead." Emaleen, a one-year-old with corduroy overalls and messy blond hair, just beginning to learn how to walk; her mother only a hand, reaching into the camera frame as if to keep Emaleen from falling. Looking at the photo was like prodding an old bruise, trying to determine its size and shape, checking to see if it had healed at all.

She'd left her mother to die alone in the woods. She'd done nothing but run away.

Arthur she could hardly remember at all. He was a featureless shadow, as if backlit by a blinding sun. She couldn't recall his face or hands, what he wore or how he had smelled. Even the outline of him was vague, but towering, as if seen from the perspective of a small child sitting on the ground and looking up.

When Emaleen was six years old and had been at her aunt's house for only a week or two, she and Liz went for their first walk together along the trail that followed the old railroad grade near the bay.

"What's that plant called?" Emaleen had asked.

"I think those are blackberry bushes, or maybe they're called marion-berries. I'm not really sure."

"How about the other name? The funny one."

"You mean the scientific name? I have no idea. We can probably look it up . . . Did your mom teach you about that?"

"Arthur taught me."

After that, Aunt Liz purchased several plant identification books and began carrying them on their walks, and for her eighth birthday, she gave Emaleen a wooden flower press. Together they learned how botanists collect the plants and press them in newspaper, how they record everything they can about where they found them and how they grew. Their walks were slow because Emaleen was always stopping with her notebook to squat beside a small plant that most people would have overlooked.

"You're very observant," her aunt said.

"Arthur told me. Sometimes flowers are so little, you have to put your eyes very close to see them."

A long time ago, Emaleen had believed something else about Arthur, but she'd learned not to talk about it. Grown-ups didn't like to hear it, and thinking about it made her physically ill. For most of her childhood, she'd done well in forgetting. When she was sixteen, though, a news story had caught her attention. She and Liz were watching TV while they cooked dinner together, and the news anchor was talking about the death of a woman in Eastern Washington. Weeks before, they'd reported that the woman had been attacked and killed by her two large dogs, and her husband had found her body in a field behind their house.

"Police now say the dogs weren't the culprits, but instead the husband," the man on the television said. "Fifty-seven-year-old George Clarke has been arrested on murder charges. Authorities say he bludgeoned his wife to death, then fed her body to the dogs in hopes of destroying the evidence of his crime."

A resonating, sickening sensation had washed over Emaleen. Was it something she'd dreamed or imagined as a child? She needed to see his face, and then maybe she'd know. She'd left the kitchen, gone to the garage, and pulled out the photo albums.

"Dinner is ready," her aunt called, and when Emaleen didn't answer, she came out to the garage. "What are you looking for?"

"Do we have any pictures of Arthur?"

"Arthur . . . Neilsen? I don't think so. Your mom wasn't with him for very long."

"Did you know him?"

"Not really. I probably saw him around at some point, but not that I remember— Oh Emmie, what's the matter?"

"It's just, I don't think it was a bear. Arthur did it. He killed my mom."

Liz was quiet, as if considering it all.

"I'm sorry," Emaleen said. "I don't know why I didn't tell you this before."

"You did. You used to talk about this when you were little."

"What?"

"You don't remember? It's one reason I took you to that therapist. Because it seemed like you had gotten some of the events mixed up in your mind. Which is understandable, after everything you'd been through."

"No, but that's the thing—I wasn't making it up. I think it was Arthur. We need to tell somebody. Like the police or something."

"I didn't think you were making it up. You were just a child, trying to make sense of something terrible. Here, let me show you something."

Liz led her to the bedroom on the second floor that she used as a home office, and she took a manila envelope out of the file cabinet.

"I saved all of this because I thought someday, when you were old enough, you might want to know more." She slid the packet of papers out of the envelope, her eyes skimmed the top sheet, and she let out a long sigh. "But I don't know. Maybe you shouldn't . . ."

"What is it?"

"It's the medical examiner's report. But I'd forgotten how explicit it is."

"Just let me see. Please."

It took a while for Emaleen to understand what she was reading.

"Rebecca Josephine Finney, Postmortem Autopsy . . . multiple deep lacerations to scalp . . . fracture to right temporal bone, contusion of brain tissue . . . dislocation of upper cervical spine, spinal cord severed . . . Puncture wounds consistent with canine teeth of large adult male grizzly bear . . . Defensive bite wounds on hands and arms . . . bruising indicates victim was alive when wounds were inflicted . . . All lesions consistent with jaw, dentition, and claw of large male grizzly."

In the packet, there was also a report from the Alaska State Troopers that included a diagram of the location and a written statement from Warren Neilsen, describing how and where he found the body.

The last pages were clippings from Alaskan newspapers. "Rebecca Finney, 26, was killed in what appears to be a bear mauling last weekend in a remote area of the Wolverine Valley. Her young daughter was safely rescued, but a local man remains missing." A later article reported, "An autopsy has been conclusive—Rebecca Finney, whose body was discovered earlier this year northeast of Alpine, was killed by a grizzly bear. A former Alaska State Trooper, with the assistance of a local hunting guide, was able to locate and dispatch the bear they believe was responsible for the attack, but due to the difficulty of the terrain, they were unable to recover the animal's carcass. The search for Arthur Neilsen has been suspended. Officials say it is likely he was killed by the bear or perished while trying to hike out for help."

These, then, were the simple, cold facts. Whatever else lurked in Emaleen's subconscious—the shifting illusions of fairy wings and witch's hair, a fur pelt buried beneath moss and earth, a man who was also a bear—it was nothing but childish imagination.

Chapter 32

The Wolverine Lodge was a disappointment. Emaleen had always pictured it as majestic, but also cozy, like a Swiss mountain resort, with honey-colored logs, large windows, flower baskets hanging from the eaves. There would be a grand main entrance, log beams overhead, plush carpet leading up to the front desk, and the light fragrance of pine.

But this place was kind of a dump—a worn-out, squat building with burnt-red paint peeling off its skinny, knobby logs. A neon PABST BLUE RIBBON sign glared in a window, and a half dozen rusty pickup trucks and run-down cars were parked in the gravel lot.

Even the so-called midnight sun was underwhelming. It was after 11 P.M., and while it was light enough to see, it was gray and bleak. A mist hung low in the valley, and she couldn't see far beyond the lodge, no mountains or river valleys or anything remotely majestic. When she got out of the car, the muffled sounds of a bar leaked into the parking lot, loud music that could have been country or rock, loud voices that were either laughing or yelling. Drunken strangers. Maybe she was in the wrong place, but back toward the highway, there was the sign—THE WOLVERINE LODGE, EST. 1935. She shoved her hands into her armpits and hugged herself against the cold. Beyond the music and voices coming from the lodge, it was quiet. The trees were a shadowy outline in all directions. Listening closely, she made out a low rumble in the distance and wondered if it was the Wolverine River.

A yipping, howling cry rose above the sound of the river. Emaleen stood completely still and listened. Another yip joined in, and another. The cries came from somewhere in the woods. It didn't sound like dogs. The chorus was echoing and haunting, and she wondered if wolves came this close to the lodge.

"Emaleen! I'm Rebecca Finney's daughter. Della is expecting me. Em-a-leen! Birdie's daughter!"

She shouted the same words over and over at the bartender, a guy who looked to be in his twenties wearing a denim vest and a thin cotton cowboy shirt, but he pointed at his ear and shook his head.

"Della? Is Della here?"

"Della?" he shouted back. "I'll see if I can find her."

The small bar was crowded, and Emaleen crammed herself between the wall beside the door and a large man in a Carhartt jacket who didn't seem to notice her. Lynyrd Skynyrd was on the jukebox, several people were playing pool in the back, and everyone was shouting over each other to be heard. A sign behind the bar read LEAVE YOUR FIREARMS WITH THE BAR-TENDER. And someone had written in pen below it, "Behave and we'll give 'em back when you leave." Emaleen wondered what part of the sign, if any, was a joke.

The man laughed at something someone had said, and he slapped the bar top hard with his big hand, startling Emaleen. Then she heard someone calling her name.

"Emaleen? Emaleen! Holy smokes!"

It was Della. It had to be. Tall and round, her graying hair in a pile on top of her head. "It's really you!" And she was hugging Emaleen, circling her with her large, soft arms and rocking her like a small child. Emaleen thought she could almost remember that smell, of beer and patchouli and tobacco.

Della pulled back and put Emaleen at arm's length without letting go. "Just look at you. My god, you're all grown up. My little ladybug." Then in

the same breath she was shouting over the noise of the bar. "Joe, turn off
the . . . turn the goddamned thing off! Joe!"

Della pushed her way through the crowd, stood on the rung of a bar-
stool, and reached up to ring a large cast-iron bell hanging from the ceiling.
She put two fingers to her mouth and blew an ear-piercing wolf whistle.

"Look who's here! Dan! Larry! Susan! Come here. You see who this is?
It's our Emaleen."

The bartender had finally figured out how to turn off the jukebox, and
the laughter and shouting slowly died down.

"Who's that, Della?" someone yelled from the pool table.

"Emaleen. Our little Emaleen, all grown up!"

"That Birdie's girl?" someone else called out.

A few people started gathering around Emaleen, talking over each
other, kissing her cheeks, hugging her, holding her hands, slurring their
words, their eyes watery with emotion or drink.

"I knew your mom ages back. Little Emaleen. You remember me?"
Cathy. Boots. Roy. None of the faces or names were familiar. "I pulled you
around on a sled. Right outside this door. You were just a tiny thing." "Your
mama was a looker." "Skinny as a whip, but she could drink us all under
the table."

Everyone was offering to buy her a beer, a shot of whiskey, because she
was—how old was she now? Old enough to have a beer, that's for sure.
And where had she been living all this time? Was she coming back to
Alaska for good?

Della must have seen some expression on Emaleen's face because she
interceded. "All right, all right. Come on, honey. Let's get you to bed before
you fall asleep standing up."

Emaleen woke in the middle of the night sweating and with the impres-
sion that she'd been having an unpleasant dream, but the details were
gone. She threw off the covers and flipped over her pillow to see if the
other side was cooler. When Della had brought her out to the cabin and
helped her make up the bed, they'd turned up the baseboard heater. Now
it was suffocatingly hot, and there was the smell of old cigarette smoke and

bleach. She got out of bed, turned down the thermostat, and considered opening the window or door, but she thought of the wild animals and the men who'd been at the bar. She switched on the bathroom light so the fan would come on and hoped it would circulate the air.

This was the cabin where she and her mother had stayed, Della had told her—did she remember it? No, Emaleen had answered with certainty. But now, in the half-light from the bathroom, everything was familiar. The card table by the window. The microwave on the dresser. The swirling pattern in the ugly brown and orange carpeting. The dank, musty odor. She climbed back into bed, and she could almost remember sleeping here beside her mother, but also being alone at night, listening to the music and laughter coming from the bar.

Emaleen slept and slept, and she could have slept for hours more, but the sunlight was a glare around the edges of the blinds on the window, and when she looked at her watch, she saw that it was nearly 11 A.M. She didn't take a shower or brush her hair, just dressed in a hurry, her curiosity rising.

When she threw open the cabin door, there was the bittersweet fragrance of cottonwood leaves, and the mountains were sudden and everywhere. Emaleen blinked against the bright, intense beauty of it. During the night, the weather had changed, the gray wall of clouds lifting and disintegrating until they were just a few wisps that clung to the highest peaks against the blue sky. Rugged mountains rose up steeply on either side of the valley and stretched in layers to the north and south, as far as she could see. Velvety green rolled across the valleys, up and up, until it broke into purplish-gray rock faces and then, on the tallest, farthest mountains— brilliantly white snow, glistening in the morning sun. It was the height of summer, yet there was fresh snow on the mountains. The green and blue and purple and white were all so vivid Emaleen couldn't pull her eyes away from the sight.

The cabin had no porch, so she sat on the single step, her bare legs stretched out on the short grass in front of her. Yellow-headed dandelions bloomed in the sunshine along the front of the cabin, and it was as if the present, this precise, dreamy moment, was a transparent overlay, and the past was the more substantial foundation, like a double-exposed photograph. She was a grown woman, sitting on the stoop in her shorts and sandals, but beneath it all, she was a little girl in her rainbow rubber boots.

"Do you remember the way?" Della asked, pulling back the curtain on the cafe window and pointing. "It's just across the parking lot there and down that trail."

"Is it okay? To just walk over there?"

"You might want to put on some long pants. Or at least spray your legs down with bug dope."

"But don't I need to be worried about wild animals?"

"Nah, just stay on the trail. It's a hop, skip, and a jump. You can almost see the roof of his place through the trees. But you can take my pistol, if it'd make you feel better? Or, if you want to wait until this afternoon, I can go with you then."

"No, that's okay. If you think it's all right."

The path led into a spruce forest that was shady and hushed, and under Emaleen's sandals, the ground was covered with a thick bed of spruce needles and the bracts and pieces of cones that squirrels had pulled apart to get at the seeds. She'd read that Alaska didn't have chipmunks or gray squirrels, skunks or opossums, but there were small red squirrels with foxlike tails. She was searching the trees, hoping to see one, when ahead, on a low bough that spread over the trail, she saw the witch's hair.

Parmeliaceae. She remembered when she first learned about the lichen family from one of her plant books. "A composite organism of algae and fungus in a symbiotic relationship . . . includes hairlike growths on tree branches with common names such as old man's beard, pale-footed horsehair, and witch's hair."

You're like a furry witch. When she got near enough, she reached up and rubbed the tangled, rough threads between her fingers and thumb. *And forest witches, they have golden eyes.*

She was continuing down the trail, touching the gray-green and dusty-brown lichen draped across the branches, when in a noisy burst, something flew up from the forest floor directly in front of her. She jumped back with an "Oh!" and saw a bird the size of a small chicken land clumsily on a nearby spruce tree. It turned its head to the side so it could peer down at her. A dramatic flare of red arched above its eye, but the rest of the grouse was a speckled brownish gray.

"Oh god," she said out loud and laughed. "You scared me."

The shock left her giddy with adrenaline, alert to every sound and trace of movement, as she continued to follow the trail through the trees and into a clearing. There was a large vegetable garden with neat rows of herbs, broccoli, carrots, potatoes, cabbages, and blooming pea vines that clung to a chicken-wire fence. Nearby, there was a small greenhouse made of sapling poles and opaque plastic sheeting. The door was propped open with a rock, and inside tomato and cucumber plants, and what looked like several marijuana plants, grew in black buckets. She heard the hum of bees and, just beyond the greenhouse, saw the stacked wooden boxes of two beehives.

A few steps farther and the house came into view. It was the most unusual Emaleen had ever seen. It was made of logs but had eight walls in the shape of a giant octagon with two stories and a complex, multisided roof that came to a sharp point in the center. As if mirroring the shape of the house, the front door featured an octagonal stained-glass window with a leaf pattern.

At first, she thought the old man was naked except for a straw hat. He was kneeling in a flower bed near the house, his deeply suntanned back to her, and, embarrassed, she considered retreating. But the man looked over his shoulder at her, and when he stood up, she was thankful to see that he wasn't completely naked. He was wearing khaki shorts with frayed edges. His stout chest was covered in wooly, white hair. His beard was bushy and white, and his long hair had been pulled back into a thick braid.

"Oh, hi!" she said. "I'm Emaleen. Birdie's daughter?"

"Emaleen Finney! As I live and breathe."

He stepped toward her, arms reaching out.

"Syd?"

"No, no," he said as he hugged her enthusiastically. "That's Uncle Syd to you."

Emaleen laughed congenially, though in truth she had no memory of the man beyond his name inscribed in all the books he'd sent her over the years.

"Your place is amazing," she said. "The garden and the flowers and everything. And this . . ." She gestured toward the flower bed where he'd been working. "It's beautiful."

"Flora Alaskana," Syd said. "Do you remember any of them?"

"Yeah, I think so. Let's see, wild geranium? And lupine." Emaleen pointed to each as she named them. "Arctic rose. And that's monkshood, right?"

"I hear you're a scientist, so how about any of that Linnaean Latin?"

Emaleen laughed again. "I guess I can give it a try? *Geranium erianthum? Lupinus arcticus. Rosa acicularis.* And the monkshood . . . I know it's related to delphinium, but I can't think of . . ."

"I haven't a clue," Syd said. "But good on you. Did you have to learn those for one of your classes?"

"No, not really. I don't know why, but I've just always been interested. My favorite professor, he talked about how domesticated plants have been bred to have these big, showy flowers. But wild plants are so much more delicate and beautiful. You just have to look more closely to see it."

"That's your area of study, I hear—botany?"

"Yeah, plant biology. I just graduated. So, I guess it's time to find a job now."

"Ah well, all in good time." He brushed dirt off his hands and knees as he talked, then put on a denim shirt and buttoned it.

"That's one reason I decided to come up this summer. There are some jobs I saw listed here that I thought I might—"

"Yes? Yes, I want to hear all about that. But first, I need to wet my whistle. Iced tea?" Syd gestured toward the house.

The inside was an open, octagonal-shaped room with a wooden spiral staircase in the center leading up to the second floor. Two of the walls were lined with floor-to-ceiling shelves so overcrowded with books that some were stacked on the floor. Displayed on another wall, stretched across the logs, was a large, brown fur with what looked like a black mane and tail.

"Is that a . . . is that a horse?" Emaleen asked.

"That's Lady Morgan, queen of the beasts," he said as he washed his hands in a basin. "She lived to be thirty-two. That's quite old for a horse. One of the dog mushers wanted the meat, and it seemed a shame to let her go to waste. So, I skinned her out and tanned the hide. Sentimental of me, I know."

Syd set two glasses and an enamel jug on a table near a picture window. The broad, wooden sill was lined with fossils, stones of different colors, and several bleached animal skulls of varying sizes and shapes. The largest barely fit on the sill.

"That's a bear skull, isn't it?"

"It is," he said as he poured iced tea into each glass.

"It's huge. Did you kill it?"

"No, no. I found that years ago, up on the North Fork of the Wolverine."

"How did it die?"

"I'm not sure. He'd been down a while when I came across him." Syd had picked up the skull and seemed to contemplate it. "You know what was odd about it, though? The bones weren't set . . . in the skull. It was malleable. Like a baby's. You know how infants have those soft spots on their heads, to let the skull shift during birth, and grow and change? It was something like that. As if the bear's head was designed to mold into different shapes." He looked intently at her, as if expecting a reaction. Unsure how to respond, she drank some of her iced tea. It was mint, sweetened with honey, and icy cold.

"That's delicious. Thank you."

Syd nodded and put the bear skull back on the sill.

"So," he said. "Tell me about this burgeoning career of yours."

"Well, it's definitely not a career yet. I've just been looking at some seasonal work. There are a couple of different vegetation surveys happening around Alaska this summer, through the Forest Service and the university, you know? And they're hiring, just like field assistants, technicians."

"And you've applied?"

"No, not yet."

"Why not?"

"They're all in remote field camps, where you're camping. Out in the wilderness."

"True enough. And?"

"I don't know if I'm cut out for it. And my aunt, god, she'd freak if she knew I was even thinking about it."

"Is she unhappy that you're here now?"

"No, not really. I think she's hoping I'll get it out of my system and hurry back home."

"Home being Washington? And what do you think?"

"I don't know. To be honest, it's kind of overwhelming, being back here again."

"Sure, sure." He stood and took some kind of tin down from a shelf. Emaleen thought he was going to offer her a cookie, but instead he said, "Let's move this operation outside, so I can have a smoke. Bring your iced tea along with you."

He led the way out and into the shade of a birch tree near the house. At the base of the tree were two lawn chairs in an Adirondack style but built of bent and intertwined twigs.

"Did you make these?"

"Yep. Willow. One of my newer projects. I need to sew some cushions for them, though. Fair warning, they're hard on the ass." He sat in one and gestured toward the other.

"All of this," she said as she took her seat, "the house, the garden, everything—you built it?"

"Not alone. A lot of good people around here. Hard workers. I figured out early on, all I had to do is come up with a few cases of cold beer and they'd show up. Started with the foundation, we dug it out with nothing but shovels and a wheelbarrow. Mixed the concrete by hand. The rock all came from a quarry downriver." He nodded toward the stonework at the base of the log house.

"That's incredible." She sat back in the chair and drank more of the iced tea. With the cookie tin on his lap, Syd deftly rolled a cigarette with a Zig-Zag paper, and when he lit it with a match, there was the whiff of marijuana along with burning tobacco.

"So," he said after he'd exhaled away from her. "Della tells me you're going out to the North Fork."

"I don't know. I want to, but I'm not sure it's going to work out. I guess Mr. Neilsen doesn't fly much anymore."

Syd leaned his head back on the chair and puffed on his cigarette. Typically, Emaleen would have been uncomfortable with the silence, but there was something easy and peaceful about being here. She watched a red-breasted robin land in the garden and hop along the rows. There was a gentle breeze, and several billowing, white clouds moved slowly across the blue sky and cast shadows along the green mountainside in the distance.

"Peculiar how similar they are, the stories about bears. All down through the ages," Syd said out of nowhere. He was still reclining in his chair, his arms on the rests and the marijuana cigarette smoldering between two fingers. "Berserkers and shape-shifters. Wild sows taking in abandoned human babies and raising them as their own. Women falling in love with boars. Girls being abducted by bears and giving birth to their children in mountain caves. Russia, Europe, North America, Japan." He poked an index finger to different places in the air, as if gesturing toward an invisible map. "Again and again. Did you know, there was a whole line of Danes who believed they were the descendants of bears?"

"Oh." Emaleen's mind reeled. Why was he saying all of this? Before she had a chance to formulate her thoughts, he was talking again.

"I encouraged her to go out there, your mother. Not that anyone could have deterred her. She had a mind of her own. The happiest I ever saw her was the day you two were leaving for the North Fork. She wanted something more than this common life, and I think she almost found it. Up in those mountains. In Arthur."

Syd looked over at her, as if considering something for the first time.

"Strange how time works," he said. "Yesterday I was sitting here, shooting the breeze with Birdie. Yet here you are, just about the age she was then."

Emaleen's understanding of her mother had long been knotted up with grief. A bar waitress who drank people under the table. A distracted mother drawn to risk and havoc. And Emaleen hadn't been able to save her—that was her deepest shame, and paradoxically, the source of a festering anger. What kind of mother puts her six-year-old in that impossible situation?

But now, as Syd described her, it was like the turn of a kaleidoscope, and a different image came into focus. Birdie. A young woman about her same age, hardly able to support herself and her child, but wanting something extraordinary.

"I thought it was going to be good for the two of you. I told her—go and be happy. But I wasn't factoring everything into the equation." Syd rested his head on the back of the chair and rolled it slowly side to side, as if weighing some argument, then said quietly, as if to himself, "He won't like it."

"What's that?" Emaleen said, rising out of her own thoughts.

"I'm going to tell you something," he said. "Warren, he makes that trip out to the North Fork all the time. He'll deny it, but he sure as hell can fly you out there. And he should. If I were you, I'd just show up at his house and ask him, face-to-face. We owe you that much."

Chapter 33

It was habit that got Warren out of bed, nothing else.
He didn't set an alarm anymore, but each and every damned morning, he
woke up at 6 A.M. sharp and no matter how he tried, couldn't ever get back
to sleep. He'd ease out of bed and take a shower, holding on to the hand-
rails Syd had installed a few years back after Warren suffered a small
stroke. He'd get dressed in his slacks and button-up shirt, because it's what
he'd always done, and then he'd turn on the coffeepot and let the dog out.
Spinner was mostly deaf now, so he had to nudge her until she startled
awake. "Come on, old girl. Up and at 'em."

Usually he'd have a toasted English muffin and coffee—he didn't have
the appetite he once did—and then he'd turn on the radio, sit in the recliner, and doze off and on until habit required something else of him. But
today was Sunday, and if he didn't show up at the lodge for breakfast, Della
would launch a search and rescue. She'd done it before. One time it was
Ruby, the new cook. Another, it was Syd banging on the door. When Warren had grumbled about it to Della, she'd retorted, "If you don't want us
pestering you, then turn up on Sunday. Or at least answer the phone when
I call, so that I know you're all right."

Warren opened the door for the dog and waited to be sure she made it
down the steps without falling. He sat on the hall bench to lace up his boots
and took the walking stick from where it leaned beside the door.

When he got outside, Spinner was already waiting for him beside the pickup. It was a mystery to him, how the dog could know the day of the week. "All right, then. Load up." Used to be he could open the passenger door, pat the seat, and Spinner would jump in expertly, but her back end was starting to give out and she didn't have the strength anymore. Instead the dog got her front paws up on the running board and waited for Warren to heft her the rest of the way.

"We're quite the pair, aren't we," he said after struggling to get her into the truck. "Not sure how long we're going to be able to keep this up."

A few words to the dog, even if she was deaf, was marginally acceptable, but he was careful not to carry on full-fledged conversations. He'd seen a few of the old women at the post office or grocery store talking to themselves outright, complaining about their electric bill or discussing with themselves what they were going to cook for dinner. It was a slippery slope—they'd probably started out just talking to the dog too.

After his stroke, his daughters had wanted to move him down to the Lower 48 to be closer to one of them. That wasn't going to happen, for any number of reasons, some of which he couldn't share with his daughters. He appeased them, though, by pointing out that he had a community of friends and neighbors that were always willing to help, and he promised he would get out of the house. Wendy had suggested he return to the Alpine church, but he had no desire to sit alone in a pew. The service put him to sleep, and the prim chitchat before and after made him awkward. He'd only ever gone because it was important to Carol.

The Wolverine Lodge wasn't much his crowd either. The bar was rowdy most nights, and he could do without the belligerence and drunkenness. But he'd found that on Sunday mornings, the bar was empty, the jukebox silent, the cafe quiet, and Della was usually in the kitchen baking her cinnamon rolls, so the windows were pleasantly steamy and the air smelled of rising dough. It reminded Warren of being a little boy back in Ohio, his mother baking bread early on a sunny morning.

Warren parked in the shade on the side of the lodge and cracked both truck windows. "Good girl," he said and gave the dog a pat on the head. She'd be content to sleep on a blanket on the truck seat until he came back with her bacon sandwich.

Warren wiped his boots on the rug in the arctic entry, then found his favorite table in the cafe by the window, where he could watch the sun tip over the mountains and pour through the curtains.

"Morning, Warren." Della handed him a laminated menu. Just like every Sunday, he looked it over, as if considering the options. "Well. Let's see what we've got here." He took his reading glasses out of his shirt pocket and put them on. Della waited with no impatience. "Well, the usual, I suppose."

Coffee with brown sugar, eggs over easy, sourdough toast, reindeer sausage fried crispy. If he ordered anything less, Della would fret over him.

"Ruby's already got it cooking." She winked at him and turned his mug right side up on the table. "Emaleen made it here already, a day or two quicker than we were expecting," she said as she poured the coffee.

Warren looked up, expecting to see the girl.

"No, no, she's still in bed," Della said. "We won't see her until ten or so. Ah, to be young again. My aching back won't let me sleep much past seven."

She took the coffeepot back behind the counter and set it on the burner.

"I don't know if Liz already shared the news with you," she said, "but she graduated this spring. Got her degree in plants or something. I'm not sure what kind of job that'll get you, but she's smart as a tack, that's for sure."

"She always was," Warren said.

"And she's anxious to see you."

No, he highly doubted that. He was about the last person on earth she wanted to see, and that was all right. He'd made peace with it, as much as a man could.

Warren was surprised when Della returned to the table, pulled out a chair, and sat down across from him.

"Listen, Warren. She . . . well, she's asking again, about going out to the North Fork. She wants you to fly her out there."

"Della, you know I can't do that."

"I know, I know. And I've tried telling her."

Warren glanced up from his coffee mug.

"Don't worry, I didn't say why. She thinks you're not up to it, so she's asking about other pilots. I don't know, Warren—I'm not sure we can dodge this."

Over the years, Liz Finney had been kind enough to reply to Warren's inquiries, letting him know that the girl was doing well in school and participating in various activities. In junior high, she was on the swim team and excelled at mathematics. Throughout high school, she earned top grades and worked summers on a groundskeeping crew. That had been enough, to know that she was cared for and loved. It did nothing to assuage the grief and guilt that had become a kind of chronic illness, but Warren accepted that pain as the least of what he deserved. Every year that went by without hearing from the girl herself, the more he was reassured. That's all he hoped for her, that she get on with her life without ever having to look back.

But that afternoon, when he heard a car pull up at the front of the house and then a soft but persistent knock, he knew a day of reckoning had arrived. He opened the door to see Emaleen Finney, a grown young woman, standing on his doorstep. She was taller and bigger than her mother had been, with wavy blond hair and a sunny face. She was wearing cutoff jeans, a university sweatshirt, and sandals.

"Mr. Neilsen? I'm sorry to bother you. I don't know if you remember me? Emaleen? I'm Birdie's daughter?" He saw, then, that she was holding her hand out expectantly.

"Yes, yes, of course," he said, shaking her hand.

"I tried to call ahead, but I kept getting your answering machine, so I thought I'd swing by and see if you were around. I hope you don't mind. Della said that maybe it wasn't a good idea."

Without intending to, Warren made a quiet harrumphing sound. "I guess you should come in."

In the entryway, he paused and looked down at her feet.

"Oh, should I take my shoes off?"

He preferred people to remove their shoes at the door, but if she took them off, she'd be walking around his house in her bare feet.

"No, that's fine."

He led her down the hall, into the living room, and gestured for her to sit on the couch. "Can I get you something to drink? I've got coffee on."

"No, thanks. I think I drank an entire pot with Della this morning," the girl said with a little laugh.

"There's water. I'm afraid I don't have much else."

"Oh, sure. That would be nice."

He could tell she was only being polite, but he was trying to find his equilibrium within the habit of pleasantries. When he came back with a glass of water, the dog had climbed up on the couch and put her head on the girl's lap.

"Spinner, get off of there."

"No, it's okay."

"I'm afraid we've gotten lax about the rules around here, just the two of us."

"She's a sweetie," the girl said as she stroked the dog's head.

Warren was gathering the piles of newspapers and magazines on the coffee table to make room to set the glass down, and the girl started helping him. "I really am sorry to intrude like this. I was just hoping to talk to you about a couple of things actually. I . . ."

"Hold on, hold on." He dreaded whatever she had to say, and he wanted to be seated when it came. "All right then," he said once he was in the recliner.

"Well . . . mostly, I wanted to thank you. For the savings bonds? It was really generous of you. I got my degree this spring. I mean, without you . . . my aunt did her best to put money aside for college . . . but because of you, I don't have any debt. That's really huge. I mean, a lot of my friends are already stressed out about how they're going to make their loan payments. And I don't have to worry about that. I mean, I still need to find a job and everything, but . . ."

The girl trailed off and Warren realized he'd been scowling as she spoke. He'd asked Liz Finney to keep that to herself, where the savings bonds had come from. Why hadn't the woman honored his wishes? But before he could process this piece of information, the girl was on to something else, talking more quickly the more nervous she got. He should put her at ease, but he couldn't muster the energy or superficial cheer.

"I wanted to see how it would feel to be here again. When I was a kid, I used to be so homesick for Alaska. But I don't know—maybe it was just because I missed my mom so much or . . ."

The girl took a drink from her water glass, set it back on the coffee table, and swallowed, as if trying to get her nerve up.

"Um, so that's the other thing. Why I'm here. Della told me I shouldn't bother you with it. But I was hoping to see the old cabin. Syd said you still fly out there pretty often?"

Warren was taken aback. Why would Syd tell the girl? He, of all people, understood what was at stake.

"He said that, did he?"

"But I don't mean to . . . if it's too much to ask, I'm sure I can find somebody else to fly me out there. I saw some ads on the corkboard at the lodge, people who do like flightseeing and stuff. I'm sure I can figure out something."

With the impatience of youth, she wanted an answer, right here, right now, but she didn't understand what she was asking. It seemed to Warren that it could only cause her more distress, but was it in his power, or even his right, to deny her? He wanted to protect her. But that wasn't the entire truth. He was protecting himself as well.

"Look, I'm sorry. I shouldn't have bothered you." The girl abruptly stood up. "I'll leave now." Spinner opened her eyes and, when she saw that the visitor was leaving, eased herself off the couch and followed the girl toward the front door.

"Hold on, hold on," Warren called after her. "Don't let the dog out. She can stay inside."

In the entryway, he sat on the bench to put on his boots. "Just give me a minute here," he said. "I have something for you."

With the walking stick in one hand, and his other hand on the porch railing, he made his way down the steps. The girl was young and healthy and surely found his pace agonizingly slow as they walked across the yard to the Quonset hut. When he reached the door, he realized he'd forgotten his reading glasses.

"I can't see well enough," he said. "It's 24, 37, 12."

"Oh, you want me to unlock it?"

Inside, Warren went to the gun cabinet, took out the rifle, and double-checked to be sure it wasn't loaded before holding it out to the girl.

"It was your mother's," he said.

"Oh. Wow."

"It's all right. It's not loaded."

The girl seemed reluctant to take it, and he could tell by the way she held it nervously away from her body that she wasn't used to handling guns.

"Your mother's .30-06," Warren explained. "It was a gift from Hank, your great-grandfather. He sized the stock down for her smaller frame. From what I understand, she shot her first caribou with it."

"Oh, wow," she said again. She gingerly touched the bolt handle.

"It's a Winchester Model 70," he said. "Pre-'64 action."

Her smile was apologetic. "I don't know what that means."

"It's a good rifle. That's all."

Warren had taken care of it over the years. The stock, English walnut carved with leaves and scrollwork, was beautiful and well oiled. The action was smooth. There was some fading in the bluing at the end of the barrel from use, but not a speck of rust or pitting. The scope seemed to be in working order too, though the rifle hadn't been sighted in for years.

"Do you do any shooting?" he asked.

"Ah, no. Never, actually. I mean, when I was a kid I had a toy cap pistol? Does that count? You know, with the paper rolls?" The girl laughed. "That is the full extent of my experience."

"Well, this isn't a cap gun. But it's fairly straightforward, and it doesn't kick too much." He took the rifle from her, keeping the barrel lowered. "You always want to point it away from people, even if you know it's not loaded."

"Okay, right."

"It's a bolt action, which means you slide this out and back in, and it'll push a round from the magazine into the chamber. You lock down the bolt handle, like this. Now it's ready to fire. This here, this is the safety. And on the scope, you turn this dial to increase the magnification. At close range, you want to keep it down at 2."

Warren handed the rifle back to the girl.

"Do you have any real shoes?" he asked.

The girl looked down at her sandals. "I mean, these—they're real, right?"

"They don't do anything to protect your feet."

"Oh, okay. Well, it's all I have with me. Why?"

He didn't have any paper targets on hand, but he found a piece of cardboard and with a marker drew a few concentric circles. He took a box of .30-06 ammunition down from a shelf and gave the girl a set of earplugs.

Years ago, in the field behind his workshop, he'd paced off a hundred-yard range, and he kept a metal folding chair and a wooden benchrest nearby. He directed the girl to tack the cardboard to the sawhorse at the other end while he set up the chair and table.

"You can shoot standing up, but it's more difficult to hold your aim," he said as he showed the girl how to load the gun. "It's always better to find a rest if you can. Go ahead and sit down there. All right, load a round into the chamber. Good. Now pull the butt of the stock snug into your shoulder. Rest your cheek on the stock there and move your eye forward just until you see the big picture in the scope. Not too close now, or on the recoil, it could come back and hit you in the eye. All right, you got the target in view? Now, switch off the safety. There you go." Warren stepped back and plugged both his ears with his fingers. "Hold the crosshairs steady on the target. When you're ready, squeeze the trigger."

The girl was a quick and careful learner, and after some practice, she was able to get a neat grouping of several shots.

"That's right, as soon as you pull the trigger you want to quickly reload. Make it reflexive, so you're not hesitating in the moment. Pull the trigger, reload. When you're shooting at an animal, do you know where to aim?"

"Um, no?"

"Normally, you want to aim for just behind the front shoulder, because that will get you into the vital organs. But if an animal is charging directly at you, you probably aren't going to have that kind of shot. So then you'll be aiming at what's called center mass of the animal. But even if you hit a leg or shoulder or miss altogether, as long as you reload quickly, you've got a chance at stopping it."

The girl's expression had turned more somber. "Mr. Neilsen, why are you telling me this?"

"It's good to know."

He'd send her with another box of ammunition, and he'd tell her to practice out on the riverbed near the lodge. Della could help her set up a target. If he was going to take her out to the North Fork, he needed to be certain she could protect herself.

Chapter 34

It was as if Della had been stalling her all morning. Emaleen was planning to drive out to the family homestead—it was only twenty minutes away, and though she had no memory or emotional attachment to it, she wanted to see it because it was where her mother and Aunt Liz had spent their childhoods. The developer had yet to do anything with the property, according to Della, and no one would care if Emaleen walked around the place.

"Wait until later this afternoon," Della said, after Emaleen finished her breakfast in the cafe. "Then I'll take you over."

"That's okay, I think I can find it. The directions are pretty simple."

"Yeah, that's probably so. I know, how about this? Help me unpack some of the boxes in the pantry first. If you don't mind."

They were quickly done with the task, and Emaleen said she would head out, if there wasn't anything more to do.

"Have you been out to the picnic table yet?" Della asked. "Of course, it's not the same one. The wood rotted over the years, and I had to replace it. But your mother always liked to take her breaks out there."

It seemed unlikely that the picnic table was really the point, but maybe Della had something on her mind to discuss. Emaleen could visit the homestead later in the afternoon, or even tomorrow. She'd told Liz that she would probably stay a week at the lodge, then another week or so seeing some other parts of Alaska before making the drive back to Washington, but there was nothing to hold her to those plans.

Della sat on top of the picnic table facing the mountains, with her feet resting on the bench, and she patted the space next to her, inviting Emaleen to sit too.

"I think your mother did a lot of daydreaming out here, looking across the river."

"Yeah?"

"She loved you so much." Della said it in an offhand manner, as if it hardly needed to be spoken at all.

"Hmm."

"What? Oh, honey." She put a hand on Emaleen's knee and looked into her face until Emaleen met her eyes. "Your mother loved you more than anything, you know that, right? That's why she took you out there. I wanted you at the lodge, so I could keep an eye on the two of you." She squeezed Emaleen's knee. "That's just how I am. But I understood why she wanted to do something different. She was trying to get a fresh start."

"I wish I remembered her more."

"She was beautiful and funny. A bit of a wild card. She had her hands full, raising you on her own, but she did her very best." She wrapped an arm around Emaleen's shoulder and squeezed her. "And look at you. All grown up. A college degree and everything. If your mother could see you now."

Neither of them spoke for a long while as they looked across the Wolverine Valley, toward the mountains. As the minutes passed, Emaleen considered getting up to leave, but Della's arm remained firmly around her shoulders.

"For crying out loud, it's about flipping time," Della said, just as Emaleen heard the sound of a humming engine that grew closer and then abruptly decreased in power. It was a small airplane, descending toward the lodge. "Come on, Emmie—quick, quick. Go get your things."

"What things?"

"That's Warren. He showed up after all." There was an excited, nervous energy about Della. "You're going out to the North Fork."

The airplane landed on what Emaleen had thought was a long, skinny field near the lodge, then it turned and taxied back toward them.

"We're going, right now? What do I need?"

"Get on some long pants and pack some extra clothes in case the weather turns. You can wear those hiking boots of mine, and grab a day-pack from the closet. Don't forget your rifle."

When Emaleen returned, Della and Warren were loading bags and boxes into the back of the airplane.

"I was worried that if you didn't show up soon, I was going to have to hug her all day to keep her from leaving." Della handed Warren a sack of dog food. "Inside the back door to the kitchen, there's a box of fruits and veggies," she said to Emaleen as she took the daypack and rifle from her. "And in the walk-in freezer, there's a black garbage bag. Get that too."

The cardboard box was full of wilted heads of lettuce, mushy strawberries, and carrots and apples that looked past their prime, nothing that looked good to eat. The garbage bag in the freezer was surprisingly heavy. Curious, Emaleen untied the top and saw what looked like beef bones and freezer-burnt fish fillets.

"You're going to have to help Warren with all of this," Della said quietly. "It's too much for him anymore, no matter what he says."

"Sure, but what's it all for?"

"I packed some bologna sandwiches and snacks for the two of you. And there's a thermos of coffee and some drinking water, in case the creek is muddy."

Della hugged Emaleen and kissed her firmly on the cheek. "You take care, all right? Warren, you've got that radio phone? I'll see you back here this evening."

Warren showed Emaleen where to step to climb up into the airplane. It was even smaller on the inside than it looked, just wide enough for the single passenger seat directly behind the pilot's seat. The harness was complicated, and Warren helped buckle her in, then handed her a set of headphones. When he climbed into his seat and put on his own headphones, she could hear his voice in her ears.

"We're all set?"

Before Emaleen answered, the airplane began to taxi away from the lodge and out to the airstrip. She'd flown in commercial jets a few times with her aunt, but this was something else entirely. Once he pivoted at the far end of the field, Warren revved the engine and the plane sped along, bouncing slightly on its fat wheels, and before Emaleen had registered the fact that they were taking off, they were in the air. Within minutes, they were flying toward the mountains, almost into them it seemed, but then they were slipping through a narrow valley.

"Group of Dall sheep on your right." Warren pointed out his side window, and there on a steep, green slope was a cluster of white spots that passed by so quickly Emaleen only caught a glimpse.

They flew through the mountain pass, the valley opened wider, and Emaleen could see the river below her.

"Is that . . ." Her voice wasn't loud enough to activate the headset, so she spoke more clearly. "Is that a moose down there?"

Warren looked out his window on the left.

"The other side," Emaleen said, but it was too late, they'd flown beyond it.

Less than half an hour later, they were descending, but to where? There was only a creek and thick brush and what looked like a small trail, but suddenly the plane was landing on the trail and coming to a quick stop before the boulder edge of the creek.

Emaleen waited while Warren shut off the engine and climbed out of the plane. He took her headphones and hung them from a hook inside the plane, then helped her unbuckle the harness and climb out. She was unsteady on her feet and slightly dizzy from the flight through the mountains.

"You used to be waiting out here," Warren said. "Ready to greet me when I flew in."

"I did?"

"I always looked forward to that." He took her rifle from a scabbard on the plane's wing and handed it to her. "Go ahead and load it. Five in the magazine, but keep the chamber empty."

"Should we bring any of that too?" She nodded toward the bags and boxes in the back of the plane.

"No, we'll take care of that later."

Emaleen watched how Warren carried his rifle, the sling over his shoulder and the rifle at his back with the barrel pointed skyward. It felt unnatural, but Emaleen did the same.

"I'm afraid I haven't kept the place up, but I know you want to see it," he said. "You go ahead. You'll go faster than I'm able. No, that's a different trail. The way to the cabin is over there."

The place had existed in memory and dream for so long, yet none of it was quite right. There were the wildflowers—bluebells and purple geraniums and fireweed stalks with flower buds just forming—but it wasn't a vast field, only a tiny meadow. The log cabin was hardly bigger than the gardening shed in Aunt Liz's backyard, and the front roofline was caved in.

"A windblown tree fell on it, years back," Warren said. "Syd helped me buck it up and move it out of the way, but I never did get to fixing the roof. Then again, there didn't seem to be much point."

"Is it safe to go inside?"

Warren walked up the steps first, tapping on the porch with his walking stick as if to test the strength of the wood. The door was slightly ajar, stuck in place by the collapsed roof.

"Probably best not to go in, I suppose," he said.

Emaleen peered through the opening. Inside, would she have found some remnant of her childhood—a toy or piece of clothing? It didn't look as if Warren had ever cleaned it out. A few rusty food cans were scattered across the floor.

"What's that smell?" she asked.

"Porcupine. You can see what he's done to the bed there. They love to chew on plywood."

They were silent for a while, then Warren said, apologetically, "It's not much to look at anymore."

"No, I guess it isn't."

When they turned from the cabin door, she saw the woodshed. There was no jarring, lucid recollection, but instead a vague unease that she didn't know how to explain. Then, past the woodshed, she spotted the cache on its tall legs. Years ago, Syd had sent her a children's folktale about Bony Legs, an old woman who ate children and lived in a hut that stood high up on tall chicken legs. Seeing the cache now, she realized she'd conflated the two images, picturing it as something much more fantastical.

"I remember that," she said softly. "Wasn't there a door on it?"

"I used moose hide for the hinges, and over time it rotted. It must have fallen off at some point."

At the base of the cache, overgrown in the grass and shrubs, Emaleen found the ladder. "Do you think it's sturdy enough?" She stood it up and leaned it against the cache. Warren pulled on the first couple of rungs and jostled the ladder.

"Seems strong enough. Just watch your step."

The cache wasn't that tall, less than ten feet, but in her child's mind it had been a massive tower, twenty, or thirty, a hundred feet in the air. As she stepped onto the ladder, the present moment was no longer a transparent overlay. Instead it was as if she were climbing up into a dreamscape, rung after rung, the summer sun bright, the colors of the trees and sky like a hallucination.

She remembered being inside the cache, looking out into the forest where the witches flew, but she didn't climb into it now. The space was small, and she felt like Alice in Wonderland, having grown much too large. A dusty old sleeping bag was balled up just inside of the entrance. Farther in, there were a few crates and boxes but mostly cobwebs and dust. She was beginning the climb down, when she noticed something on the floor of the cache. It was a thimble, on its side like a tiny cup that had been overturned.

She picked it up and, without thinking, tried to put it on her thumb, but of course, it no longer fit. The thimble might have once been bright and shining silver, but it had turned the dull shade of lead.

Thimblina.

Emaleen tucked the thimble into the front pocket of her jeans.

"All right then." Warren let out a long breath, as if preparing for something, and led the way back down toward the creek.

"Are we leaving already?"

"No, we've got something else to take care of."

At the airplane, he unloaded the sacks of dog food, the boxes, and the garbage bag from the back of the plane and handed them to Emaleen, who set them on the ground nearby.

"Over in the bushes, there are a couple of five-gallon buckets. Would you mind getting them for me?"

"What are they for?" she said after she'd found them.

"Makes for easier carrying." He set one of the plastic buckets beside the garbage bag and began to untie it.

"I can get that, if you'd like," Emaleen said. "Where do you need it?"

"It's heavier than it looks."

She picked up the sack and put it over her shoulder.

"I'm all right," she said.

"You sure you can manage with your rifle?"

"Yep, I'm good."

"Set it down for now. This'll take me a little while."

Using a pocketknife, he cut open one of the sacks of dog food and poured it into a bucket until it was half full. Emaleen could have carried an entire bucket of dog food, along with the garbage bag full of bones and fish, and the rifle, but she didn't know how far they were going, and she was sensitive to the fact that Warren seemed embarrassed by his limitations. He had certainly once been taller and stronger than she was, but now he had the stooped, frail frame of an old man. He walked slowly, one hand on his walking stick, the other carrying the bucket by its metal bail. At the far edge of the airstrip, they passed a campfire ring formed from granite boulders and two large rounds of wood that looked like they'd been used as chairs. "This is where Syd and I set up camp, when we stay the night."

As she followed, she slowed her pace to keep a few strides behind. The well-used trail passed through tall alders and willows and then into a forested area with a mix of spruce and birch. That's where she first noticed the woven-wire fencing, well over six feet high, that ran from one tree to the next and, above it, another kind of wire secured with plastic insulators.

"Why is this fence here?"

Warren was struggling with the bucket. He stopped and set it down frequently, resting against his walking stick, sighing loudly as if frustrated, but he didn't answer her question. A rank odor grew stronger the farther they went, like an animal pen or zoo exhibit that hadn't been cleaned frequently enough, a feral stink of urine, feces, and rotting food.

"Don't worry about the fence," Warren said. "I haven't had to keep it electrified for years now."

When they came to a gate, there was a shallow steel trough just the other side of the fence. Warren carefully tipped the bucket against the fence and emptied the dog food into the trough, then took the garbage bag from Emaleen and untied it. The frozen pieces of salmon he put into the trough, but the bones he threw out into the muddy, foul pen. When he was done, he tapped at the trough with his walking stick.

At the metallic drumming, something stepped out from behind a large spruce tree inside the pen. It was him. His fur was shabby, and he moved like a decrepit or sick animal, slow and flat-footed. There was the one ear that hung off the side of his broad head and the scar across his muzzle. He didn't look up at Emaleen or Warren, but he shambled in their direction with his head down, the nostrils in his black, leathery nose flaring as if he tracked some scent.

Emaleen slid the rifle off her shoulder and grabbed on to the bolt action, just as Warren had taught her.

"It's all right," Warren said in a low tone. "You're safe on this side of the fence."

The bear was so close now that Emaleen could have reached out and touched him, but he did nothing to acknowledge her presence. He shoved his head into the trough and nosed through the dog food and frozen fish.

"I don't understand. In the old newspaper articles, it said . . ." That terrible, old feeling—the torrent of anger, grief, and fear—roared so loudly in Emaleen's head that she couldn't hear her own words. "I thought someone killed . . . I thought he was dead."

"That probably would have been the right thing to do." Warren stared straight ahead, clenching and unclenching the muscles in his jaw.

Emaleen turned from the pen, away from Warren, and strode quickly down the trail, nearly at a run, not thinking about where she was going but needing to go somewhere. She walked out of the woods, past the old firepit, past the airplane, without seeing anything.

When Warren found her, she was standing at the edge of the creek, the rifle still hanging from its sling on her shoulder, as she threw rocks into the water, one after another. Without speaking, he sat down on a nearby boulder and rested the walking stick across his knees.

"I used to try to tell people, when I was little," she said after a while. "Everyone said I was making it up. That I was just upset because of what had happened to my mother. But I always knew it was him." She picked up a rounded piece of granite and threw it as hard as she could into the water. Warren was quiet, as if it were still her turn to talk.

"Is he ever . . . himself?" she asked. "Because it's him, isn't it? That's Arthur."

Warren nodded. "It is him. But my son—I haven't seen him since your mother died. I used to hope he would take off the pelt, so I could see him one last time. It could be shame. He can't face what he has done. Or, I don't know . . . maybe this is who he was all along."

They were quiet for a long time, and she didn't throw any more rocks but just watched the clear water rush past. Warren cleared his throat. "Anything I say is a pittance against all that was taken from you. But I am truly . . ." She could hear the anguish in his voice, but she didn't look at him. He cleared his throat again. "I am truly sorry, Emaleen. I never should have allowed it to happen. Any of it."

A calm exhaustion was settling over her. Her natural tendency was to shy away from conflict and anger, but this was different. She wouldn't allow herself to become complacent. All of her life, she'd lived with the bear. As a little girl she'd had a recurring nightmare in which she was running through a thick, brambly forest at night. In the shadows behind her, the animal and her mother merged together into a writhing death shape that roared and screamed as one, and Emaleen kept running and running, until the sounds were muffled and small.

And again and again in the light of day, she had imagined a different ending. She didn't run. She didn't leave her mom. She killed the bear. With a gun, with a knife, with a snare around its neck. Again and again, fury and shame hot in her belly, she had tried to solve the problem of how a little girl can save her mother.

"We should bring the rest of the food up there," she said and set off for the airplane.

"There's no hurry," Warren said. He was slowly getting to his feet, but she was already picking up the other sack of dog food and marching toward the trail.

She could significantly outpace him. She would have enough time.

When she got to the pen, the bear was lying in the mud between the trough and the spruce tree, less than a hundred feet away. He was sleeping with his head turned to one side, rested on his front paws. Along his back, his fur was short and thin, as if it had been rubbed away. Emaleen quietly lowered the sack of food to the ground and eased the rifle off her shoulder. She pulled back the bolt handle and loaded a round into the chamber. He didn't react to the sound. Five bullets. It would be enough if she quickly reloaded, shot, and shot again. She raised the rifle, put her eye to the scope, and found the round of his back, then lowered the rifle very slightly until the crosshairs were in the right place. *Aim for just behind the front shoulder, because that will get you into the vital organs.* She pushed her thumb to release the safety and placed her index finger on the trigger. She needed to do it now. Warren would be coming. Her arms were getting tired.

"Hey!" she shouted. "Hey! Look at me!"

The bear lifted his head. She raised the rifle again and the image through the scope was perfectly focused—his eyes, small and dark in his huge head; the blond-tipped fur along the top of his brow; the haze of tiny flies that hovered over him. Emaleen lowered the rifle and angrily brushed away tears. She needed to be able to see.

"You can pour that right into the trough," she heard Warren say. He was walking along the fence line toward her, carrying the bucket.

"Oh, okay," she said, trying to make her voice sound normal. Warren took out his pocketknife as he approached and cut open the sack. Maybe he hadn't seen. Maybe he didn't know her intentions.

"He looks sick," Emaleen said. "What's wrong with him?"

They were sitting on a driftwood log down by the creek. Warren had retrieved the lunch Della had packed, and though she had no appetite, Emaleen took the sandwich and bag of chips that he held out to her.

"He's old," he said. "Grizzly bears don't live nearly as long as a man. It doesn't help, the condition of his pen. Usually this time of year I'd let him out into the larger corral. He has more room, and I have a chance to clean out the pen. But the fence is in bad shape . . . there's rusted wire, trees that have come down . . ."

"Syd showed me a bear skull at his cabin," Emaleen said. "He found it out here somewhere, and he said it was like soft or something, like it could mold into different shapes?"

"He reads a lot, and he has a lot of theories." Warren leaned over and picked up a green stone from the water-worn rocks. "It doesn't much interest me, though. All the hows and whys, they don't change anything, do they? Not for you or your mother."

He rubbed the dust off the stone with his thumb. He often thought of the day he found Arthur by the river. He should have left him there, turned his back on the baby and walked away. For good and bad, though, we are each bound to our own character. He tossed the stone into the creek.

"Why doesn't he break through the fence?" Emaleen asked. "He could, couldn't he?"

"I suppose. He's just trained. Syd and I kept it electrified with marine batteries, but it wasn't easy. You've got to recharge them and keep the fence clear of brush. After a while, we realized he wasn't testing it anymore. He's fed, and there's a little stream that runs down through the pen, so he's got water. He believes there's no way out, and he doesn't have any reason to try."

"But what would you do? If he broke out?"

"I'd bait him back in, the same way Syd and I did it when we first caught him."

"But what if you couldn't? Like what if he wouldn't go back?"

Warren looked at her with a gentle, pained expression. "I won't let him hurt anyone else, Emaleen. If that's what you're asking. I'd shoot him if I had to." He gathered the sandwiches and chips that neither of them had eaten and stood up from the log.

As he began walking back toward the airstrip and the plane, Emaleen called out to him. "Hey! I could help. You know, with the fence? And cleaning out his pen."

Chapter 35

For several days they didn't return to the North Fork.
Emaleen drove to Warren's house each afternoon, but he was so slow and meticulous about everything, and there was not much she could do to speed up the process. He spent most of one day getting his chainsaw ready—sharpening the chain with a round file, changing out the spark plug, cleaning the air filter, mixing gasoline, and adding bar oil. Emaleen stood by, handing him tools when she could, but mostly she just watched the minutes drag by. Another afternoon, he searched for hours for a specific come-along he said he needed to stretch the fencing. U-nails. Wire cutters. Loppers. He muttered to himself as he wandered around the inside of the Quonset hut with a handwritten list on a clipboard.

"I'm going to stick around here for another week or so, I think," Emaleen told her aunt from the telephone in Della's office. "I'd like to help Mr. Neilsen do some work around his place."

She didn't mention Arthur, or the fence, or the rifle that she'd grown used to carrying.

She still thought about killing him. There would be justice in it, but maybe also mercy. When she passed the pen, she watched for some sign of recognition or cognizance, but the most he did was flick his good ear at the bothersome insects or rub his muzzle against a front paw, rarely even

opening his eyes. She had the urge to provoke him. She clapped and whistled, and even thought of throwing a stick at him. If he looked at her with
clarity, and in his eyes she could see some indication of the man he'd been,
would she be able to pull the trigger?

While Warren began inspecting the fence, Emaleen was unloading supplies from the airplane. The third trip up the trail, as she carried a bucket
of tools, wires, and nails, she watched the bear get to his feet and shake his
entire body, like a dog, the loose skin sliding back and forth across the
hump of his back, a cloud of dust rising from his fur. She waited to see if he
would turn his head in her direction, but he shook again and shuffled a few
steps. He scratched at the ground with his long claws and flopped onto his
side with his back to her.

Emaleen continued past the pen, through the trees, to where Warren
was using the loppers to cut brush away from the fence.

"I'm afraid we're not going to get much done today," he said.

"But we just got here."

"Along this section, the fence is rusting and coming apart. I thought
we'd be able to re-stretch it, but this all has to be replaced. I've got several
rolls in the shop. I just didn't think we'd need them so soon."

"You go get it. I'll stay here and keep working." She couldn't leave room
for him to say no, because this might be her last chance.

"The weather's good now, but it can always change," Warren said. "Or
something else could come along to keep me from flying back out here
today."

"I'll be fine. You'll only be gone for, like, an hour. I can get a lot done if I
stay here." She began dragging cut brush away from the fence and putting
it into a pile, hoping to convince him by a show of effort.

"I suppose I have emergency gear in the plane," he said. "A small tent, a
sleeping bag, and a few other things in a dry bag."

She cut a sapling spruce tree with the loppers and threw it onto the pile.
She could hear Warren making quiet sounds to himself, clearing his throat,
starting to speak, then stopping. She kept at the work.

"Well, all right then," he said finally. "I'll set some things out by the airstrip, just in case. You'll stay right here until I get back? And you'll keep
your rifle in arm's reach all of the time."

"Definitely."

As soon as she heard the airplane's engine fade into the distance, she dropped the loppers, picked up the rifle, and walked back toward the pen. Her heart was pounding. She couldn't do it like before. But Warren had said it himself—if he got out of the pen and was a danger, he would shoot him.

Before she approached the gate, she readied her rifle. The bear was asleep, sprawled on his belly with his head outstretched on the ground like a bearskin rug. She watched him carefully as she unlatched the gate and dragged it to the side, and she raised the rifle. When he roared and stood up to his full height, when he charged through the gate and lunged at her, then she would shoot him, again and again.

He didn't move, only blinked a few times and closed his eyes again.

With the rifle still in position, she shouted, "Hey!" and kicked at the trough. He lifted his head. She thought of the bear skull on Syd's window-sill, and realized he was even bigger. If she put her two hands on top of his head, her outspread fingers wouldn't be able to span the distance.

He yawned. He was getting up, slowly and with much effort. He took a few steps. She pulled the rifle butt firmly into her shoulder, but he wasn't coming toward her. He was going to the trough. He put his head in and snuffled at the old dog food without eating any of it.

Emaleen stepped in front of the open gate. "Hey!" she shouted again. "Don't you see this? Come on!" *Come on, you goddamned son of a bitch. Show me who you really are.* She wouldn't be afraid of him any longer.

His movements were cumbersome. Though he wasn't particularly fat, his large frame caused his steps to take on a rolling, side-to-side motion. When he got to where the gate had been, he paused and seemed to sway slightly on his feet. He lowered his head and sniffed at the ground, then took another step forward, and another, until he was out of the pen. Emaleen backed away. If he was too close, she wouldn't be able to see clearly through the scope.

He didn't advance toward her, but began walking along the fence line, away from the gate. After a short distance, he raised his nose into the air and turned into the woods. She needed to do it now, before he got away. But it felt wrong. He was so passive and weak. He went a few paces, then stopped, his head hanging low, his breathing labored. He looked back over his shoulder, as if to see if she were still nearby, and started walking again. Holding the rifle with both hands, she followed.

The scene was like a primeval dream—the massive, shabby bear lumbering through the spruce forest, sunbeams breaking through the branches and touching on pale-green lady ferns and Arctic rose brambles. The air was warm and calm and scented with spruce sap, and several yellow swallowtail butterflies rose and fell and rose again in erratic flights from one flower to the next. When the bear stopped to rest, he raised his nose in the air. *Shoot him. I have to do it now.* But then he was walking again.

Ahead, the land dipped into a gulley where the spruce trees and prickly rose bushes gave way to alder bushes, ostrich ferns, and broad-leafed devil's club. As she scrambled and slid down the steep incline, the smell hit her—cold earth, rotting wood, and the astringent, medicinal aroma of the plants. From the brush, she heard branches breaking and the bear's paws squelching in mud.

It was the place of her nightmares. In a shadowy alder gulley like this, he had killed her mother. She wanted to turn back, run away to safety. But she wasn't a child. She had set him free, and now she had to finish this. She followed him into the brush.

When she emerged from the thicket, the bear was walking up a game trail that traversed the gulley. He reached the top and disappeared. She couldn't lose sight of him. She ran up the trail and when she crested the rise, the bear was going down the other side. Below was a small beaver pond. The near shore was a grassy marsh, but on the other side, the bank was steep and mossy.

She knew this place too. Jumping off the beaver house into the deep, dark water, then rising with a gasp to see Arthur swimming up to her. *There you go, little one. There you go.*

Did he remember too? Maybe he'd come here to remind her of the joyful, gentle times they'd had together, an unspoken acknowledgment of all that had once been and all that he'd taken from her.

Or, he was just an old animal, incapable of regret or affection, seeking the water to soothe his aches. Emaleen sat on the hillside overlooking the pond. She had a perfect shot from here. She rested the rifle on her lap. The bear waded through the horsetails and coarse grass, the water rising up his legs, his chest, until it must have been deep enough for him to swim because he slid into the pond until only the top half of his head remained above the surface. She imagined his four paws paddling slowly beneath him. It seemed effortless and lazy, as if he were floating rather than swimming, and then he put his head underwater and vanished. When he came up again, he was nearly to the beaver house.

"Arthur," she called out. It felt absurd, speaking to him, but she didn't know what else to do. "We have to go back, okay?"

The bear turned in the water to face her, clearly responding to the sound of her voice. He swam in her direction and when he got to the marsh, he walked through the grass until the water was low on his legs. He stopped and shook his head and entire body so that water droplets sprayed from his fur in a great arc.

Emaleen held the rifle in both hands.

"Arthur? Do you understand me? It's time to go back."

It was difficult from that distance to see if his eyes were focused on her, but he ambled up the hill toward her. There was nothing aggressive or sudden in his movements. Emaleen stepped backward off the game trail and let him go by.

As he passed within an arm's length, he turned his head in her direction and their eyes met. The skin on his upper and lower lids was black, but at this angle, there was a glimpse of the whites of his eyes and his irises caught the sunlight so that they glowed a warm amber.

"Arthur?" she said.

The bear dropped his gaze and blew air out of his nostrils in a huffing sigh. Then he started walking again, his head low, his gait a rolling side-to-side, his giant paws silent on the forest floor.

She didn't know the exact route they'd come by, but she had no doubt that he was returning in the direction of the pen—across the ridge, down into the alder thicket, through the spruce trees and wild roses. The journey seemed much quicker, whether because he was revived or because she knew where they were going. At the fence, he turned and followed it until he reached the open gate, and then he walked through.

Emaleen dragged the gate closed and latched it.

Chapter 36

Warren looked out the side window of the airplane and saw Emaleen at the edge of the airstrip, waiting for him. He could picture her as a little girl, jumping up and down and waving her arms in excitement, but of course she wasn't a child anymore. She held up a single hand in greeting.

Along with the rolls of fencing, he'd brought a candy bar and a 7 Up for her, thinking of how hard she would have been working while he was gone. When she met him at the airplane and he offered them to her, though, her "Thank you" was subdued. He felt foolish. She'd probably outgrown junk food.

"Mr. Neilsen? I'm sorry. I have to tell you something."

"Is everything all right?"

"I'm fine. Everything is fine. It's just that . . . when you were gone, I . . . I let him out. Of his pen."

"What . . ." Warren was so shocked and confused he could hardly find the words. "Why in God's name?"

"I'm so sorry. But he's okay," she went on. "I had my rifle, and I didn't let him out of my sight. All he did was go to a pond. He swam around for a while. And then, when I said it was time to go back to his pen, it was like he knew what I meant. He went right back in, and I latched the gate."

"The risk you took . . . you could have been . . ."

"I know. I know. But everything's okay now. It won't happen again." She picked up a roll of fencing and put it on her shoulder. "And we have enough time. We can still get a lot done."

At the pen, Warren saw why the girl had confessed. The change in the bear was quite noticeable. He looked content, stretched out and sleeping in the sun. In places, his fur was still damp, but where it had dried, it was fluffy and clean.

"I imagine it felt good to him, to be in that cool water," Warren said.

"Yeah, I think so."

"It was dangerous, what you did. But it was kind of you."

"No, it's not like that. I thought . . . I don't know what I thought."

Warren was impressed when they reached the brush piles. Despite all the goings-on in his absence, she'd still managed to clear a large section of the fence.

"Let's see how it's looking farther down the line. Maybe we can just re-place this part," he said.

She set down the roll of fencing, picked up the loppers, and followed him.

"Did you know that he's the one who taught me to swim?" she said. "That summer. I'm not sure, but I think it might have been at that pond. He would toss me up in the air, so I could splash down into the water. We called it rocket, or something like that."

Warren stopped in his tracks. It was bewildering, how closely grief ran alongside joy.

"We used to do that, when he was a little boy," he said. "We'd take him to a lake near our house and swim off a dock there. I would put my hands under his feet and count down, four, three, two, one, and launch him up like a little rocket."

The girl made a soft noise, almost a laugh but more of a soundless out-breath.

Warren was stunned by her youth and energy. It'd been a long time since he was around someone her age, and though Emaleen was inexperi-enced at working in the woods, she picked up the skills as quickly as she'd learned to shoot the rifle. There was so much he couldn't do anymore, and he knew he would have to move slowly and carefully. But it was an embarrassment that he couldn't even manage the chainsaw or roll away the logs.

Emaleen stepped in, respectfully and patiently, eager to learn. The Husqvarna chainsaw was almost too much for her and her arm muscles must have been burning from the weight, but she didn't back down. He showed her how to work the choke and the pull cord to fire it up, and how to judge a log's pressure points so as to keep the bar from binding up. Don't let the chain touch the ground while it's running, he told her, and he'd only had to say it once.

The corral encompassed more than an acre, and over the next days, they discovered how extensive the damage was. Three large trees had come down on the fence, posts had rotted, and long stretches of the woven wire had sagged and rusted beyond repair. "I didn't know it was this bad," he said apologetically. "The time got away from me."

Alone, he never would have been able to do any of it, and he told her as much.

"I'm glad to help." And she seemed so. Even as she wiped sweat from her forehead and swatted away mosquitoes, even as she bucked up logs and dug fence-post holes and wrestled with the wire fencing, she seemed glad.

Every day, she brought peanut-butter-and-honey sandwiches—one for herself, one for Warren, and one for the bear. The first time she tore a corner off a sandwich and tossed it into the pen, the bear sniffed at it, licked it, then picked it up with his teeth and, with the back of a paw, shoved it into his mouth.

"I guess he likes that all right," Warren said.

When the bear began walking toward her, she held the sandwich through the fence.

"Don't let him take it from your fingers," he said.

"Oh," she said, withdrawing her hand.

Remember who he is. They were Carol's words. He couldn't bring himself to speak them out loud.

Emaleen tossed the rest of the sandwich to the bear. "I was thinking, maybe we could build the fence longer, so he could go to the beaver pond."

Warren didn't want to disappoint her. Extending the fence that far would require an entire summer's worth of work, and he wasn't sure they had that much time.

"Let's just see how it goes, all right?" he said.

Surely she would decline, but Warren offered—Emaleen was welcome to stay at his house. She could take one of the guest rooms, she'd have her own bathroom with a tub, and she could wash her clothes without going to the laundromat in town. It wouldn't hurt his feelings, though, if she preferred being at the lodge cabin.

"Oh, that would be great! Are you sure you wouldn't mind?" she said. "I don't want to put you out at all."

"No, it's no trouble," he said. "My oldest daughter visited a few months back, and she washed all the sheets and made up the room before she left."

"I mean, I'm so grateful to Della. She's not charging me anything to stay there. But it's, well, it's a little depressing. The bar and everything . . . I guess it's not my kind of place."

With those words, his sense of kinship with the girl grew. "I've always thought much the same," he said.

That evening, Warren poked garlic cloves into a moose roast Syd had given him. He rarely prepared full meals anymore, with only him and the dog at home. It was enjoyable to be cooking again. He wore Carol's apron as he peeled potatoes and carrots, sliced onions, and packed it all into the roasting pan along with the slab of seasoned meat.

"I like your apron," Emaleen said, and he thought perhaps she was teasing him, but then he saw her kind smile.

"It was Carol's," he said.

"I thought maybe."

As he prepared dinner, Emaleen noticed a burned-out bulb in the overhead light fixture. He feigned surprise, but it had been that way for weeks. He was no longer confident enough in his balance to get up on the stepladder. Without offering or asking, Emaleen found the folding stepladder and a new lightbulb in the broom closet and changed it out.

"There," she said cheerfully when she was done. "How's that, Mr. Neilsen?"

"That brightens up the place, doesn't it? Thank you very much." He opened the oven door, slid in the roasting pan, and set the timer. "You used to call me Mr. Warren, when you were a little girl."

"Really? I don't remember that."

"Just Warren is fine, though."

Over dinner, he asked more about her degree and her plans for the future. She described the jobs she'd seen advertised around Alaska, but she worried she wasn't tough enough to work in a field camp. "Look at yourself," he replied. She held out her arms and laughed. She was sunburned and mosquito-bitten, and even though she'd worn long sleeves, she had scrapes and scratches up and down her arms.

"Did you say Professor Lundeen is heading up that study in Fairbanks?" he asked. "I've known her for a lot of years. If you'd like, I could give her a call and vouch for you."

"Oh, that would be amazing."

"I seem to recall that first day when you and your mother came out to the North Fork, you were asking all about the wildflowers in the meadow there by the cabin. You had an interest even then."

"It's because of Arthur, you know. I remember this incredible sense of wonder when he was teaching me the names of the plants and how to tell them apart. It was like my eyes had been changed and I saw everything differently after that." Emaleen pushed at the food on her plate with her fork. "It's weird, when you think about what happened, but I wouldn't be the same person if I'd never known him."

They both ate quietly after that, and Warren was afraid the evening had turned somber. But it didn't last. Soon, she was asking about the cabin at the North Fork, how he and Carol had built it. He left the table to get the photo album from those early days. As he flipped through the pages and described the photographs, Emaleen ate second and third helpings, apologizing even though it pleased Warren. When he said it was all right, she fed a few small pieces of moose roast to Spinner, who had been resting under the table with her head on Emaleen's feet throughout the meal.

"I'm afraid I don't have anything for dessert," he said.

"That's all right. I'm completely stuffed—it tasted so good."

"You know what I do have?" He went to the refrigerator and jostled through the jars of condiments at the back of the shelves. "Somewhere in here. There it is. Dandelion mead. Della made it last summer."

"What does it taste like?"

"I'm not sure. Should we give it a try?" Warren pried off the bottle cap with a church key and poured the honey-colored liquid into two wineglasses.

"Cheers," Warren said, and they touched their glasses and each took a sip. It tasted like summertime—sweet, floral, and slightly bubbly.

"Oh wow, that's delicious," she said.

"We could take it outside, if you'd like. Usually the mosquitoes aren't too bad on the back deck."

Spinner followed them onto the porch, where Warren sat in a patio chair and Emaleen took the porch swing. It was the golden hour, the low sun casting a glow that turned the colors to richer shades—the brilliant magenta of the fireweed blossoms, the leafy green across the hayfields, and the dark green of the forest, with its spruce and cottonwood and birch. In the distance, the evening light brought the mountains into heightened relief so that the rock faces and ravines and jagged, snowy peaks stood out vividly. The air was warm and gentle, and everything was quiet, except for the echoing, lovely trill of the hermit thrush songbirds.

"This is how I always remembered it," Emaleen said quietly. "I missed it so much when I was a kid. I'm not sure it's like this anywhere else."

Neither of them spoke for a time, and it was a comfortable silence. Eventually, Warren went back to the kitchen and brought out the bottle to pour a little more into each of their glasses.

"I feel kind of bad for him," she said.

He knew who she meant. "I should have put him down," he said. "It would have been less cruel, perhaps. But I couldn't bring myself to do it."

"No," she said. "I couldn't . . . I don't think I'd be able to either."

"I have so many regrets that, at times, it has been almost intolerable," he said.

They sipped their dandelion mead and looked toward the mountains, the girl rocking slowly on the porch swing.

"I ran away," she said.

He didn't know what she meant. To come here from Washington, she'd run away?

"My mom was dying. I saw it, and I left her. I ran away." Warren started to speak, but she interrupted him. "No, I know what you're going to say. That I was just a kid, that there was nothing I could have done. But I didn't even try."

"Is this what you've believed all this time?" he said. "Don't you remember the day that I found you? I was flying over and I spotted you on the riverbed. When I landed, you came running to me, and do you know what you said? 'We have to help my mom.'"

"What?"

"That's what you said. Over and over again. Your feet were bleeding, you'd walked for hours. All by yourself. But you weren't running away from anything. You knew you couldn't save her on your own. And you knew that the North Fork would eventually lead you to the lodge. You had a blanket and a flashlight in your backpack because you were smart enough to know it was going to be a long trip."

"Really? I don't . . . I don't remember any of that."

"It was one of the bravest acts I've ever witnessed in a child."

She made that out-breath that was almost a laugh but almost a sad sigh.

"I've never thought of myself that way," she said.

Chapter 37

The skies were pure blue when they returned to the North Fork, and by ten in the morning it was already hotter than it had been any other day. As they approached the pen, two ravens and several magpies flew up from the trough. The bear was lying in the shade of a tree nearby, flies buzzing around his head. His eyes were open, but he didn't blink.

"Is he okay?"

"I don't know," Warren said. He tapped the trough with his walking stick, and when the bear shifted his head slightly, Emaleen was surprised at her own relief. Just two weeks ago, she'd planned to shoot him.

"He really hasn't been eating at all," she said. "Maybe it's because it's so hot."

"Maybe," Warren said.

The heat slowed their work. Emaleen was soaked in sweat and had to stop frequently to drink water and rest. She worried about Warren too. "I've got this," she said as she unrolled the new fencing. She persuaded him to sit on a spruce round while he talked her through how to work the come-along to stretch the fencing, and how to anchor it from tree to tree with the U-nails.

"Take your time," he told her more than once. "There's no rush."

They were so close to being finished, though. By lunch, they might be able to let the bear out into the larger corral. He'd have fresh greens to eat and the shady forest to walk through, and she'd have the afternoon to clean out his trough and pen.

At noon, she was closing in on the last section of fence when Warren suggested they take a short break. She set down her tools, and they walked back to the pen with their lunch. The bear was standing at the gate, his head low and his sides heaving as if from exertion.

"Hey there," Warren said softly.

The bear didn't respond, just stood with his front paws wide apart as if to steady himself.

"What's wrong with him?"

"I've never seen him like this before," Warren said.

Emaleen took a peanut-butter sandwich from her backpack and tossed a piece to the bear. It landed by a front paw, but he didn't seem to notice. She waved another piece through the fencing, hoping he would catch the scent of it.

"Could we let him out so he could go to the pond?" she asked.

"I don't know."

"It made him feel better last time. And we're both here, with our rifles."

Warren was making the sounds he did when considering a decision, a humming kind of grumble. "All right then," he said.

As Emaleen unlatched the gate and dragged it to the side, she heard Warren working the bolt action on his rifle. For a long time, though, the bear didn't move. When he finally took a couple of steps forward, through the gate, he stumbled. Emaleen moved toward the bear, but Warren stopped her with his hand.

"Let him be," he said. "There's nothing we can do."

Slowly, the bear began walking along the fence. Emaleen wasn't sure he was strong enough to make it all the way to the pond, but he kept going, she and Warren following with their rifles, the bear's strides taking on more purpose.

"Shouldn't he start going that way?" she asked, pointing in the direction of the pond. When Warren didn't answer, she looked back to see that he was falling behind. He was stepping carefully over the uneven ground and leaning heavily on his walking stick.

"Are you all right, Warren?" she called.

"Just slow going. Keep an eye on him. I'll catch up."

But the bear wasn't going to the pond. He continued along the fence until he reached a corner post and then he kept on straight into the forest, toward the mountainside. He was traveling more quickly now and Emaleen had to jog at times to keep up.

"Emaleen! Emaleen?" She heard Warren's calls, but she couldn't see him anymore.

"I'm okay!" she hollered back. "I'll keep up with him!"

"No! Leave him! I don't want you going alone!"

"I'm fine! I've got my rifle. Don't worry. I'll be careful!"

Emaleen followed the bear on and on, through the forest, through a grassy marshland and across a treacherous bog where they both struggled to keep from sinking into the black, watery mud. When they were at last on dry ground, the bear lay in the shade of a stunted black spruce tree. Sitting on a grass hummock, Emaleen took off her sweatshirt and tied it around her waist, and then wiped dead mosquitoes and mud off her face with the hem of her T-shirt. She could hear Warren's shouts in the distance and she knew that he must be worried, but she couldn't leave the bear.

There was the trickle of water nearby and she searched until she found a small, clear stream that came down through the moss and boulders. She knelt at the edge and slurped water from her cupped hands. She'd forgotten how it tasted, like ice and rock. "There's water to drink over here," she called to the bear.

His moan was growly and pinched, as if he were in pain. He was trying to stand but was only able to get his front legs under him. He sat for a long time, his head low and his front paws braced against his weight. He moaned again as he raised himself to all fours.

"Arthur. You should drink some water."

But the bear turned toward the mountain and began walking again.

Life is hard. It was something Syd had told her when she was visiting him again the other evening. He described the tiny chickadees coming to his feeder each winter with their hearts racing and their feathers fluffed against the cold. The yearling moose chased off by their mothers and left to fend for themselves. The snowshoe hares dodging the constant hunt of the lynx and owls and hawks. All that hunger and fear. And then Syd was recalling friends and family he'd known over the years. Those who were addicted and abused, lonely and discontented. People like Birdie and Arthur, who tried and tried but never found their footing. It was a miracle, not that life had come into existence, but that it endured. Dying, that was the easy part. He confessed that he'd stolen that line, in one form or another, from Hemingway. He'd gone to his shelves, handed Emaleen a book, and told her to read it when she got a chance.

They were above the trees now, she and Arthur. The old bear stopped often, panting with his giant head so low that his nose nearly touched the ground. Where was he going? Emaleen sat to rest on the tundra.

The blueberry bushes and Labrador tea, the cinquefoil and spirea, were all in bloom. Eight months out of the year, this slope was buried in snow. The conditions were extreme—nothing but rock and wind and meager soil. So much left to happenstance and incredible endurance. Yet life thrived, unfurled its leaves toward the sun, and poured hope into its tender, fragile flowers.

They'd been traveling for more than two hours, and she thought she could hear an engine far away. Warren was searching for them. She faced back down toward the creek valley, but the plane wasn't anywhere in sight.

They were in the high country now, and Emaleen could see for miles across the mountain ridges. The shrubs and stunted spruce had been left behind for moss, stony ground, silvery caribou lichen, ankle-high bushes, and flowers she only knew from books. She wanted to stop and study every one of them—their toothed and heart-shaped leaves, their petals in delicate hues of purple and yellow and pink, the tiny hairs along their stems, pollen like gold dust on their stamens. She longed to pull off her hiking boots and socks and walk barefoot across the tundra, but she knew the soles of her feet were too soft-skinned.

There wasn't enough time anyway. The bear was continuing at his slow, steady pace, and she followed. They were on a narrow ridge that rose higher and higher toward a peak, and up ahead, she saw a large white branch laid out on the green moss. Curious, she left the game trail and, when she got closer, saw that it was a single caribou antler. The main beam was thick and nearly three feet tall, and the many points were stained the color of rust.

A memory stirred, fragmented and blurry and maybe not even real. Her mom coming home from the mountains with her face burnished by wind and sun, her hair wild. Tart blueberries pouring out of a canteen instead of water. She'd spent the night alone on a rock, she said. There had been so many stars. And a giant's teeth. A ring of mushrooms where the witches and fairies danced. Caribou marching across the sky with their antlers bleeding.

They were so far from the cabin now that Emaleen began to worry about how long it would take for them to get back. When the bear approached a shale slide that looked frighteningly steep and dangerous, she called to him, "We should go back! Arthur!" But the bear staggered on, traversing the mountainside along a game path. Each step sent shards of dark-gray rock crumbling and tumbling down the slope. *We all make this trail. The bears and moose and caribou.* Emaleen followed.

All those years ago, on a hot summer day, she and her mother and Arthur had climbed up here to play in the snow. Surely this couldn't be the same place, but the bear was crossing a velvety-green alpine bowl, toward a drift of snow. He was too weak to slide and play, but if he just lay there for a while, maybe it would give him some relief. The bear did not stop, though. He kept on, past the snowdrift and over the top of a ridge.

They had passed through a range of mountains and were now looking down into a different valley. Far, far below was a broad, braided river, and on the other side, the artificial glint of metal in the sun. Emaleen was light-headed with vertigo and déjà vu. Was that the Wolverine Lodge?

The bear had sprawled on his side, his head on the tundra and his paws straight out in front of him, his chest heaving up and down. Emaleen sat nearby and watched him. He'd come all this way intentionally, to be in this specific place. She wondered what memories or meaning it held.

Soon she would tell him it was time to go back to the corral. It would be a long journey, but it would be easier going downhill. When they got there, she would give him a peanut-butter sandwich, and tomorrow, she would take him to the pond for a swim. For now, he just needed to rest.

But the longer he lay on the tundra, the more labored and shallow his breathing became. His mouth was open and his gray-pink tongue lolled out onto the moss. He didn't move or flicker his eyes; there was only his rapid panting. *It must feel like he's drowning,* she thought.

"Arthur?"

She was still frightened of him, but she hated his suffering more. She left her rifle on the tundra and crept closer. He was positioned with his throat and belly exposed, and for the first time she noticed the painful-looking scar that ran thick and jagged from under his chin down the front of his chest.

"Arthur?"

He didn't respond, even when she reached out and put her hand on his front paw.

It was strange to be this close to him. Even in his weakened state, he radiated a wild force that raised goosebumps across Emaleen's skin. His claws were several inches long and golden-hued. The fur on his paw was dense and silkier than she'd expected, and she could feel the underlying bones. Like the widespread fingers of a man.

An eternity seemed to pass. A bumblebee hovered among the lowbush cranberry blossoms and then was swept away by a breeze. A little, soft-brown pika darted out of a crack in a rock and disappeared just as quickly. A fuzzy, orange-and-black caterpillar crawled across a circle of lichen on a stone. Above the river valley, a raven wheeled and soared among the wind currents. The old bear panted and whimpered, and Emaleen grew chilled from the mountain air, but she kept her hand on his paw.

By the time Warren flew over in his airplane, she knew that Arthur wouldn't ever leave this mountainside. The plane descended toward the ridgetop where she sat, and Warren tipped the wings in her direction. He had spotted them. He circled out over the river valley and flew back over them. She remembered the protocol. Waving both arms in the air was a sign of distress, a call for help. With tears in her eyes, she raised one arm and waved at Warren. *I'm all right. Everything is going to be all right.*

It was evening when the end finally came. The old bear's frenetic panting reached a horrible crescendo and his neck and legs straightened as if he were trying to stretch out, and then it stopped. The silence was complete. The blond-tipped fur along his back rippled in the wind, but he no longer breathed, and the surface of his eyes slowly turned dull and opaque. He was gone.

Emaleen let out a shuddering sigh, as if she'd been holding her own breath all this time. It was late in the evening, but the sun wouldn't set until nearly midnight. She didn't have to leave him yet.

For half an hour, she searched along the ridge. She picked fragrant artemisia and Labrador tea. She hiked down to a snowmelt stream, and at its edges she found shooting stars, forget-me-nots, and pink plumes. She climbed up on a rocky slope where the purple mountain saxifrage, white-and-yellow avens, and kinnikinnick grew. She filled the pocket of her sweatshirt with the sprigs and flowers, and then she went back to Arthur. Sitting cross-legged at his side, she carefully took each plant out of her pocket and placed it along the ruff of the bear's neck.

When her pocket was empty, she stood up from the tundra, adjusted the rifle strap on her shoulder, and began the journey back.

She'd believed that she was bound to the two of them, that their dangerous power would forever dictate who she was and how she moved through the world. They would always be a mysterious part of her, it was true. But her life was her own. She had come to understand their true names and, at last, she could say goodbye. Birdie, Arthur. Mother. Bear.

Acknowledgments

I had the tremendous good fortune to work again with editors Andrea Walker and Mary-Anne Harrington and my longtime agent, Jeff Kleinman. Thank you all for your brilliant insights and patience. It was a joy to have the Snow Child team back together again.

At Tinder Press in the UK, thanks to Alexia Thomaidis, Caitlin Raynor, Ollie Martin, Ellie Freedman, and Eleanor Wood. At Random House in the United States, thanks to Carrie Neill, Briony Everroad, Jennifer Rodriguez, Taylor Noel, Virginia Norey, and Naomi Goodheart, and I am particularly grateful to Andy Ward and Alison Rich for coming to the rescue with this wonderful title. Also, thanks to Lorella Belli at Lorella Belli Literary Agency Limited, and at Folio Literary Management, Sophie Brett-Chin and Chiara Panzeri. For the stunning cover art, thank you to illustrator Anna Morrison.

Thank you to Karl Braendel and Kiche Braendel, who not only shared their vast knowledge and firsthand stories about Alaska's brown bears, but also allowed me to join them for two weeks in their remote hunting camp on Kodiak Island. Thanks to ecologist Kathryn Baer and environmental scientist Zachary Baer, for helping me to chart Emaleen's future prospects and guiding me through the maze of common and scientific names for Alaska's plants. Thank you to Ruth Hulbert, for the beautiful botanical illustrations. Thanks to Mary Ann Cockle, owner of Fireside Books and copy editor extraordinaire. And thank you to the entire crew at Fireside Books, who helped welcome this book into the world.

My biological father, my mother, and the father who raised me are all gone now, but through their genetics and how they lived their lives, their support and encouragement, they made me the writer I am today. I will always remember them with love and gratitude: Gary Kline (1952–1977), Julie Hungiville LeMay (1954–2019), and John LeMay (1949–2022).

Most of all, thank you to my husband, Sam, and our daughters, Grace and Aurora. You were by my side every step of the way, reading and listening to every iteration of every chapter, offering invaluable advice, and, most important, giving me courage. This novel would not be what it is today without the three of you. I love you with all of my heart.